THE DIEMEN
ALEXANDER

Marie Heitz

Clan Destine
PRESS

First published by Clan Destine Press in 2023

PO Box 121,
Bittern Victoria 3918
Australia

National Library of Australia Cataloguing-In-Publication data:

Marie Heitz

THE DIEMEN ALEXANDER

ISBNs: 978-1-922904-41-6 (paperback)
          978-1-922904-42-3 (eBook)

Cover illustration and design: Sam Lyne

Design & Typesetting by Clan Destine Press

Clan Destine
PRESS

www.clandestinepress.net

This book is dedicated to Suzy Cooper and Nelli Noakes.

Part I

Chapter I

For his final school year to start well, Luke needed a big nasty fire on kunanyi. Maybe not as big as the '67 fire, back when it was called Mount Wellington, but enough to kill a decent whack of stuff, incinerate plants and animals, insects and worms, pollute the water, choke the streams with ash – an all-round disastrophe. And that's what he got.

The fire was a preview of his ecological nightmare. He'd wished it and it had happened.

Sick with guilt, he mooned about the house, till little sister Gatta finally said, 'You didn't cause it, you dick. But if you did, could you wish typhoid – no, the clap – on the school board?' Then she shook her head sadly. 'No, not gunna happen. They'd need to have crotchal parts to infect.'

They were both at home: Luke for his month-long Self Directed Learning Unit, the one only übernerds got to do, the one he'd stupidly cornered himself into needing the fire for; Gatta because she'd been suspended yet again.

No, he hadn't caused the kunanyi fire. If he had powers like that, his biceps would be guns, not just the barrels, and skanky economics teacher Hansen, not Luke, would have the jellyfish spine. But Luke hadn't just wished for the fire, he'd needed it, and needing it had been his fault. It started with that stupid argument in Hansen's economics class, when Hansen had put up those graphs of historical temperatures. Said he was teaching them critical thinking! BS! He'd lifted the images from a climate denialist website! Meek geek Luke had bashed his knees on the desk as he stood up. His ears blushed neon. But his voice was clear: 'Those only show narrow time periods and places. They prove zilch. The test of true science is that it can make predictions.'

'Well, go on, Luke Schache, True Scientist,' Hansen had said, 'make one.'

'The mountain is going to burn this summer. We will have caused it. Us. And a million animals, whose fault it isn't, are going to die.'

Then, to underline his commitment and his piss-poor selection of battles, Luke had made it the subject of his SDLU: "A Photo-essay on the Effects of Fire on a Landscape: kunanyi/Mt Wellington."

That's why he had to go up the mountain today, to photograph the wished-for wreckage, get the "After" pictures of the "Befores" he'd already got. Without the fire, his photo-essay would be a flop. He could still have wangled a pass on the SDLU, but he needed a distinction for next year's uni scholarship. To study Meteorology. Or Environmental science. Environmental law. Anything to try to help the nearly fucked-up planet. And afford Gatta's school fees.

He didn't want to go back up. Everything leading up to the fire – his stupid, horrible wish, weaselly Hansen, climate denial, the whole selfish exploitation of Earth – was wrongness. All of it. Wrong. And his triumphant reaction – standing on Collins Street in the middle of the CBD his face turned up to the ash raining down as the sky bulged with orange smoke – made him want to vomit.

His sister got all that (like Mum didn't, but who would know? It's not like she was ever home). She just Gattesquely ignored it.

'Get up there, Luke, do it. Take your pics while shit's still smoky – woo, vibes!' Gatta had waggled black painted fingernails. 'It's not like it can take revenge on you.'

Last night, it had rained – lucky, blessed, undeserved rain – and put out the fire.

So Luke went up. Cycled to the top of Lenah Valley Road before hiking up the fire trail where the bush was unburnt. Here, he was cradled in the familiar comfort of living, sensate trees: leaves basking, roots seeking, feeling the vibrations of his passing feet.

Then he reached the bottom of the Old Hobartians Track where all soft green life ended and blackness began.

The first hurdle: the new sign which read *Danger. Do Not Enter. By Order of Wellington Park Management Authority.* Averting his eyes, he folded his knees and elbows through the orange and black tape. Of the genes that were haphazardly distributed between him and Gatta, almost all of the rule-breaking had gone to Gatta.

On the other side of the tape rose a desolate slope of blackened boulders and scarified soil pierced by skeletal trunks. Luke, wearing black right down to his beanie, was the same colour as absolutely everything. He pulled the beanie further down over his blond hair and, feeling painfully illegal but at least not very spottable, started up the steep rock steps.

To his right he heard the chuckle of the New Town Rivulet. He was surprised to see the water. Normally the creek was invisible behind a dense wall of brush, bright with ferns and pink mountain berries. Seeing it shocked him: the water was coal-skinned, unreflecting and unlit, the only colour the occasional glint of rainbow sheen where it pooled behind clumped debris. Luke hurried past.

The smoke had largely cleared but the rain that had doused the inferno now steamed back from a thousand acres of charred trees – thick, acrid and bitter. He stopped, coughing. His throat was closing and his heart thumped. He clasped his chest, trying to calm his breathing.

'Hey!'

He looked back down the slope. A man stood on the fire trail below, pointing at the sign. Luke waved. The man shook his head in disgust but made no move to pursue him.

Go, before he changes his mind.

Luke hastened on, slipping on the greasy ash-covered stone. Eventually, he lost purchase completely and slid sideways, and thumped into a tree trunk. A brief creak was the only warning. He hurled himself sideways into a bush, which had become a cluster of black pitchforks, as a dark mass crashed down right next to him. The bough shattered, showering him with sparks.

He rolled away, slapping at his clothes. Slithered into an ashy puddle. Took a breath. Examined himself: a lot of scorch marks on his clothes, a few small burns on his forearms. The huge tree-limb was still burning, spitting sparks. *An accident. Not revenge, stupid.*

Luke stood up. He was shaken and filthy. And hot. He took off his beanie, which helped, and dreamed of snow. A lock of blond hair fell in his eyes, the only non-black parts of him. Now he felt exposed. He could still see little people on the fire trails below, which meant they could see him. But there was no way the beanie was going back on. And no way he was giving up. He took two handfuls of ashy soil, scrubbed them into his pale hair and face – an SAS commando in Lenah Valley – and kept going.

His first photo site was near the Lost World track junction, another four hundred metres up, and it was hard going. Steep and slippery, and the only handholds were covertly hot tree limbs. Worst were the concealed puddles, so full of debris they looked like solid ground till he stepped in and his foot disappeared into a warm oily stew, and soft unidentified lumps nudged his ankles. He wished fervently for traditional freezing Tasmanian bushwalking mud.

At the North-South mountain bike track junction, Luke glanced around for the mountain bikers. Not even extreme mountain treachery would usually deter those loonies, but today it had. He gripped the straps of his pack, took the next hazardous step and wished he'd picked up an unburnt fallen branch earlier, for a walking stick. Or a weapon.

He stopped again. It wasn't the heat making him uneasy; it was the enormous silence, thick with the lost, which pressed against his skin. So much angry death.

Seven-year-old Luke had made his mum stop by roadkill, insisting the dead wallabies and possums were crying to him; *cold, cold, naked, alone*; had dragged their bodies into the shelter of the bush. Now, on the charred mountainside, a tumult of stilled voices – animals, insects, even the trees – prodded at him. He wanted to run. *It wasn't me.*

'You're a dick.' Gatta's words again. 'This is what you came for. It's perfect. The pics will be sensational.'

He pushed himself on, which helped to distract him. Just ahead and upward was the first rock overhang, a natural refuge, draped in gentle greens, which had always been good for a rest. He should have been ready for what it looked like now, but he wasn't.

What faced him was a blackened hollow. Worse, the empty air bulged with presence. It was as though the newly dead had summoned all the old dead to witness: all past ages and past lives were present here, and more real than him. He felt like an intruder, offensively alive: shoes crunching, breath rustling, eyeballs rotating, jointed limbs moving.

'Okay, I hear you,' he said, backing out. 'I am standing up for you. That's why I'm here.'

He still wanted to drop to his knees and ask forgiveness. For the human-caused fire that had killed; for himself. Or to run away.

He was being intimidated by rocks – *rocks?* – his brain must be drying out.

Instead, he cast around for water, but he'd forgotten all the usual watercourses would be choked with ash. The first pool he found, he submerged his bottle under the charcoal scum. The first mouthful was bitter and spiky. He spat. Tried hard not to think of burnt spiders. The second scoured his throat like whisky. Would drinking whisky help his wussiness?

He drank two more bottles of smoky grey water and told himself he was less spooked. He was still as hot and wet and dirty as a human compost heap, but had recovered enough to keep going. He might have another hour of climbing to his first photo, if he could even recognise the site.

Above him loomed the dark bulk of kunanyi. The peak had vanished in a roiling mass of black cloud, which stretched gigantic fingers over the town towards the Derwent River and the sullen lump of Mount Direction on the further shore. The sun pierced low underneath and lit brilliant whitecaps on the iron-dark river. Wind gusts struck the water and swept the waves southeast in harried flocks.

Luke might be about to get very wet. Wetter. But he had to *get the freakin' pictures!* He went on, the familiar path unrecognisable. What had been a tunnel through green – the dark, shiny, almost military green of satinwood; the silver and green of musk; splashes of brilliant lime moss; and the olive of the stringybarks; with sprays of mauve and pink cheeseberries, the extravagant scarlet-cupped sunburst of the waratah – was now an open wasteland. Only the blackened hulks of the bigger trees remained. But centuries of footsteps had followed the contours of the land and worn a shallow depression that his own feet could still follow, if he left them to it.

After 45 minutes of dogged ascent, his feet took a sharp left and stopped. He turned. This could be the right place.

Yes. Across the river, the peak of Caves Hill lined up with the sharp indent of Geilston Bay. Luke fumbled for his camera, wiped his fingers marginally cleaner on his shirt and brought up his comparison photo.

The original scene had framed a mountain pepper nestling in a tumble of boulders, each boulder draped with lichens in a mosaic of mustard, bone white and rusted orange, with a shaggy toupee of moss. He recognised the boulders, though now they were just three prehistoric stones with their heads shaved. *Hmmm.* He could try some shots with different slants of light, highlight the contours, their bare boulder-ness.

He rubbed the back of his smutty hand on his chin and started shooting.

Caaaark!

Three huge shadows swooped overhead, coal-black against the dark clouds, revealing a flash of lemon as they wheeled. Yellow-tailed black cockatoos, with their harsh, oddly melancholy call. It matched their diffident character, in contrast to the truly demented screech of the white, sulphur-crested thugs. Three more swept by, their peculiar rowing flight more than usually awkward in the leaden air. They made him think more than ever of pterodactyls: huge but clumsy fliers, painfully beaky, only barely adequate at being dinosaurs.

Caaaark, the yellow-tails repeated, then suddenly stalled in confusion and broke away into separate steep dives.

Luke stared. This was totally uncockatoo-like. Then his hair prickled. Tingles danced up and down his arms. The world cracked in half. The stringybark behind the pepper he'd photographed exploded and vanished, vaporised in a deafening bang.

Luke was thrown by a giant hand and landed on his back, only distantly feeling the impact, unable to hear or see.

Time passed, not measurable. Clear and utter peace. Luke floated on it, his heart beating serenely and very slowly in his chest; thunder pulsing against his skin. He opened his eyes to purest white with starbursts of silver, which gradually formed into bruised and angry clouds, close as a ceiling, lit by searing arcs of lightning.

'Oh shit.'

He heaved himself to his feet, swayed and nearly fell. His muscles squirmed like jellied eels inside his skin and his vision was still speckled. Then the sky hurled down second bolt of lightning, so close he felt the heat, and he plunged headlong up the track into the Lost World.

The rain battered his back like a waterfall. His world disappeared into the slashing grey torrent. He staggered blindly forward. Somewhere, surely close, was a rock overhang. The freezing rain turned stinging, fusillades of hailstones bounced, and he pushed ahead desperately.

The huge dolerite shelf loomed out of the grey maelstrom, a cloven mass which had crashed down the mountain some unimaginable time ago to land here. He slithered underneath it past a chest-high boulder, retreated as close to the back wall as he could, and drew his knees up to his stomach. His heart pounded painfully. His palms were torn up and he shivered uncontrollably from cold and shock and adrenaline. The clatter of the hail and almost continuous thunder were like a physical force. But here he was out of their reach.

Luke shrugged off his pack, took out his beanie and rain jacket, and folded his entire long skinny frame into its damp Goretex embrace. With his beanie pulled down to his neck and his sleeves to his fingertips, he wasn't warm but no longer heading for hypothermia.

When his heart rate slowed, he wormed two power bars from his pack. He ate only one. The weather was so biblical, emergency rations might be needed on one of the next forty days. Instead, he extracted his camera. He reviewed his photos with a spreading smile: the burnt images were so stark they could almost have been taken in black and white, and with the sun appearing and disappearing between repeated exposures, he had a choice of grim contrast or muted melancholy moods. Gatta's opinion would help; she was annoyingly but usefully unerring about what worked and what was "a total pants-down".

Above the background drumming came an ominous crack, followed by a clattering thump. A charred tree crown juddered over the rock shelf. A moment later, a stream of blackened soil and gravel coursed down the slope next to the overhang. Larger rocks tumbled with them and, in the jumble, a small, forked branch.

Whoa, a branch with a head! *A tiger snake!*

Not a snake; it had legs. Blue-tongue-goanna-sized but way skinny. Whatever it was, it looked dead. Ish. Unmoving, pale belly up, half-submerged in black mud.

Luke unfolded his legs and picked up the creature. It drooped over his palm, cold and limp. It might be dead, but didn't reptiles slow right down in cold without necessarily going all the way and dying? If it was dead, wouldn't it be stiff?

Gently, Luke wiped away some of the mud with his sleeve, opened his jacket and cradled the poor beaten animal along his left arm against his stomach. It was very cold. Much colder than him. He felt his own heat flow into the little body.

Maybe he'd been given a chance to save something, however small.

Chapter 2

Luke leant back against the rock and closed his eyes. The hail had stopped, the rain was easing and a sense of peace spread through him from where he held the lizard. Huh! Helping must create its own warmth.

Then his left palm felt faint strokes. He looked down.

Yaah! The lizard was licking him. Lapping at his bloodied hand! Its eyes were still closed, its two tiny nostrils dilated. Luke just managed not to jerk his hand away. The licking didn't hurt, just tickled and, yeah, it could feed on his leaked blood. He didn't need it. But didn't lizards carry diseases? If it licked an open wound, wouldn't he get some weird blood infection and die?

He moved his hand. The lizard stopped licking but didn't move, didn't open its eyes. Luke couldn't even see it breathing. Luke barely breathed himself. They both waited.

Then, inspired, Luke slid his right hand into his pocket and extracted his last power bar. He managed to peel back the wrapper one-handed and poked it in front of the lizard's nose.

For a full minute, nothing happened. Then the little nostrils opened again. Its dark flanks moved as it breathed. It opened its eyes and flicked out a long tongue. One of its front legs reached forward to grasp a protruding nut. Luke let the bar go.

'Go on,' he said.

The lizard swivelled its head to look up at his face. Its eyes were a murky mustard, till a pair of inner lids slid upward to reveal them as brilliant yellow, with a vertical slit, like a cat. Its head was black and it now looked more like a tiger snake again. The eyes regarded him for a second, then it commenced to eat the bar, quite unhurriedly. Luke watched in fascination.

It took fifteen minutes to eat the bar, which Luke thought was a magnificent effort. He would have had to eat a basketball to consume an equivalent amount for his body size. After it finished the last crumb, it took several deep breaths.

'I'd burp now,' said Luke.

The lizard looked at him again, that extraordinary yellow, then laid its head against Luke's stomach, stretched out comfortably and closed its eyes.

Huh, what? He was in a cave on the mountain with a weird reptile taking a nap in his lap. Maybe he'd really been blasted unconscious by the lightning and this was all some hallucination while he lay in the rain, waiting to die. He dug his fingernails into his torn palm, the palm the creature had licked. Ouch! Nope, not a hallucination. But he needed to wash that hand. The rain had stopped and all around him the mountain was shedding water in chuckling rivulets.

Careful not to disturb the lizard, Luke reached over to a clearish puddle. If he died of something stupid, his mum would kill him. Gatta would dig him up in order to kill him. He swished his hand in the water.

Hand rinsed, Luke sniffed the air. It had nearly been washed clean of its heavy char smell. Sunbeams slanted across the mountain. The sun was low. Time to get home. And fascinating as it was, he couldn't take the lizard from its own habitat. Rescuing it would have to be enough. Feeding it power bars was probably wrong too; could give it whatever the lizard equivalent of lumpy jaw was. Though it had been an emergency.

He gazed down at it tenderly.

In the changed light, its black head looked more bluish, a deep beautiful glow like a late evening sky. Its colour became more intense the longer he looked. He'd never seen a reptile like this, not even in pictures. Never even heard of one, and he'd never see one again – but he did have his camera.

Though the lizard exuded relaxation, Luke moved carefully, manoeuvring his camera to capture a picture of the whole animal, then closer detail of its head, limbs and long ridged tail. It seemed awkwardly put together. Its general shape was snaky but it had a deep chest and prominent shoulders, quite over-engineered for its delicate forelimbs. The rear limbs were much more muscular and the toes were thick and partly webbed. It had a long tail, with a prominent central ridge running its entire length.

Luke frowned. He remembered a picture of a lizard from the deserts in Northern Australia, a large lizard. A monitor? A water monitor? It had the same tail, for swimming. What was a northern swimming lizard doing on a mountain in Tasmania? Their neighbour Brendan might have a zoologist friend who could explain it. But he needed detailed photos.

Gently, he turned the animal on its back. It draped itself bonelessly over his hand. There was a ridge down the deep chest as well, like the keel of a boat. He took several photos from different angles. Then he tucked away his camera, shuffled out from under the overhang and stood up with the lizard stretched contentedly out along his left arm Nearby, he found a sunny spot, still far enough under the rock ledge to provide some protection from predators. He placed the lizard on the rock, ignoring the tug in his chest.

Its eyes flashed open.

'Gotta go.' Luke said. 'Bye.'

The lizard bounced up onto four legs, head and tail raised like flags. The yellow eyes blinked twice. Boy and lizard regarded each other, before Luke shouldered his pack and turned down the track. The way was easier now it wasn't obscured by rain and the deluge had washed away some mud. But it was precarious going downhill and after a dozen steps he had to stop.

Immediately a line of sharp tugs ascended the back of his pants. He looked around to see the dark little body and a tail swinging in mid-air as it scrabbled around the side of his pack, then swarmed up to the top. He felt a little nudge on the back of his neck. Slowly, he reached around to the top of his pack and touched the lizard with his fingertips. It felt smooth and warm and relaxed. Then, not painfully but firmly, it nipped his finger.

Luke hesitated. He could try putting it on the ground again, but he had no chance of outrunning it. Bizarrely, it had adopted him. Or perhaps it had adopted a source of power bars. In any case, at this point Luke had no choice but to continue down the mountain with it on his back. He tried to ignore the fact that he was grinning.

He scrambled and slithered his way down to the fire trail and squirmed back under the orange warning sign. The sign had been absolutely truthful and it had done its best.

'Sorry,' he told it. Then he reached around and plucked the lizard off the top of his pack. It curled its tail firmly around his wrist. Somebody must have told it looking a man in the eye was important.

'You might think this is a good idea,' he said, 'but I'm sure I'm not allowed to remove a wild lizard from a national park. And even if I could, I probably need a licence for you or something. So nobody had better see you.' He put it on his shoulder, tucked his shirt into his pants and snugged the waistband of the pack tightly around his middle. Then he lowered the reptile inside his shirt. It wriggled, fitting its tail around the contour of Luke's body. He peered down into his shirt. The lizard was lying on its back. Its pale belly was now washed in aquamarine. It looked very comfortable. Luke snorted and shook his head.

When he reached his bike at the top of Lenah Valley Road, the sun had dipped below the forest crowns but he still had the light of a long summer evening to get home. The air was crisp, not cold. Someone had even started a barbecue. Just as Luke's nose registered the sausage notes, he felt a scrabble against his stomach and a moment later the lizard's head emerged at his top button. It rotated directly to the source of the smell.

'Ha,' said Luke. 'Well, at least we'll know what else to feed you. You can't live on power bars.' He nudged it back down inside his shirt.

As he threaded his way on his bike towards South Hobart he got colder and wetter. The streets were soaked. At least he'd have a good excuse for his bedraggled clothes.

'You've survived worse,' he said, as the little snaky body curled more tightly against his skin. The evening was growing cooler. Luke jinked to avoid an ancient Corolla with a bucket-hatted driver who had swerved unexpectedly round a puddle. 'You might even survive the ride home.'

Bugger. If he came off his bike and they got separated, the lizard would be lost in the strange world that Luke had brought it into. The lizard was Luke's responsibility. He slowed down.

The Huon Road became the narrow lane of clapboard houses and randomly assembled greenery that was his street.

Mum's Audi was in the carport. Hmm. He'd stow his bike on the back veranda. Maybe he could avoid Mum till he'd changed his clothes and figured out what to do about his passenger. He wheeled his bike up the side of the house, clucking at next doors' chooks.

Mum couldn't know. She'd freak. And she'd tell her brother, and Ty would do something awful to the lizard, because that's the kind of thing Ty did.

Chapter 3

'You look like a dead seal,' said Gatta, from the back door.

'Thanks. I thought I looked like a commando. Where's Mum?'

'Not the commando SEAL, the *arf arf* sort. Ty has taken her to Sydney to look at his new Flexig lab.' Gatta scowled.

Anxiety spiked within Luke's relief. 'And offered her the manager job?'

'Yep. And she heard from Anders yesterday about their trust fund. Seven years after the divorce and they still have to argue about it. Christ! She's mega-skint just now, and after Anders' gabbing, the single mum jitters are even worse. Ty is mega-smug, because it makes her likely to accept the job. She's just too chickenshit to tell us.' She rubbed her ankle tattoo with the opposite bare heel. 'You really do look like crap. Want to get changed and eat some kickarse pasta?'

Luke's stomach replied with a rumble and he started up the steps.

'What's with the funny walk? Did you fall off your bike?'

'I found something. Or it found me. But I need to get inside. I'm cold.'

The kitchen was full of warm light and the smell of cooking. Luke nearly threw himself face down in the saucepan. He wasn't alone. The lizard appeared at his collar, warmed up and ready to eat.

'Holy shit! You've got a tiger snake. I don't know that they eat pasta.' Gatta made it a policy not to be scared of anything but her hands were up, martial arts defence style, a mop-headed half-sized white Bruce Lee.

'It's a lizard,' Luke said. 'Well, I'm not sure what it is but I don't think it's dangerous, at least not to me. And I'll put money on its eating pasta.'

He lifted the creature out of his shirt and placed it on the kitchen table, where it stood with head alert but tail resting placidly. Under the hanging light it was a deep indigo.

'Christ on a stick!' Gatta leaned forward cautiously. The lizard's eyes glittered in the light. She pulled back her sloppy jumper sleeve. 'Should I let it smell me? You don't think it will bite?'

'It likes the taste of blood,' Luke said.

She looked at him suspiciously.

'It licked the blood on my hand but it had lots of chances to bite me and it didn't. Well, it nipped me once, but that was just for encouragement.'

Gatta squeezed one eye shut and glared at Luke with the other. Then she looked at the creature, which regarded her calmly. 'You'd better not!' she warned and held her hand in front of its face. Its head swayed slightly from side to side, its nostrils dilated and its tongue flickered. Gatta's hand betrayed her by trembling. The lizard licked her finger.

'*Yaaa aa aaah!*'

'Don't assume it likes you,' Luke said. 'Your hand probably smells like your cooking. But I think we've established that it doesn't bite. Us, anyway. I'm going to get changed. We'll see what it does. It wouldn't let me leave, before.'

The creature watched him leave the room, but showed no signs of following.

'What should I feed it?' Gatta yelled after him.

'I don't know. Wait till I get back.'

When he returned, Gatta had set the table. The lizard stood in the middle like a centrepiece, surrounded by the crockery. Gatta had set a bowl in front of it.

'I'm surprised you didn't give it a serviette,' he said.

'I couldn't find one that matched. Did you notice it changes colour?'

The lizard's head was now ruby, shading back though its indigo trunk to a midnight-blue tail.

'Wow! Way cool!' said Luke. 'It sort of didn't quite always look the same but I thought that was the light. I thought only chameleons could do that.'

'Badassical. Do you reckon chameleons have better table manners than regular lizards?'

'I don't think they do tables much. But I don't want to put it on the floor.'

'Yes, it's way too pretty. And I don't like calling it *it*. We have to find out whether it's Harry or Meghan.' Gatta rubbed heel on calf. 'Lukey.'

'Yes, Gattacus?'

She pointed two fingers back and forth between them. 'It's not just hearing us, it's listening! It's following us so hard its nearly pressing *like*.'

'Yes,' he said, and the lizard's head swivelled back towards him. 'This is way weird.'

'I so agree,' she said. 'I think Mrs Google is going to be very busy after dinner. But your Luke-stomach is about to leap out of your throat and eat both of us, and then we'll never find out what it is.'

He put spaghetti marinara on both their plates and paused. The lizard watched with wide yellow cat eyes. Luke filled the little bowl in front of it. Its inner eyelids dropped and it fell to eating.

'Freaky,' he muttered.

'It's got to be a he!' announced Gatta. 'He was waiting to be served.'

She offered the lizard a lettuce leaf. It flicked out its tongue briefly but showed no other interest. 'Definitely a he.' They watched, transfixed as its little ruby head moved efficiently around its bowl.

After the meal, the lizard – now mainly dark blue, with a receding tinge of red about its head – comfortably fell asleep amid the plates.

'Okay, time to ask Mrs Google,' Luke said. 'I've never seen anything like it and I don't know if there's many Tassie reptiles that size. There's something called a monitor in the Territory which looks like it.'

'Him,' said Gatta, 'and we're not going to find him on the net.'

'We haven't looked yet.'

Luke fetched his laptop. The Tasmanian Parks website listed seventeen lizards: a mountain dragon, fifteen skinks and a blue-tongue. He worked his way methodically through all of them. The mountain dragon could change its skin colour but was far too stocky, as was the blue-tongue. Their lizard was shaped most like a mountain skink ('You found it on the mountain,' Gatta pointed out), but was about six times the size. None of the animals had the ridged tail and were obviously the wrong proportions but Luke refused to miss one out.

'Let's see the monitors,' Gatta said, her shaggy dark head bobbing restlessly next to his shoulder. Luke clicked on the link to Mertens' Water Monitor. They both gasped. A huge powerful snakelike lizard stared confidently at the photographer. Its sinuous body ended in a long muscular ridged tail.

'It's him,' Gatta said, 'but better looking.' She glanced guiltily at their lizard. 'Sorry.'

'Not quite,' said Luke. 'The monitor's eyes are yellow, but I can't see any lids. And its pupils are round. Eyes are probably important. And the Mertens' shoulders don't look lumpy and his chest is flatter.' He scrolled down. 'Let's see if he can change colour.' They both read intently. 'Doesn't look like it. At least, it's not mentioned.'

'Maybe he's a half-breed,' Gatta said. 'Like his mum was a chameleon and his dad was a monitor.' She looked at the lizard with sympathy. 'Similar to me.'

Luke grimaced but didn't reply. The subject of their possible non-matching fathers was best left at a truce. 'Different species can't interbreed. And I think chameleons and monitors are not just different species but different, whatchamacallit, genuses. Like really not related.'

'Well, he's a genius for a lizard. He's for sure figured out how to boss us around. Definitely a he, straight-up?'

Luke rolled his eyes. 'Well, let's see if we can figure out that part at least.' He googled *Lizard; sex*, looked at the results, flushed and hastily typed *Lizards; gender*.

Gatta hooted. 'Could you try to be, like, more awkward?'

Luke ignored her and studied the screen. 'Looks like if you've got male and female lizards, the males are more colourful, have bigger heads, are more aggressive and do more push-ups.'

'What?'

'Yes, they do push-ups, look.' He clicked on a video. They stared at the image of a pretty yellow speckled skink on a red gravel road doing rapid push-ups without apparent effort.

'Hah, pretending like he's not busting,' jeered Gatta. Gatta could do more push-ups than Luke but no one else knew this. 'He doesn't look like the push-ups type.' She pointed at the prone, now nearly black reptile in the middle of the table and whispered, 'His arms are really wimpy.'

Luke kept reading. 'The males have got two bumps just behind the ummmm clo-aca, which is the word for their bum, between the abdomen and the tail.'

'Two bumps?'

'Yes, they've got, um, two penises.'

'Two penises? What for?'

'I don't know what for. They're called hemipenes and they're inside the body.' Luke scrolled further down and turned an even deeper shade of scarlet. 'You can stroke upwards from the tail and make them stick out.'

'No news there. You're doing an impressivo colour change yourself, btw.' Gatta cramped sideways with laughter.

'It says don't try to do this to the lizard yourself – get a professional.'

'A professional what? Lizard stroker?' she choked.

Luke said woodenly: 'The females have no bumps but two little red dots in the same place. We might be able to tell those.'

'What – now?'

'Yes, now. We are so not having this conversation again.' He reached for the sleeping animal. It reacted not at all as he turned it over. Luke and Gatta leaned forward and peered at it in silence. After a moment she reached out a black painted fingernail to the base of its tail. 'Here. Two little bumps. No red dots. Agreed?'

'Okay, agreed,' said Luke. 'He's male. We are not doing any stroking.'

'I'm glad that's settled. It makes him so much more of a person.' She added generously: 'You can name him now.'

'Name him?'

'Totally. And now he can have a proper name, not something dicky ungendered like Bobbie or Kim or Tyler.'

Luke knew not to respond to the jibe at their uncle but felt a pang for his mother. He looked at the lizard. 'Nothing comes to mind.'

'Your chance is gone. I'm going to call him Alexander.'

'Alexander?'

'Yes, cos he could conquer the known world by the time he's thirty,' said Gatta, who'd knocked off the whole week's history unit in an afternoon. 'It took him half a day to get off the mountain and get two slaves a hundred times his size.'

Luke looked at Alexander and saw a creature with more potency than he'd had a minute ago. His sister had a knack for changing the world into something more vibrant and charged with meaning. Or maybe she simply saw what he missed.

'Maybe his slaves had better do his dishes,' he said.

'He's not doing them. He's got no hands for a start,' she said, gathering plates.

'Actually, it's weird because up on the mountain I gave him a power bar and he held it in his front foot, paw, claw, whatever, to eat it. I didn't think lizards did that. But I guess there's all kinds of stuff we don't know about him or reptiles generally.'

There was a death ray sound. Gatta groped in the labyrinthine pockets of her jumper, extracted her phone and made a face. 'It's Mum.

Had to leave in a hurry. Have you had dinner? XX.

'Hah!' She typed a reply at lightning speed.

Luke grabbed the phone from her. The text read:

Yes. It was delicious and lovingly prepared. Thank you sooo much. You are a domestic goddess.

He deleted the last three sentences and pressed Send. 'It doesn't help,' he said.

Gatta's eyes were shining. 'She's the chameleon, you know. At work, she's this super-organised people manager.' She put on a fawning warble: '"Holly helps us all be our best selves",' then spat, 'Here at home, she's the queenest queen bitch ever. She hates *you* because you look like Anders. He's your father! It's your fault you look like him? What are you going to do, dye your hair black and try to be shorter?'

'She doesn't hate me. And you have to stop pretending you think you have a different dad. You make it so hard for her to be nice to you.'

'It was her fault Dad left. And now Brendan's never here either.'

Luke sighed. 'It's his job to be away.' Brendan, their next-door neighbour, was a geologist. 'And it's us he likes; it's not like they're partners.'

'They would be if she stopped letting Ty run her life.' Gatta slammed the saucepan in the sink.' I just don't get why she can't get over her and Ty being foster kids together. One day even Brendan will get bummed out and some babe will take him away and we'll never see *him* again either!'

'Oh wow!' Luke said. 'Look at Alexander.'

The lizard was still prone but his colour was now a vivid moving patchwork of purple, green and yellow, the borders drifting and swaying. It made them seasick to look at him.

'God's undies!' whispered Gatta. 'Do you think he's getting feels off us?'

Luke shook his head wordlessly. Their anger dissolved into awed bewilderment. The swaying patterns slowed and faded.

'Dogs can smell fear, supposedly,' said Luke. 'Maybe it's something like that.'

'He's not like anything. He's going to change our lives, isn't he?'

'I don't know anything except he's decided to be with us for the moment. And that he's really into colour.'

Alexander was drifting back to blue, with residual tints of mauve and green that now looked much more harmonious.

The humans washed up. Gatta put the bowl she'd given Alexander in the cupboard with hers.

'We're going to bed,' said Gatta when they'd finished. 'Do you think he needs to pee-pee?'

Luke frowned. 'I don't think reptiles wee. I think they do this combined thing, both things together.'

'Number one and a half? Well, won't he need to do that?'

'No idea. I don't know how often they need to.'

'He's in the house. Shouldn't you start, like, toilet training him?'

'How do you suggest I do that? And why me?' said Luke, irritated.

'You remember Fatso? Brendan went outside with him and peed in the garden till he got the idea and they'd pee together.'

'Alexander is a lizard not a Labrador! And it took Fatso six weeks.'

'All the more reason to start early. And Fatso was stupid. Alexander the Great conquered the world. He didn't have time to learn things slowly.'

Gatta's reasoning was so illogical there was no way to argue with it. Going her way was simply easier. Luke picked up Alexander and laid him along his forearm. The tail curled gently around his upper arm and Luke's heart tugged again.

He went onto the back veranda, the air crisp on his skin. It smelt clean-washed. Alexander's tongue flickered, tasting it.

'Well, at least she's got to see us pretend,' he said and set the lizard on the grass. He flushed.

'I don't know why I'm such an idiot,' he muttered, as he lined himself up out of view behind the Christmas bush. He unzipped his pants. He couldn't see Alexander. 'Bloody idiot,' he repeated, but in fact there was a novel freedom about peeing outside in the dark. Afterwards, he waited a few minutes, enjoying the cool prickle of grass against his toes, the lemony scent of the myrtle, and having nothing trying to kill him or argue with him. Then he sat on the veranda step.

Five minutes later there was still no sign of the lizard and Luke realised he'd been a Championship dickbrain. How would it know it was time to come back? What had possessed them to assume it was like a pet? They'd seen what they wanted to see: a miraculously human-smart creature which intuitively understood them. Who wouldn't want that? In reality, it was a prehistoric reptile with an unknowable brain. Frozen in the storm, it had sought warmth and food and protection. He had stupidly and selfishly taken it out of its own world into an alien one with fatal dangers: dogs, cats, cars, chemical poisons. He felt wretched, and with every passing minute that no lizard emerged from the darkness, more wretched still.

'Nailed it?' Gatta's shadow fell on the step.

'He hasn't come back.'

'He will. He's out there exploring.'

'No, he's lost.' Luke tried not to show his anger. The lizard was his responsibility. He had let Gatta suck him into her fantasy. 'Maybe not lost, but he's got a lot more world out there. And his real home to go to. He won't come back.'

'Lukey, he will.' She sat down next to him. They waited in silence until it was too dark to see further than the lawn edge and they were shivering. Luke couldn't make himself put his arm around her.

'I'm going in,' he said finally. 'You should too.'

Luke went to bed as miserable as he'd ever been. The whole photographing the fire thing had been excruciatingly wrong. He'd had a fall-back position in case of no fire, but really it was like he'd willed it into being. Not just fire-tolerant plants but precious rainforest incinerated, and thousands of animals: wallabies, pademelons, potoroos and bandicoots, echidnas and possums, baby birds in their nests, those who couldn't flee, injured or orphaned or burned to death. He felt so sick he retched.

And what had possessed him to go beyond the warning sign? He could have died at least twice and what would that have done to Gatta; to his mother? Taking the lizard home was the next in his string of stupid decisions. Letting it escape into the darkness was the latest.

'You're just feeling sorry for yourself,' he snarled. 'It was cool and you thought it liked you and now you've lost it.'

He imagined laughter at stupidface Luke. No, he was hearing real laughter. Gatta.

He got up and padded down the corridor to the kitchen. His sister was sitting on the back step, hunchbacked…no, in a doona, and talking to her left shoulder. Alexander was back and Gatta was midnight venting like she used to with Fatso. Luke was about to interrupt when he heard his name.

'…ace choice in Luke. He's peace and love in human form. Thinks if he believes enough in goodness, he'll make it happen. Well, la-la land there, buddy. He couldn't make it happen for Mum and Anders. You know, Mum used to be a mum when we lived in Sydney and had a dad? Anders. Mr Blond Perfucktion God. And I was the nasty troll child.'

For seven years, Gatta had fiercely stoked her bitterness. Luke bent his head against the cool window. He knew what was coming next: the conversation she'd overheard hiding up the ash tree after her Sissy Frocks Bonfire. Between Anders and Ty.

Sure enough, Gatta repeated Anders' words: 'He said, "I cannot be the father to such a daughter." Then Ty, Black Belt in Biotech, says, "Two blue eyes don't make a brown." And Anders went back to Krautland three weeks later. Ty busted up Mum and Dad to get his sister back. And he used me to do it.'

'Not the whole story, Gatta,' Luke mumbled. She refused to blame Anders for not bothering to research the small print of eye colour inheritance. Anders had wanted a career wife as little as he wanted a tomboy daughter. A son in his image hadn't been enough. He'd seized on the infidelity excuse to leave. And Gatta had seized upon Ty to hate.

'The only good thing about Ty is he's only ever here when Mum is. He lives in his Tosser Tower in Dynnyrne. And Mum, Mum allegedly lives here but she's at work, like, all the time. Because she prefers meano goblins to us.'

Immunoglobulins. Mum and Ty at Flexig made stuff normal people couldn't even pronounce. But there was no point talking to Gatta now – she was on a rant because they both knew they'd lose their mother to the job in Sydney. Holly's children wouldn't be enough to keep her here either. Any more than it was enough for Dad.

Luke tiptoed back to his room.

He woke to darkness, deep silence and cold. Luke groped for his tangled covers. A fold of blanket was wedged against his chest. He reached under his armpit to pull it out and felt not a blanket but something smooth that wriggled, and a tiny but unmistakeable flick of a tongue on his finger.

'You idiot,' said Luke. He was unaccountably, ridiculously happy. 'I could have rolled on you. Who knows what colour the mush would have been?'

He picked up Alexander and laid him on his bare chest. The lizard smelled earthy and faintly metallic. Four sets of claws prickled. He lifted Alexander above his head to tuck him under the top edge of his pillow.

'Try to stay there,' Luke instructed. 'If you come down here, remember I warned you.' He giggled. Nothing he did was making any sense, but Alexander had chosen to come back. And he seemed to have the knack of unmooring Luke from his careful, rational self.

Chapter 4

Luke awoke sweating in sunshine – the sun hit his bedroom at 5am in summer – bruised all over, with his hands on fire. He'd been thrown by lightning, battered by hail and smacked himself a dozen times while careering about on the mountain, and had only hastily washed his shredded palms. Now his mal-used body was taking revenge. Everything hurt. But he reached up and found the tip of a tail beside his left ear and felt at peace. Not because Alexander had returned, but because while sleeping, his brain had untangled itself and produced a solution.

He rolled out of bed and manoeuvred himself gingerly into a pair of boxers and a tee. The boards creaked in the hall but Gatta would sleep through Armageddon and his mother, who wouldn't, wasn't home. The light-flooded kitchen was nearly as warm as his bedroom, so he grabbed his laptop and a glass of milk and took himself out to the veranda.

He set up the laptop on the apple crate next to the little stone Buddha, and got started. The sun climbed. Tiny silvereyes twittered and fussed in the grevillea. Luke heard nothing, frowning and hunched, occasionally stretching his hands.

'Oh good, it's Luke,' said Mrs Fazackerly from next door's garden. The stumpy figure of Audrey was behind her, already wearing her hat.

'Morning, Mrs F.' He rubbed his eyes. 'Good morning, Audrey.'

'Oo,' said Audrey, waving her chubby hand.

'Luke, I need to let the girls out. Their run is muddy after the rain and the wet isn't good for their feet. Can you be hawk scarer while I get Audrey breakfast?'

'No worries, Mrs F.'

The old woman opened the wire hatch and chickens spread out onto the fresh grass, darting and bobbing. Luke looked around quickly. There was still no sign of Alexander. He was not so big that a determined chicken, with allies, couldn't fight him off. If he got bigger… Luke would worry about that later. Though if his plan worked, he might not have to.

Gatta appeared, yawning, in her violently purple and yellow tartan pyjamas. Best not to mention what he'd overheard last night.

'Alexander came back. How did he get in? Didn't you close up?'

She stretched mightily. 'I doona-ed up, stayed out till he got back. He was cold and moving kinda slow so we doona-shared and had a talk. I told him not to stay out so long because it stresses you out. Then he went to find you and I went to bed. Want some brekky?'

'Yes.' Luke's stomach, which he was sure was sentient, gave a muted roar. 'I've found out some stuff. That website I looked at about lizard sexes? It doesn't apply to monitors. And he isn't a normal monitor anyway. So we don't really know what sex he is.'

Gatta shrugged. 'He's a he.'

'Not that it's relevant anyway. We can't keep him. We'd have to get a licence for a start and keep him in a cage and feed him frozen mice. That is just so far off working for me, and Mum would go clear off her nut.'

'I knew you'd say that,' said Gatta. 'So come and have brekky and we'll figure out how to get him back on the mountain.'

Luke stared, suspicious. Why wasn't she fighting?

Gatta ignored the look and continued blandly. 'Mum texted. She'll be back this afternoon. Is your phone off? She only texts me when she can't get you.'

'Same as why she talks to me – she's not big on going to work with claw marks on her face.' Luke closed his laptop.

Audrey had come out to look after the chooks. She was sitting on the grass in her hat, surrounded by chickens, everyone looking for snacks. She would give them all the beetles but sometimes kept a worm for herself carefully wiping off the soil and stroking it tenderly first. Luke and Gatta enjoyed her joyous hugs but had learned to avoid her kisses. She looked up and waved.

'Oo. Atta,' she said.

'Fifty years of eating worms. The path to health and happiness,' said Luke.

They waved back and walked into their kitchen.

Alexander had made his way up into Luke's weathered Tasmanian Oak shelving. He was propped up on his front legs between two jars of preserved peaches and looked expectant. His colour was back to indigo, with tints of dark blue drifting back and forth across his shoulders.

'He looks bigger,' said Luke.

'I think he looks cuter.'

'He's been eating a lot. But he'll fit inside my pack. I can ride up above the Lost World on the road and walk down.'

'You don't have to ride up the mountain. I want to come and I want to go by bus.'

Luke was dismayed. Having Gatta along was bad karma. 'We can't. There is no bus.'

'There's the Hobart Explorer. You can get off at different places and shit.'

'Do you know how much that costs!?'

'You notice Alexander is listening again?'

The reptile's gaze was switching between them as they spoke. He was more upright and his eyes were luminous.

Luke refused to be distracted. Gatta had a habit of creating real world problems that he had to sort out. 'For the two of us that'll be 40 bucks or something.'

'Not if Hamish is driving. I'll sort it with Lucie. You get brekky. I want Russian Caravan tea, thanks.' She grabbed her phone and started her lightspeed texting. Luke went to protest but she held up a stop hand. Just like Mum. He risked decapitation if he pointed this out.

As Luke was setting the cereal down, he felt a sharp scrabble on his leg followed by tugs on his boxers and shirt as Alexander swarmed up his back, over his shoulder, and then down his arm onto the table.

'Ow,' he said belatedly.

'The Luke ladder!' whooped Gatta. 'Look at him conquering the world!'

'One human leg at a time,' muttered Luke, rubbing his calf.

Breakfast was punctuated with death ray noises and bursts of texting from Gatta. Alexander chased nuts around his bowl with his nose and splashed milk gaily.

'You sure you're not related to Fatso?' asked Luke. The lizard's bowl was empty. Alexander looked at Gatta, who obligingly poured him more cereal. Her phone buzzed again.

'We can get on the bus near the Livingston Street corner at eleven,' Gatta said. 'Lucie asked Hamish to help out. He's cool with it.'

'He can't be! It's his first job! If his boss finds out, he's *gone*.'

Gatta shrugged. 'If he doesn't help, he's even goner. In *World of Warcraft*, she's a Death Knight – anger, cruelty, vengeance, all that good shit – and he's just a noob DPS schmuck."

'So she can, what, virtually kill him?'

'Much worse. She's his Guild Leader. She can freeze him out so he can't play. That's dick-drop-off serious. Anyway, he's going to pretend to scan our phones so it all looks legit. His boss won't know.'

Luke threw up his hands in defeat. 'Get some proper clothes on then,' and he left to get changed.

The first problem arose when they tried to put Alexander in Luke's backpack. They could lower him in, but when they tried to zip the top he thrashed and scrabbled and hissed. He wouldn't quieten even when Gatta told him he was handsome and brave and why wouldn't he sleep after breakfast? As soon as they unzipped the top he sprang out and wriggled straight up Luke's arm to his shoulders, adding more scratches to his forearm. He looked erratically green and purple and his tail twitched.

'Okay,' said Gatta. 'You'll just have to wear your hoodie.'

Luke gestured at the sun pouring through the kitchen window. 'Kill me now.'

Chapter 5

They set off into the bright morning. The deluge had swept gravel driveways down the hillside and spread them in swathes across the road. Anthony from two doors up, with his manbun and baggy shorts and crocs, was shovelling the remains of his garden walkway back into a battered wheelbarrow. To Luke's hoodie he said, 'You feeling okay, mate?'

'Flu,' said Gatta.

By the time they reached the Huon Road, Luke was sweating and irritable. Whenever they were out of sight of people he flapped his hoodie up and down to create a breeze around his neck. Each time he did this, Alexander hissed softly. According to Gatta, he was blue, so they assumed it was a hiss of approval.

'I'm not doing it for you, Butthead' grumbled Luke.

The orange Explorer bus appeared. It crunched to a stop and a stony-faced Hamish pretended to scan their phones. They sat in front of a group of Chinese tourists, Luke hoping that anything odd on his part would look like Western weirdness and that they wouldn't have enough English to tell anyone local about it anyway. A fit elderly couple in matching Mont hiking shirts nodded at them. Gatta beamed in return, to encourage goodwill, while Luke scowled to discourage conversation. The couple smiled uncertainly.

'This is going well,' Luke fumed under his breath.

Gatta grinned idiotically.

The bus ground upward. The windows were all closed. Luke was starting to steam, and so apparently was Alexander. As the bus swung wide to make the turn onto Pinnacle Road, Luke felt claws approach the open front of the hoodie. He dragged Alexander back by the tail. Moments later, the lizard made another attempt, which Luke caught just in time. The elderly couple looked at them curiously.

'Eczema,' said Gatta, miming scratching her neck.

'You should have told them I had lice,' muttered Luke, red in the face from heat and embarrassment and rage. He reached his hand inside his hoodie, took a sweaty grasp of Alexander and managed to hold him more or less in place till they reached the Springs, where the bus stopped. The bushwalkers gathered their poles and packs and departed. The Chinese remained and the bus pulled out. Luke and Alexander maintained their hot, miserable stalemate, till Hamish slowed for an uncharacteristically confident pademelon who was fossicking by the roadside. The tourists exclaimed happily and there was a flurry of phones and cameras.

Luke took advantage of the activity to open the window next to him. When the bus moved off, a cooling breeze washed over his face. He sighed with relief and opened the side of the hoodie slightly. Alexander hissed and gave a lurch, his rear claws digging painfully into Luke's neck. Luke lost his grip on the slippery body and grabbed frantically to hold the front of the hoodie closed. Alexander writhed and clawed for purchase. Luke struggled to his feet.

'We're getting off,' he snarled and marched to the front of the bus where Hamish, enslaved by a teenage witch but no dummy, had pulled the bus over.

Luke flung himself onto the verge, mumbling thanks to Hamish, and barely allowed the bus to accelerate before releasing his cowl. Alexander launched himself into mid-air past Gatta, and made for the undergrowth. Luke threw his pack at Gatta and stripped off the hoodie in disgust. It was slimy and putrid with sweat. He preferred not to think about what contribution Alexander had made.

'Mm, eau-de-boy,' said Gatta. Luke glared.

The lizard had dived into a heap of stringybark ribbons and was rolling ecstatically like a dog in a possum carcass. Then he popped up, looked at Luke and Gatta and raced off up the forest edge on hind legs. In motion, his awkward shape was transformed, the powerful hind legs balanced by the tail, so he seemed to barely deviate as he flowed around ferns and grass clumps.

'The new winger for the Hawks!' said Luke. He felt lighter and cooler and indescribably relieved. Alexander was now safely back in his own territory, or nearby. What he did next was up to him.

They followed at human pace. The fire had stopped short of the Pinnacle Road and here they were walking in an intact forest of yellow gum and stringybark, which dropped away steeply to their right. Far below, the Derwent sparkled blue.

They couldn't see Alexander. His colours had turned to rippling shades of olive and emerald so they saw occasional moving grasses but nothing animal. After a time, Gatta stopped and said: 'Can you see him?'

Luke squinted. 'No.'

'Should we keep going?'

'Yes. If he wants to find us, he can.'

But by the time they reached the top of the Old Hobartians track they still hadn't seen any sign of him.

'What do we do now?' Gatta asked.

'I don't know. This is where I wanted to take him, or a bit down the track to be away from the road.'

They waited indecisively. Somewhere up the slope, a currawong clinked. Gatta kicked her boot against the grass. With a brilliant burst of scarlet, a lizard appeared, flashing into view right at their feet. He sparked alternating colours of blue and red, like a police car.

'He was there all along!'

Alexander had his tail in his mouth and was performing rapid circles in front of them, still flashing red and blue.

'The little bastard,' Gatta said. 'He's got a sense of humour!'

He stopped, looked up at them and hissed. Then he turned tail and darted down the track.

'He looks in charge now,' said Luke as they followed. The lizard seemed impatient, zipping ahead and returning, bounding over the smaller boulders and slithering down the larger ones. He was now bright red.

After a few minutes of scrambling, they slowed. Alexander faced them in the middle of the track, propped on four legs with his tail high. He waited for them to stop, hissed and disappeared into the brush.

'I think he just threw us a *Chill Here*,' said Gatta.

'We don't have any choice,' said Luke. 'We can't follow him into that.' Dense flowering cheeseberry surrounded them. The burnt smell was strong now. 'I could do with a drink,' continued Luke. 'There's a stream a bit further on.'

'He meant us to wait here,' said Gatta.

'Do you realise how totally bizarre that sounds? He's a lizard. He's got a brain the size of a Malteser.'

'Bruh, Mr Leslie has a brain the size of a…brain and he's a total clown shoes. And what about Audrey?'

'Audrey has Down syndrome. Her brain didn't come out like other human brains.'

'Well, can't Alexander have something like reverse Down. For lizards?'

'Now you're being a nit.'

'Well, Christ on a unicycle! Look at that!' she mouthed.

Alexander was moving carefully up the steep stony path towards them, hopping onto rocks like a kangaroo. It wasn't that which made their jaws drop. Between his two front limbs he held a broken eggshell. It was grey, slightly marbled and about twice the size of a hen's egg. He hopped closer and laid it carefully at their feet.

They squatted down. Luke reached out to touch it, hesitated, and looked at Alexander. The lizard's eyes were bright, the cats' pupils wide. Luke picked the egg up. Two broken halves were placed inside each other. The shell was thick, much thicker than a chicken's egg, with a creamy white interior which looked pitted and crumbly.

'I think it's his own egg,' said Gatta, awed.

'Maybe,' said Luke, puzzled. 'But this egg is really old.'

'How old?'

'I don't know. But it looks sort of weathered.' Luke touched it gingerly. The outside looked and felt like worn granite. The inside was gritty.

'It's not made that way?' asked Gatta.

Luke pulled out the inner half and handed it to her. 'No, it's very hard but looks sort of scratched up, see?'

'What do we do with it?'

'I don't know,' said Luke and continued, very firmly, 'but we need to do what we came here for.'

'Okay,' said Gatta.

He looked at her warily.

'You're going to do it anyway, Luke. And it doesn't matter; I know what the outcome will be.'

'Hmph,' said Luke, more relieved at her easy agreement than annoyed at her condescending tone. He shrugged off his pack and took out a ziplock bag of power bars stripped of their packaging. He tipped the bars into a pile in front of Alexander, hesitated, and placed the eggshell carefully off the centre of the track. He stood up and cleared his throat. He felt very foolish.

'Alexander.'

The lizard hissed. He was navy blue.

'See, he knows his name,' whispered Gatta.

Luke started to say goodbye, felt idiotic, waved, which was just as bad, and gave up.

'Come on,' he said to Gatta, and started back up the track. He only half-believed what Gatta was certain of, and his chest was tight.

There was a flash of a snaky body on his left as Alexander overtook and then turned to face them, head cocked accusingly. His tail twitched.

'Okay,' said Gatta. 'Do we agree that this question is sorted?'

'Yes,' said Luke and scooped up the lizard against his chest. Twenty claws dug emphatically into his shirt. They collected the power bars, which were now officially Alexander's, and the eggshell.

'All your worldly goods,' said Luke. And sighed. His moral self was appeased, but their problems had barely begun. Beginning with how to get Alexander back down the mountain.

Gatta read his mind. 'I know how we'll do it,' she said. 'Get Mr Handsome home on the bus.'

'I am so not wearing that hoodie again.'

'No, too freakin' hot. I've got a cool way. Watch and be awed, bruh.'

Gatta took her shirt apart, ripping each sleeve off the shoulder seam.

Luke gaped. Gatta had been covering her arms since Grade 8 and never shared why, but Luke suspected it had to do with winding up their mother. After the first fully sleeved six months, and some furtive conversations between Holly and Tyler, her mother had touched Gatta's arm as they washed up after dinner.

'Darling, why are you always so rugged up?'

'Oh, it's the *self-harm* conversation,' said Gatta, and added with lacerating contempt: 'Why would I cut myself? I'm not the one with the problems.'

Holly had left the kitchen tight-lipped. And the mystery arms had remained concealed since.

Now Gatta was calmly knotting the torn end of one sleeve, creating a bag. Her arms were alabaster white, toned and perfectly unscarred. Luke watched, fascinated by the smooth movement of her muscles under the skin, like a living statue. She looked up and grinned.

'Vampire arms,' she said. 'How about this for Alexander's ride home?'

Luke frowned doubtfully.

'Come here, Hunkasaurus.' She picked up Alexander and tried to lower him into the open end of the sleeve. His tail didn't lash, but it swayed. Luke gently folded it near his body which he accepted, and pulled the bag up to cover him.

'Now what?' asked Luke.

'Approach,' she ordered. 'Hold him here,' gesturing at her waist. Then with Luke holding the lizard's weight, she lifted her shirt – Luke managed to avert his eyes without dropping the bag – and buttoned the cuff of the sleeve through her bra strap. Alexander lay snug against her stomach in his pouch.

'What do you think? Solved, no?'

She was right. Her oversized shirt fell loosely and as long as she didn't lean back, there was no tell-tale reptile-shaped bump to be seen.

'Okaaaaaaay,' said Luke, still doubtful.

'It'll work, okay? I'm cool, he's cool. Let's have some lunch.' She lifted Alexander out. They found their way to the stream and comfortable boulders and shared the power bars.

Again, Luke wrestled with the question of what they should feed Alexander over the long term. Animals were no different to humans in eating what they liked and thereby killing themselves, quickly or slowly. He wasn't sure whether Mrs Google could help much; nothing seemed to apply to Alexander.

'What do you think we should feed him?' he asked.

Gatta, telepathic as ever, said, 'Don't sweat it, Lukey. We just all agreed he can decide stuff for himself. We give him whatever and see what he eats.'

Luke was partly convinced.

They made their way back up to the road and Gatta stowed Alexander away. When he settled into the makeshift bag, his outer lids were down.

Their bus pulled up. Hamish's face went from sour to startled when he saw them. Bone-white girly deltoids had that effect. Gatta beamed at Hamish and they settled in the rear seats. Luke pulled out the eggshell. It didn't reveal anything more. Gatta tapped one half with her black nail, first carefully, then harder.

'It seems really strong. And if that grey stuff is meant as camo, it would hide well in stones.'

'Yeah, the shell's strong, it'd survive lying on stones.' Luke frowned. 'I still think it looks old. I wonder if it really is Alexander's. He doesn't seem old. But I haven't a clue how we'd find out.'

'Brendan might know someone,' said Gatta doubtfully.

'We can't tell Mum,' they said together.

'And if Ty sees him...' said Luke. The memory came to both of them: Ty in his Italian suit, standing on their lawn like the grass was an offence. His two sudden gliding steps to the left, the reach-down and the flick of his wrist. The tiger snake, head bashed out against the veranda post, tossed aside. Gatta put a protective hand over her stomach.

'Anyway, it's not like we can ask Snoozeosaur.'

They both looked down. Alexander was asleep.

Luke snorted. They'd made exactly zero progress. He stowed the eggshell halves away in his pack, wincing as he folded them into his stewing hoodie. It smelled like the Black Death in there.

Chapter 6

As soon as Hamish set them down at the Livingston Street corner, Luke's anxiety amped.

'We don't have a plan for Mum. Or Ty.'

'If she takes that stupid job, she'll leave us here because *schooool*, and she'll be home, like, never.'

Luke nodded glumly. 'But she'll have Ty keep an eye on us. So worse.'

'We put Snoozeosaur in my room. It's a no-Mum, no-Slime zone in there.'

'And when he gets out?'

'We catch him. *Aaargh, what is that thing!* We never saw him before. We put him outside. If Ty's about, we'll make him run like buggery or throw him over the fence.'

Luke faced her. 'And dogs and cats and cars?'

'Lukey, Lukey.' Gatta knuckled his nose, but tenderly. 'He did his own midnight lizard thing last night and he came back. He's decided to live with us.'

'I can't believe I'm letting this happen.'

'It's not your decision. He's going to do what he does.'

'Well, we still better get home before Mum does. We'll maybe sneak this past her but we'll get bugger-all past Tyler.'

They were within sight of their house. No new parked cars. 'Slimeball defences good to stand down,' said Gatta.

Luke was showered and climbing into fresh clothes when the front door closed and his mother's heels tock-tocked up the hall. By now, Gatta would have sorted Alexander and put on standard nothing-to-see-here Gatta gear. Mum didn't need her alert levels upped by bare vampire-white arms.

'Hi Mum,' he said, emerging into the hall.

She stretched up to give him a peck on the cheek. They'd been the same height the year Anders left – rubbed noses for goodbye. Now with every centimetre he grew, she was more remote.

'Is Gatta home? We all need to discuss my job.'

Ty stood watching at her back like he always did, like he'd placed himself in her life. They mirrored each other: sheaves of black hair, classic tailoring, clear pale skin and cool blue eyes, restless but controlled, compact, precise; existing in their own armed camp of two. As ever, Luke wondered how much his mother's camp was a prison. He wanted to slip messages past the guards, ride in through the palisades and rescue her. It was easier than accepting that she herself was one of the guards and that he and Gatta were part of the world she wanted to keep out.

He waved vaguely. 'She's about.'

They went to the kitchen together. Gatta faced them in front of the big window. She had on a shapeless sweater and a semblance of her Ty face, the poking-the-toad one, but her eyes were darting. When she saw them, they betrayed a tinge of panic. Something must have gone very wrong: Gatta had a No Panic policy.

'Oh, Mum, there you are,' she said, too loudly. 'How was Sydney? Funky restaurant? New shoes?'

Luke managed a quick sweep of the room behind Mum and Ty. His heart nearly stopped. On the highest shelf were the cookbooks, and resting on the cookbooks, his tail snaking down the spine of Ottolenghi's *Plenty*, was Alexander. He was examining Stephanie Alexander's *Kitchen Garden* with his flickering tongue and he was a lovely wash of aquamarine.

'Tyler has given me a job opportunity,' Holly said tightly. 'We went out for dinner to talk it through.'

'And did a nice evening at Tetsuya's persuade you?'

Alexander had come out in green blotches. His tail was swishing. Luke was in agony that the movement would catch someone's eye.

'You might, *Agatha*, for once,' said Tyler to Gatta, 'attempt a divergence from rudeness. Just for variety.'

Agatha. Her birth name was one of the million things Gatta couldn't forgive Anders for. Ty used it liberally.

Alexander vanished. He didn't run over the tops of the books or leap in the air or fall. He simply wasn't there. Luke gaped. Then he caught a flash of a yellow eye. He couldn't pinpoint where.

'Let's all sit down,' Luke croaked and pulled Gatta across to the dining table, leaving the seats opposite for Tyler and Holly so their backs were to the shelves. 'What's the job, Mum?'

According to Holly, Luke could usually be counted on to be reasonable but Gatta, however resigned, would fight at every street corner. Holly was oblivious to any undercurrents, but Tyler, ever alert for subterfuge, seemed instantly to pick up on the atmosphere. His gaze flicked around the room.

'What happened to your hands, Luke?' said Holly.

'Came off my bike.'

She nodded, then let out a breath. 'Ty is expanding Flexig into Sydney. He wants me to set up and run the lab.'

Tyler put a hand on their mother's shoulder. Gatta snorted.

Holly pushed on. 'You know my job here is a dead end. He's offering me the Sydney lab – which should be extremely profitable – as a share in the business.'

If he slid his gaze across the shelves, Luke could get an idea of Alexander's outline but when he tried looking directly, he couldn't see him at all. The illusion was impossibly perfect. The lizard's head was now over a corner of the shelving, the buttress piece Luke had chamfered with one of Brendan's wood chisels. Luke could admire the close join he'd achieved, the grain of the upright, the slight difference in colour of the horizontal, on Alexander's skin. Further to the right, on the lizard's body, was an exact image of the jar of Mrs F's pickled jalapeños, labelled in her meticulous teacher's writing.

Gatta said, 'More money for Lisa Ho and Manolo's then?' Her hurt at abandonment was talking, but this was incendiary. On purpose?

Luke kicked her under the table. 'Not the time,' he said through gritted teeth. They needed to discuss this with their mother, but much more urgently they needed to catch an invisible lizard before he changed his mind and became visible. They needed to agree to everything, finish the conversation quickly.

Gatta ignored him. 'Why isn't Ty going up there himself? Cheaper to send you?'

'Your school behaviour predicts a lifetime of defrauding Centrelink,' said Tyler. 'If it were different, you might understand.

Behind him, a jar of pickles rocked precariously, then the crockpot on the bottom shelf rippled. A red tail lashed against the floorboards. Tyler registered the panic on Luke's and Gatta's faces and whirled around.

'We see through you, slimeball,' yelled Gatta, her first diversionary tactic having misfired.

Tyler pushed his chair back. Holly grabbed his arm, mistaking his intent to investigate for anger. Gatta deployed her snigger, usually guaranteed to produce blind rage in anyone over thirty, but they were out of time. They needed an emergency change in strategy. Luke could see the whole ridge of Alexander's back now, a menacing red advancing towards Tyler's ankles. Their only chance was somehow to make him disappear again.

Luke strove to let calm wash through his brain; he pictured a wave of cool blue sinking through him and into everyone in the room. He held both arms out, palms down, his right hand gently over Gatta's. She started to snarl, then powered down, uncertain but trying to synch with him. Luke was determinedly not looking at Alexander, focusing instead on Holly, who was still restraining their uncle.

Gatta said, 'I'm sorry.'

That got everyone's attention. It took Tyler half a second to spot the tactic – Gatta was smiling queasily – but by then the emotional temperature had dropped, even if it was by three people being stunned. Two of them stared at her. She repeated, 'Yeah, I'm, like, sorry.' She squirmed. 'Ah, maybe we all need to go and chill.'

Tyler frowned. Gatta always, always, advanced gleefully towards a fight and counted a win as emerging the largest smithereen. He scanned the room, trying to pierce through to whatever they were hiding. Gatta's face was in a rictus, like a chimpanzee about to attack. Luke's pulse accelerated to thrash metal and his cool blue cloud was dissolving. He needed more help. He squeezed Gatta's hand – come on, Gatta, you do have reverse gear – and miraculously she understood. Her fake smile melted into genuine serenity. Together, they exhaled. Luke knew he didn't need to look for Alexander now and Tyler knew that they'd won. Won something.

He tried to restart the battle. 'Sorry for what? Today or the last five years? Sorry for being a heartless little reptile?'

Gatta retaliated with the nuclear option: she smiled into her mother's eyes. 'I do want to talk about your new job, but today's gone a bit...' She waved a hand.

Holly smiled back uncertainly.

Tyler started to reply but his sister stopped him. 'Yes, Gatta, we'll do it tomorrow. Let's all have a bit of time out.' She rose. 'Come on Ty. We've got work at the lab.' She looked at her children. 'You can manage your own dinner...?'

'In the bag, Mum,' said Luke.

The adults left. Holly had visibly refocused, relieved to divert her attention from the hard stuff back to her job.

Ty was slower to leave. He had unfinished business. Anything deliberately kept from him was a threat and no threat could be ignored.

Chapter 7

As soon as the door closed behind them, Alexander reappeared on the kitchen bench. His tail was still a demonic red. The rest of him was doing a subdued version of his police car strobe When Luke picked him up and held him against his shoulder, the red receded a little.

'Mum's not asking, she's going,' said Luke.

'Yep, doing a runner. But *he* is staying,' said Gatta. Her jaw trembled halfway between rage and tears. She managed to laugh. '*Little reptile!*'

Luke felt like crying too but a subject closed by Gatta had a hunking great padlock on it. Instead he said, 'Did you really have to make everyone so angry so fast?'

'Yeah, sorry. I was trying to make them so mad they'd leave and not spot him.'

'Could you believe his camouflage? If he were a computer, the processing power that would take is insane! Even if he loses it when he gets mad himself.'

Alexander was now almost all aqua and bonelessly relaxed. Luke stroked him. A trail of iridescence followed his fingers down the lizard's back. As the sparkles slowly faded, Luke felt a little less sad.

'He communicates with his skin,' said Luke. 'And he disappears when he feels a threat.'

'He reads us so fast,' said Gatta. 'How does he do that?'

'Fatso did it too. I think it must be smell or something. And tone of voice.'

'Yeah. Did you notice he did his zap-out as soon as Ty started talking? Maybe he can hear evil,' said Gatta, seriously. Then she brightened. 'He does know his name, and when you're talking to him. Watch this: Alexander!'

His eyes blinked open.

'Luke,' she said, pointing at him. The lizard made a faint gravelly sound that might have been *oo*. She pointed at herself. 'Gatta.' Alexander thrust his snake head forward and back, bobbing like one of Mrs F's chickens, and hiccupped.

'Okay, so he isn't built to make people sounds. But he understands them.'

Luke scratched his ear. 'Maybe we're seeing stuff we want to see.'

'Nup.' Gatta tossed her hair and planted a kiss on Alexander's neck. Indigo ripples spread from the touch. 'You are the coolest,' she whispered. 'Come on, Technicolosaurus, let's go out and name the neighbourhood.' She scooped him off Luke's shoulder and placed him on her own. Both of them had turned the same excited shade of pink.

'Stay away from people. I don't think the world's ready for him yet.'

Luke sat down with his hands in his hair. For two days, he'd felt like a kayaker in unknown rapids, carried forwards, paddling vainly for control, never able to relax long enough to plan a course. He opened his laptop. His body ached and his brain felt battered.

What questions to ask? How to ask them? Were there other animals like Alexander? Was he a one-off, a mutant, or had he arrived here from another country – South America? – and, if so, how? Where did the egg fit in? Alexander looked like he'd sussed out human motives incredibly fast, but how much did he understand, really? How did other animals communicate with people?

Luke began to type.

For hours he sat and grumbled, got up and paced, sat down. Through the window, the shadows lengthened from the west and the lemons in their tree turned gold.

The door banged. Gatta appeared in the doorway. 'We're hungry! And I think he's nearly dead.' She put her hand on the table. Alexander negotiated his way down her arm and crawled up to Luke. His head was an unenthusiastic pastel pink and his body mostly slate grey. He sank down and closed his eyes.

'You look like a half-sucked mango,' said Gatta to Luke.

He raked down his wild hair. 'I've looked up a lot of stuff but I don't know how much it helps.'

'We're all pretty wasted.' Gatta brandished a chef's knife. 'Food will save us.'

Luke took it from her and started chopping mushrooms for an omelette.

'I wonder if he likes jalapeños,' said Luke.

'He was checking a lot of things out,' Gatta said. She reached in her pocket and scattered a handful of bush nuts and berries on the bench.

'He'd run up and, like, stick his nose at anything like this. Sometimes he was like, nup, straightaway, sometimes he'd sort of nip them and spit.'

Luke peered at the assortment. 'Any idea what his tastes are?'

'Nup. But he was looking for something.' She pointed at blue gum and candle bark buds. 'It for sure wasn't gumtrees. I picked those for him and he didn't even sniff them.'

'Hm.' Luke went back to chopping. 'Maybe he's got a deficiency of some sort. Like when cows lick salt.'

'Or like having a caramel slice deficiency at Banjo's Bakery.' Gatta whisked the eggs. 'Actually, no, it wasn't like that. He was really serious. And he didn't find whatever he was looking for. He learned about a hundred words as well. I told him the names of things. He was listening.'

Luke cocked an eyebrow.

'Yeah, weird, being a boy and all. But he got every word.'

'That's what Mrs Bunton says about her cats. And that they can read. It must be them that read all her newspapers.' They grimaced, remembering being asked inside to look for the missing Sabrina. They had spent a nightmare afternoon groping in the foetid dark of the Georgian sandstone house, which the old woman had turned into an airless stinking dungeon. Piles of newspapers rose past the windows, scattered with lumps that might have been food or faeces, human or feline. They eventually found Sabrina's mummified corpse under a divan, dead a lot longer than *last Sunday*.

'He's way smarter than a cat.' Gatta started cooking the egg. 'And he's friend, not an alien overlord.'

'I'm not sure what he is,' said Luke.

The glory of butter and egg wafted through the room. Alexander's outer lids slid up. Luke, setting out tall glasses on the table, had a sudden image of Godzilla lying between the glass towers of Tokyo. Another animal that hadn't fit.

'I read a lot of stuff,' he said, 'but I don't know what it means. I couldn't find another reptile that looked like him, anywhere in the world. But there are four-and-a-half thousand species. They keep finding new ones, in jungles and stuff. What he most looks like is a Varanus, a monitor. But his chest and his shoulders are wrong. I think he might be some kind of mutant.' He looked at the lizard between the glasses. 'Like Godzilla, but nicer.'

'Godzilla meant well,' said Gatta, sliding equal amounts of omelette onto three plates. Luke frowned.

'I also read that you can overfeed reptiles and it's bad for them. A carpet python can get by on a couple of mice every six weeks. And if they get fat they can get sick, just like people.'

'He looked hungry today,' said Gatta. 'And does he look fat to you?'

'No, but he's getting bigger.' He held his forearm along Alexander's body. 'When I picked him up yesterday he was as long as this.' He pointed from his fingertips to the inside of his elbow. The lizard was now obviously a good three centimetres longer.

'Maybe he grows when he's invisible,' said Gatta.

'He looks more tortoise-y now.' said Luke. Alexander already had an omelette-sized lump at his midsection. Once again, he'd ignored the lettuce and cucumber, though he did enjoy exploding a cherry tomato between his teeth.

'Mum and Ty can't find out about him,' said Luke, sweeping up the last mushroom.

'We've got it sorted,' said Gatta. 'Alexander!'

His head turned, instantly more red.

'Camo!' she said.

Without moving, he disappeared. As before, the illusion was complete, with the shiny white edge of his bowl, the water glass and the grain of the wooden table visible where his head and forelimb had been. Only because he'd tried it before could Luke get an idea of his outline by flicking his eyes back and forth across the table.

'Belgium,' said Gatta, and a lizard was back on the table.

'How did you teach him that?' exclaimed Luke.

'He taught me. I was flat out teaching him new words, saying *pothole*, or something useless, and he hissed. Then he gave me a look like OK does in physics when he wants attention.'

Luke shivered. OK was Mr Klaassen, not named for being agreeable but for Zero Kelvin, the temperature of his stare. Luke looked at Alexander with new respect.

'Then he zapped out for a second, then zapped back and gave me the look again. He wanted the word for that. So I said *Camo*. We practised it. Then he zapped out and wiggled a bit, or maybe he didn't do it completely – anyway he wanted me to know he was still there. He was waiting for the word to come back.'

'Belgium?'

'I needed something I wasn't going to say by accident.'

'Well, it works. But that is so…' Luke waved his hands uselessly. 'Those things are all concepts. Only humans think like... I just don't...' He pushed his hands against his earhole, trying to stuff in thoughts that were too big.

'Chill,' said Gatta placidly. 'He did it and I bet he can do lots of other things and we're going to find out about all of them because he can stay now.'

Okay, now Luke had to stand up. Every time he thought he could fit Alexander into the world he understood, a new impossible thing blew his mind. He paced around, straightening chairs.

'If he's a mutant, he has a squillion complex mutations; and I can't even start on what he just did. If I could even get the basics, starting with the egg. Lizards don't lay *hard* eggs – they're sort of leathery. We need some help but I don't even know how to ask, let alone who, even if we could ask without looking like we had a little Godzilla at home in the bedroom.'

'Brendan?' said Gatta.

'Of course!' Jeez, the chance to offload some responsibility! 'We don't have to tell him everything and we can ask him who to ask. But he's been out of network for a week.'

'Text him,' said Gatta, stacking dishes. 'He'll call when he's in range.'

'Maybe we can ask him about Mum too.' Luke had to raise it, padlocked or not.

'Mum? Brendan's a bloke, not her bestie. And they haven't talked for, like, four years.'

'They did when we first got here, after the divorce, and there's stuff he might know about the settlement. Money stuff,' said Luke.

'Why do you want to ask about money?'

'Mum sent me an email about her Sydney job while you guys were exploring. No, we don't get a say. She's going to do it. She'll be up there weekdays but she'll fly back if we call and say we need her.'

Gatta looked at him bleakly. '*Hi Mum. I think Luke died last week because he smells, but I've gone blind from vitamin deficiency and I can't find him.* But what's with the money?'

'She says she needs the job because of school fees and debts and the mortgage, but I don't get it. The mortgage on this place wouldn't be big.'

'It's not about money. She's trying to ditch Hobart and us. Remember when Slimesuit was like, *She wasn't made to have kids?* Whatever.'

Luke agreed but always found himself defending their mother. 'Anyway, you should text her. Maybe you could stick with being nice as the new strategy.'

She gave him the finger listlessly, but started stabbing at her phone. Luke picked up his own phone.

> Hey Brendan. News about Mum. And we have questions re geology and biology. Could you help or send us to someone? Call soon? Thx.

Gatta wordlessly handed him her phone. Her text read:

> Sorry I was a bitch. Ty makes me mad. Pls can we talk without him. G.

Luke couldn't remember her talking sans sarcasm to their mother since the beginning of high school: the start of the Hidden Arms Era. He gave her a hug.

'Thanks, Gattacus.'

'S'okay,' she muttered.

Chapter 8

Alexander didn't wake up when Luke took him to his bedroom. Luke hesitated in the doorway. Where to find a spot for him? Somewhere concealed, but where he could get out easily. And not too cold. Lizards needed warmth, even if they could live on the Mountain. Eventually, Luke opened his top drawer, which was a lizard hop from his mattress, and placed Alexander under the socks, leaving the drawer half-open.

He'd gone to bed and it was past midnight when his phone rang.

''Lo, Brendan.'

'Luke, sorry it's late. We're drilling down in the gorge from six tomorrow and I won't have network again. You okay, mate?'

'Uh, yeah, good.' And it was nearly true. Luke had never known Brendan not to be able to solve something, or make it not scary, which was the same thing. But explaining was hard.

'I, uh… we've found something. I, um, can't tell you about all of it because you might get into trouble, or,' he stumbled on, 'we'll have to give it back, or to someone who won't–'

'I get it,' Brendan said. 'You can't tell me. You're good at doing the right thing so I'm sure you're doing that now. Fire away.'

Luke's grip on his phone eased. 'We've got something else. I'm not sure how it ties in. It's an egg.'

'I take it you didn't find it in the fridge. Do you know if what's inside is alive?'

'Uh, no, I mean a broken shell. And I think it's, like, really old but I'm not sure.'

'So you want to know what kind of egg it is and how old?'

Just having the conversation made Luke more relaxed than he'd been in days, maybe weeks. He was suddenly furious at his own dad for leaving. I shouldn't have to carry all the shit.

'Uh, yes. Exactly.'

'And you would rather the person you asked didn't tell anyone else?'

'Yes.'

'Well, as it happens, I think I know someone.' Brendan's voice lightened with amusement. 'I'll text you her details. It's Emeritus Professor Joy Cantrell. She's a geologist but big on the biosciences side. She's always had a low bullshit threshold so she's made enemies but she's got the right kind of friends. Including me, I suppose. And she knows all about having to withhold information till the right time.' His laugh came down the phone. 'They haven't managed to completely get rid of her yet. I'll email her now. She'll pick it up in the morning and text you an appointment. Will that work?'

'Yes, sure.' His surrogate dad, unlike his biological father, always delivered. 'How's the work going?'

'You mean, when am I coming home?'

'Sort of both.'

'Not sure. If I could make the rain stop and get a replacement drill bit, it could be end of the week. The terrain's a bastard. But if I put in an incomplete survey or someone later finds rare earth where I missed it, I stop getting jobs.'

An adult explanation.

'And what's up with your mum?'

Luke relayed the contents of his mother's email, finding his voice unexpectedly hard to control. He gave up. 'She's going to go and Ty's going to be here all the time and I want to know why and it all sucks.'

There was a long silence. Then Brendan said, 'Ah shit.' Luke heard him scratch his stubble. 'Sometimes that woman needs shakin. Not for what she's doing, I admire that, but for still treating you like a little kid. You're not.'

He seemed to come to a decision. 'She'll kill me for telling you because this is really hers to tell, but here goes: she invented a biotech device–'

'UC186,' said Luke. 'It's a drug delivery thing, a folding designer protein that transports a precise dose through skin, which is hard. 186 means it took 186 goes to make a working one.'

'Well done! Both you and her. That's why I do rocks. But when Anders left, he took her start-up down. Never mind how, but he did. She owes about eight, maybe ten million, because she wouldn't declare bankruptcy and she wouldn't sell the patent. I think your hyena of an uncle is a guarantor for her repayments, though he didn't tip in any cash. If Flexig is opening a branch in Sydney, I reckon they're using it to relaunch her product.'

Luke had got stuck three sentences back. 'My mum owes eight to ten million dollars?'

'Thereabouts. She'll make it back, no worries, if they can get that technology to market. She's high-end smart, is Holly. But my guess is Ty is her silent partner, so he'll make a mint. He's a whole different kind of smart.'

Luke wasn't sure who to be most angry at. 'Why didn't she tell us?'

'Dunno. Ashamed? Thought she'd scare you? Worried that telling you would make her lose her nerve and sell out? But if I'm right about the relaunch, she needs this thing to succeed.'

Luke stared up at the faint outline of the ceiling rose. Anders, who had left. Anders, who had sent that infinitely cruel email to Gatta saying he wasn't her father. Anders, who had vindictively tried to destroy his wife's life work. And Ty, who went on and on about self-reliance: Ty was just a tapeworm. Luke didn't need to be angry at his mother.

'Luke, you there? Don't be too hard on Holly, okay?'

'It's all good. I think I can even get Gatta to help out.'

'*Angry Agatha* helping her mum? Top effort Luke. You've discovered more than an egg.'

'Yes, um, thanks.'

'No probs. Though after blabbing, I might just keep hiding down the gorge for a while.' Brendan sighed. 'Look, I have to get up in three hours. You'll hear from Joy in the morning. She'll see you if she can. Try not to waffle. Have your facts straight, including what you do and don't want to tell her. She'll be okay with that. She's not okay with having her time wasted.'

'Understood. Night, Brendan.'

'Night Luke. Hug your sister for me.'

Chapter 9

In the morning, Alexander appeared not to have moved, entirely cocooned in socks except for one dark blue hind leg. But security was an illusion; there were people, institutions, for whom Alexander would be irresistible, the rarest, most fascinating thing they'd ever seen. The most valuable.

Eight million dollars' worth? Ten?

Luke was about to talk with some of these people. He went into the kitchen to think about things that didn't make him overflow with self-disgust: the sun slanting clear from the east, lighting the last white flowers of the leatherwood, picked out against the glossy green. Familiar, unthreatening, morning things. He focused on nectar and birds, black and white liveried New Holland honeyeaters, hopping and flitting among the flowers, curving their beaks into the petals, *jick jicking* to each other. A flash of a yellow patched wing, a swoop and an insect snatched from the air, then a *phseet*. Effortless agility, grace. Feeding. Life sustaining itself by using other life. *Exploitation*. It was natural.

His brain had swerved back to swampy territory: Alexander was worth a mint. Would money bring his mother back?

'No!' Luke said aloud. Alexander was himself, not a Merc or a Beemer, not Luke's to sell. And the more defenceless he was, the more it was Luke's responsibility to protect him from danger, which currently included Luke.

His phone rescued him by chirping. It read:

UTAS Life Sciences Building, Room 391, 10am. Joy Cantrell.

He had a shock of mixed relief and anxiety. Even over a text, the professor sounded formidable, demanding of facts and clear thought. And he hadn't been ordering his thoughts at all; in fact, his questions had grown woollier and more wayward every time he went near them.

The source of his angst crawled in from the hall, a dark dull green, a lizard-shaped avocado. His lumpy shoulders and spindly front legs looked more even more awkward and rigid than usual. He stopped in the patch of sunlight in front of the fridge, regarded Luke with porridgy brown eyes and sank to the floor.

'Well you made it before Gatta, though that's no feat,' said Luke. He stepped over the basking lizard to fetch the stone-like egg. Fifteen minutes of thinking later, he was a little clearer about the questions he wanted to ask Professor Cantrell, mainly by avoiding the murky parts.

He heard a hiss. Alexander was erect, yellow eyes brilliant with the look that threw ice needles.

'Whoa, okay! You've got my attention.'

As Luke watched, Alexander ran a gumnut highlights reel on his body: images of the gumnuts, acorns and bush fruits Gatta had gathered, all projected with hyperreal intensity. After the last, there remained a wavery olive blotch – and a demanding stare.

'You're still looking for something. It's okay, we'll help you look.' Luke no longer bothered wondering whether Alexander understood him. But how did it work? Alexander's own language wasn't words. How could he possibly understand theirs? His skin was his communication. But since he was plainly designed for communication, who was he supposed to be doing it with? There seemed to be only one of him.

'Well, that was full-on. I think we both deserve bacon and eggs to recover.'

They ate approximately equivalent breakfasts. What would happen if they kept feeding him this much? Would he stop eating? Now almost hemispherical, he waddled back to his patch of sunshine and fell asleep.

Gatta wandered out in her bilious pyjamas.

'I need to go to the uni,' he told her. 'Brendan found someone for us to talk to.'

She yawned and stepped carefully over Alexander. 'Smells like bacon. Looks like a pig. I'll take him to the Botanical Gardens.'

'How did you know I was about to suggest that? Did he run his catalogue past you too?'

'What? Nope.' She yawned again, hugely. 'But yesterday he wasn't just sampling, he was searching. He needs more material. We'll find a heap of stuff to test out at the Gardens.'

'You two obviously have your own chat room,' said Luke to Alexander. 'And you were bordering on rude.'

Alexander opened his eyes. He made a sinuous movement. A lizardy shrug? Then his blue skin faded to silver, ripples flowed down it and green fronds appeared, waving gently. Luke realised he was looking at a sunlit stream bed, water flowing over smooth stones, there on his kitchen floor. The image was clear in every detail. Its serenity reached across the room and washed though him.

Gatta laughed. 'I think he's saying *Peace, bro.*'

Luke shook himself. 'Did you get an actual vibe from that pic?'

Gatta fluttered her fingers over her heart.

Luke rubbed his face. 'I can't even.'

His little sister squeezed his shoulder. 'Go with it, Luke. He means well.'

'Like Godzilla? I'm not sure I like that he's *making* us feel things. We don't get a choice.'

'I think we do. Anyway, is that any worse than all the other choices we don't get?'

Chapter 10

Luke put on his newest shirt, swiped at his shoes with the brush, wrapped his exhibit in a clean tea towel in his pack and biked off past the relaxed jumble of dry-stone walls, wavery pickets, trailing vines, leggy roses and festively messy stringybark ribbons hugging their satiny trunks that constituted front gardens in his street. As he approached Huon Road, the pickets became pointier, whiter and more prim. Fences sprouted gates and rooflines straightened. But all the structures were still festooned, nestled or totally swallowed in plant life.

How did the billions of people living in inner cities, totally detached from growing things, manage? Why didn't they wither up and drop into dust? Maybe they had; they just didn't know it. Luke pictured Sydney's streets heaving with apparently living people strolling in their Skechers and white earbuds; in reality all empty rustling husks, unknowingly dead.

Life Sciences. The building entrance was marked by two gigantic elephant seals facing off in glorious grey fibreglass. It was 9.55. Luke banged through the front door to find himself surrounded by taxidermy: one display showcased the Tasmanian tiger looking defiant rather than extinct; and the other, Antarctic birdlife, featuring an insouciant Adelie penguin suspended mid-backflip. Luke's confidence rose slightly. Humour was allowed here.

He made for the stairs. The stairwell had a three-storey mural of the ocean, floor to surface, and he wanted to stay there, drowned in its blue. Instead, he surfaced onto the worn lino of the third floor and hurried on, counting door numbers, passing noticeboards, conference research paper summaries, other dull green branching hallways, biohazard warnings prohibiting entry and, unexpectedly, framed delicate line drawings of aquatic ferns. The corridor seemed endless. But there was only one door left. It didn't have a number and it was closed.

He took a breath, knocked and opened it onto a reception area. Its walls were lined to the ceiling with shelves stuffed with files. Opposite him was another closed door.

Guarding this door from behind a desk was a set of imposing shoulders clothed in olive drab and the top of a black-haired head patterned with cornrows. Then she lifted her face. His first and only rational thoughts were that she was far too young to be Brendan's professor, and how many years older than him was she? Then his mind was swamped in images: he saw queens – scholar queens, judge-queens, warriors – but all queens. Boadicea, Cleopatra, icy Elizabeth in her jewels.

'Luke Schache,' he heard her say. 'Exactly on time.' Then her voice receded to nothing. He smelled dust and blood and heard a thousand spears, longbows, rifles, thump against chests in tribute; saw the line of her jaw lift as vanquished sweat-soaked enemies slumped into the dirt.

'*Hello*? On time but actually forgot to get out of bed?' Her voice was deep. Not gravel, thought Luke, not the riverbed, more like the river. Like a West Indian cricket commentator.

She was looking less amused and more irritated. 'You are Luke? And you do talk?' Her head cocked sideways, forming a long line of muscle from her jaw down to the delicate hollow at the top of her breastbone.

'Yes, I'm sorry,' he said. Later, he'd rather have pulled his tongue out through his backside than have it say the rest of what it said to her: 'Do you play cricket?'

'AFL. Why, do you want me for your team?'

'You remind me of Michael Holding.'

'My ancestors might have passed on all the colours of the rainbow to me, but I'm not a middle-aged Jamaican man.' Irritated was rising towards angry.

Luke knew he desperately had to retrieve the situation but his brain was shorting out, seizing on random words: rainbow? Was she LGBTIQ+? Trans was possible. He had never thought about whether he was open to a trans relationship, but decided instantly that he was. Or maybe she was... 'Rainbow like Sue Bird and Megan Rapinoe?' The magnetic, formidable sporting power couple.

Her green eyes were arctic. 'No, like Sudanese, Danish, Fijian and Chinese heritage. And I think you'd better get out of here before Prof arrives.'

But it was too late. A crisp voice behind him said, 'Good morning. Luke? I'm Joy Cantrell. What's wrong, Shona?'

The professor was at least a head shorter than him, even in her heels and immaculate grey bun in which few blonde strands remained. She looked like a Swedish air hostess in a classic 1950s advertising poster.

'I don't know what you heard about him,' Shona said, 'but he's an utter idiot.'

'Well, I've had at least forty years more experience of dealing with idiots than you, so we'll see how I get on. And he's an idiot with a half-hour timeslot.'

Professor Cantrell led him into a tiny windowless inner office and offered him the chair opposite her desk.

'Brendan isn't an idiot and doesn't ask for trivial favours. What do you want to ask?'

Luke's brain settled back into calm order. He was reassured rather than intimidated by her manner; and reason was how *he* operated. He unfolded the tea towel in his hands. 'We found this and we want to know where it came from and how old it is.'

She pulled the tea towel towards her but made no move to touch the egg. 'And you found it on the mountain?'

He nodded.

She examined it more closely then looked up, puzzled. 'It's not exactly my field, but an explanation for this doesn't come easily to mind. It's a big egg, and egg size is proportional to bird size.' She rummaged in a drawer while continuing. 'It's too small for an emu. The Tasmanian emu got hunted out pretty early and I think it was a bit smaller than the mainland one. Maybe a shy albatross, but kunanyi would be way out of its territory, same for a Cape Barren Goose.' She produced a tape measure – her fingers were unexpectedly thick and gnarled – then stopped as she saw his face.

'What? Brendan said you had information you couldn't share. I respect that but try not to waste my time.'

Luke cleared his throat. 'What if it's not a bird?'

'A reptile?' She shook her head. 'Most of them have leathery eggs. Not all of them, true. And its surprisingly hard to predict between species. But none that fit down here. Saltwater crocodile eggs would be the right size and they're hard, but there hasn't been a Tasmanian crocodilian since the Triassic. Too cold. Besides, this thing flew.'

'Flew?' Luke's confusion was plain.

'Or flies. Look at the shape.'

'It's like, egg-shaped.'

She raised her eyebrows over her glasses and made an impatient beckoning motion.

'I mean,' Luke said, 'it's not spherical.'

'Exactly,' she said. 'Berkeley did a huge study of 50,000 bird eggs – 1400 species – only a couple of years ago. The eggs with the most ellipticity and asymmetry, that's length and pointiness, produced birds that were the strongest fliers. They thought it had to do with streamlined body shape.'

Luke thought hard. 'What about animals, birds that have to swim?'

'Very good!' The professor looked pleased. 'Penguins also have long pointy eggs. What else did you think about your egg?'

'It's very hard. And it's a sort of blotchy grey. So we thought it might have been laid in the open, around stones, which is what the camouflage is like. And maybe the parents weren't always around to protect it.'

'Excellent observations and plausible conclusions.'

'Some of them were my sister's,' said Luke.

'Good for her,' she replied but she sounded abstracted. She was examining the shell with a magnifying glass. 'There's something odd about the top layer. Usually mum puts on the final layer of calcium and mixes in some colour just before she lays the egg, but this seems to be different altogether. And it's uneven.' She looked at him over the top of her glasses. 'Can I keep this for a week or two?'

He hesitated.

She took off her glasses and laid down the magnifier. 'Look, Luke. I know I haven't helped you much, except to confirm you have something very unusual. We haven't been able to get onto the age of the thing, your other question, and I can't tell that by looking at it either. To get any further, I'll need to use a microscope and some comparison materials, maybe chromatography if I get really stuck, and I'll need material for DNA. We might be able to get close to the age with amino acid dating, but I'm not sure if it's outside the scope of the technique.'

Luke said quietly, 'It's not mine.'

'Well, can you make a decision on behalf of the owner? I assume you haven't stolen it.'

Luke looked down at his knees. This was the bigger question. He now faced a larger choice: either Alexander was an animal dependant on Luke or he was something new. Sentient. A friend.

He realised he'd already made the decision.

'No, I didn't steal it. The owner gave it to me. He knows I've taken it this morning and he trusts me. And I'll trust you. But nobody else can know about this yet.' He placed his hands on the table. 'The egg *is* from some kind of reptile.'

'Thank you, Luke,' Professor Cantrell said formally. 'I acknowledge your trust and understand that secrecy is the most important principle here. I'll do what work I can myself. If someone else does an analysis for me I can disguise the source. If I can't find a way to do that, I won't do the test.'

Luke had never been addressed so like an equal by someone he felt so unequal to. Unable to speak, he nodded stiffly.

The professor smiled. 'Thank you for trusting me with this intriguing puzzle.'

Luke was exhausted when he returned to the outer room. Shona stood with her back to him, braids in a thick rope to the middle of her back, her face in quarter profile. At least this time when his imagination took over his brain he was halfway prepared. As she scooped a stray few strands away from her face, one elbow up, he saw two fingers drawing the string of a compound bow up to her cheekbone: a horsewoman at full gallop. She turned that fierce, wildly beautiful face towards him.

He struggled to shape his words into something vaguely sensible. 'You look like you'd rather be outside.'

'So do you.' She laughed, not unkindly.

'So do we all,' said Joy Cantrell. 'I'm late, but it was very interesting. Luke will need to come back to see us in a week or two, Shona. I'll text you when I have some news, Luke.'

'Thanks,' said Luke then added. 'Sorry, but I have one more question.'

'Quickly then.'

'You mentioned a Tasmanian crocodile from the, ah, Jurassic? I didn't know we had a dinosaur. What's it called?'

'From the Triassic. *Tasmaniosaurus triassicus*. Technically it's not a dinosaur, or a crocodile. There's an abstract of Martin Ezcurra's paper on the wall down the corridor.'

'Just after Gandalf,' said Shona, closing the door behind him.

He realised why he needed directions to a wizard when he came to the dog-eared poster of a windblown Ian McKellen leaning on his staff, above the words: *So it begins. The Semester.*

The next poster was behind glass, dense with words and meaningfully entitled: "The Osteology of the Basal *Archosauromorph Tasmaniosaurus triassicus* from the Lower Triassic of Tasmania Australia." He searched the tiny text and cramped tables for a recognisable picture of a placidly chomping head with weeds trailing from its mouth or a roaring biped with tiny knitting hands and far too many teeth.

A long brown finger reached past his shoulder, pointing at a crowded line diagram. 'This is the guts of it,' said Shona.

He jumped and his knees actually wobbled, but he made himself look at the picture. 'It looks like an island archipelago in the Caribbean.'

She laughed. 'It's a diagram of all the bones found and Ezcurra's re-measurement of them. It took me a solid week to grasp it all.'

Luke wondered whether he was imagining a heat field emanating from her body. 'Why isn't there a picture of it?'

'The author isn't sure enough of what it looked like to put one in that kind of publication. Here, I've got one.' She scrolled through her phone. 'Or at least somebody's idea of it, based on the bones we found here and the skeletons of overseas animals we think are relatives.' She held the screen up to him. She smelled of grass and diesel fumes.

His heart accelerated, not because of her scent but because the animal in the picture looked like a stocky Varanus, a monitor. Its front legs and head were more massive than Alexander's and its neck shorter but it could have been his cousin.

'How old is it?' he asked.

'About 230 million years – 50 million years before *Jurassic Park*. They found it on Knocklofty. About two kilometres thataway.' She pointed past him.

His heart was hammering in his chest. 'Do they know what it ate or anything else about it?'

'Definitely meat. They found a nearly intact jaw.' She pointed at a tiny brown photograph with a lot of mean-looking serrations. 'And it had a very good sense of smell.'

Despite the jolt this gave him, he was incredulous. 'How do you figure that from a skeleton?'

'We studied it last year. The inside of the skull had a huge space for the bit of brain that interprets smell. It's one of the highlights of the paper and what makes our guy important.' Her voice was trailing off and she was looking at him intently. 'Why are you so interested? Is this relevant to why you came to see Prof?'

'Um, I'm interested in dinosaurs and it's so cool that we have a local one,' he said, not exactly lying. Her green eyes narrowed. He was thinking that he'd last approximately thirty seconds under interrogation, when his phone pinged. It was Gatta.

More weird shit @ RTBG. Mum meeting us at home. Cu.g.

'It's my sister,' he said, smiled weakly, and spread his hands in a what-can-you-do gesture. 'I need to go, sorry.'

She looked doubting. He was unfortunately reminded of Michael Holding's nickname, which was Whispering Death.

But then she smiled suddenly and said, 'I'm going to allow you the Sue Bird reference as a compliment.'

Chapter 11

Luke unchained his bike. 'Don't be an even worse idiot,' he told himself, aloud. 'Alexander is a lizard. You're hearing hooves and thinking zebras.' He swung his leg over the seat. The bike was getting too small. 'No, not zebras, unicorns!'

Shona's arm pointing towards Knocklofty – meaningless as a direction, but what a heart-stopping line that gesture made down her chest to her waist. And the name on her shirt pocket – an area he couldn't look at more than fleetingly – was Garang. He tried its shape out on his lips.

He was late. Mum's car was in the driveway and he hadn't told Gatta about the debts yet. Luke paused to gather himself on the front veranda.

Above the front door was a reminder of how badly their family financial chats could go: Luke's Rose Window, leadlight design and craftsmanship by Luke, glazing by Brendan, had been a surprise present for Holly's birthday. Their mother had withheld admiration and delight until she ascertained what the materials cost. Gatta was furious. Another miserable post-divorce birthday. Their poverty, which they mostly ignored, was confronting on birthdays. And when Luke thought about school fees. Or when Gatta, an expert op-shopper, flaunted it.

The kitchen was in a state of wary truce, with the two sides encamped across the table, hands clamped around respective mugs. Gatta had promised to be nice but was having difficulty executing this fully. Holly wore the resigned but determined look he recognised from her long-ago extraction of a plastic giraffe from an infant Gatta's nostril: the process was going to be painful but the outcome was never in doubt. Both of them looked hugely relieved to see him.

'Hi Mum,' he said. 'Let's go sit outside.'

'Good idea,' said Gatta, too heartily, and got up. Over Mum's head he raised his eyebrows and mouthed 'Alexander?' at her. She shrugged, which was unhelpful. His gaze swept round the room, but there was no sign of a lizard, visible or camouflaged.

They settled themselves on the back veranda, placing their mugs on the apple crate next to the little stone Buddha.

Luke knew his mother was girding herself for the effort of justifying her abandonment of them. He saved her the trouble. 'Hey Mum. We – well, I – know about the debt.'

Two pairs of amazed eyes swivelled to him.

'Who told you?'

'Brendan.' Luke, looking at Holly, mentally encouraged Brendan to stay down the gorge. 'I asked him because I knew there was more than the mortgage.'

'That still wasn't his to tell,' said Holly.

'How much is it?' asked Gatta.

'As of today, about 8.2 million.'

Gatta gaped. 'How did you–'

'It was Dad, wasn't it?' said Luke.

Holly stared somewhere past Luke's ear for a long time. Then she said, in something like her normal voice, 'He made the major investors pull out. But the fuck-up was mine. I could have stopped them but I didn't have the spine.' Her lip twitched. 'Then.'

Luke and Gatta were open-mouthed at more than the unimaginable sum of money. Mum swearing?

And Luke had thought spinelessness was solely his department. 'But you still own the... thing,' he said.

Holly gave a tiny, tight smile. 'If I'd declared bankruptcy, I would have lost it.' She swallowed some tea. 'I decided from then on, everything was up to me. My future. Your futures.'

'And you decided on working,' said Gatta, equally tight. 'If you had done bankruptcy, you wouldn't have a debt and wouldn't have to work so much and wouldn't need to go away now.'

Luke realised suddenly that he'd been looking straight at Alexander for the last minute. He was six metres away in the tree daisy, resting across two low branches. He was not projecting shiny leaves and happy daisy flowers, but he was a good background dark green. The end of his tail, though, was swaying and purplish. Luke shot Gatta a warning look. *Don't get mad now. Do not.* 'But it's important, isn't it, Mum? UC186.'

Holly's eyes came alive. 'There's nothing else like it. Anywhere.'

Luke felt a jolt. He knew his mum was smart, but for the first time he saw the other person she was – the scientist, whose soul was in their invention.

'Big Pharma spent decades trying to make this. I saw it, long ago, the shape of it – the shape is the function – and I kept going till I brought it into the world. Something that had never existed. *Every single human* will be helped by this. Everyone who needs immunisation, antibiotics, cancer treatment, everyone. And it's mine. My company, Transcend, owns it.'

But Gatta continued, 'So if you wouldn't do the bankrupt thing, how does the paying back work?'

'It's a business mortgage. I negotiated extended repayments.' Holly's voice was flat now. She was looking in the general direction of the blackwood, not far to Alexander's left.

Gatta persisted. 'Why didn't Uncle Ty help you pay it? He's loaded, isn't he?'

Holly looked directly at them for the first time. Luke nodded idiotically to keep her looking at them and not at the tree daisy, where the swinging tail was now mauve and moving faster.

'I wouldn't let him. Ty looked after me when our parents died, through some awful foster homes and worse institutions. He worked two jobs while we both studied so we could have more, look better, be successful by looking successful. But the Transcend debt…' She looked like she was swallowing bile. 'After Anders, I didn't want anyone paying for me ever again. I don't ever want to feel owned. The person who pays for us is me.'

Gatta's face was working, grimly resisting the implication that all this might justify the years of mothering she'd been denied.

Then Luke saw Alexander descend from the tree and stalk towards them, his crest smouldering crimson against the green grass. Mum was looking down. He bared his teeth at Gatta and frantically gestured at the advancing shape. *Gatta! You're arcing him up!!*

Gatta sprang up, touched her mother's arm and walked away down the veranda steps, blocking her view of the lizard.

Her mother was so surprised at the apparent expression of sympathy that it shocked her into thinking out loud. 'Every day you look more like Anders,' she said to Luke. 'You sound like him. But you're not him. And you're so good for your sister.'

Gatta was pacing the grass with her arms cradled in front of her chest. It looked as if she was hugging herself for comfort, but Luke knew she was holding Alexander under her sloppy jumper, soothing both of them and concealing him all at once.

Holly went on. 'Tyler buys me all the things I need, clothes and,' she gestured to her elegant pixie cut and immaculate nails, 'what I need to go to work and feel like the person everybody thinks I am.'

Luke didn't want to think about how much of the resemblance between Holly and Ty was manufactured by Ty. Would it help, though, if Gatta understood their mother's appearance had a purpose beyond preening?

Gatta came back up the steps with her arms low around her midsection. She gave Luke a tiny nod. To Holly she said, 'You've had an insane amount of crap to deal with – from Anders, from those dick-brained investors, from Ty – who is a shakedown, I don't care what you say.'

Holly shook her head wearily, but Gatta went on: 'And. So. Much. Shit. From. Me.'

Luke was stunned. Gatta was actively making peace. For the first time in seven years. For Alexander's sake.

'You have to go to Sydney and do this job and you should and I'll stop giving you shit. I'll try. But one thing…'

Holly's equally stunned face went back to wary.

'You've dropped the f-bomb. Means I can drop it now.'

Holly laughed, a sound Luke had forgotten. 'Just be careful where you drop it.' She sighed. 'Your suspension. What you did was funny, this time, and probably true, but the school board had no option.'

Gatta's *Unsuperheroes Gallery* of teachers had been secure in WhatsApp, but freed into the wider world by a Year 10 fan whose fannishness exceeded her understanding of security.

Wander Woman, whose outdoor ed classes had been lost on the Mountain more than once, was affectionate in tone; and The Flash – unfortunate pairing of no jocks with voluminous shorts on sports days – also, more or less. Mary the West Coast Eagle was an honorary member named for the painting in the school chapel of the supernaturally serene Blessed Virgin, resplendent in gold leaf and Marian blue, the Eagles' AFL colours. Miss O'Malley frequently called on her help to survive her demonic Year 9s. But other entries were less fond. The Man of Steal, who Gatta fingered for thefts that had been blamed on students, became Betman when she spotted his urgent attention to horse racing during class. Watchmen and The Handyman, both too queasily attentive to the Year 8 gym classes, and Speederman named for his amphetamine use had required the school to take legal advice.

Holly shut her eyes for a moment, closing the subject. 'Luke, can you supervise her next three weeks' homework?'

Luke nodded. Making him responsible was delegation genius. Gatta was incapable of making him look bad and also capable of completing three weeks work in a week. Gatta made no comment, her expression bizarrely beatific. Luke wondered what colour Alexander was now.

'And I'll be home most weekends,' said Holly.

Luke exchanged a glance with Gatta as they mentally downgraded "most" to "occasional".

'You're leaving soon?' he asked Holly.

'I've got a flight this afternoon.'

So, Luke was right; this hadn't been a consultation but a briefing. He tried not to let his mood sag. Mum in Sydney was nearly like Mum in Hobart; already they sometimes went days without seeing her.

'Tyler will be around this evening to check in.' Back to briskness, she pecked them both on the cheek and disappeared inside to pack.

'Thanks for that. And for what you didn't bring up,' said Luke to Gatta.

Gatta was prone to bringing up the subject of her paternity in suspension-related conversations. Her first suspension, three years ago, was for asking Mr Afanasthasiou whether he was her father, on the basis of being a hairy dwarf. This was a week after Anders' email and after Gatta had told Holly she'd believed what Anders had said. Holly's rage, never seen before or since, only confirmed to Gatta that Anders had told the truth.

'No biggie. On our walk, Piglet and I,' – she caressed her reptilian lap – 'agreed not to bitch out.'

In which mind or minds had this agreement been negotiated? How much free will did Gatta have in making her screaming character U-turn? What was scarier – believing Alexander really was manipulating their emotions, or that he and Gatta were going insane?

Chapter 12

Holly's taxi backed down the drive as Luke assembled cheese and apricot chutney sandwiches. Alexander wove about the kitchen bench, patterned in shades of red and brown that jostled together as he moved.

'Hah!' said Gatta. 'He's reminding me. He's spent the morning hiding in leaves, when he wasn't off smelling blood.' Alexander sniffed a sandwich. 'Why didn't Mum just freakin' tell us?'

'She couldn't tell us when we were kids, then she wasn't around enough to notice we weren't kids anymore, then it just got too hard.'

'I can't even. She's an *adult*.'

'Maybe she couldn't admit she had something else as important to her as we are. UC186. She can't see it fail or go to someone else. It's hers. It's *her*.'

Gatta squinched up her eyes. 'If she'd been a man, they'd have given her a medal, or a grant.' Then she grinned. 'Big Love. Go Mum!'

It looked like Gatta's pro-Mum position might be permanent. And that she'd accepted Holly's invention as a deserving rival for her attention.

'Go Mum.' Luke handed her a sandwich. 'Food. Then tell me about the Botanic Gardens.' He slid a second sandwich in front of Alexander.

'There was a bunch of homey losers playing nasty rap, no cans, up the front of the bus. Everyone else was busy being pissed at them so we sat up back and I pointed at stuff and taught him words. When we got off, we didn't even make it through the gates. He did the turbo chook straight under the fence into those fields that sometimes have cows.'

'The Government House Gardens?'

'Yeah. Lot of trees. Bimbo me stood there and called like he was my dog. Then some random told me this wasn't an off-lead area.' Her mouth made a cat's bum. 'We're gunna have to carry Fatso's lead, for the dog look. Anyway, when he came back he wasn't zippy, and kind of poo brown. He gave me these.' She pulled out a few shiny acorns from her pocket. 'But he didn't look thrilled with them.'

Alexander devoured his sandwich with more determination than enthusiasm, though Gatta noted he'd sucked up the last chutney molecule. She doled him out another large spoonful. 'Chihuahuasaurus has had a hard day. I think he wishes he were bigger.'

Another Luke-sized lunch inside the lizard. 'He's doing his best,' said Luke.

'Anyway, after that, things went screwy. We went into the middle bit of the BG to that monster tree – it looks sorta like the ones he liked. He was zipping around, not really in camo but hard to see, so that was okay. Then I heard the homeys. They'd got, like, right into one of the man-eating plant displays, from Brazil or somewhere, and were doing rapper shit.' She threw a rapid succession of obscene hand gestures, her face furious. 'And taking selfies and trashing plants. One of the volunteers was yelling at them, but they were such total fuck-ups.'

Gatta grinned evilly. 'Then the volunteer came back with a spade. She was, like, garden gnome size, but really mad. They tried to get out but fell over each other and the plants got revenge. They cut themselves on that grass that looks like swords.'

'Swordgrass,' said Luke, unnecessarily.

'Yeah. I think there was that barbed wiry creeper too. Anyway, when they got out they were all bleeding and pissed off. That really threw him.' She indicated Alexander, who was still restless, not in his traditional post-food coma.

'He hates nasty. He was totally red and hissing and spitting at them like he wanted to tear out their eyeballs. When I grabbed him, he nearly bit me! Everybody was still checking out the douchebags, so I took him inside the conservatory. He even *felt* hot. There was, like, nobody there so I threw him in the fountain. It's okay, he can swim. He can hold his breath forever too. He sat on the bottom and went green. A kid saw him, but little kids see witches and flying reindeer and shit.'

She sighed. 'Slaying it, not. But we still had this mission. So I had a brain zing and took him to the oaks. He took off into the leaves and kept bringing me these.' She dug out more acorns, each a little different: fatter or longer or more cone-shaped. 'Then he took me to this thing.' She extracted her phone and showed Luke a picture of a dowdy tree with mid-brown leaves, not much larger than a bush.

'He collected a lot of its nuts. It was weird. He kept smelling them like he wasn't sure and trying to bite them and looking frustrated. It was obvious he wanted me to take them home. So they're in your sock drawer in a sock. I figured you had him sleeping there.'

She expanded the photo of the nondescript tree. At its base was a stake with a weathered label. '*Quercus cryptogermanii*, Hungarian Oak. Eurasian,' read Luke.

'Why is it called the Hungarian Oak if it's German?' asked Gatta. 'Did the Hungarians steal it or something?'

'I don't know. It sounds like it lives over a wide area, but not naturally in Australia. Crypto means secret.'

'Hungarian but secretly German. It's a botanic-y spy? Sorry, unhelpful. It's not the answer anyway. We'll do the gardens again tomorrow. We only saw about a third of it.'

They both contemplated Alexander.

'You know, he's looking sad, Lukey. Maybe he's still hungry.' She reached for the chutney jar.

'Don't give him more of that,' said Luke. 'Let's try him on an apple. The shape will be a challenge.'

'I don't think he needs any more challenges,' muttered Gatta, but she put an apple in front of Alexander. He regarded it dully. Then his tongue flicked out. He roused himself, waddled towards it and opened his mouth. It was too large and smooth for him to get any purchase with his teeth. He breathed in and out against its shiny surface, slowly turning Granny Smith-coloured. After half a minute, now almost fully green, he glared at the apple.

'I don't think he likes apples,' said Gatta.

But then he gave a little leap, heaving his chest on top of the fruit, stabilising himself with his splayed back legs and tail. His front legs held the apple like he was subduing it. Luke and Gatta watched, startled, as he slashed into the apple with the side of his mouth. It was like watching pork roast being sliced on a cooking show. Except the razor-sharp carving blade had serrations, which reminded Luke of the small brown picture he'd seen only this morning.

'Did you know Tassie has a dinosaur?' he said.

'Cool! Is that what you found out at the uni?'

He pushed his hand through his hair. 'I didn't find out much else, except that we're not all that stupid. The prof wasn't sure about his egg either. She's going to try to find out more.'

'Was she, like, scary?'

'No, but her assistant sure was.'

'Let me guess, he was small, and dumb and gassing himself up on boss petrol.'

'She wasn't a man and she definitely had brains.' He shivered. 'She wasn't little either.'

'Oh, like the Heemskerck?'

The Heemskerck was one of the less offensive *Unsuperheroes*. Mrs De Vos, history teacher, Australian bridge champion, Dutch, and as majestically round-bottomed as her ship namesake, was not entirely unamused when she discovered why her history class had such enthusiasm for the early Dutch navigators. Luke liked her.

'Not like Mrs De Vos.' He started clearing plates.

'Lukey,' said Gatta, 'spill!'

Luke gave up trying to hide his blush. 'She was, uh, really tall and had, um, muscles. She looked sort of African-Asian and she had these,' – he drew fingers over his scalp – 'like plaited dreads.'

'Cornrows,' said Gatta. Her mouth fell open. 'You've met Shona!'

Alexander was manoeuvring slices of apple into his mouth with his front claws.

'You've heard of her?'

'I've met her. She gave a women's AFL clinic at school. She's a goddess. She moves like–' Gatta attempted a spring-heeled leap which became a collision with the fridge.

Luke's single attempt at a ruck contest had looked uncannily similar. His opponent, about twice Luke's weight, hadn't bothered leaving the ground.

'Well, not like that,' said Gatta, picking herself up. 'I was totally crap at the clinic cos I'm so small. But I really want to play! It's so unfair only the boys got to play till last year.' She flushed too, remembering. 'Shona told me I had smarts and heart and they were the most important things, and I could be a champion midfielder. She's got incredible eyes.'

Luke nodded.

'She came out of the change room and the boys were frothing.' Gatta giggled. 'Soooo hard being a boy. But then she demoed some drills and the poor babies, they were shitting themselves they'd be asked to help. She couldn't ask them, cos they were boys and she's sort of a teacher.' Gatta looked regretful, 'But she'd brought some of her team. They were awesome dudettes but like–'

'Cubs around the she-wolf?'

'Exactly.'

'Anyway,' said Luke, needing to move the conversation to less unsettling territory, 'she showed me a picture of *Tasmaniosaurus triassicus* – 230 million years old. They found it on Knocklofty and it looks like they've only ever found one.'

'It must have been lonely,' said Gatta.

'They found it in a quarry, so there's probably chunks of its relatives in the walls of the old sandstones in West Hobart. Thing is,' he grimaced, 'the reconstruction looks like him.' He gestured at Alexander, who had finished the apple and was settling, drifting from green towards a gentle shade of aqua.

'I know that's ridiculous,' he said as Gatta opened her mouth. 'Pretend I didn't say it. Your goddess was standing behind me turning my brain to goop.'

Gatta said, far too casually, 'Maybe the goddess is someone to ask? She must know what to look for in identifying lizards.'

Luke's throat closed at the thought of talking to Shona again. He shook his head. 'Dead ones, maybe. The prof has his egg. Most likely he comes from South America and some stupid reptile person smuggled him in.'

Gatta shrugged then pulled her troll face. 'Mum said Ty's going to turn up at dinner.'

'Then we need to get him out of the way.' They looked at Alexander speculatively. 'More meat?'

'I can defrost a packet of mince, like, an hour before our dinner,' said Gatta. 'He'll sleep for a week.'

'Good plan. I'm going to google some more reptiles. Fossils and real ones. And oak trees.'

'I'm going to Netflix with Apple Murderer.'

'I wonder how he'll suss out a screen?'

'He's a screen himself – he'll be all over it.'

Gatta was right. She chose *The Man from Snowy River* on the basis it was nearly prehistoric, had mountains in it and rivers and Australian accents, mostly, so Alexander would feel at home. When Alexander first saw the Victorian High Country on a ten inch iPad screen: toy horses and tiny people, all of which smelled not of themselves but of metal and plastic, he flinched, hissed and tail-lashed, then stalked around the back of the screen, tongue flickering suspiciously. He emerged seeming satisfied with the arrangement. When Luke walked in on the closing credits, Alexander was stupefied – two hours screen time too much for his first try? – but managed to wave a miniature Akubra on his skin in greeting.

Nothing made sense. 'All the animal species that communicate well live in groups,' Luke said. 'Otherwise there'd be no point to being able to. Why is he alone?'

'How old did you say Tassiesaurus was? Two hundred million years? Maybe he's been waiting that long for someone to talk to.' She picked him up. 'Come on, Piglet.'

They fed him a hearty chunk of mince, mixed with herbs, egg and Worcester sauce, 'Because he's not a barbarian,' said Gatta. Afterwards, he was indeed piglet-shaped and almost comatose.

'He looks like he's been clubbed,' said Luke, tucking him in among the socks.

Chapter 13

The front door opened and closed as Gatta was dishing up stir-fry and Luke checking on his oven-roasting pine nuts. Ty entered the kitchen the way he entered every room – pausing first as though securing a perimeter. His presence was more than usually unsettling. He had never been there without Holly; and his elegance looked out of place beside a fridge splattered with Post-its and the row of battered tins on the sideboard, bookended by pickle jars that sprouted charred wooden spoons. He – and their mother – looked natural in Ty's kitchen, which was stainless steel, vast and uncluttered as an ice floe

'Ah, cooking,' Ty said. 'A constructive life skill.'

Neither of them answered. Ty was obviously snooping for what he'd been cheated of last time. Alexander seemed settled but Luke still fervently hoped Gatta could hold out, not engage, and Ty would leave.

'Mum taught me,' Gatta said, miscalculating. It was so obviously an unnecessary lie that Ty took a chair and folded his hands. Usually Ty ignored them. Luke suspected that, perversely, he had a greater regard for Gatta, who was at least combative, and that he took Luke's habit of conciliation as a weakness. Now Ty was composed, waiting for what would reveal itself.

Then Luke smelt something acrid. For a disorientating moment he thought he'd absorbed an Alexander talent and smelled Ty's personality. *Idiot. No, you forgot the pine nuts!* They'd now be irretrievably burnt.

'Damn!' He jumped up, heaved them out of the oven and dumped the tray by the sink. 'Gatta's got the cooking. I can only do the charcoal makeover.'

'As useful as the biblical burnt offering. A financial contribution to the household from both of you would be more effective.'

This was blatantly unfair to Luke, who had just lost his long-term job at the servo to the owner's sulky son, though he was expecting to get it back within the week. It may have been less unfair to Gatta, whose sporadic babysitting jobs had almost completely dried up after a couple of "brat-related" incidents. But if Ty wanted to push Gatta's buttons, unfairness to Luke was a superlative choice.

Luke went to forestall her at the exact moment he heard a tiny but distinct thump from the back of the house. He immediately diagnosed the sound: a half-asleep lizard pulling itself up to the lip of his sock drawer, in the dark, teetering on the edge, maybe the tail catching in a sock, then overbalancing and plopping to the floor. He couldn't remember whether he'd left his door open.

Luke had lost control of several things.

'Like the financial contribution you've made?' Gatta's voice was rising. 'Keeping Mum's nose just above the surface of the shit pool, so she'd need your job, and when her invention comes good you rake in half the money?'

'So the teenage satirist,' said Ty, who had been shown the *Unsuperheroes*, 'also grasps research and development. And finance.'

Alexander sleepwalked in through the door behind Ty. He was a deep blue and horribly visible. Luke was sure he could hear his tail scraping on the floorboards. The reflection in the window in front of him – surely Ty would see it in seconds.

'Alexander! Camo!' Gatta yelped.

Alexander's eyes blinked bright yellow and he vanished.

'What?' said Ty, startled.

'Alexander Camo,' spat Gatta, making her panic look like rage. 'Online fraudster. Investment schemes. Took Lucie's mum for everything.'

'Camo?'

'Pretended his grandfather came from Hungary, no, Poland, to work on the Hydro, like Lucie's mum's dad, to suck her in. He had too many like, c's and z's in his name…it was something like Camonuszkiewicz.'

When she was lying under pressure, Gatta's imagination would take off like a startled bird; Luke hoped it would fly nowhere close to a Flemish-speaking country in central Europe. He saw the floorboards behind Ty distort, a slow ripple moving unsteadily to the left. With a tiny insistent scraping sound.

'What you're doing isn't fraud,' said Luke, calming, mediating, drawing attention, making noise. 'You're investing in mum's invention, aren't you?'

The tea towel hanging from the oven was writhing like it was being pulled on by invisible claws, which it was. Luke's heart sank. He was out of ideas. And what was Alexander doing? He'd just eaten the equivalent of a Christmas lunch and should have been unconscious till Thursday.

'I'm making it possible for her to work on it,' said Ty, drawn into a civilised conversation against his will. 'My company's support is persuasive for new investors.' He twisted around to scan the room; somehow missed the towel movement. 'Fraud. Now I hope you wouldn't be taken in by anything like that, Agatha. I'd hate your Thatso lesson in gullibility to have been a waste of my efforts.'

Uh-oh. Extreme provocation. When Gatta was five, Ty had convinced her that Thatso, the stuffed dog version of Fatso, and Gatta's indomitable companion in every endeavour, was magically fireproof. Naturally, this had resulted in his traumatic death when she flaunted his superpower to Luke.

Gatta went extremely still.

Ty went on. 'I could've advised you before your most recent misdemeanour to better choose your enemies and bide your time.'

'That's your life advice, then?'

There was a clatter as the tray of burnt pine nuts tilted and slid into the sink.

Gatta leapt up. Apparently clumsy with rage, she grasped the tray more firmly than it needed. 'I think the subject of burnt things can be disposed of, like these.'

She took the tray outside but didn't return from the garden. Ty waited, puzzled at her refusal to rejoin the fight. After a time he nodded at Luke, who had been no fun, and left.

Luke held his head. He needed a holiday. He thought of that moment of pure emptiness, suspended outside time, after the lightning on the mountain in the rain. As an alternative meditation, he did the washing up.

He found Gatta on the back veranda, sprawled on a chair, holding Alexander on her lap. 'What was with him?' he asked.

She shrugged. 'No clue. I didn't need to *Belgium*; he just faded back in when we got out here. He was trying to eat the burnt nuts.'

'He was hungry? How is that possible?'

'I don't know. He's superhuman, remember. Anyway, he didn't like them and went back to sleep.' She stroked Alexander. He responded with faint iridescence, a trail of tiny jewels in the darkness.

Luke stretched his whole length, then draped himself over his chair, dangling his arms to the boards. He felt unutterably tired, his head crowded with clamouring voices. He looked out at the silhouetted line of trees. Somewhere from the back of the garden he heard a cricket chirring. Or was it a frog? Lemon myrtle floated on the air. The peace of the evening settled over him, opening his heart to the warmth of the world.

What?

Luke sat up and rubbed his eyes. That mellow feeling was delicious, but oddly foreign. He looked at Alexander, supine on Gatta's lap. By the light from the kitchen, Luke could see the lizard's back: dark green treetops were swaying hypnotically across his shoulders down to his tail.

'Alexander! Stop that!' he said. The treetops stilled and the mellowness gradually subsided.

'Were you getting that?' he said to Gatta. 'Like a drug?'

'*Choof choof, ooooooohh,*' she said. 'Nice, wasn't it?'

'Actually, it's scary. I don't know what he's doing. Tuning in? Trying to help? We need to stop him doing it.'

'What's the harm, Lukey? Anyway, he stopped when you asked.'

Luke wasn't reassured.

Chapter 14

The next morning, a cool southerly was blowing and Mrs F's chooks were grumbling in their shed when Luke got researching. By the time Gatta arrived for her semiconscious stumble round the kitchen, he had a small pile of printouts.

'Gah,' she said, peering at the top one. She took a huge gulp of Russian Caravan tea. Luke was getting really sick of smoky smells. Thank god she'd got over her Lapsang Souchong phase. 'What's this? Looks like a bunch of islands.'

'It's a diagram of all the bones found for *Tasmaniosaurus triassicus*.' He handed her another printout. 'Here's the reconstruction.'

She squinted at the two sheets. 'Not many bones to magic up a whole dude out of.'

'Exactly. And get this: the bones they found are the skull, the top of the neck and the pelvis, that is the hips, and some back legs. One or two bits of ribs and some stuff they're not sure where it goes.'

She looked at the next sheet, which was a photo of Alexander, then back at the reconstruction.

'How did they figure out the shoulder and chest bits?'

'They figure our guy is a relative of some others in South Africa and India, so used that as a guide.'

She was grinning. 'So we don't really know whether—'

'We don't know anything. We've got bones of an animal that lived two-fifty-odd million years ago and there have been at least two major extinctions since then.'

'So Alexander could be the Tassiesaurus.' Her face was a little pink. 'We have to ask Shona.'

'We can't. I'll look like a total tool, which she already thinks I am and—'

'I've already asked her.'

'You've what??'

His sister retreated behind the table and held the cereal packet defensively. 'I PM'd her last night. We can meet her after footy training at the uni tonight. She lives up here somewhere, so she can give us a lift home.'

'Well, text her and tell her it was a mistake and you're sorry and – wait – you told her about Alexander!'

Alexander wandered in, wearing his morning dark green, which was quickly gaining a fringe of red. He paused in the middle of the floor, his head jerking back and forth as they spoke. Then the green started to ripple soothingly.

'Don't you even start,' Luke snarled at him and banged outside onto the veranda.

There was silence from inside. Next door, Audrey was sitting on the grass sharing worms with the chickens. The chickens were mostly in her lee. She had Whitney on her lap and was stroking her. Only once, years ago, Mrs F had cooked one of the chickens. Now they were allowed to die of old age and she and Audrey buried them solemnly around the yard. Audrey still talked to the underground ones, though she didn't share worms with them.

Gatta crept out. 'Luke, I'm sorry–'

'It's done.' He sighed. 'And you're right. We can't handle all this. We were going to have to trust someone eventually, even if it's...' He circled a hand.

Gatta sagged with relief. 'I'm like totally certain she's solid, Luke.'

'From meeting her once,' he muttered. But Gatta, though she was all-or-nothing in her judgements of people, almost never missed. 'You sure about going back to the Gardens with him?'

'He's still looking for something. I think we were close. There were a lot of other trees in the BG like the Querky he hasn't checked out yet.'

'*Quercus*,' he said. 'Oaks. You know I looked up the translation of Wurmbaum and it's wormwood, which is actually not an oak. They make flavourings from it and also absinthe, which can be poisonous.' He shrugged. 'More for the "Weird Stuff that Doesn't Fit" file. 'You want to get brekky and we can go?'

Alexander was now longer than the width of Luke's shoulders. He seemed anxious to be accommodating and settled himself agreeably with his tail down Luke's shirt, hidden under a scarf. Luke felt a surge of affection as the lizard snuggled against his neck. Then he frowned at

Gatta, who was winding on her own scarf. 'I can't tell if my feelings are real or if he's choof-choofing me.'

'What does it matter? It's the same as the feels that people, dogs, everyone, get off each other all the time.'

At the main gate of the Royal Tasmanian Botanic Gardens, Alexander showed no further interest in the Government House Gardens but he glared and hissed across the road at the Beaumaris Zoo.

'He didn't like that place yesterday either,' said Gatta.

'I don't know how he can know. It's been closed for over fifty years.'

Above the chained gates, the zoo's name was picked out in mosaic, an ironically cheery white on blue. The zoo's history was welded to the gates in grey metal bas-relief: an elephant, a lion, a bear and a monkey, long-forgotten, and the last Tasmanian tiger, remembered. Each stared hollow-eyed from its metal cage – lonely animals, far from home, whose future was to die in their prisons. Which they had. Maybe their misery had sunk so deep into the soil of the site – like petrol into the condemned ground of an old service station – that it still drifted over the place like a pall and Alexander had sensed it. Or maybe he was feeling Luke's and Gatta's response to the old zoo. He would have looked like a cat with its hair on end, if he'd had hair.

'Come on, dude, we're about seventy years too late,' said Luke. 'And besides, things are better now in zoos.' Though he wasn't sure of that either.

They entered the gardens.

'The oak garden is over there.' Gatta pointed to their left. 'But the map shows more oak leaf drawings that way.'

A flock of blondes fluttered by, swiping phones, flicking hair, and selfie-ing their way down the green avenue. Alexander had disappeared into dark broad-leaved ground cover. A minute later, they heard a sneeze. He emerged, patterned like the leaves.

'He's a European Wild Ginger,' said Gatta, reading the plaque.

'And he's allergic to it,' said Luke when he sneezed again.

Alexander sneezed once more and waggled his head irritably. They continued past the sandstone conservatory but slowed when a large group blocked the path. Luke couldn't see Alexander, but heard a tiny sneeze from the cyclamens.

He approached one of the RTBG volunteers. 'Ah, excuse me.' Luke's height should have been intimidating but the school yearbook caricature of him was a Nordic stork with glasses. He didn't actually wear glasses, just looked like he should. He made any woman over twenty-five, and sadly many younger ones, feel motherly. The volunteer smiled at him. 'Yes?'

'What's happening here?'

She pointed to the Subantarctic Plant House, where the crowd was densest. 'We have a celebrity, an *influencer*,' she said proudly. 'Taylah Simon. Eight million followers. She's promoting fake fur as part of her campaign against animal cruelty. The Gardens have let her take pictures in the Cold House and bring a couple of huskies. It's splendid publicity for us.'

Over the heads of the crowd, Luke spotted Taylah: long thin denim-clad legs, a thick jumper cropped above her smooth flat belly and huge black winged sunglasses. The *influencer* wasn't wearing the furs. They were piled in the arms of a shorter satellite woman with the same hair and masklike glasses, this time in rose. To the side crouched a wiry man in a polar fleece and beanie, fondling the necks of two sitting huskies. The photographer was setting up a shot, the crowd behind him.

'The huskies are the grandchildren of the last huskies the Australian Antarctic Division had at Mawson Base,' said the volunteer. 'We've had them before, at the Husky Picnic. They're so good with the kiddies.'

The huskies sat obediently, turning their heads away and licking their lips as the celebrity twirled the furs in front of their noses, an ice axe and mitts looped over one elbow. The crowd closed in, some of them too close to the talent. Rose Glasses shooed them out of the shot.

Gloss and pouting. 'Not my style of animal activist, but good on her,' Luke said to Gatta. 'We won't get through here. Is there another way?'

'Around the back of the conservatory.'

As they retreated, Luke could still hear the occasional sneeze, the last quite close by. From behind them came a strange coo, followed by giggling. Did a dog make the cooing noise? Luke turned.

Twenty metres away, Taylah Simon, now draped in fur, was squatting with an arm around each dog. One had dropped its shoulder and she was trying to haul it back up. The handler, out of shot, was frowning.

Then Luke saw the episode that would be shared and retweeted by the eight million followers, in high-def and slo-mo. It was all about teeth and eyes: Taylah's teeth, impossibly bright between her wide Ruby Woo'd lips; the husky's eyes suddenly wild; Taylah's smile freezing; and the husky's teeth bared, swinging, the curving spray of saliva perfectly captured by the camera. Then the snarling dog was facing of her.

The handler leaped in. The audio caught her "Oh my god" as she fell back. The ice axe and mitts slapped down to the ground. One cork wedge flew high. There was a confusion of whirling fur and tails. The other husky was howling.

Luke pushed through the crowd. The handler had pulled back the snarling husky. Rose Glasses and a white-faced girl were holding the other one. Taylah sat on the ground, keening and clutching her left knee. Blood ran down her wrists and dripped from one elbow. It was the exact shade of her lips.

'Has anyone called an ambulance?' Luke called.

'Doing it,' said Gatta, beside him.

He lowered his voice. 'Where's Alexander?'

She patted her shoulder.

'Let's get him away.'

They hurried back up the path. Behind them, the babble was rising. Someone was crying. Gatta led them to the field of oaks, because it was as far from the scene of fear and cameras as they could get. Alexander sprang away. He wasn't using camouflage, just changing his tone from olives to bright greens as he slid between stems and fronds.

'He's got no red,' said Luke. 'What was that all about? Do you think he set off those dogs?'

'I don't know,' said Gatta. 'He wasn't giving me anger vibes. Besides, why would he?'

'I don't know either. But I couldn't see why the husky went nuts.'

'Dogs don't really like being hugged,' said Gatta, kicking at leaves. 'Especially not by people they don't know.'

'Those dogs are trained for public situations,' said Luke. 'Something else happened.'

Gatta shrugged. 'Not our problem. Hey, he isn't interested in any of these trees.'

They were entering a grove of stolid trunks with thick, deeply fissured bark and spreading crowns. Normally Luke would have considered how foreign the oaks looked, how their shape was sheltering compared with Australian trees that mostly seemed to reach skywards, and whether the difference was to do with sun exposure. Today he was rattled. The savagery they'd witnessed was so sudden and inexplicable. Surely Alexander was involved somehow, though he hadn't gone near the dogs and seemed placid.

Alexander had set a course towards a particular tree; Luke was unsurprised it was the Hungarian Oak. Alexander was purposeful, casting around, beagle-like. Periodically he picked up an acorn and deposited it with Gatta, who obediently cached it in her jumper. Luke thrust his hands in his pockets and frowned.

'Let's go.' Gatta held up a handful of small dark acorns. 'He's not really happy with these but I think he's done.'

The death ray sounded in the grove.

'Holy…' Gatta handed Luke her phone. It was a text from Lucie:

OMG!!! Luke was there!! With a photo. And a Twitter link.

'Holy Christ,' said Luke. At #TaylahDogAttack, the pic showcased the teeth – Taylah's and the husky's. It would have 400 000 retweets by the evening. The texted photo was a blurrier shot of the crowd, Luke's head overtopping everyone. They stared at the pictures, depressed.

'Grrr.' Gatta replied:

So? Luke didn't do it. You've spotted a wiraffe, not a werewolf.

Chapter 15

When they got home, Luke's stomach was knotted in a ball. Dog attack this morning, facing Shona this evening. 'I need to go take more post-fire photos,' he said.

'Cool,' said Gatta. 'I'll get Alexander some lunch then we'll do Netflix language lessons. I'm thinking *Storm Boy*. He's not ready for *Annihilation* yet.'

'How do you know he's getting any words anyway?' asked Luke.

'How? Watch this! Alexander!'

He was tasting the air around the oven. His head swivelled towards her. 'Horses.'

Manes flowed, smooth equine shoulders bunched as the brumbies galloped over a ridge in the Victorian High Country. Between the stove and the kitchen table, across the lizard's body.

'And one from our walk – bike!'

An image of a battered Giant hybrid replaced the horses.

'Thanks, Alexander,' said Gatta. 'Also, you asked him to stop giving you the feels last night. He did, right? Obvs he understood you.'

Luke was not as amazed as he expected to be.

He rode up to the blackened emptiness on the mountain to find it still crowded with unresting ghosts. Unresting because the inferno that had killed them was not part of the natural cycle of fire and regrowth, but unnatural, human-caused, intense beyond regeneration. Again, they pressed up against him.

It was humans that killed us. You, human, remember us.

His imagination was nuts lately. Ghosts. And communicating with a lizard. How much of either was imaginary? And did it matter, as long as he treated both ethically? He tried to infuse the ghosts into his photos, create the memorial they demanded. Or he demanded of himself.

When he got home, Gatta was sitting on the front veranda eating cashews and apparently feeding them to the other canvas deckchair. Alexander was in full camo then.

'He's not a girl, so cashews won't make him fat,' she said.

'How was *Storm Boy*?'

'He really liked the pelicans. And the cormorants. But I kept getting interrupted by Lucie. There's major fire about the huskies.'

He sat down next to her, moving Alexander. He'd become accustomed to picking the slight distortions in light that betrayed his outline.

'People are posting footage on Taylah's Facebook page,' Gatta said.

'We need to look at it all,' said Luke. 'I'm still scared Alexander caused it.'

Searching frame by frame on Luke's computer – for an odd shimmer snaking over jeans or white shagginess – they found something else: the blue tip of the ice axe blade hidden in fur and the yellow line of the shaft down the husky's front leg.

'The spike is on the dog's foot!' said Luke. 'And when she drags the dog up, it digs in.'

'You stab, I bite.'

There were streams of comments along with the footage, many calling "regretfully" for the dog's destruction:

Surprise, surprise! It takes a wild animal to show you what *animal cruelty* really means.

It's a wolf, Taylah, not a dachshund!

Huskies are unpredictable. That's why they're sled dogs, not handbag dogs, ha ha.

'What are we going to do with this?' said Luke. 'What if they put the husky down?'

'Let's see if there's more about Taylah,' said Gatta. 'They took her to the Royal Hobart.' She flicked through pages. 'Not good. No, really bad. She's had to have surgery. She's going to sue everybody.'

She looked into the middle distance. 'Okay, I'm going to take an ice axe-y still from the footage and send it to Lucie.' Her thumbs got busy. 'Sorry/not sorry, Taytay.'

Alexander crawled up Gatta's leg and onto her lap. He was a muted navy.

'Hey, Pelicosaurus. You know, I think he liked pelicans because he wants to fly. His walk is getting like, more awkward.'

'I'm with him there,' said Luke. In an hour he would see Shona and his legs were likely to forget what order to walk in.

'Poor baby,' said Gatta. 'Shona is an awesome babe. But you're actually pretty cute. And you've got some freaky show and tell.' She stroked Alexander. 'You've never been seen before in the history of, like, forever.'

Chapter 16

When they got off the bus on Sandy Bay Road, the southerly had filled in and whitecaps were rising beyond the Derwent Sailing Squadron. Alexander's head craned towards the penned yachts. Towards sound? The ringing percussion of halyards on masts? No, his tongue was flickering: he smelled the river. The only water he'd ever known was rain and streams and puddles.

'Time for that later,' Luke said, clamping the restless lizard onto his shoulder as they crossed the road to the playing fields. They passed the lower ground, the rugby domain, all grunt and thump and heaving buttocks. The floodlights came on as they neared the upper field where the women were training. Luke had never seen women's AFL. He expected it would be like women's cricket, skilled but depowered.

'Are the tackling rules the same for AFLW?'

'They're like that.' She gestured across the field, at a gleefully ferocious scrimmage. Luke had somehow expected women to be more inhibited in visiting damage on each other. He flinched as two clinched forms crashed into the turf together. The women rolled over, looked skyward and laughed.

'Wow.'

Alexander watched with lively interest from his perch on Luke's shoulder. He was a placid blue, with just a maroon highlight down his crest.

'He gets that they're enjoying themselves,' Gatta said. 'Friends thwacking the bejesus out of each other.'

'I thought only men did that,' mumbled Luke.

'Well, they don't get all the fun now. I don't see Shona.'

'Over there,' said Luke. They'd been looking for her tell-tale height but she kept herself low, weaving through defenders with a hip flick and a chest fend. Her smile gleamed in the fading light. When she saw them, she tapped her wrist, flashed open fingers and pointed over her shoulder. Luke took in the red-gold glow of her skin, her decathlete's build, her athletic grace, her confidence in her body. How could his mouth be dry if his guts were water?

'Ten minutes,' said Gatta.

The players reassorted their groups and spread out as Luke, Gatta and Alexander continued around the perimeter. Behind the goalposts, broad concrete steps ascended to a carpark and the university buildings.

A cluster of four coaching staff consulted in front of the steps. A woman tapped rapidly on a tablet while one with spiky hair sketched positions and trajectories in the air. The bull-sized man opposite was nodding. He had the relaxed geniality of a very large man who'd never had to exercise dominance because he'd never not possessed it. He laughed expansively, clapping his meaty hand on the shoulder of coach next to him. The second man was a head shorter, with greying hair, but his legs in his shorts were muscular and his feet looked light.

As Luke and Gatta walked along the top of the steps, Alexander stopped casting about and tasting the air and fell motionless. Luke suddenly became conscious of an absence, like a power failure when all the nearly inaudible hums actually stop. They had acquired a sense of Alexander that was beyond seeing his shape or hearing his movements or feeling the emotional auras he projected. Even when he was invisible he still felt there. He was visible now, but their sense of him had gone. Bizarre! The lizard had weight and his claws pricked though Luke's jumper, but the feeling of his presence had disappeared.

Luke stopped just as Gatta turned towards him. She stared at Alexander. 'Hey, what's happening, little man?' He was battleship grey, peering down the oval with his yellow eyes. She touched him. A trickle of his substance returned, but it felt colourless, alien and unfeeling as a Soviet-era building.

'Is it something out there?' Luke scanned their field of view.

A fair girl in a too-big jumper was on the steps looking anxiously up at the big coach. Her eyes were in shadow under the lights and her face looked hollow. Was she a player? She was smaller than the other women on the field. The big man spoke, gave her a one-armed hug, pushed her gently away and threw her a football. The two female coaches were walking slowly away. The grey-haired coach had jogged off and was dropping orange cones onto the grass in a large square.

'Nope,' said Gatta.

Shouts came from the distance as Shona's long shape hung atop a leaping pyramid of other players, her rope of hair flying like a pennant. She came down in a crouch with the ball in hand.

Alexander shifted his grip on Luke and, just like that, he was back.

'Hey, Ghostosaurus, what happened to you?'

They both felt a little pulse of calm and reassurance.

'Well, that was nice,' said Luke, 'but it wasn't an explanation.'

Luke couldn't rationalise the uneasiness he felt. Maybe from being about to talk to Shona? She stood in a knot of players in front of the clubrooms.

'How are we going to do this?' asked Luke.

'What if I take him for a walk and you fix it with Shona?'

The world saw him give his scarf to his younger sister against the cooling evening, after which she gave him space to talk to babes. The babes appraised him as he approached. Their sleeveless football jumpers showed toned shoulders. They radiated relaxed physicality. Luke didn't know any women like this. Of the sporty girls at school, the downhill mountain bikers had wiry muscles and crazy courage – maybe just craziness – and the rock climbers had steely hands and minds, but none were so casually at ease in their bodies. Much more at ease than him.

'Evening, Aryan Brother,' said a young woman every bit as fair as he was and only a handspan off his height. 'Looking for a leg up?' She gave a little rucking hop towards him.

'Easy, Bec, you might break him,' said her smaller friend, shaking out her topknot.

'You're right. And he's quite cute. Even though he's only a baby.'

Another woman joined them. She looked like the model Adut Akech, as graceful but even taller. The three women inspected him, heads cocked sideways. He felt like a stick insect, impaled on three pins. The tall blonde – Bec – shook her head. 'Not a footy boy.' She made a circle of finger and thumb: his puny arms. 'Catwalk maybe, if he could grow stubble.'

Luke's sense of injustice overtook his shyness. 'Okay, so you looked great out there, better footballers than me, no question, but what's with the insults?'

The smaller woman stepped forward. Her pale face and determined expression was that of a Victorian era heroine wearing a throat brooch and lace-up boots, not a sleeveless footy jumper. 'I'm Emily,' she said. Yep, Victorian heroine. 'Most of us have had to put up with a lot to get to play this game. It's been really hard to get this,' she swept her arm over the playing fields, 'for training, even at this time of year. But that's not your fault.' She held out her hand. Heart pounding, Luke shook it.

'You should be captain, Emily, not me,' said Shona from behind her. 'This is Luke, ladies. He's not the enemy.' She applied a pretend chokehold to Bec and they snarled at each other. When they turned back to him, Bec was smiling.

'Sorry,' she said.

'S'okay.'

'And Luke and I have business to discuss with his sister.' They looked around the grounds which were now deep in twilight. Gatta was near the cricket nets.

'Saturday, Bec,' said Shona, 'and don't eat any young men between now and then.'

Bec giggled and patted Shona's bum. Luke decided to hate her after all.

Chapter 17

'Becs has a huge chip on her shoulder. Big chip, big shoulders,' Shona said to Luke as they walked around the perimeter

'Noted.' Luke was acutely aware of the distance between her shoulder and his. His skin prickled with her nearness. He looked across her, ostensibly for Gatta, and caught the shine of sweat on Shona's curved upper lip and along the lifted line of her cheekbone. Looking down was no safer. Down there he discovered her silky bronze calf and his sudden ambition to be a sock.

By the time they reached Gatta, Luke's chest felt upside down or reversed or something and he'd almost forgotten what they were doing here. He stepped away from Shona to Gatta's side. Shona looked the pair of them up and down in amazement. 'Are you sure she's your sister?' she asked Luke.

'Half-sister,' said Gatta.

'Which half?'

'The inner half,' said Gatta, flushed and big-eyed like a five year old. 'You've got a big club.'

'Lots of, um, strong women,' agreed Luke.

Shona's smile was very white in the dark. 'That's the Hobart and the Uni clubs. We share training grounds and alternate venues every week. We share the coaches as well, which is good for everyone.'

'Who are the coaches?' he asked, to hear Shona's voice again.

'The big guy, Phil, is our head coach. He was one of those legendary players.' She sighed. 'His cred was a huge part of getting us funding, players, a comp, everything, but he doesn't really know how to coach women. He doesn't want us to go hard – it's like we're all his little girls. These women love the physicality.' She flexed an arm with a clenched fist and an alarming heft of muscle. 'It's no accident both teams have lots of basketballers.

'Adam, the other coach, has helped a lot there. He's not much bigger than many of our players so he understands how to get them to use the weight they've got, as hard as necessary. But he's low key about it. And he doesn't compete at all with Phil. He only started coming to support his wife when she was playing.' Shona's voice softened. 'Then she got sick and stopped coming but he stayed. We still see her sometimes.'

'And the women coaches belong to the other club?' Luke asked.

'Yep. Pip and Maddie. They're married to each other, with twins who've come to training from birth. Those boys have twenty-four mothers.' Shona laughed. 'Now, what have you brought to show me?'

Gatta clutched her bulky scarf and looked at Luke. He took a deep breath. The silence lengthened.

'To do with what you brought Prof?' said Shona. 'Gatta said you have something else?' A note of impatience was creeping in.

'We do,' said Luke. 'Best just to—'

He lifted Alexander out of Gatta's scarf and set him on the grass. Shona frowned and crouched down. Alexander regarded her with lizard stillness.

'It looks like a monitor. A Varanus. Except, there's something wrong with its front legs, like a congenital deformity.' She straightened up. 'Is this it?'

'He's a he, not an it,' said Gatta, 'and don't be rude; he understands what you're saying.'

Shona almost rolled her eyes. 'I was right the first time I saw you. Except you're both idiots.'

'No, you were wrong,' said Gatta. 'Alexander. Red.'

Alexander blinked from blue to crimson. Then, at Gatta's prompts, black, blue and a particularly pleasing green.

'He's metachrotic,' said Shona faintly. 'And he *does* understand you.' She crouched down again. 'Does he understand anything else?'

'Lots of things,' said Luke. 'Lots more than we even know about yet, I think. But we didn't want to ask you about his party tricks. We're trying to understand what he is and how he came to be here. I think each question could help answer the other.'

'Yes,' said Shona. She chewed on her rope of plaits, which made her look as little-girl-like as a six-foot-two MMA-capable football goddess could. 'I'm cold. And hungry. Why don't we grab something from the Tacotaco van and sit in my truck?'

Soon the interior of Shona's ancient Ford Courier twin cab was steamed up with four bodies (even if one of them was ectothermic, as far as they knew), twelve tacos and eighteen serves of hot sauce. Alexander was in back with Gatta.

'Okay,' said Shona, stashing the two leftover tacos on the dashboard. Luke struggled to process the sight of his queen pulling lettuce from her teeth. The cabin space was small and she filled a lot of it. She asked, 'Where did you find him?'

'On the mountain, near the Lost World.'

'What did—'

'No,' said Luke. 'That's two questions.' He glanced at Gatta. 'It's our go.'

Shona laughed, settled her long limbs and half-turned towards Luke. The carpark floodlights shone down the planes of her face. It was an effort to look at her and also talk.

'Alexander,' he called, 'come here.' He hadn't tried that before — without even considering why, he didn't think of it as a command — but was confident that Gatta had covered it. Alexander clambered sleepily over the transmission and the handbrake and onto his right thigh.

'Just suppose...' Luke hesitated. 'No, let's not suppose anything. Think of the bones of *Tasmaniosaurus*, the ones that were found. Would he fit them?'

Shona sighed. 'Where do I even start?'

'Crocodiles are 200 million years old,' Gatta said, proving Luke wasn't the only one who could use Google and that her mind-reading extended beyond her brother.

'And didn't change much in that time. Um, mayyyybe...' Shona rolled her eyes. 'Okay, I'll play.' She leaned forward to study Alexander. 'His skull and his jaw look pretty close.'

'He could smell a flea on your dog,' said Gatta, inaccurately but making her point.

Shona's clear green eyes interrogated Luke. His insides did a wrestling move, but he nodded. 'He has an awesome sense of smell. At least as good as a dog. Like you told me about *Tasmaniosaurus*.'

'Huh.' She reached a graceful forefinger out to Alexander's shoulder. 'The forelimbs are, ah, problematic. But we have no forelimb or limb girdle bones from *Tasmaniosaurus*. The hind limbs could be the same.' Her finger hovered above the line of his crest. 'It would help to know how much of this is bone.'

'Alexander,' said Luke. The lizard, who was mostly asleep and dark blue with yellow fringing, opened his eyes. 'This is Shona.'

Alexander raised his head. The yellow bloomed.

'You can touch him,' said Gatta. 'It's pretty obvious when he doesn't like people.'

Shona hesitated. Alexander dropped himself off Luke's thigh and crawled across the seats onto Shona's.

'He also has a way of answering questions you haven't asked,' said Gatta.

Luke wanted to avoid a deeper discussion of Alexander's understanding just now. 'It's your turn for a question,' he said.

Shona rested her hand gently on the length of Alexander's back and her face became conspicuously peaceful. Luke felt a little jolt. He examined himself for uninvited serenity vibes, but couldn't detect anything alien, only anxiety, longing and strangled lust. He looked at Gatta. She shook her head.

'Does he do any other colours?' asked Shona.

Time for the big stuff. 'Yes, lots. He, ah, does pictures.'

'Pictures?'

'Alexander: dog.' On the yellow skin appeared an image of a husky and a moment later, a mongrel terrier. The terrier licked its nose.

Shona gasped and yanked both hands clear of Alexander like he'd scalded her. She cast from side to side as though searching for an explanation in the seatbacks or the windscreen.

'I'm sorry, I have to get out.'

Alexander slid off her leg. Without taking her eyes off him, she scrabbled at the door handle then backed out of the truck. When Luke and Gatta and Alexander got out more sedately, she was standing under one of the light poles.

'You okay?' Luke asked.

She nodded. Her hand was at her throat.

'Sorry,' he said. 'We've had longer to get used to him. We wanted to know if he could be related to *Tasmaniosaurus*. But also whether you'd heard of any other animal who does what he does, but I guess we already knew the answer to that. There is nothing like him, is there?'

Shona shook her head and walked away, her figure a shifting node in the geometric patterns of floodlight across the oval. Eventually she returned.

'You want to share the last two tacos?' asked Luke.

She grinned at him gratefully and he could have personally ground the corn for a state-wide supply of taco shells. They sat on the tailgate and chewed. Gatta and Alexander sprawled in the tray, sharing the remaining hot sauce.

'Okay,' said Shona. 'The first question is easier to think about, if not to answer, so we'll start with that. As Gatta pointed out, crocodiles are still here, looking close to what they looked like in the late Triassic. They probably made it through two worldwide extinctions by having very slow metabolism when they needed to and being able to eat nearly anything, even if it's been dead a long time. So if they got through, something else could have. It's not impossible that Alexander is a relative of *T.t.*'

'Except,' said Gatta, 'where are the two hundred million years of skeletons in between them?'

'See? The half-brother is on the inside,' said Luke, tapping his forehead.

'Maybe underwater,' said Shona. 'Crocodiles are amphibians and became more and less aquatic depending on conditions over the ages. He,' she gestured at Alexander, who was licking chili sauce off a claw, 'looks like his species could be recently aquatic. Anyway, what am I doing on this side of the argument?'

'How can we prove it?' asked Luke.

'Depends on whether you want to,' said Shona. 'So far, you seem to want to keep him a secret and I understand why. I know Prof is doing research on something you brought in. She hasn't told even me what the thing is. But studying the real live him,' she shook her head, 'would take a collaborative effort between a lot of unis. We'd need a complete genome sequence, which is hard enough to do on any species that hasn't been sequenced before, let alone a brand new one. Or freakingly old one. Summary: no way could you do it on the quiet. So you'll have to decide whether to give up the secrecy. Now, about the other stuff–'

'Yes,' said Luke. 'There are chameleons and, squid that…'

Shona rubbed her arms. 'Not in the ballpark. He's not just mimicking his environment, he's doing a *concept*. And he was doing a perfect picture.' She shivered. 'A *moving* one.'

Luke cleared his throat. 'On mimicking the environment. You might as well see this. Alexander. Camo.'

Shona was partly prepared, but she still grabbed the wall of the ute tray for support. 'Christ!' Then she flinched as Alexander's claws scrabbled on the metal, advancing on them. Luke felt him climb onto his leg, making his way to Shona.

'He wants you to trust him,' he said, suddenly realising this. He took Shona's hand, allowed himself a moment of bliss, and placed it gently on Alexander's invisible back as the lizard clambered onto her thigh. Her eyes widened and her body froze, except for her hand, which trembled but remained in place. Luke reluctantly removed his own hand. Shona's stilled, apparently hovering over her mid-thigh, as Alexander settled. Luke saw tiny wisps of steam appearing above her right knee, showing where his nose was, probably exhaling hot sauce. After a long moment Shona started moving her hand over Alexander's body, cautiously feeling his contours. Gradually she relaxed. Alexander brought himself back slowly, like a solidifying ghost.

No sudden movements to startle the deer, thought Luke.

Shona looked up at the night sky and blew out a long breath. 'Man,' she said. 'I'm not scared anymore but I think I should be. I'm trying to decide whether I'm more blown away by the invisibility or by the human thinking. This will take high level, big horizon thinking. And time.'

'There's a problem with that,' said Luke. 'At least for Gatta and me and probably him. He's getting bigger.'

Shona looked down at blue and gold Alexander, whose head and body measured her thigh. His tail was curled around her buttock. 'He's no bigger than a poodle.'

'Four days ago he was the size of a banana. Plus a tail.'

'Four days ago?!'

'He eats however much you give him and he's always hungry.'

Shona ran her hand over her tight cornrows. 'Well, stop feeding him.'

Luke and Gatta looked at each other, then at Alexander, who seemed unperturbed, then back at each other. Did they just expect him to understand that? And did he?

Shona said, 'Crocodiles can eat every six months if they have to. Because they don't have to put energy into keeping their temperature up, like mammals, extra food they just turn into more crocodile.' She rubbed her arms again. 'It's getting cold and we need to go home. We need to think. I take it I can talk to the Prof? She's proved she's good at secrets.'

Luke frowned. 'Could you just talk, um, theoretically?'

'Theoretically, how? "Hey, Prof, how would you sequence an undescribed species which might be a dinosaur?" Her brain is the sort that can figure out nearly the whole cow starting with a hamburger patty.'

'I don't know. Yes, talk to her,' said Luke. He stroked Alexander's head. 'I wish I could ask him.' It came out before he could stop it, but Shona didn't laugh.

'Maybe someday you will,' she said.

Chapter 18

On Tuesday evening, Ty walked into their kitchen again, with his left hand across his chest, blood soaking the cuff of his suit jacket. Luke leaped up from his computer. Alexander was outside. To Alexander's exquisite emotional senses, Ty's routine unpleasantry would feel like a choking cloud of nasty. Had the lizard leapt into the cloud and attacked its source? Ty looked like he'd won a fight, not lost one. Would they find Alexander's body on the road?

'Dog fight,' said Ty, heading for the bathroom. 'You may wish to tend to the distressed.' By which he plainly didn't mean himself.

Luke grabbed a torch and hurried out with Gatta. Angry dogs could still mean Alexander was involved; Luke still didn't trust what had happened with the husky.

It was fully dark except for a yellow pool under the streetlight, where their neighbours clustered with the silence of something ended. Someone was crying; Anthony's little daughter from two doors down, her face pressed against her father's stomach, his hand cupping her head. His other hand held a spade.

'Is anyone hurt?' asked Luke.

'No one,' said Anthony, 'except that.' He gestured to a mound of brown fur on the footpath. 'It's the one that went for Kurt last week.'

'And it went for Ty? Unprovoked?'

'Ty got out of his car and the dog just grabbed his arm. I tried to hit it with this, got it once, it might have let go, but your uncle just pulled it in – towards him – and shoved his hand further down its throat.'

'He killed it?'

'Held it down till it choked. I knew he was a cold bastard, but Jesus.' Anthony's large hand covered his daughter's ear. The other bystanders had started to drift into the darkness.

'Whose is it?' asked Gatta.

'There's no tag,' said Anthony. 'We should take it into my yard, I guess.'

He gave his little girl's hand to Gatta and Luke helped him carry the dog into his garden.

Later on, back in their own kitchen, Ty sat in his shirtsleeves, elegantly trousered legs casually crossed. His jacket was carefully folded over a chair. His hand was bandaged but he looked otherwise unperturbed.

Gatta stared at him. 'You killed that dog.'

'It attacked me.'

'But you didn't have to. And it wasn't the dog's fault – it was the owner's for his shit job training it.'

'I agree. He is the one at fault and the one that deserves the retribution. Had he been there, I would have dispensed it. But he wasn't.'

'But the dog–'

'And the dog, by law, would have to be put down, so I was doing it a favour.'

'You're unbelievable,' said Gatta.

'No, I am reality,' said Ty, and left.

Gatta stood with her fists balled in the middle of the kitchen, eyes glittering with angry tears. 'He is fucking psycho. Real people have feels. *I am reality*. Who even talks like that?'

Luke said nothing. Ty had grown up without compassion and interpreted kindness as weakness, certainly in Luke. What they saw as cruelty, Ty saw as life lessons. Or maybe it was both. If Luke ever woke up to a day when he saw the world like Ty did, he'd top himself. Luke just wanted Ty away from them, especially away from Alexander. 'Where is Alexander?'

'I don't know, but I don't think he was there.'

A quick search found Alexander lying under a chair on the back veranda. 'He's legless,' Gatta said. He was a luxuriant aquamarine, almost spherical around the middle and radiating contentment

'So he had nothing to do with it,' said Luke, relieved. 'But what was Ty even doing there? And–'

'Why did Ty send us outside?'

'Pure fuckery?'

'I don't think so.' Luke strode back to the kitchen and his laptop, heart already sinking. He opened it. 'He's been in my search history. The dog was a coincidence but Ty used it to get us outside. And he's found the pages on *Tasmaniosaurus* I've been looking at. And extinctions and reptiles.'

'No biggie.' said Gatta. 'Everyone knows you're into boring, obscure stuff.'

'Oh, no.' The thought hit him like an ice shower. 'My phone was on the kitchen bench. And the auto-lock is, like, five minutes.' He snatched up his phone and opened his photos. The top picture was not the last one he'd taken but one of Alexander in a patch of sunlight on the kitchen floor. They stared at each other in horror.

Gatta snorted back her tears. 'We haven't broken any laws.'

'It all depends on what Alexander is. If he's valuable, we're minors and Ty could legally take him from us. And he would. If Alexander's not a threatened species, Ty could legally kill him. Now we *really* need to know.'

Which led to what he'd been longing for and fearing all week. 'We have to talk to Shona again.'

Chapter 19

They couldn't talk to Shona for nearly another week, during which Luke's stomach migrated unpredictably back and forth from his chest.

Late that night, Luke rang Holly. As he dialled, he realised he wanted to talk to the new Mum, the one he only partly knew. Did she realise he might not be the son she thought either?

Hey Mum, I'm stretching what humans understand by sentience. And human responsibility toward animals. That stuff has always been important to me. No, sadly he couldn't talk about that.

'Hey, Mum. How's the inventing? No, you aced the inventing years ago. The money-raising? Not your favourite thing?'

'Yes. No. Correct both times.' She sounded harried.

Luke imagined her at her desk in a darkened building. 'You've been running the lab all day and the money isn't raising?'

'Hah.' She gave a bitter laugh. 'It should be called begging. I'm putting together a pitch to Paladin Finance, another venture capital firm. Typically, they want 80 per cent of the company.'

'I heard that was called vulture capital.'

Her laugh was more open this time. 'How old are you again, Luke?'

Older. You weren't there to see it happen. But you are now. 'It was economics class.' At least Hansen was as cynical on capitalism as on climate.

After fifteen minutes, he rang off. They hadn't discussed him and Gatta at all.

The week that followed provided fresh challenges. Luke wrestled with his bushfire photos and fulfilling his promise: charging the wasteland images with the presence of the lost. Gatta claimed to be dealing with her geometry and algebra units by teaching them to Alexander but they seemed to spend most of their time watching movies. Some of them were in Swedish, 'So he can read the subtitles, and why would he be offended by nudity? He doesn't wear clothes.'

Gatta's death ray frequency rose. On Thursday morning she said,

'Okay, executive summary.' It was the first time in a decade she had quoted her mother without sarcasm. 'After Lucie put out the ice axe pic, about a thousand people jumped on and were, like, duh, obvious. But Taylah's parents are saying so what? The dog still bit her and she has nerve damage. So they're suing the Gardens, the council and the husky guy and now they're also suing Fauxfurall, who they say made her use the axe. It's like a troll-for-all with people digging up stuff on Taylah and how she's been mean to her pets and eats veal. But it's still looking suss for the huskies.'

'Typical. Tiny-minded, nasty all round. And execute the blameless.' Bitter generalisations were not Luke's style, but they were both miserable. Feeding Alexander less had been a struggle. They'd immediately rejected the idea of not sharing mealtimes but a trial of lettuce and cucumber coated in chilli sauce failed. He licked the sauce off then stared at their meatloaf till they gave in. Feeling guilty, they ate far less themselves and dinnertimes became joyless affairs, morally correct and nourishing to nobody.

To track their progress and convince themselves all the agony was worthwhile, Luke started photographing Alexander every morning in the same sun patch on the boards in front of the fridge. For the first few days of the new regimen, Alexander's alarming growth stopped. Then on Friday, he was eight cm longer. Luke thought he could detect that smugness had a colour.

'Look at this,' Luke said to Gatta, flicking between photos.

'Cool. He's smarter than us.'

Luke bared his teeth.

'Ooh, hangry Luke. Sorry. Any clues in your socks?'

His sock drawer had acquired a rich and complex scent not unlike truffles.

'Oh bugger,' said Luke, picking up a cricket sock with a brown streak. A wisp of white down was stuck to the dried blood. He banged out to the veranda.

'Where are you going?' asked Gatta, on his heels.

'To count Mrs F's chickens. Damn, there's a new hole under the fence. Oh, hello Audrey.'

Audrey gave them her beaming wave.

'Audrey would have noticed if one of the girls was missing. Even if she can't count, she'd know.'

'Oo. Atta,' said Audrey. Then she laughed and waggled her chubby arm in a way that unmistakeably meant "snake". Or snake-shaped lizard. 'Ssssss,' said Audrey happily.

'I don't get it,' said Luke. 'He's obviously been over there, but she seems very cheerful about it, which she wouldn't be if he ate one of the girls.' Oh shit. 'Unless he did his doping hypnotising thing on her?'

'But it would wear off and the chook would still be eaten, right? Besides, they're all there.'

'You're right. But he's for sure eaten a whole something.'

'I wonder if any of Mrs Bunton's cats are missing.'

That night they abandoned the deprivation policy and ate celebratory heapings of spaghetti. Afterwards, Alexander sprawled gold and blue on the sideboard, Gatta burped on the sofa and Luke, half in a pasta trance, opened his laptop and read about eating. Specifically, how ancestral crocodiles survived the Permian Triassic Extinction by lying in a century of darkness eating slimy dead things. So when Ty materialised in the doorway, nobody was prepared. Luke, after a slack-jawed moment, closed his laptop. As signals to Ty went, this was a red arrow pointing at the Guilty Party. If he'd just left it open, the page would have rightly bored the pants off any sensible person.

Gatta, realising Ty had already seen Alexander, hiccuped and said, 'Belgium. Hmm. For some reason I just woke up and thought of something boring. Why would I do that?'

'Ah, the opening insult. Never mind. Perhaps this presages thoughts on other boring subjects, like economics and a career and self-sufficiency,' said Ty. 'What is that thing?'

Gatta glanced at Alexander who was aggressively purple and yawned. 'A freebie from the museum. They were giving away old exhibits.'

'Exhibit of what? Gargoyles? It's not even an actual species.' He walked up to Alexander and stretched out his hand.

'Rubber ones,' said Gatta.

Ty had Alexander's head in one hand and body in the other. 'I can't fathom it,' he said. His hands were wiry, the opposite of office-soft. Casually they bent Alexander's neck. 'Why would a purported scientific organisation waste money on this kind of garbage?'

Luke's head felt unstable on his neck. When Ty had killed the snake, had they heard a double sound: had he cracked its neck before crushing its skull against the post?

'It's playful. I'm donating it to the junior school,' said Gatta.

Ty flexed Alexander's neck. 'To further their ignorance? When children need facts on the real world, instead they get drivel like this. Cartoons, fantasies.'

Alexander, miraculously, was allowing himself to be bent, not blinking, not breathing – enduring. But his colour...

'So you wouldn't approve of it going bright pink then?' said Gatta.

Ty's hands jerked away. Alexander, rigid, dropped onto the sideboard with a soft clunk.

'Like those mood rings we tried? The ones you bagged because they turned anger-red?'

An excess of disgust propelled Ty out the door.

Luke and Gatta sagged pale-faced on the sofa. Alexander faded towards shades of blue, which became movements. Jagged movements. Rising and falling. Janet Leigh in a motel shower.

'Jesus! He's doing *Psycho*! What were you thinking, Gats?'

'Chill. He wants to wash Ty off him. It's the only shower scene he knows.'

For the next three days, Ty ignored them. They considered asking Holly to discourage his visits, but Luke found himself avoiding the subject of her brother when they spoke on the phone. Instead, they talked about things they'd never discussed. Her project mostly, and adult conversations where they discovered in each other interesting people who talked about science and philosophy and ideas. Mum as friend. Who knew?!

Alexander was also making social advances. He wasn't eating Mrs F's Barnevelders or Orpingtons but rather visiting invisibly with them and Audrey. If the neighbours hadn't long been averting their eyes from her snacking habits, they would have seen her drop worms from a height and clap when they vanished into thin air. From the way he was growing, he was also eating something much larger than worms; something with bones, based on the little piles of scat with bone chips they started finding under the tree daisy. And from the blood on Luke's socks. So, control measures having failed, they left the back door ajar in the evenings. Luke called this a pragmatic arrangement; Gatta called it caving.

They preferred not to think about what the possums called it. They were now out there in the dark with Alexander.

Chapter 20

Talking to Shona meant going to the Tasmanian Cricket Association ground the next evening where Uni Women's was training with Hobart. Travelling on a bus with Alexander was getting harder by the day. Draping him around his shoulders made Luke look like a hunter lugging a wallaby he'd shot. Alexander had to go in a backpack, which fortunately he accepted when bribed with beef jerky. Or toast, which he loved madly but was messier. When they got off the bus they let him out to walk the short distance from the Victorian terrace houses of the Glebe up the hill to the ground. A few European trees were crammed into narrow front gardens and leaves drifted about their ankles. Alexander gave a couple of green acorns a desultory sniff.

'He's gone off the acorns a bit,' said Gatta.

'He's still got a thing for the ones we collected,' said Luke. 'He knows exactly how many he's got. I took one out of his drawer to take a photo of it while he was asleep. He came galumphing out and gave me the ice dagger look until I gave it back. Then he bit it and spat at it and took it back to his drawer.'

'Can't live with 'em, can't live without 'em.'

They no longer worried much about Alexander at night. People were unconscious of him, though he made dogs sniff and cast around nervously. Cats fled.

At the cricket ground, the floodlights put each player in the middle of their own star-shaped penumbra, turning the field into a giant spider's web with the strands stretching and rebounding as the players moved through their drills. Their boots kicked up the smell of grass and earth.

Luke and Gatta skirted an equipment store to the old wooden benches. A small person was perched on the end. She looked around as they approached. They couldn't walk around her without jumping over the fence or a bench so they stopped. She was cocooned in a full-length puffer jacket, the sort that Gatta called 'wearing a sleeping bag', and her head was swathed in scarf.

'Hi,' said Luke. All he could see of her was large dark eyes and a wistful expression. 'They look great, don't they?' He gestured at the players on the field, then stopped. 'I mean, enjoying themselves, I mean I'm not perving or anything. This is my sister.'

The woman laughed – a richer sound than Luke expected – smiled at Gatta, and looked less wistful. 'I'm not perving either. They do look great.'

'Ah, do you play?'

'I used to. I've been sick.' Longing had crept into her voice. 'You look like you could play.'

'I'm tall enough but one of the coaches at school told me I had less mongrel than *Hello Kitty*.'

She laughed again. 'These girls love being a pack of mongrels.'

'Being mongrels and being a pack.'

'You've got it exactly. I wasn't great at the mongrel either. Much better at dodging tackles than crunching people. I'm Rosie. Nice to meet you. You're kind of... restful to talk to, you know.'

'That's Luke,' said Gatta.

That's when he felt the touch of something he recognised. Alexander had wrapped a blanket of comfort around the woman, relief from sorrow and pain. Luke suppressed his disapproval; he would have done the same thing himself if he could. He had been trying to do it, with words.

Ahead of them, Bec burst out of a pack of players with the football under her arm. Shona was behind her but losing ground. Then she launched herself, horizontal in one impossibly long line from her boots to the end of her fingers. She caught Bec's waist, trapping one arm, and pulled her down. A whistle blew. The blonde and dark heads lay together on the turf, panting. The other players pulled them up and they wandered back to the clubrooms and the coaches.

Rosie touched Luke's arm, sketched a wave and started walking after them.

Luke felt Alexander's presence vanish again. He looked around; he couldn't see him.

'Where is he?' he asked Gatta.

'He was under the end of the second row. I think. I don't see him. And he's gone off the air again.'

'Nothing we can do,' said Luke. 'We'll wait. Shona knows where we are.'

Their breath steamed on the night air.

'That woman, Rosie,' Gatta said.

'Yeah. She's lovely. And it's bad, whatever it is.'

He watched Rosie reach the group and the assistant coach, Adam, hurry over to her. Luke had already guessed she was his wife. Adam's concern was obvious, even from a distance. His arm went around Rosie protectively; she curled into him. He turned her away from the group and kissed her. Their foreheads stayed touching.

Luke felt a twinge in his chest. In making himself a sanctuary, Adam grew larger, but made Rosie's luminous beauty look more fragile, almost transparent. All his competent masculinity – which Luke longed for – couldn't protect her from whatever was eating her from within. Luke felt sad for her but he couldn't help a stab of jealousy.

The larger coach, Phil, was laughing. He had herded four of the women together and was resisting their efforts to break out of the circle of his enormous arms. They staggered together like a multi-legged drunken animal. Pip and Maddie were trying to secure their toddlers, who were launching themselves at the legs of any passing player. Some of them surrendered to the tackles by falling to the grass. Everywhere, humans were holding each other, making Luke hollow with longing.

The chief cause for his feeling was walking towards them, swinging a towel and car keys. Luke's sense of Alexander came back; he was somewhere nearby. Luke had a pulse of fear, but he wasn't sure of what.

'Hi Luke, Gatta.' The lights behind her, or maybe it was the heat from Shona's body, gave her a faint misty aura. 'Let's go. I'm hungry.' She looked down at Alexander. 'Wow. The non-feeding regime's going well, then.'

Alexander hissed, showed off all his teeth and pretend-bit her calf.

'We tried,' said Gatta. 'He's been finding other stuff somewhere. Leaving bones and ick around.'

'Roadkill?' asked Shona, unlocking her ute.

'Could be,' said Luke. That was better than the image of Alexander killing a live animal.

'Crocs eat carrion,' said Shona, letting Gatta and Alexander in the back and getting behind the wheel. 'Most carnivores do if they're hungry.'

'I'm not sure how we can stop him,' said Luke. 'Besides, I think we've got a bigger problem.'

'Bigger problems need more brainpower and brains need food,' said Shona. 'Budgie Smugglers?'

'What?'

'*Budgie Smugglers*, on Collins Street. They make killer burgers, really cheap.'

Budgie Smugglers turned out to be crammed with old motorcycle parts and middle-aged motorcyclists. Three of them rose from their stools when Shona walked in. A moment later she was enveloped in creaking black leather. She looked over their heads at Luke and Gatta and shrugged. 'Friends of my brother's. Can you order?'

Luke was getting really tired of watching other people hugging, especially Shona.

They parked next to the trees in St David's Park and started on the burgers.

'Okay,' said Shona. 'Hit me up with the bigger problems.'

'What do you think a modern-day *Tasmaniosaurus triassicus* would be worth?'

'Worth?' Shona stared at him.

'In money. Or suppose you could convince people you had one. What could you sell it for?'

She looked taken aback. 'It would be the biggest discovery in–'

'In the history of history,' said Gatta.

'Well, of palaeontology anyway,' said Shona. 'You couldn't possibly put a value on that. What it would mean for evolutionary biology, understanding the extinctions, physiology. I mean we don't know anything about Archosaurs or even dinosaurs except what we extrapolate from their bones. We're probably wildly wrong about the rest of it, what their hearts or lungs, or even blood, immune systems... I don't know where to start.' Her eyes lit up. 'Ooh, their DNA!'

'No, not the scientific value,' said Luke, though he loved how excited she was. 'I really do mean money. If it's so significant, surely someone somewhere would want to buy it.'

Her ravenous look turned ferocious.

'No, not us!' said Luke. 'We couldn't sell him. He's himself; we don't own him. But what if someone else found out?'

'Sounds like someone has. Okay, we'll get onto who later.' She took her last bite of burger and licked her fingers, which Luke found disturbing.

'Let's see. If you *had* found a living *Tt* there's no question it would be big. Automatic Nobel Prize-big. Then, depending on its physiology, any new research could translate into medical knowledge.' She contemplated the chips they had kept for afters.

'I suppose it's a question of who would buy it and how much money they had. The three biggest places for palaeontology would be the BBC universities – Bristol, Bremen and Columbia. They'd have millions for something like this, especially Columbia.' She took a chip. 'If you wanted to maximise the money, and I'm getting the feeling your someone does,' – Luke nodded gloomily – 'you'd play them off against each other. Ten million. At least.'

'Ten million?' said Gatta.

'That's what I was afraid of,' said Luke.

'We should have got the *Tt* to pay for dinner,' said Shona. 'Now who do you think is after him?'

They told her about Ty while they shared the last chips.

'But,' said Luke, 'this all depends on whether Alexander is really a *Tt*. Or I suppose if Ty could convince someone he could be. That's really why we're here, to find out where the prof has got up to on the eggshell.'

'She's got me helping. That's what PhD students are for.' Shona gave long-suffering sigh. 'Amino acid dating can't be used at less than a thousand years. The shell is less old than that. We had someone look at the crystalline structure. They said they can't be at all accurate because crystals don't change that much, but at a guess more than a hundred years but probably less than five hundred.'

'Okay.'

'There's not much else. Our analyst said there might have been biological material on the inside layer, so Prof sent a sample off in case any DNA survived. It's been tricky because we can't use the usual uni resources. Prof is calling in favours from private labs.'

'So we're not much further,' said Luke. *Ten million...*

'No further at all.' Shona peered over the seat at Alexander. 'We need to be looking at him. An X-ray of his bones. But I don't know anyone with elastic morals and a backyard X-ray machine. Or better still, a 3D CT scanner.' Then she hit her forehead. 'What a dumbarse! Why are we doing DNA on the egg when we've got him! He must be sloughing skin like crazy, the way he's growing.'

'Would that look like prawn crackers, just not so pink?' asked Gatta. 'There are some of those in your sock drawer, Luke.'

'But how does his DNA help when there's no *Tt* DNA to compare it to?' he asked Shona.

'If he is a *Tt* we can't compare him to anything,' she said. 'If he's not, he'll be a *Varanus* and have *their* DNA, so that'd prove he's not a *Tt* but a monitor with unusual front legs.' She looked guiltily at Alexander then coughed. 'When I made the crack about him getting bigger and he made like my leg was food—'

'He was joking,' said Gatta.

'You know that's another dimension more screwy? More unheard of?'

Luke and Gatta nodded.

'Another ten million dollars worth of unheard of,' said Luke.

'Our very own Filthylucrosaur,' said Gatta.

Chapter 21

They drove up to South Hobart in silence, except for the snuffling of the uncounted-million-dollar lizard probing the seat crevices for escaped salt grains. When Shona turned into their street, Gatta said, 'Delish burgers but I'm still hungry. Want to come check out my cheese toast? With hot paprika? If Toastfiendosaurus will let you have any?'

'Why not,' said Shona. 'I can pick myself up some prawn crackers.'

Luke had always thought their kitchen looked okayish, with the long window onto the garden and his and Brendan's well-turned carpentry. But with Shona in it, even in a faded cotton jersey and grass-stained shorts, he saw its worn edges. Gatta was banging in cupboards, gathering plates. He and Shona looked in opposite directions. He was mystified to find her as uncomfortable as he was.

'So, Gatta texted me about this Taylah what's-her-name thing?' she said to fill the silence.

'It got weirder,' Gatta said. 'Show Shona Lucie's Facebook page, Luke. Remember that woman who was holding the second husky after the attack? Her friend got a vid that shows the dog's teeth don't ever actually touch her.'

Luke ran the footage on his laptop. The new angle revealed a clear two centimetres of air between the husky's teeth and Taylah's knee. And something else.

'Look! The way the axe jerks when she falls. She's slashed herself with the blade!' said Luke.

'There's no question the dog didn't touch her,' Shona said.

'Is she still suing?' asked Gatta from behind a cloud of red spice.

'It doesn't say. She's back in hospital for a wound infection they're blaming on the dog. But the trolls are in armies now.' Luke scrolled quickly. 'There are pics of a pet pony she supposedly starved – some of them look photoshopped – neighbours who say she poisoned their dog...'

'What were you two doing at the Botanical Gardens anyway?' asked Shona.

'Alexander was obsessed with acorns.'

'Acorns? A bit out of season. Did you find any?'

'Yes, last year's mostly. But he only liked one sort. I got a picture. He doesn't like you touching his stash. Not that he ever does anything with it, except to bite one occasionally, like he's checking they still taste awful.' Luke turned the screen towards Shona.

'*Quercus cryptogermanii*. The Hungarian Oak,' she read. 'Connection?'

'Hold on. Über-toasties,' said Gatta. She proffered a plate of cheese toast smothered in paprika. Alexander was performing rapid circles on the floor, whacking his tail on chair-legs and the fridge. He got his own plate of toast, plain and nearly black. 'That's the way he likes it,' she told Shona.

'Well, sort of likes it,' said Luke. 'Watch this.' Alexander plunged into the toast pile in a frenzy of black crumbs, throwing fragments in every direction, then hoovered up every last one, all in the space of a minute. Then he glared and hissed at the plate. 'It's like he's expecting something else.'

'Marmalade?' suggested Shona, chewing her own toast. 'Amazing,' she said indistinctly. 'Smokiness in layers. The different smokes in the toast and the cheese and the paprika.'

'That's it,' Luke shouted. 'Smoke!' He jumped up. 'Remember when Ty was here, when Alexander should have been zonked but zombie-walked out here after the burnt pine nuts? *He needs his acorns burnt!*'

He retrieved some acorns, wrenched the grill control to max, and tossed one under the grill. Alexander's head drew up like an angry gull, but after a few seconds his tongue flickered. With the faint burning smell, a red spot bloomed between Alexander's eyes. It reached a brilliance they'd never seen then expanded, as if it was his true colour welling up from within.

'Gats, the rest of them,' Luke said.

Gatta scattered the rest of the acorns onto the tray. Smoke drifted from the grill. Alexander stretched to maximum height and as the smoke curled around him, the fiery patch flared down his flanks to his tail and intensified till his whole body glowed the incandescent red of molten steel. So bright, the smoke haze and their faces were tinted crimson. He turned his yellow eyes to Luke, who knew they'd reached the most momentous hour of Alexander's life.

He as asking.

It felt like he and Alexander had reached the top of the bridge, clambered over the safety rail and were looking down. They could turn back, or they could jump. Alexander had seemed compelled to gather the acorns, but what came now was a choice, which hadn't come with instructions. He was scared. He wanted Luke to choose for him. Or for Luke to commit to a journey with him.

Thinking further wasn't going to help, so Luke didn't. He pulled the charred acorns from the grill and offered them up. Alexander stretched out a claw and took one, placed it within his jaws and bit. It shattered. Luke's own mouth shared the feeling. He almost spat.

Alexander swallowed it awkwardly and reached for the next. He regarded the acorn solemnly. They were committed. He ate it.

The smoke swirled, bitter and acrid, stinging their eyes and throats.

'Smoke alarm will go,' said Shona and reached up to unscrew it. She sat down. 'What's going on?' she whispered. 'Do I sound delusional if I say he's making it look like some kind of initiation ceremony?'

'It feels really important to him,' said Luke. 'But really, I've no idea. He could be a lizard teenager trying his first line of coke.' He was trying to joke but he couldn't feel either sacredness or daredevilry from Alexander, just uncertainty. Where there should have been… something. Conviction at least.

They watched in silence as, with each acorn Alexander ate, his internal glow faded. By the last one, he was a dank lilac and his posture was stiff and bent. When his light had drained completely, the kitchen seemed cold, dingier, the windows murky and smoke-stained.

After swallowing the last fragment with difficulty, Alexander was motionless. Then he dropped to the floor, and walked a slow circle, shaking out his limbs. He looked buckled, beaten. He stopped, his head sank, and Luke was flooded with fear, a sense of being pitifully small in the path of an approaching nameless monster. He fell to his knees and gathered the lizard up against his chest. Then he and Alexander were folded into the circle of Shona's and Gatta's arms, as they kneeled together in the growing dark.

Part II

Chapter 22

That night Luke dreamed of AFL: starting in the ruck against a stick-armed boy. Except, as he approached, the boy sniggered. He followed the boy's stare down to his own naked, concave chest, then across to the boy's interchange bench, groaning with mountainous drip-nosed trolls, wielding troll clubs. Luke looked wildly around for the umpires but they had fled or been eaten. The trolls, in Collingwood Magpie jerseys, bared their broken teeth and thumped their filthy boots on the earth. The thumping grew louder and the stench of their panting reached out to choke him.

He woke gasping in the dark. Alexander was crawling around the floor, his tail thumping against the bedposts. He blundered into the dresser. Luke slid out of bed and groped for him. Alexander crept up against his leg and they rested against each other, calmer together. When Luke got cold and slipped back into bed, his unease immediately returned. He reached down for Alexander's shoulder, re-establishing the calm. Though it felt like two small boys holding hands in the dark, it would get them to morning.

Luke was nearly asleep before he realised he could still smell the trolls.

At first light, Alexander followed Luke into the kitchen. His usual morning green had darker patches – an avocado that had missed the fleeting window of ripeness. Alexander moved like his insides, too, had passed their best. Luke offered him some muesli, which was dismissed with an irritable tail flick. He held up a couple of eggs, was rewarded with a feeling like his stomach had wrapped itself miserably round his spine. 'Not enough then?'

Gatta walked in just then, at least an hour early for her. 'Phew,' she said. 'Morning breath alert.'

'He's had that all night,' Luke said. 'I guess I kind of got used to it. He's just projected "starving" at me. We need to feed him a heap but I don't know of what.'

'Sorry we don't have a bullock on hand,' said Gatta to Alexander, 'but maybe the butcher has some like, spare parts.'

Luke's bike trip to the butcher took twenty minutes. He procured a huge bag of bleeding bones and assorted offal, enough to last a good few days. It lasted till lunchtime. What unnerved them most was not Alexander's overwhelming hunger, which he projected at them so nakedly it was impossible to withstand, or the pervasive smell of rottenness that hung around him, diminishing slightly when he ate – it was his uncertainty. Alexander had always been sociable and curious, sometimes playful, sometimes irritable, sometimes demanding, but he'd never been less than confidently himself. Now he was timid and it scared them. He reached out with his unease and bound them to him; the further they moved away, the stronger it became. They couldn't tell whether it was coming from him or from themselves, but they gave up wondering and simply stayed with him.

Luke brought his laptop out to the veranda because Alexander refused to move from the sun, and talked to him because talking was calming. About aperture and shutter settings, and the rules of cricket.

In the afternoon, Gatta had Netflix in her bedroom for him, plus an enormous bag of jerky. She was vindicated in discovering that his interest in subtitles transcended nudity and existentialism, so she paused the beginning of *As Good as it Gets* for a quick rundown on the alphabet. The combination of movie and jerky relieved his distress almost completely for nearly 140 minutes, but his smell was growing stronger. Stoically, Gatta streamed *Red Dog*, looking for strong animal role models, (having forgotten the fate of the kelpie).

They staggered out of her room in the late afternoon, Gatta clutching an empty jerky bag and frowning.

'The smell is bad,' she told Luke. 'Sorry.' This to Alexander. She'd always been for open communication over tact. 'And he's kind of warm. Like he's getting to be his own heater.'

'Yes, I'd noticed,' said Luke. 'I don't understand that at all. Reptiles aren't supposed to be able to generate heat. I wonder if it's a fever.'

'His skin's getting like the highway on a hot day. His pics are going blurry.'

'Blurry?'

Gatta shimmied. 'Our game. I say a word and he shows me the pic for it. He remembers the words no problem. He's never missed, even stuff he learned a week ago. But today his pics are not sharp, like my phone after I dropped it in the sink.'

Gatta's phone vibrated. 'Oh crap. Crap crap. The Goblin's coming. Mum's doing a flying visit from Sydney and she's bringing him.'

'Shit,' said Luke. 'I don't know if we can leave Alexander in another room now. He'll make a noise or come out.'

'I'll go sulk in my room with him,' said Gatta 'We've had a fight or I've got female problems, yada yada, or you have no idea. Just business as usual. Any of that will work.'

Luke was on his laptop when Ty and Holly turned up. Next to his mother, he felt taller than ever. He thought of Shona's coach, Adam, growing bigger around his sick wife, as he put both arms around Holly. 'Welcome home, Mum. Hi, Ty.'

She startled. It had been years since hugging was routine, and Luke's chest had been much smaller then. She laughed. 'Hi, little Luke.' She hugged him back. 'I'm sorry I have to be back in Sydney tomorrow. Ty thought we could come for an early dinner, then work after.'

She frowned and turned her head.

'What is that *smell?*' said Ty.

Luke had forgotten about the smell. 'Possums in the roof. I think. I can deal with it later.' He fervently wished Gatta was there to do the lying.

'Maybe deal with it now. It's daylight,' said Ty. He was alert. Luke never put off maintenance.

'I'll have to borrow a ladder from Mr Jensen.' Luke had two ladders, one of them Brendan's, but Ty couldn't know that, couldn't drive a ladder and had certainly never touched a possum, dead or alive.

'There's a stepladder in the laundry,' said Ty. 'Where's the manhole?'

Luke's heart plummeted as he pictured the roof access above Gatta's dresser. 'Uh, I'm not sure. I think you can only get in the roof from under the eaves. I'll get the ladder. Why don't you uh go outside for a drink?'

'The roof access is in Gatta's room,' said Holly, looking at Luke with concern.

Once again, he'd succeeded only in directing suspicion to the right place. Ty was striding towards Gatta's door. Gatta could, what? Throw a tantrum and refuse entry to her room? Could they possibly miss Alexander if he went camo in such a small space? You could just about follow your nose to him.

Ty threw open Gatta's door.

'What, you don't have to knock when you're over thirty?' She was hunched on her bed with her phone, scowling.

Luke couldn't see a lizard-shaped lump under the doona, nor an indent on the bed, nor a shimmer in the corner. Alexander wouldn't have agreed to go far. Could she have stuffed him under the bed somehow? The rotten smell was strong.

'Excuse us, Agatha,' said Ty. 'There appears to be a…creature in the roof space. We need to get up there.'

Luke's heart nearly stopped when he saw the access cover was fractionally askew. How the hell had Gatta managed to get Alexander up there?

'Here's the ladder,' said Holly, unfolding it.

Luke stepped forward. 'I can–'

'I'll do it,' said Ty. 'Holly's always telling me I need to get more practical. Like you.' He smiled. Then stepped up the ladder, pushed the cover aside and poked his head into the space. 'There's something up here.' His voice was muffled. 'I need a torch.'

Luke had time to wonder whether Alexander, ravenous and irritable, would bite Ty's head off.

'Here,' said Holly.

Behind her, Gatta gave a slight nod to the window.

'I'll go look where they might be getting in from,' Luke said.

Next door, Audrey was peering into the chicken house and chuckling. Her mother was at her back door. Audrey waved at all of them.

'Sssssss,' she called and wiggled her arm.

Mrs F would think only one thing.

Luke watched her grab a shovel and march down the lawn to kill the snake.

He couldn't call out to stop her without alerting Ty and there wasn't time to intercept her. She'd discover Alexander and one of them would be seriously bloodied or worse.

Then he saw the Buddha. About eight cm tall and made of granite, meditating on the apple crate. Without further thought, Luke picked it up and threw it at Mrs F.

Luke could hit his wicketkeeper's gloves from seventy metres; he could hit a shovel from twenty virtually with his eyes shut. There was a clang and Mrs F stopped, amazed. From the corner of his eye, Luke saw Ty appear at the back door. Mrs F recognised the Buddha at her feet and looked at Luke. He grimaced desperately at her and mouthed, 'No.'

Would she make the connection? Mrs F's coldness to Ty was intense; he'd never acknowledged Audrey.

From the chook pen came a cheerful *pock pock pock*. Mrs F took Audrey's hand, nodded at Luke, and nudged the Buddha into a patch of maidenhair fern on her way back to the house.

Chapter 23

During dinner preparations, Luke and Gatta heard a disturbing sound. Ty was humming as he set the table. Later, over Holly's risotto, he said conversationally, 'I didn't find anything in the roof space. And the smell was less up there. Maybe it wasn't a dead possum.'

'More cheese, Gatta?' *Not Agatha? What was going on?* 'Maybe it was a particularly malodorous live animal that saw me coming and escaped to the neighbours.' He speared a tomato. 'Perhaps we have a unique species, an Australian skunk?'

Holly stared at her brother. Ty was never fanciful. Smiling, he raised his eyebrows at Luke and Gatta.

Okay, so he knew. And now they knew he knew. What next? Unlike a normal adult, he'd always treated them as equal opponents not as children. Preparing you for the real world.

Gatta was unnaturally still. Bereft of ideas.

'Mum,' Luke said, 'your drug delivery system, UC–'

'186,' said Holly, relieved to be on familiar territory.

'UC186. You said it was,' Luke rotated a hand, 'a folding peptide which is alternately hydrophilic and hydrophobic to get through the skin layers.'

'UC. Oozy!' Gatta came to life. 'It oozes through.'

Holly laughed. 'Both. Exactly right! Yes?'

'You said the thing can bind to almost any drug so it's an alternative to almost any tablet or needle. Which means an awful lot of money.'

'Yes, Luke,' said Ty. 'Money. Does this offend you?'

'It also means an awful lot of used backing patches. Are they biodegradable? Affordable in the Developing World?'

'Luke, the world doesn't care whether you save it or not,' said Ty.

But Holly was pursing her lips. 'No, not biodegradable so far.'

'With all that money you could…' said Luke.

The conversation continued on safe ground but Luke struggled between talking with his mother and sending reassurance towards unhappy Alexander.

Dinner dragged on into the next century, but as soon as Ty's tail lights disappeared, Luke was in Mrs F's backyard.

'Safest to leave him over there,' he told Gatta when he returned. 'Ty knows he's here somewhere and he's biding his time. He'll be back. Alexander hates it but he knows he's got no choice. He didn't try to follow me back.' He smiled a little. 'I think the chickens are helping. They're cuddled all over him. Either they're enjoying his warmth or he's got them hypnotised into a chooky love-fest. By the way, how did you get him over there when he's been welded to us since last night?'

'He did a *Red Dog*. I heard "possums in the roof" and he had to go. Then I messed with the manhole thing.'

When Luke was in bed, with the day stilled, Alexander's mental keening grew stronger, a thin clear note of misery. Luke tried to pull Alexander's suffering to himself, imagined it disappearing into a mirrored pool. He looked for an image of reassurance to send back: cinnamon toast; planing timber, the fragrant curls dropping. He wasn't sure whose wretchedness diminished with this, but it certainly worked on him.

He awoke like someone had slapped him. He sat up, straining for a noise, heard nothing but deep silence. A calm stripe of moonlight lay across his knees. Regardless, something had struck him almost physically: the absolute certainty of danger and urgency. There was only one likely cause.

He pulled on a jumper and slid out down the hall. The back veranda was mostly in shadow, but nothing moved there. He eased open the door, the click of the lock loud as a hammer blow, and crept out, crouched over, keeping his body below the railing slats. The moon was high and a third full, showing an empty lawn bordered by impenetrable black. He peered between the gaps, waiting. Anyone hiding under the trees would be invisible, but might have seen him come out the door.

He waited, until the danger kicked in his chest. It pushed him on, duckwalking to the end of the veranda where, through the cyclone fence, he had a view of Mrs F's yard and the chicken coop. The lawn was clear. The chooks were quiet. Luke's heart was slowing, and he was wondering whether it was his stupid brain inventing another troll story when he saw movement at the top of Mrs F's walk. Not just movement: someone holding a long thin object. The dark shape separated from the shadow of the satinwood and entered the back yard. It had to be Ty, coming to steal Alexander.

If Luke had acted like himself and stopped to think, everything would have been different, but he didn't. He was at the far side of the veranda in four strides and vaulting the rail in pitch darkness. His toes sank in soil and there was a brief waft of basil. He bounded over the vegetable bed and across the front corner of his house back into moonlight. When he made the top of Mrs F's drive, Ty was halfway down the lawn, pausing to adjust the rod, which had a noose at one end.

Do something! But what? Ty was about to capture Alexander. Hurt him, maybe kill him in the process. All of Luke's frustration and fear and hatred – of his own weakness as well as of Ty – rose into a wave of rage. It swept him down to the bottom corner of the house where Mrs F had propped the shovel. He grabbed it and, without breaking stride, raised it over his head and swung. He should, with his fury, his fast-bowling action and the heavy shovel, have rendered Ty's skull and brain into mulch. As it was, the shovel glanced off an overhanging branch changing its trajectory. It smacked Ty partly on the shoulder, but still hit enough of his head to drop him like a stunned heifer at the abattoir. He fell face forward and was still.

The shovel slipped from Luke's fingers. His knees buckled and he sank to the grass beside his uncle. Had he killed him?

A fragment of the old Luke managed to retrieve a first aid lesson he had paid Luke-like attention to. He slid his trembling hand around Ty's neck till his fingertips – oh thank god, thank trees, thank fuck – hit a rapid pulse. He bent double and nearly sobbed with relief. But now his rational self had to sort out what his primal self had wrought. He wobbled upright, made his way down to the coop, which was completely dark inside, and called Alexander's name. The answering hiss trailed off into a new sound, a bubbling croak. There was a shuffling noise; a drowsy clucking from the chickens. Alexander's snout appeared at the moonlit doorway.

'Hang in there,' said Luke.

He ran back to his house, his bedroom and his phone. When he turned, a figure was in his doorway. For a horrified moment he saw a crouched Ty – or his ghost – then Gatta whispered, 'What's happening?'

'Ty came for Alexander. I hit him. He's unconscious and we have to get Alexander out before Ty wakes up, but he's sick and can't walk far. I have to–'

'Call Shona,' she said with him.

Shona was groggy but said, 'Luke?' She didn't say "It's two in the morning," or "Do you know what time it is?", which meant a lot, but he was too freaked out to realise that till later.

'I'll be there in five,' she said after he explained. 'I'm going to coast down the road so you won't hear the engine. I'll bring a tarp.'

Could a woman get any more perfect?

Luke pulled jeans on over his boxers then he and Gatta returned to Mrs F's. They edged down the path. Luke hadn't bothered to arm himself. He couldn't hit Ty again.

'Where is he?' whispered Gatta. The lawn was empty.

'He must have woken up and gone. He can't have taken Alexander! They were both stuffed. But I'll check.'

Alexander had dragged himself further out of the coop. Even by moonlight, he was pale. Luke put a hand on his neck. His skin was hot and crackled but the familiar current of their connection still flowed.

Together, Gatta, Luke and Shona lifted Alexander onto the tarp, took the corners and stumbled up to the road. To Luke, Alexander's pallid body seemed to float behind Shona, invisible in darkness. They slid him onto the tray of the ute and pushed the vehicle to the bottom of the first hill before Shona switched on the engine or the lights.

She lived a few minutes further up the mountain, and once they turned off the Huon Road, there was no streetlight at all, only the silvery trunks of the blue gums and the occasional letterbox gleaming as the headlight beams swung across them. Their tyres rattled onto gravel. A minute later they took a sharp left turn and bounced into a narrow rutted driveway. A darkened house loomed on their left but Shona drove past and stopped by a semicircle of yellow light spilling out of her front door onto a tiny veranda. They carried Alexander on his tarp to the door.

Inside was a square metre of sunken entry with wooden steps up to a floor which rose to waist level on three sides.

They placed Alexander gently in the space on the right. His breathing had slowed.

'He feels calmer than he has all day,' said Luke in surprise.

'Maybe it's the feels from us. He's in a safer place than he's been for a while,' said Gatta.

'We'll figure it out in the morning.'

Luke caught Shona giving him a lopsided grin.

'Better get you home so you don't look like you've been out bashing people all night,' she said.

Chapter 24

Luke was back at Shona's by eight in the morning. Daylight revealed her house as a narrow two-storey wooden cabin with a tall, steeply pitched roof and a central stone chimney. The single large downstairs room was arranged around a central stone fireplace. A bathroom/laundry was tucked way to the left, a kitchen alcove ahead, and on the right, stairs led to a bedroom. It had been built by Daroslav and Jozef, long dead carpenters who neither knew nor cared about Australian building regulations. Two of thousands displaced by WWII, they had journeyed to the bottom of the earth to build Tasmania's hydroelectric dams and then this house.

The front door was open to relieve the smell.

Inside, Shona crouched beside Alexander. He was the colour of spoiled cheese and exuded waves of distress. He lifted his head to look at Luke, managed a flare of rosy pink over his neck, then had to reposition his legs and tail.

Luke placed his hand on the lizard's rump and nearly jerked it back. The scales felt hot and crackly but doughy underneath, like the old foil-backed insulation Brendan had pulled from their roof. Alexander had welcomed his touch but winced at even slight pressure.

'He's not good, is he?' said Shona.

'No,' said Luke. 'He's much worse than yesterday. And I don't understand any of it. How can he even have a fever? He's a reptile.'

'We need a vet.'

He nodded. 'But I don't know how we're going to explain Alexander. And even if we found a vet who would understand and we could trust…' he looked around hopelessly, like he expected a saintly veterinarian to emerge from the stone fireplace or pop out of the laundry, 'I don't have the money to pay one.'

'I know somebody,' said Shona slowly. 'We'll have to worry about the money later. I'm not going to try to get treatment for free – vets get too much of that and I'm sure you're good for it in the long run – but it's someone trustworthy who definitely has the smarts. It's just that…' She came to a decision. 'It's Rosie. You met her at footy training. She was wearing a down coat.'

'She seemed nice, but isn't she sick?'

'Anorexia. And yes, she's doing badly. But this might help her as well as Alexander. When she started playing footy with us she was improving, putting on weight and getting strong. She mothered the younger girls.' Shona smiled, remembering. 'Kept bringing them food. Then started eating some of it herself. It was like she improved having other people that needed her to be fit. Helping Alexander might help her too: she'll know she has to be at the top of her game.'

'Well, if you think—'

'Luke. We have no idea what we're doing,' said Shona.

'Okay,' he said. 'Ring her.'

Luke went home. When he returned, Rosie was standing in Shona's doorway, enveloped in a quilted coat. Her eyes were still huge but they weren't wistful – they were worried. From Alexander came pain and fear and hunger. The fear lessened when Luke arrived, but the hunger increased with the smell from his backpack, which was full of cow parts. Luke laid his cheek next to Alexander's.

'Hi Luke. My fellow failed-mongrel.' Rosie gave him a quick smile. 'Shona told me what was happening. I don't know quite what Alexander is, but that doesn't matter for now – he's a saurian and they all have similar physiology. This sounds like a couple of common problems that happen to reptiles with inexperienced carers. You've never looked after one before?'

Luke shook his head, both ashamed and hopeful. If they'd missed something, maybe Alexander would get better easily once they fixed it. Though Rosie's face said it wouldn't be easy.

'Many reptiles get dysechdysis – not shedding properly. Usually because they don't have access to water. And they get metabolic bone disease, where their bones don't grow right, from the wrong diet. Lack of water makes this worse and they can end up with kidney or heart failure. Or secondary infections. He looks like there's something wrong with his skin and his bones or joints are painful. And he's got a fever. How did you give him access to water?'

'Um, we didn't, um, organise any, as such. We thought he'd ask.'

Rosie frowned. She'd probably heard stupider things but Luke couldn't think of any. He wanted to crawl away.

'I need to examine him more closely and I don't want to get clawed or bitten. We'll need restraints.'

'He won't hurt you, whatever you do,' said Luke.

Rosie shook her head and started removing her thin rubber gloves.

Shona said, 'He had painful handling yesterday, including by me, and all he did was cooperate.'

They compromised on Luke holding Alexander's jaws and Shona his powerful back legs. Luke felt their every touch on Alexander and every movement in his own bones and skin but also his reassurance from their care. Alexander even projected a weak glow of comfort in return. Rosie's face seemed all bone and eyes, and though he could see the tendons slide under the gloves and white skin of her hands, they were sure and methodical. Rosie relaxed and grew more confident as she examined him, getting in close to study his eyes and jaw with a magnifier. She straightened up, more worried than before.

'It's not just his skin. The smell and the fever are probably from an infection, or maybe a toxin. But he's got swelling, oedema, of his tissues, which might kidney or heart failure. I can't feel big kidneys or bladder stones but his heart feels enlarged.'

'He might have a four-chambered heart,' said Shona.

Rosie looked at her strangely. 'He's a lizard, a Varanid, not a crocodile. Three chambers.'

'Well, we're not sure what breed he is,' said Luke. 'He's some kind of crossover.' Then he flushed, because how could he possibly have any credibility?

Rosie ignored him, politely. 'What I really can't understand is how he's making his fever. Reptiles get fevers – it's part of their immune defence. But they raise their temperature with behaviour, moving into warm areas.

'There are more things I don't understand. I need more information. I'll get equipment to take blood and tissue samples, some examination gear, maybe an ultrasound if I'm lucky.' Her voice was less certain. 'I haven't been doing much work at the practice lately so they might not let me borrow it.' Then she stretched her hand to Alexander and Luke felt a pulse of comfort again.

'I'll be back tomorrow. In the meantime, make sure he can drink as much as he wants. And give him a long bath in water that's at his temperature. Regardless of where his temperature is coming from, we shouldn't try to lower it.'

As Shona looked around the small cabin uncertainly, Rosie said, 'Or at least a good wash, if you have nothing to bath him in.' She left the house energised by purpose.

Luke and Shona were alone. Luke suddenly found the ceiling buttresses intensely interesting. Honey coloured. Geometry of shadows. He said, 'I like your place.' He gestured at the rafters. 'The craftsmanship. And, ah, cosy.'

'Thanks. I thought from the look of your work on yours – Gatta told me – you'd like mine.'

'Brendan's and my work.' *She'd thought about his work, and him?* He flapped a hand. His hands felt too big. 'Should we wash Alexander? Outside maybe?'

Shona grinned. 'There's no way we'd fit three of us in my shower. I barely fit in it myself.'

Shona in the shower… He had to get outside. 'I'll give him lunch first.'

They fed him on his tarp outside. Luke was used to seeing Alexander swallow quantities about half his size, which now approximated an Alsation, but Shona gaped in amazement. 'Well, appetite is a good sign, I think.' A whole shinbone disappeared. 'Though that looks a bit unhinged.'

Luke was testing the temperature of their tub of water. 'You didn't tell Rosie everything about him,' he said.

Shona handed him a sponge. 'I thought that was up to you. We'll have to tell her more, especially about the acorns because if it's a toxin, there's your source. They kill horses and cows sometimes but lots of animals eat them.'

Shona kneeled opposite Luke and began sponging Alexander's neck. 'See if you can find out some more about the Hungarian Oak.'

Pearls of water beaded on her forearms. The sponge-bath was thorough and splashy and far too short for Luke.

He went home, oblivious to the cooling afternoon, taking Shona's shortcut down the property, across the gully and its icy stream and over a hill onto the Huon Road. At home, pots were on the stove and Gatta was on the phone.

'Hold on, Mum, Luke's here.' To Luke, 'Mum never left for Sydney. She's at Emergency with Uncle Ty. She says he was attacked by an intruder outside his house last night. Lowlife hit him with a baseball bat!'

She covered the mouthpiece and whispered, 'He's trying to point the finger away from you, obvs. You'd have used a cricket bat,' then said into the phone, 'Hold on, Mum, I'll put you on speaker.'

Their mother's voice came out tired. 'He's going to be okay, but his shoulder is really bruised, he can't drive and he's probably going to have concussion. He'll be off work, but he's refused to have me stay, so I'm flying out later.' Anxiety and irritation crept in. 'I think he's being irrational, which is totally unlike him. I need him rational to get Paladin on board with Transcend.'

'You won't get the money?'

'Ty said not to worry, he'd find it himself. But that's even stranger. He doesn't have that much.'

Ty's game of finding Alexander had turned serious. Luke nearly thought, nearly said, *Mum, I can find it*, but he didn't.

Holly continued, 'In the meantime, I have to try to run the lab here from Sydney until he's back on board.'

'So you'll get home at three in the morning and get up at two,' said Luke, surprised that his anger at Ty was stronger than his guilt.

'Yes,' she said, then laughed. 'But I've asked him to pay me a CEO salary and 100 shares per day. That'll motivate him to get back.'

'It's about time he paid you what you've always been worth,' said Luke. Words the old Luke couldn't have said aloud. And the old Luke's voice had never possessed that steely edge. His mother wasn't protesting so he voiced another thought, long unspoken. 'Mum, why does Ty hate me?'

He heard an intake of breath, almost saw his mother's hand cover her mouth. Knew that the silence meant she wasn't rebutting him. That time was past. When she finally spoke, she sounded detached, like she was talking pharmacokinetics. 'You were Anders's golden-haired firstborn son.'

Gatta mimed shielding herself from Luke's dazzling rays, then rolled her eyes and mouthed, 'Duh!'

'You smiled at everyone, charmed everyone.' Holly's voice wavered. 'You had everything.'

'I was a baby!'

'Then you were a child. And children were Ty's first enemies.' Holly sighed. 'And you bound me to Anders maybe much longer than we would have been together. I must go. I'll talk to you from Sydney, okay, Luke?'

She rang off.

'Running away.' Gatta sounded more sad than bitter. 'Big applause, Luke. You've got further into Planet-Mum than we have in forever.'

'And Planet-Ty. She might physically live here, but in every way that matters, she lives there. I wonder why.'

'He's convinced her that nowhere else is safe.'

'Could we convince her it's safer with us?'

Gatta stared. 'Luke, you've got that all doodle-doo-a-cock. She's the adult.'

Gatta disappeared to her room and History while Luke sat down to study acorn toxins. It was a struggle. His brain kept diverting to Shona's bare ankles. And stealing his mother back off his uncle.

Chapter 25

Shona was hosing off the veranda in T-shirt and faded cargo pants when Luke arrived the following morning. 'You'd think he was a herd of tigers,' she said. 'I had to get up in the middle of the night and find a couple of dead wallabies to feed him, otherwise neither of us would have got any sleep. I actually have two jobs as well as a PhD to finish. And a house that normally smells pretty nice. We have to recruit more help.'

She coiled the hose in perfect loops and said more quietly, 'He's getting sicker. We really will need more hands to care for him. But we can decide after Rosie's been. She's on her way.'

'I'm sorry. Sorry to drag you into this.'

'Thanks for the sentiment. You're older than when we first met, you know.'

'Less stupid?'

Shona waggled a hand. 'Hmmm. Certainly more violent.'

Rosie arrived and slammed the door on a middle-aged Subaru Outback. A large messenger bag was slung over her shoulder. Her cheeks were pink. 'How is he?'

They walked through the open front door. Alexander's smell was now distinctly rotten and increasingly penetrating. His skin was mottled, grey and greenish. He stirred little when they arrived and barely raised his eyelids. Before, the strongest currents in his distress had been pain with surges of hunger; those were still powerful, but now above all else was fear. Luke wanted to hold him, but touch would hurt.

'He's worse isn't he? I take it he got a bath and has been drinking, but it doesn't look like he's shed at all.' Rosie frowned. 'But he looks… bigger?'

'Yes,' said Shona calmly. 'Bigger by a backpack full of cow and two dead wallabies.'

'That's um…surprising but it's a good sign. Appetite is good,' said Rosie.

Luke nearly laughed. Was Alexander nudging Rosie's thinking as well as sending his pulse of reassurance? He managed that for Rosie, even as he got sicker. Keeping his vet onside?

She repeated the survey of his skin and body from nose to tail, less happy as she went. 'I want to take some samples and give him an antibiotic shot and I want to examine inside his mouth and his rectum.'

Luke glanced at Alexander, wondering if her last word had come up in his language lessons. With Gatta, there was no telling. Alexander appeared unperturbed.

'Those things are uncomfortable,' continued Rosie, 'so I'm going to try a manoeuvre that sometimes puts lizards to sleep. You should hold him, for everyone's safety.'

With Luke and Shona in the same positions as the day before, Rosie put one gloved hand under Alexander, low on his belly, and the other over his closed eyes. 'When I press on his eyes, I can cause a vasovagal response, exactly like a faint. I'm feeling his heart rate, and I can tell if it's working.'

Rosie's fingers pressed gently but firmly over Alexander's eyes. She looked focused and sure. She was not as pale and seemed to have more energy than the day before. Then Luke realised Alexander's signal was fading, as it had that evening at the training field on what felt like weeks ago. Shona made a small noise. Luke looked at her startled face. She too had internalised his background hum without knowing it and had felt it fade. Her eyes questioned him. He nodded.

'It's working,' said Rosie. 'His heart rate was about 100, which is very high by the way, and it's right down now, less than thirty.'

'I feel it working,' said Shona, wonderingly. Alexander's presence in Luke's mind had vanished. His body had sunk so completely it felt dissolved.

'We'll start with his mouth.' Rosie reached for some tubes and a spatula.

From outside, there was a crunch of tyres followed by a car engine switching off. Adam was in the doorway by Alexander's tail, face creased with worry.

His face was like a pilot's in an airline ad: Mature. Dependable. Children and adults would automatically look towards him in an emergency, whereas they would instinctively step carefully around Ty. 'You weren't answering your phone,' he said to Rosie.

'Sorry sweetie,' she said. 'I had it muted because I thought this was going to be tricky. I'm okay. I had breakfast. I did.'

Adam looked like he, too, was putting off a conversation till later. He leaned closer and wrinkled his nose. 'Your patient looks odd. And pretty sick.'

'He is,' she said, 'but the vasovagal trick is working a treat. He's a good boy but he's in a lot of pain so I wouldn't have been able to do this stuff,' she held up the spatula, 'without it.'

'Opiates work on reptiles,' Adam said as Rosie gently eased the spatula between Alexander's teeth and opened his mouth.

'Yes. But he's off the books so I can't get any through the practice. And this is working.'

Luke felt disloyal but he said, 'He's in pain all the time. And he's frightened.'

'Pet owners are just like parents,' said Adam. He smiled at Luke in a way that made them teammates. 'I'm a paramedic. I listen to a lot of parents.' He appeared to have a brief internal dialogue then looked from under his flight captain's brows at Luke. 'I can get you some opiates if he really needs them. Just to make life easier for my wife. Nobody needs to know.'

Rosie was taking swabs from Alexander's mouth. 'Adam, I don't want you to do that. And I'm doing fine.'

'Don't let her overdo it,' Adam said to Luke and Shona. 'She really feels this is important but she can't afford to get sicker. My priority is my wife so I'm going to help you if I can, but if she starts getting worse, which she does when she's not putting herself first, I'm not going to let her come. That's if she doesn't collapse first.'

'Really, sweetie, I feel great,' said Rosie, capping a swab. 'Now I need to do a rectal exam because that's a much better way to feel his organs. So we'll roll him sideways a little. I'm going to take a blood sample from his tail too.' She smiled at her husband. 'I'll see you at home,' then turned her full focus to her patient. Adam's jaw clenched momentarily. He waved and walked out.

Rosie worked with swift, economical movements, which was fortunate because just before she finished, Luke felt a tweak from Alexander's mind and tone returning to his neck muscles.

Shona noticed it too. 'He's waking up.'

They heard Adam's engine turn over as Alexander started to thrash. Luke wasn't sure if he felt the surge coming with his mind or through his hands, but he leaped back as the lizard's jaws gaped and a mouthful of razor-sharp teeth swept past him. Alexander's head swung towards the doorway and Rosie, his back legs launched him up despite Shona's powerful restraining hands, and his tail lashed around behind her, striking the coat rack, gouging his tail and spattering the wall with blood.

'Alexander! It's Luke.'

Alexander's eyes swung back to him and stopped, peering dully. His tongue flickered. His head swayed from side to side and his tail dangled uncertainly, dripping blood, then he sank to the floorboards again and was still. Luke was stunned. He'd never felt such a naked blast of rage and violence. Alexander, who had seemed so frail, could obviously summon up a scarily dangerous strength.

'Okay, we're not doing that again without sedation,' said Rosie. She was quite calm, unlike Shona, who was as shaken as Luke. 'I'm actually sort of glad he did that. It shows that a lot of systems, like his heart and muscles, aren't as far gone as I thought. And we've got a free tissue sample.'

She reached over to the wall and picked up a piece of bloodied grey flesh. Luke and Shona shuddered. Rosie dropped it into a sample container then turned to Alexander's tail. 'Poor boy,' she said, tenderly. 'You just woke up a tiny bit too soon. I know you didn't mean it.'

Luke was not sure. Alexander had been so angry, not just reacting to pain. Now, though, he seemed dull and confused. He didn't react when Rosie dressed the gash in his tail. At least his pain and fear were muted.

Rosie packed up her equipment. 'I think his temperature is higher, though I didn't get an internal one yesterday. It's 43 degrees today, which is very high. We shouldn't try to get it down because it's helping his immune system with his infection. I've given him an antibiotic. That'll bring it down if it works.'

'Umm, about that,' said Luke, realising he should have raised this earlier. 'You mentioned the possibility of a toxin. Well, there's something he ate a lot of the night before he got sick.' He brought up his phone picture of the Hungarian Oak acorn.

Rosie shook her head. 'Acorn poisoning can be severe but usually gives animals gastrointestinal problems before everything else. His gut is definitely healthy. And fever wouldn't be a big thing.' She considered. 'Unless it's some kind of allergy.' She shook her head again. 'I really don't understand the fever. He shouldn't be able to get that hot without a heat source. He's never had it before, has he? When he hasn't been sick?'

Luke shook his head.

'I think we'll stick with standard management and let it go. We're okay till it gets over 48 degrees. That's when it starts breaking down tissue and he's really stuffed.'

She tapped her lips with a thoughtful forefinger. In vet mode she looked whip-thin, sharp and strong, rather than frail. 'I really wish I had an ultrasound. He might have abscesses, especially around his chest – he's very sore there. And an X-ray. And someone else to discuss him with. There really is no chance of bringing him down into town, is there?'

'No,' said Luke, immediately.

'It's your decision,' said Rosie. 'I'm hoping the antibiotic will start helping. Keep giving him plenty of fluid and washing him in warm water. If he wants to eat, feed him.' She gave a Luke a smile that warmed him fully as much as Alexander's choofing. 'You're having a hard time but you're doing your best. If it's possible to fix him, we will, the three of us.'

When Rosie had gone, Luke and Shona carried Alexander outside for his wash.

Shona said, 'Has he always given you that – whatever it is – that feeling in your head that he's there?'

'Yes, at least I think so. He also sometimes, ah, tells you how he's feeling.'

Shona was pouring warm water on Alexander's shoulders. Her gold-bronze arms glowed against the lizard's pallid skin. Water splashed on her T-shirt, making wet patches on her abdomen. 'Go on,' she said.

'Mainly he does it with colour, though I'm not sure whether he's communicating on purpose or whether it changes automatically with his feelings. Like us blushing,' said Luke, who was doing exactly that. Shona was giving him her full attention, which was scarily wonderful, like meeting an orca.

'But sometimes I'm just sure, completely sure, he's feeling a certain way and I think somehow he's telling me.' He compressed his lips and looked at the ground. 'And sometimes I think I'm going nuts.'

He looked up straight into her green eyes. 'Not crazy. Go on,' she said.

'He definitely can tell how *we're* feeling, Gatta and me. Especially if we're stressed or angry. It really upsets him.'

Shona laid her long hand on Alexander's back. A few yellow blooms rose on the lizard's skin around her fingers. 'I think I'm getting that he needs us around,' she said. 'I had a pet Varanus when we lived in Broome. That's how I met Rosie, and how I know she has expertise in reptiles. My Smaug, who was a water monitor, kind of enjoyed my company.' She stroked Alexander, which made Luke's back tingle disturbingly. 'It's more than company he needs now, though. He needs pretty much constant care and food and bathing.'

'I'll bring an old blow-up paddle pool from home,' said Luke.

'Good, but I can't stay here with him all day. I've got a garden maintenance job with clients I can't lose, and tutorials to prepare for the students. That's before I even start to think about my PhD. And you need someone with you who can drive. So,' she held up a hand when Luke started to speak, 'I'm going to ask three girls from the team to help. Loyal ones.'

Luke's stomach sickened. 'What if Alexander doesn't like them? What about what he did this morning?'

'If Alexander doesn't like them, he'll let us know,' said Shona. 'If we have to do anything close up, it should be you or me with him. If you're worried about privacy, I get that, but I don't think we've got a choice. The girls aren't vets or zoologists; they're not going to ask awkward questions.'

Once again, Luke felt both trapped and out of control, but they did need help and he couldn't volunteer anyone. Mrs F had brains and the physical and moral courage of Geronimo but she also had the sole care of Audrey. Gatta couldn't drive, legally. Brendan wasn't there.

Shona left after they finished Alexander's wash. Washing produced revolting water but neither removed loose skin nor diminished the smell. Still, Alexander roused himself enough to eat. The butcher was giving Luke a discount but he would need his job back soon.

He made himself coffee in Shona's galley-sized kitchen and admired the workmanship. The builders could true a plank and place a keystone and the only building design they knew had lasted several centuries.

Beyond the kitchen was a conservatory, with glass that stretched the height of the house. It was expansive and cosy, lit by the sun filtering through a grove of silver-trunked flowering gums.

Luke took his coffee into the conservatory, collapsed into an armchair, closed his eyes. He tried to be the sunlight on his skin and think of nothing at all.

Instead, his brain showed him Alexander in a red mist eating burnt acorns; the doomed animals on the gates of the Beaumaris Zoo; a shovel descending on Ty's head.

Chapter 26

Gatta rang. 'I need to be helping,' she said. 'I bet nobody's Netflixing with him. He'll crack it soon.'

'He already has. It wasn't Netflix withdrawal,' Luke summarised.

'Duzz'n matter. I'm coming. Anthony said I could borrow his bike.' To Gatta, this was not totally an outrageous lie, as Anthony had once told her she could borrow a skateboard. 'I'll get it.'

She rang back thirty minutes later. 'Bike's good. But we have a Slimeball problem. There's a white car lurking up by the primary school with somebody inside not doing anything except breathing out poison gas.'

'Now we know why he took time off work.' To track them to Alexander. 'Get the bike out through the block upside of Mrs F's.' He gave the remaining directions. 'And can you bring the paddle pool?'

Gatta was there in twenty minutes. She settled on the wooden steps next to Alexander with two bowls of hot chocolate, which she reasoned was comfort food for everyone, even carnivores, and fired up her Netflix app.

Something eased in Luke. This morning, Alexander had been enmeshed in fear, then that inexplicable spasm of violence, leaving just confused dullness, which had infected Luke. He couldn't help Alexander.

Gatta seemed immune, or could bury her concern so deep she still blithely broadcast confidence. They were watching a show that purported to be about animals but, from the squealing tyres and conspiratorial whispering, sounded like a heist movie. Alexander must have been soothed by the intellectual rigour of analysing the subtitles; he felt almost mellow.

Shona returned and, for a second, Luke thought there were two of her, framed in bright doorway light.

'This is my sister, Nyabol,' she said.

Apart from being two tall imposing black women, they were in all other ways opposite: where Shona crackled and snapped, Nyabol cooled, emanating repose even when moving. Shona's skin glowed where Nyabol's swallowed light. She was a summer midnight, velvet and blue-black.

Nyabol laughed. 'The girls in the team call me Bolly. And she's not my sister. But we think her grandfather stole my grandfather's cattle.'

'You're a Dinka?' asked Luke, who had spent a school term mentoring a thirteen-year-old Sudanese-Aussie fast bowler who, by the end of the term, was taller and faster than him.

'Very good!' said Nyabol. 'No, I'm Nuer. The Dinka,' she nudged Shona, 'they are the cattle stealers.'

A rumble announced the arrival of Bec, in a lowered Falcon XH with mismatched panels and a lumpy cam V8. Or possibly, thought Luke, that fuck-you noise was just a metal file through the muffler baffles. Bec grumbled in the doorway: 'I hate your driveway. But I know I was only invited for my ute, so here it is.' She perched a hip on the raised floor opposite Alexander and Gatta. Her straw-blonde hair was scraped up in a tight ponytail. 'Emily couldn't come – family-ish. So,' She pointed both forefingers at herself.

Chips on both shoulders? wondered Luke.

Shona introduced the women to Alexander. Bec arched an eyebrow. Nyabol was gravely polite.

'There are ground rules,' Shona said. 'Alexander knows we're friends. But he's crook and in pain. So if he gets upset, he can injure someone, or himself.' She indicated his tail bandage. 'He won't do it on purpose, but that's no comfort when you've lost a hand. So neither of you should handle him without one of us. Also, stay clear of him while he's eating. It can be, um, challenging to watch.

'Also,' said Luke, 'he's got a fever. On the vet's advice, we aren't trying to bring it down, because it might be helping him. And he engages your feelings, which is an indicator of how he's going. So let us know if you're feeling something, ah, unexpected, when you're around him.'

Nyabol was taken aback but nodded slowly. Bec couldn't help herself. 'Woo-woo,' she said, waggling her fingers.

Shona ignored her. 'Bolly, you and I and Gatta are going to give Alexander a bath. Luke and Bec, you two are going out for roadkill.' Both women flinched, which Shona also ignored. 'It's his normal diet, so it should be better for him than just animal parts. And it's free. Though do try to get stuff that's relatively fresh.' She grimaced. 'The older corpses smell tastier but the house won't thank me.'

On their way out, Shona tossed Luke a pair of worn leather gauntlets. 'Don't lose them, they're my work ones.' He slid them on, put his skin where Shona's had been. Bec put on a tradie swagger. Great.

'I didn't pick you for Boy King of Snakes,' she said as she swung the Falcon onto the main road. 'When you haven't got your blah on.'

'I met Alexander by accident,' he said. 'And I have my blah on all the time.'

Bec had a straight nose and a wide, full mouth which all looked distinctly fine when she laughed.

Hostilities suspended, they made a good team. Her driving was aggressive but skilled and when they stopped to inspect a carcass, she pulled into a position that protected Luke from traffic. They found two relatively fresh wallabies on Waterworks Road and a potoroo on Ridgeway which the crows had started on, but Luke slung in the back anyway in case they couldn't find anything else. On the way down he had a thought.

'Could you go past Deegan's Road and take the next left?' he said. 'There's something I'd like to check on.'

She noted he'd slid down in his seat. 'It's something hinky? Come on, give.'

'There might be a white sedan opposite the primary school,' he said reluctantly. 'If there's a man in it, he'll be staking out our place, trying to follow us to Alexander.'

The bottlebrush hedges of the school appeared. And the white car. Luke sank further in his seat. 'Drive straight past.'

But Bec slowed and examined Ty closely as she drove past. When she sped up, Luke jerked up. 'I told you to drive straight past! Now he's going to be suspicious of this car and of you!'

'You think he's a threat, so I need to know what he looks like, right?' She executed a neat tight turn back onto the highway. 'Not a bad-looking dude, but, phew, anger issues, right? Who is he?'

'My uncle,' muttered Luke.

'Looks like he doesn't do blondes,' she said, primping her hair.

'He doesn't like anyone,' said Luke, 'except my mum.'

'Is that a bit weird?'

Luke wasn't listening. He was trying to remember whether he'd heard another engine start in a pause over the XH's rumbles. He angled the rear-view mirror to see the road behind and squinted into the late afternoon sun as Bec rounded a bend. 'Pull over now,' he said, sounding like a different Luke.

'Can't.' On their left they were up against a deep cutting of Triassic sandstone, rich yellow in the sunlight but at the moment notable for being high, hard and in the way.

'Shit,' said Luke. 'Soon as you can.'

Bec accelerated, then swerved into a slight indentation centimetres from the rock. They waited. A minute went by and nothing passed them.

'You think he might have followed us?' asked Bec. 'Angry, but really that smart?'

'Smart, definitely, born suspicious. And yes, angry. Did you see anyone?'

'There was a car behind us but I don't know what colour. Then I lost it. I should have been paying attention. I was stalked once.' Bec started the engine. 'The world's full of creeps.'

Luke didn't reply. His mind was on Ty: smart, bitterly vengeful and now injured by Luke.

Chapter 27

When they pulled up at her cabin, Shona was with Gatta was under the trees, emptying the paddle pool onto the thirstiest plants. Would that turn them into Stinkwort? Luke unfolded himself out of the car and hefted up the three dead marsupials in their tarp. 'Tas Roads takeaway,' he said. 'Alexander okay with Bolly?'

Gatta nodded. 'He definitely likes her and he's asleep. You okay?' Luke was never offhand about dead animals.

'Ah…' A buzzing was coming from the house. He hurried uphill and found Nyabol adjusting a floor fan to blow over Alexander. She met his eyes, cool as the air.

Luke struggled not to let his voice rise. 'We asked you not to try to bring his temperature down.'

'You are a man,' she said. At least it wasn't *boy*. 'You do not care for babies. I have bathed him and he is too hot. Babies, when they are hot like this,' she fluttered her hands in front of his face, 'they have seizures.'

'He is not a baby,' Luke said. 'He is a reptile, and he's sick. He might be dying. And this advice comes from a vet who treats reptiles.' He didn't wait for a reply but turned off the fan, coiled the cord and carried it to the back of the room. Nyabol hadn't moved when he came back to sit by Alexander.

The lizard's outline looked more uneven, with swollen areas like bruising under the skin, his green mottling now large, ugly moist patches. He was almost silent in Luke's mind, just the background hum. Luke wished he could ask him what to do. Was it time to give up? Give him to the professionals? Luke was unmoored, in control of nothing.

He went outside to where Gatta was handballing a footy with Bec and Shona, said to his sister, 'Keep an eye on him,' and walked into the forest.

Down by the stream, someone had done a half-arsed job stringing a three-strand boundary fence on drunken star pickets. An extra was left rusting and half-buried. He curled his fingers under one of the stepping stones and wrenched it clear of the soil. Shoved the nearest picket upright with his knee, tried not to think of Ty as he lifted the stone above his head and crashed it down. The picket sank a miserable centimetre in the clay. He drove the stone down harder, lifting and striking till the rock slipped from his fingers and splashed back into the water. He staggered back and sat down, hard.

'We're never, ever going to be able to move that fence now,' said Shona. She sat down beside him. Luke could hardly lift his head. He looked down at his bleeding hands.

'Bolly says she's sorry,' said Shona. 'And Bec hasn't done so well with men. You're actually doing a good job there.'

Luke nodded dully. Cold water was flowing over his shoes but he couldn't be bothered to move them. Then he lifted his head. He realised he'd been hearing music for a while, a garage band, a truly bad one. 'What is that?'

'That,' said Shona, 'is the *Flaming Dongers*. They never get up before three, and they play all night. Start like this, then get worse. You can't get within three metres of them without getting a second-hand high, but they're harmless, really nice guys actually. You pretty much can't hear the music from the house. It has to struggle out through all the fumes first, then there's the trees.' She sighed. 'Feeling any better?'

Luke shrugged. Then he felt guilty – a sure sign he was returning to himself. 'Bec told you what happened on our drive?'

'Yes. Who knows how much of a problem that's going to be.' She rubbed her forehead. 'There's something else. I don't know whether it's related. The lab the prof sent the DNA sample to has lost it.'

Luke shifted his feet from the stream. 'Lost it?? How can that happen?'

'Samples do get lost. Usually it's mislabelling. But for DNA samples, that's almost unheard of because of cross-contamination precautions. They'd actually lost it before I rang the last time, but they thought they could find it. Now they've fessed up. It could be a coincidence but–'

'They've got no explanation?' Luke was incredulous.

'Nope. They're incredibly embarrassed, of course. I'm going in person tomorrow, see if I can find out anything else. I suppose it's possible that somebody stole it.'

'We've still got the egg – plenty more samples there. And Alexander of course. But if Ty stole it and he is really tracking us, he's serious.'

'You might have whacked a bit of seriousness into him too.' She grinned. 'Serious whack.'

Luke felt far from good, but he felt better, sheltered by green man-ferns and calmness, except for surges of limp death metal played by good guys, and looking at an upright fencepost. And Shona was joking with him.

'I never actually said thanks,' he said. 'You never once stopped to say "What is this shit?" You just took on all this stuff and ran with it.'

Shona wrapped her arms around her knees and rested her chin.

'It's okay,' she said. 'About that, Bec and Bolly are smart girls so they–'

'Won't do what I tell them.'

'They don't always do what I tell them either.' She smiled at the ground, then scratched her chest. 'I wish Em could have come. She's better at people than I am.' She looked uncertain now. 'She'd know what to do about Rosie.'

'How is Rosie?'

'That's the problem. I don't know. When I knew her in Darwin she was happy and fit, played midfield – her style is all assists, setting up the plays, making the others look good. And she worked full-time. She was helping Adam get over his first wife – she had cancer, I think. Then down here, playing with us, she was flying, then somehow she wasn't. Everyone tried to help, especially Adam – he'd joined us by then. All he could do was shield her –from work and responsibility when she wanted to do more; the over-exercising. We didn't know what we were doing – I don't think anyone does with anorexia. The more we tried, the worse she got.' She rubbed one boot on the other, trying to work off the wet clay. 'So Adam's really careful about her now. I don't think he even likes her coming to spectate. It's not because of him. A few of the girls tried to come on to him – he's pretty dishy – but he truly doesn't see anyone except Rosie. He's really worried.'

Adam. Intelligent, compassionate, resourceful. Already knew about Alexander. Could they ask him…? No, he only cared about Rosie.

Shona went on, confirming Luke's thought. 'He's only helping us for her sake. If he thinks she's putting too much into us, he'll pull her out.'

'And Alexander isn't getting better and I'm not helping by not letting her do the tests she needs,' said Luke.

Shona rubbed her boots again, shifted on the ground.

Luke stood up. His feet were icy now. 'I go on like I've got this connection where I know what he's thinking and what he wants, but really? How can that be happening? What's more likely – I'm hearing voices from a lizard? Or I've discovered something incredible and I want to keep it to myself, so I tell myself that's what he wants? If so, I'm helping him to die.'

'Luke,' said Shona, looking up at him under the silky dark green blackwood canopy. 'You said I never stopped to ask what this is. But I did. And I don't think you're crazy.' Then she said: 'I'm not the best judge of delusions but I do believe in you.'

A tingly heat started in his chest.

'As for selfishness, you're the least selfish person I've ever met.'

Luke risked a glance. Every detail of her seemed hyperclear, vibrating. They resonated inside him.

She was studying a shieldfern frond, gently uncurling one of the feathery tips between her fingers. 'As a girl growing up, all the boys seemed so immature – it was worse for me because I was so big. Poor mum – after three hulking boys she wanted a little doll daughter, like her. Obviously, that's not what she got.' She hunched her shoulders in a way Luke identified with.

'I never tried at sport till I got to AFLW. But science, that's different. I always loved it and wasn't going to pretend I didn't.' Her fine nostrils flared. 'So all the boys were small. I think I made them feel smaller, but I couldn't do anything about that.' She looked up at him. 'You're not small. And in a few weeks you've got much more – not pushy – assertive.'

All Luke's responses had knotted themselves into a tight squirming ball inside his throat. 'I had to.' It was all he could say. His voice seemed to belong to a faraway floating Luke. So did his hand as he reached out to pull her up.

Chapter 28

When Luke and Gatta got home, Ty's car was gone from their street.

Luke thought he'd never feel clean again, after a day being soaked or splattered in mud, blood, sweat, roadkill and decaying reptile. Even in the shower, the stink wouldn't wash out, seemed bonded to the inside of his nose.

Over pizza, Gatta, typing with her pinkies, checked the Taylah news on Facebook. 'She's social media deaded. And she's still in the private hospital with that infection, the one the dog didn't give her.' She shoved in a crust and continued, indistinctly, 'And they've dropped the suing part – though maybe they could have another go at the Bot Gardens. One of the homeys, Jason McTurd, just got in the same hospital with an infected foot!' She laughed, spitting crumbs. 'They could both sue the Gardens for having like, dirty soil.'

Luke's brain, which had wound down with exhaustion, drumming hot water and carbs, spooled back up. 'Who is all this stuff coming from?'

'Surprise, she's got lots of ex-friends. And someone who goes by Pan-Pan works in the hospital, animal lib fanatic...his job is, like, *history* if they find out what he's saying, but it's stuff like: *She'd have the dog executed for what she did to herself. POS!!*'

A question nagged at Luke, but he didn't know what it was.

They made their Ty-evading plan for the morning: Luke would drag his bike around the cricket oval, to a road entry out of sight of the house. Ten minutes later, Gatta would set off straight up the Huon Road and abort if she was followed. It didn't feel like a good plan, but they were two kids on bikes. Luke thought Bec could have come up with a better one, though it would probably have involved screaming handbrake turns and possibly ramming.

In bed, Luke called Holly. 'Hi Mum. Frazzled? Or crushing the thirty hour day?' He didn't get the laugh he wanted.

'The work is okay. I run all the lab operations in Hobart so setting one up with new staff and machines up here is kind of fun, actually. It's Ty. He's supposed to be at home but I can't reach him most of the time and when I can he's not thinking about his business.' Luke heard her drum the desk with frustration. 'Or mine. We have a critical meeting with the rep from Paladin and I need him.'

The person who'd hit Ty with a shovel had thereby risked his mother's project. Had Luke subconsciously hit him for this reason? To remove Ty, try to replace him? Rescue his Mum by selling the golden reptile? Now Alexander was sick and they couldn't fix him, surely revealing him to the authorities could be justified? He was probably worth even more than his mother needed.

'When's the meeting, Mum?'

'The day after tomorrow.'

If Alexander wasn't better... 'So you need Ty up there by then.'

'Yes. And functioning normally. He's acting like he did when we were kids.'

'Like how?' said Luke. Kids? Ty had never been a kid.

'He's obsessed with whoever hit him. As kids we ended up in a lot of rough places. I was small and pretty and Ty thought he had to protect me. But he was small too, so he'd always have a weapon, always. And he wouldn't wait. When he smelled a threat, he'd get in first, as hard as he could. He wouldn't stop even if the other kid couldn't hit back, just keep going until the other kid was finished.'

Finished. Not only snakes and dogs. Humans. Children. 'That's just cruelty.'

'He thought he didn't have a choice. And most times we moved, he'd have to do it again. But it worked.' Holly sighed. 'I just hope he gets it out of his system soon. How is he even going to find this man? I'm sure it was one of those random things.'

Luke felt sick. Shona had said he was the least selfish person she'd ever met, and here he was, contemplating selling Alexander for his mum's debt. Was he wanting Alexander to stay sick so he could sell him? He shook his head. Ty mustn't find Alexander. Or him.

'I hope things work out, Mum. I wish I could help you.'

'I know you do.'

He didn't tell Gatta about the phone call.

By the cricket oval with his bike the next morning, he watched the cavalcade of SUVs barrelling towards the city. Ty wouldn't be fooled by their plan, so he'd have to copy the teenage Ty's strategy: the pre-emptive strike. What you did when you didn't have a choice.

Luke pushed off into the stream of SUVs, glancing behind every few seconds. Had he guessed right? There. The white bonnet and upright grille. Luke counted to ten then ripped the bike into a tight turn. The white bonnet didn't slow. Luke shook out his right shoulder. Wait, wait.

Ty saw the rock just before the windscreen crazed in front of his eyes. A second later Luke's other rock hit the passenger side and the whole screen went white.

Luke whipped his bike around and raced off. He looked behind. The white car had dropped back. He let his legs slacken a fraction, risked another look. Glass fragments were exploding out onto the white bonnet as Ty, driving with one hand, bashed out the windscreen, with what? – a tyre iron? The white car was only a hundred metres behind.

Christ! An ancient truck overloaded with firewood pulled out in front of Luke. What was the idiot doing carting firewood in February? Now he was boxed in between a steep hillside and a wall of SUVs, the truck in front and, behind him, Ty. With fifteen hundred kilos of car and a tyre iron.

The truck farted, fell back and belched smoke on a gear change.

No thought. Luke swung out between the truck and the queue of head-on Toyotas, glimpsed sparse grey hair and stubble and a shaking fist in the truck driver's window before he shot out in front of the bonnet. Now he had to pray for oncoming traffic. If he could stay close in front of the truck and go slowly enough that Ty remained stuck behind it – no problem there – he might just get away with it.

He was a hundred metres from a right-hand bend and the bush track. Just before he reached it, he slowed even further. Heard the truck's revs drop.

Then he flung himself and his bike into the ditch above the culvert. The truck changed gear. Luke heard it pass, followed by a smoother engine. He jumped up, ignoring the fire down his left arm and leg, and sprang up the track, dragging the bike. He threw it behind the first big thicket. He didn't know how long it would take Ty to realise his prey was no longer in front of the truck, or if the wood-carting old bastard would pull over to check on the arsehole cyclist, but he had fifteen seconds to get over the rise.

He made it in twelve.

There was no pursuit.

He stumbled down into the patch of rainforest and nearly fell into the stream. His legs wobbled like a toddler's and his left elbow was a mess of dirt, gravel and blood, his brain as close to beaten as his body. Fighting wasn't his natural state like it was Ty's.

And Ty had only just started.

Chapter 29

Rosie and Shona stood outside the cabin in urgent discussion. They broke off when Luke staggered from the blue gums, dripping blood. When he explained, Shona was thoughtful and Rosie horrified. Luke waved them off. He needed to sit down, but mostly he felt pulled to Alexander. Inside, he felt the heat pouring off Alexander, heard his shallow panting.

Shona came in, looking less like a goddess and more like an all-night rave survivor. 'We've had a rough night,' she said. 'Rosie's got some news too, though we're not sure what it means.' She shrugged. 'That seems about standard for him.'

'Clean that arm first,' said Rosie. 'At least we have buckets of antiseptic and bandages.'

When Luke got back from the bathroom, he caught the end of Rosie protesting, 'He always makes me huge meals. I did have lunch when I got home.' She turned to Luke. Her haunted look changed to focus. She gave him a quick smile. 'I got the results of some of the tests. His blood clotted – something funny there – so we can't determine anaemia or infection response, but his liver and kidney function are nearly normal. What we can't work out is what his tissue sample tells us. I've sent blood and tissue for culture, to find the bug, but that takes days, so I got some quick and dirty microscopy, which can give us some idea. This is where it gets weird again. A lot of his tissue is riddled with some tiny bacterium; it's intracellular, *inside* his cells.'

'What does that mean?' asked Luke.

'Something super-rare in Tasmania, like a rickettsia, which causes typhus, or listeria, but the lab isn't sure whether it's those. It's getting worse because there's more of it in the deeper, healthier-looking muscle than in the rotting stuff.'

'Where could he have got it?' asked Luke, sickening. Two others were in hospital with mysterious fevers from septic skin and muscle.

'Hard to know,' said Rosie.

'He's getting hotter,' said Gatta, who had slipped in.

'I don't know what his temperature is now,' said Shona, 'but it must be more than 48 degrees. He's cooking.'

Rosie nodded. 'One positive. The microscopy shows why the other antibiotic isn't working. I've brought something more effective against intracellular bugs.' She held up a box of ampoules, then looked at Luke with something like desperation. 'We so need a CT or ultrasound to find the source of this!'

Luke pressed his fingers on his eyes. Who wanted Alexander to remain secret – the lizard himself or Luke? And now he couldn't trust his own motives anymore. Mum's meeting was tomorrow.

'I might have found someone who could help,' Gatta said. 'That guy online – Pan-Pan – I tracked him onto militant animal rights sites. When he was in Victoria he dished info to activists who busted into factory farms. He knew labs and X-ray places they could go with sick rescued animals and stay off the books. He might know somewhere in Tassie we could go.'

'You think he'd talk to you?' asked Shona.

'He already has,' said Gatta. 'I gotta say, he's cute, I saw a pic, and he must be smart to be an X-rayer, but he might also be dumb as Taylah. He's right into animal rescue ninja stuff but it was easy to suss out who he is.'

'Okay,' said Luke. 'Rosie, you give him the new antibiotic and we'll give it 24 hours. Then if we have to, we ask Pan-Pan.'

Rosie nodded reluctantly.

'We also have to do something about his pain,' said Shona. 'Especially at night. During the day, he manages. At night,' she dropped her head, 'the only thing that helps, a little, is eating, and the only things big enough are the wildlife. I am not getting up anymore and driving around in the dark hoping to see another furry thing that's been smashed by a car. I'm not hitting any more possums on the head to make sure they're dead enough. He can't go through another night without a painkiller.' She realised she was glaring at Luke. 'Sorry,' she muttered.

Beaming at her would have looked demented but he nearly did. Yesterday she had called him mature. Now she was asking for his opinion. He swallowed, tried to sound like himself. 'I agree. Rosie, can you help?'

'I think so.' She gave a worried smile. 'Morphine has the best track record for reptiles. Adam found me some.' She looked more unhappy. 'I didn't ask how and I don't like it, but I would have had trouble getting any legally when Alexander's not a patient of my practice. Anyway, we should try a test dose. If it works, I can also take more blood tests and give him the new antibiotic in his tail vein.'

'Let's do it now,' said Luke.

Managing Alexander was getting harder with his increasing size, and parts of him slimy and hard to grasp. Then there were his spasms of lashing out with a mouthful of carving knives. Luke felt confident he could predict or at least avoid any sudden violence, so he put himself at Alexander's head with Shona at his tail and Gatta assisting Rosie. They all locked eyes and Luke nodded.

Rosie's gloved hands snapped the glass ampoule. She drew up half, took Alexander's foreleg in one hand and slid the needle carefully into the muscle at the back. Gatta flinched. Alexander didn't react. Luke gave them a thumbs up. They waited.

In the quiet, Luke heard the first gusts of the northerly, tossing the bark and leaf litter, bringing the scent of flowering gums through the open door.

Here, inside, the prick of Shona's sweat mingled with it, the angles of her face were sharper than a few days ago, the hollow at the base of her neck deeper, gleaming. His thumb would just fill that hollow if he lay his palm against her chest, lined his fingertips along her collarbone, he thought, wonderingly. The pain in his torn elbow and hands was falling away, dispersing like wisps of fog in sunshine. He floated, bathed in something infinitely soothing and sustaining, like cream or liquid silk, both warming and cooling.

A bayonet stabbed through his brain. A second jagged stab came and a third. In his brain, in Alexander's brain. Alexander, who had just received an injection. In that mind, the stabs fell through nothingness and the lizard was now utterly still but Luke felt the spasms coming.

'He's fitting,' he yelled.

'He shouldn't be.' said Rosie.

'He's not breathing.'

'He shouldn't have to, it's not long enough to affect–'

'He's not breathing.' Luke looked around frantically. He could do CPR, but Alexander's snout was far bigger than his mouth. His whole head would have to go between the teeth.

Alexander's legs began to twitch. He had to find some way of sealing his jaws and Rosie wasn't helping, fumbling in her bag.

Another searing slash nearly cut his brain in half. For a second he floated;

dimly he saw Alexander's hind legs kick back and Shona leap sideways. He needed a tube, a pipe, a big pipe…

'Gatta,' he shouted. 'That drink bottle. And a knife.'

She was back seconds later with Bec's half-full water bottle and a large kitchen knife. Thank god for smart sisters and non-reusable plastic. He grabbed the bottle by the throat and hacked off the bottom, unscrewed the top. Then he turned to Alexander. All four limbs were jerking and his jaws, with all those razor teeth, twitched and snapped. Luke hesitated.

'Here.' Shona was next to him with two folded towels. She dragged them over the teeth, tearing the cloth, but they were out of time. Luke grasped the towel-padded upper jaw and pushed the bottom of the bottle into Alexander's mouth, put his mouth to the bottle's throat and blew. He remembered just in time to turn his head but, as it was, Alexander's rank returning breath nearly took his ear off. He blew in a second and a third time, nearly blinded when more electric spasms ripped through his skull. He and Shona found a rhythm, she holding the jaws and nodding when she felt the muscles relax, he breathing in the spaces and pulling back from the putrid breath that washed back out. Alexander's jerks lessened; the blinding stabs in his own head subsided to flickers.

Now he could see what Rosie was doing. She was waiting, holding a syringe and an ampoule ready, not breaking it yet. Then Alexander was back – not awake, but his hum was there, low but steady and beautiful. The lizard's lungs took in their own first breath. Luke sat up on his heels.

Gatta lay her cheek on his back and shivered.

Shona handed Luke another towel with a less than steady hand. 'You're bleeding,' she said. He was. The right side of his jaw was slippery with something which didn't feel like it was his. He wiped it with the towel.

'I didn't expect that to happen,' said Rosie.

Luke almost laughed.

'Reptiles can go a long time without breathing, without it doing them harm.' She was nearly bone-white and beginning to tremble. 'It must be with his temperature, and his metabolism so high, and needing so much more oxygen, but I had no idea… I was unprepared…and then you…I nearly lost him.'

Her face crumpled.

Luke pulled her into his arms. She was so thin it felt like her heart was encircled by ribs alone and beating her whole chest. But her arms went around him with surprising strength. They clung to each other. She smelled of sweat and peaches.

A shape blocked the light from the doorway and Adam's voice said, 'Well, it looks like something went well.'

'Extremely well,' said Bec from behind him.

Rosie looked up and said, crying and laughing. 'Oh Adam. I nearly lost my first patient, except Luke rescued us.' She loosed one of her arms and trailed it in Alexander's direction, then tapped Luke on the chest and mouthed "Thank you". Her hair and brow were smeared with blood.

Adam eyed their faces. 'Who's bleeding?'

'Oh not me,' his wife said, absently wiping her forehead. 'I just gave the morphine, only half an amp, it shouldn't have... Then I was out of the way. But Luke put his head in the croc's mouth.' She gave a small laugh. 'Literally. So that's where the teeth got him.' She pointed at his jaw.

'I don't know whether to call you a hero or an idiot,' said Adam to Luke.

'Forgot he had teeth,' said Luke. 'So, idiot. Without Shona, he would have bitten my head off.'

'It's usually the vet that cops the bites, so well done on that front at least,' said Adam. 'But Rosie, you must not have read the dosages. You told me the responses were predictable.'

'I only gave him half an amp, that's 2.5 milligrams and–'

'He's okay now,' Shona cut in. 'And we need to take more blood and give the antibiotic. Shouldn't we do that while he's still sedated?'

'Do you think it's safe, Luke?' asked Rosie.

Luke nodded without hesitation.

'Wait a minute,' said Adam.

'It's okay, darling. Luke can read Alexander and knows where he's at.' She put a hand on Adam's shirt.

'Right, like he knew he wasn't going to get his head bitten off?'

Luke realised he'd been hoping Adam would help them. Not just with Alexander but against Ty. Now he looked more than annoyed. Jealous? Luke's blood was on Rosie's hair. He stepped away from her.

'That animal is dangerous and you're taking too many risks. You're not going near him.'

'I'll do it,' said Shona. 'I used to give injections to Smaug.'

Luke cradled Alexander's head in his hands while they did the procedure, Gatta handing Shona syringes and ampoules. Luke held his lizard's head not for their safety – he could hear Alexander clearly and would know if he were about to react – but to demonstrate that safety to everyone else, Adam in particular. Adam stood behind Rosie by the fireplace, arms wrapped around her, looking bigger, as usual. Her eyes were anxious, guilty for not helping, not doing her job. Around them stalked Bec, head down, hands shoved in pockets, occasionally scowling at Adam. Yup. She'd hate overprotective behaviour in men.

'Luke. I'm done.' Shona was frowning at him. 'You need to clean those scratches. We should have done that straightaway.'

In the tiny bathroom, Luke confronted a stranger in the mirror. He wouldn't have turned his back on that man in an alleyway. The eyes. Did they look older, like Shona thought? Horny, like Adam saw them? They certainly looked overamped. Two shallow parallel cuts ran along his jawline. They had stopped bleeding but were slightly ragged and would leave a scar. It wasn't the scar that made his stomach clench, it was Alexander's fever and the fevers of two people currently in hospital. Was he about to join them? Should Rosie give him an injection like Alexander's?

Outside, Rosie's high clear voice said, 'We should have a debrief and a cup of tea.'

'Before you do that,' said Adam, 'do you have the rest of that ampoule?'

'It's on the floor near my bag.'

Everyone was around the kitchen table when he came out, except Adam.

'Not here,' he said. 'Could you have put it somewhere else in all the excitement?'

'No, I'm very careful,' Rosie said, annoyance surfacing

'Alexander could have kicked it,' said Gatta. She wanted this resolved. Tea was brewing and crumpets were in the toaster. 'Kicked it out the door, or he's lying on it.'

Adam frowned. 'I know they're…unofficial, but you do need to keep track. Have you still got the second one?'

She had, but the first ampoule remained lost, though they didn't try to move Alexander or search much outdoors. Everyone had sagged off the high and comfort food was waiting to comfort. And why did they need to account for the morphine?

Adam paused at the top of the steps, pulled Rosie close and slid a wrapped sandwich into her coat pocket. They shared that look that shut out the rest of the world. Then, holding Rosie's hand, Adam turned to the rest of them.

'This isn't going well,' he said. 'I don't know why that animal isn't in a hospital, I don't like you using Rosie's loyalty, and I don't like what it's doing to her.'

Rosie started to protest but he put a finger across her lips, turned it into a caress. 'Yes, I know it's your job and your friends and a special patient.' He cast a not quite contemptuous look at Alexander. 'But you're going close to being used here and it's not helping your health or your judgement.' He glared at the rest of them. 'And you're going to get paid.'

'Yes, she is,' said Shona to his departing back.

Chapter 30

'Hey, I could do with one of those sangers he slipped you,' said Bec to Rosie into the silence. Adam's engine had receded. 'Come on, gimme.'

Rosie handed her the thick packet. They drank tea and ate till everyone felt better; except Luke. Everybody seemed to think he was an adult. Shona. Adam. Ty. Lately, Mum. But adults just produced bigger messes. They could lose Rosie because Adam was jealous of Luke. He'd dented Mum's chances of getting finance by bashing Ty. Did that mean Luke owed her the money?

'Hey Lukey.' He finally heard Gatta speaking. 'Rosie asked whether you were good with Alexander getting a quarter dose of what made him go tectonic.'

'Yeah.' Luke still felt dazed.

'Here, have at another one of these,' said Bec, handing him another crumpet and backhanding butter off her chin. 'Hell, have two, you and I are on Tas Roads Takeaway again soon.'

Rosie regained her lustre in running the debrief. Nyabol arrived and Shona left before Bec and Luke set off looking for usable roadkill.

After a fruitless half-hour in which they only found entrails that smelled even worse than Alexander, Bec drove toward the city and back north.

'Collinsvale,' she said.

'Good for wallabies.'

But the crows had got there first. Luke and Bec been on the road for three hours by the time he slung the second almost intact carcass in the boot.

'Mind if I try for a back-up plan?' asked Bec as Luke peeled off Shona's gloves.

'Sure.'

She sent a text off. They'd hardly spoken during the whole trip, equally preoccupied.

'We'll wait five.'

They were parked on a hillside with the windows down. A broad cloth of green unrolled gently below them, all the way to the forest edge, dotted with cows standing knee-deep in paradise. The air was fresh, enlivened by the smell of cattle. It was air that allowed the mind to open; or maybe things could be more easily said in wide spaces. Or Bec didn't like stationary silences.

'What's your Mum like?' she asked.

'What do you mean?'

'You and Gatta, you're tight. And not flush. It's like your olds aren't even around.'

Luke was startled. He'd hadn't thought Bec was interested in families. 'Mum's around, but she works a lot. Even more just now. Dad left when Gatta was little.' He gave the shorthand story, which was technically true but misleading; it left out Ty's role. He wondered suddenly whether Bec could help him understand it. 'I take it your olds weren't around much either? And you didn't have a brother?'

She gave a bark of laughter. 'I asked for that. You're right and wrong. I did have a brother but I didn't have a brother like you.'

'But you had a mum. If someone grows up serially fostered, does it make them hate everyone? Except who they grew up with?'

'You're talking about your stalker uncle? Not necessarily. Getting your teeth kicked in by people you trust turns you suspicious. And you can't always tell the monsters right away.'

'Even kids?'

'Monsters start as monsters, I think.' She gave him a sideways glance that became surprisingly kind. 'Anyone who hates *you*, Luke, is trying super hard. Or a World Series hater.'

Her phone chimed. 'We're on. Back-up came through.'

They burbled down the hill through the late summer smell of a scrub fire somewhere. 'My brother,' Bec said, 'different story. We knew who Brayden's dad was – obvious where the shittiness came from. Mine?' She shrugged. 'I don't want to know.' She downshifted near *Ink Slave Tattoos* and turned into Allunga Road. 'Mum had boyfriends, too bad so sad for Bray and me. I don't see Bray – he only wants cash – but some of his mates are okay. We're swinging by Dylan's.'

The wide black ribbon of the Brooker Highway took them to Granton, down on the river, where the northerly wind riffled the tannin-dark water. Tight squadrons of grebes poked around in the inshore rushes. Further out, the black swans' rear ends were little black haystacks pointing skywards.

After a time, Luke said, 'Who's Dylan?'

Bec grinned. 'Dylan did a stretch in Risdon two years ago, bashed a guy – who knows what really happened. He got put in a program. Animal partnerships. This is a guy who didn't know which end of the dog to feed and they put him with horses. He totally got into them, they loved him back and, the lucky bastard, a breeder gave him a job when he got out and he's still got it.'

Luke waited while she treated a couple of RVs like mobile chicanes. The open river gave way to purple tinted marshland, herons and hovering long-fingered swamp harriers.

'I suppose you've never checked, but if you try to find out how many racehorses are bred every year in Australia, you can't. That's not an accident. Horses eat a lot and most of them don't win. There are thousands of spares, which are all supposedly rehomed. But *thousands*? Where do you find that many moony teenagers or middle-aged hippie women with properties?'

Luke's heart sank as he caught on. 'So they "die", get buried, become grass to eat for new racehorses that might win?'

'Yep. But there's another way to make an extra buck out of them. Down the road, they're breeding greyhounds which also cost money to feed and they eat meat, not grass. Breeder's not stupid. Dylan needs his job for all kinds of reasons. He gets to look after his babies. But eventually he has to joint their carcasses.'

The Falcon swung up into the hills. They met Dylan at the roadside near his clapboard cottage on the stud. Bedsheet curtains drooped behind the cottage windows and barbed wire roses scraped at the last paint from their frames but the roof sat straight and the fences were immaculate. A pair of fillies, a chestnut and a bay, stood together with hind legs cocked, their manes streaming in the wind towards the visitors. Dylan was scrawny, wearing a flannel shirt, his wrists blue with old tattoos. By his side was a lumpy grain sack, dark and wet at the bottom. His sullen face came to life when Bec got out of the car.

He called past her to Luke, 'Hey, man, you got a redback spider female here. Escape quick.' The grin was grotesque, his teeth a tumbled ruin of nicotine and neglect.

Bec punched him, hard. 'Thanks Dee-Dee. What's happening?'

'Same shit. Here's your order.' He lifted the sack with unexpected strength, swallowed. 'Good cause?'

'The best,' said Bec and gave him a quick fierce hug.

As they drove away, Luke saw Dylan in the mirror, picking up a front hoof of the bay, which had its nose down the front of his shirt.

'He tells himself he can make the nags so healthy they can run fast enough to stay alive,' said Bec. 'He's not going to be able to do it much longer. He'll shoot himself instead of them. But probably he'll shoot the breeder first.'

Luke tilted his head back on the headrest and let the breeze dry the sweat on his neck.

Where did the right to dictate others' lives and deaths come from? The animals burnt on the tinder-dry mountain, the huskies Taylah blamed, the dog who'd attacked Ty. Slow greyhounds, slow horses. Luke and Alexander? The usual justification was ownership. The law covered some of it, the grey areas people wrote to suit themselves. Or maybe the laws were the wrong laws. There was a quarter of a failed racehorse in the boot, after all.

Chapter 31

The light had turned golden when Luke and Bec pulled up in front of Shona's cabin. Bec switched off the engine. They sat in the silence for a moment, then a distant wail and crash filtered up through the gums. The *Flaming Dongers* were warming to their evening's work.

The crew was in the conservatory, waiting for Luke to help administer the smaller test dose of morphine. Nyabol and Shona were tired and pensive, whereas Gatta vibrated with suppressed excitement. Outwardly at least, she maintained her airy optimism. Luke thought of the image of brumbies galloping over the Victorian Alps, their shapes flowing over Alexander's shoulders. It seemed a lifetime ago. Today, those shoulders could only answer his fingers with a faint blush of yellow. How long could they wait for the antibiotic to work? How long before asking for help from the uni?

The morphine was administered without incident. When Luke felt the cool, soothing tide flow around him, he shook himself free and let Alexander slide into the dreaming waters without him. They double-checked the dose and wrote it down for safety. Bec and Nyabol left.

'Stay for a bit. I've got news,' said Shona. Luke hadn't seen her smile for a long time. Would she ever smile at him again if he, the least selfish person she'd ever met, sold Alexander? They returned to the conservatory with Gatta.

'I've been in town, investigating.' Shona's voice was sober, resigned rather than angry. Her tone suited her navy pants and the white pleated shirt that softened her shoulders. She could have been running a medium-sized investment bank.

'I paid a visit to the lab that lost our sample,' she said. 'I said I was there to see if I could help sort out whether samples had been mixed up. The receptionist was huffy till I suggested that we'd keep using them if we could find a reasonable explanation. And I was standing. Sometimes – rarely – my appearance can be a positive.' A tiny smile.

'I'd have agreed to anything,' Luke said.

Gatta jiggled with impatience.

'Anyway, she let me look at the visitors' log. All of them were regulars except one: Robert Coombs, a rep from Aalto, not one of their usual reagent suppliers. She remembered he was very persistent and insisted he come into the lab to see what Aalto could offer. Aalto has no Robert Coombs working for them. I checked. If it was Ty, he's pretty desperate. The lab community is small and there's a big chance he'd be recognised.'

Luke fingered the dressing on his left elbow. 'It's no news that he's desperate. But I don't know that his lab can do DNA analysis. That's a bit specialist for Hobart, isn't it?'

'Google says his Sydney lab will offer it when it's up and running.' Shona glanced over her shoulder into the main room. 'I think we've got more immediate problems.'

'But *we* may have more help,' said Gatta, the words bursting out of her. 'Pan-Pan – his real name is Elliot, which is actually much cooler – he's a radiographer. He takes X-rays. And he'll take some for us if we need them.'

'Why does he want to help?' Shona said warily. 'And where's he going to take them?'

Gatta was less triumphant. 'At the Hobart Private Hospital.'

Luke and Shona were aghast but Gatta regained herself. 'He thinks it could work. He's on night call tomorrow and normally it's, like, totally dead between about one and six.'

'It's a hospital!' said Luke. 'How are we going to get him in?? Hospitals are full of people. They're hardly not going to notice a… crocodile.'

'Nah, we got this. The back entrance goes straight into the department. We get him on a trolley, right? Elliot says there's an infection protocol, where the patient and everyone else is totally dressed up in gowns and masks and shit and you couldn't tell if it was King Kong in there. Except KK'd be bigger. And Alexander would be lying under a blanket. And he sure smells like he's got an infection.'

Shona said, remotely, 'You trust this man's judgement?'

'He's really wants to do it and he's the one who'll lose his job if we stuff up.'

Two pairs of disbelieving eyes bored into her.

'Okay, maybe he did sound a bit too hot on the ninja thing. He's really fired up on how Taylah is "emblematic of systemic animal exploitation" and everything that's wrong with how we spend so much money on health for useless people and nothing on animals. He wants to be, like, the activists who free the pigs and set fire to research labs.' Her expression turned sober. 'I think doing his job feels so wrong it's killing him and he has to do this other stuff to keep himself going.'

Luke stared at his filthy shoes. This was a familiar theme today.

'I don't think it helps that if Elliot does lose his job it's going to be spectacular. He might get off on that.' Shona growled. 'He and the plan sound crazy, completely fruit bat. Alexander seemed a bit better today, seizures notwithstanding, so if we pray hard, we might not have to implement it.'

They got in Shona's truck for the trip home. As they passed the silent house to the right of her drive, Luke said, 'Whoever lives in that house doesn't seem to be home much.'

'Two of my brothers,' said Shona. 'They're on the cray boats for the uni holidays. They were home while their boat worked out of Kettering but they're up the East Coast now.'

'You have brothers!' said Gatta. 'They must be pretty—'

'Big?'

'Awesome,' said Gatta.

'Well, actually, they're both.' Her laughter filled the small cab. 'We bought this place from an old woman whose son lived here. She didn't know he had a big hydroponic weed operation going. That's what all the crappy sheds with vent fans and monster locks are doing here. The son came back one night and my brother Ilo caught him.' She laughed again. 'He won't be back. And we've got keys to all the padlocks now.'

They stopped near the culvert for Luke to pick up his bike.

When they got home, Luke's jaw was bleeding again. He thought about Alexander's teeth and hatred of meanness, and Taylah's bleeding knee. Luke's suspicion crystallised to a near certainty.

After pizza, it took them another hour and a frame-by-frame examination of seven husky videos to find it. Until the very last one, he hoped he was wrong. But there it was: the frame with the husky's hind leg and, half a lizard's length away, the rush stalks unnaturally crooked.

'Alexander was there,' Luke said. 'Taylah did spike the husky, which turned on her and she fell, but it wasn't the axe that sliced her knee. He bit her.'

Luke paced, staring out the window. His heart pounded. With every beat, his cuts throbbed. 'And I think he bit Jason too, one of the homeys you saw.'

Gatta's face was reflected in the glass. She nodded. 'Do you want me to ask Elliot what antibiotic she's being treated with and whether it's working?'

'Yes, if he can.' Gatta's fingers were already dancing. 'And can you ask him what the staff think of Jason? What kind of guy he is?'

'On it.' Without pausing her typing she added, 'You know the answer. You know Alexander can smell evil.'

After dinner, Luke rang his mum.

'Hi Luke. Is everything okay?' She sounded strained.

'All good.' *Except I've become a violent thug. And I've been bitten by the same teeth that put two people in hospital with blood poisoning.*

'Are you sure? Ty is being very non-committal about you two when I talk to him. He's not even criticising you.' She laughed without humour. 'He's so irrationally cheerful, I want to get his head rescanned.'

'We're not seeing much of him.' *Last time, he was bashing out the windscreen I'd buggered, with a crowbar.* 'All ready for your meeting tomorrow?'

'No.' Her voice was now equal parts puzzlement and annoyance. 'Ty says to put it off for another day. I hope he knows what he's doing because it makes us look sloppy where we need to look professional for Paladin to invest in us. But he's still telling me he'll find the money. He says he's close.'

Chapter 32

Luke dreamed of a green field and a running white-gold horse. Trailing it slowly was Dylan, bending occasionally to pull weeds, which came up with a soft plop and great lumps of yellow clay. When he saw Luke, he brandished one, grinning with his ruined teeth, and he held not earth and roots but lumps of pallid rotten meat and wormlike arteries. He dropped them in a grain sack. The horse wheeled, and Luke saw blisters of pus rise beneath the skin and gobbets of dead flesh drop from her golden flanks as she ran.

His ringing phone woke him at seven. Shona's voice was too level. 'I think we need to do those X-rays. I haven't been able to get Rosie – her phone has been on the blink lately – but I don't think we need her for the decision.'

'Okay.' Luke struggled to shake off his nightmare. His limbs felt leaden and his eyes wouldn't focus. 'What's happened?'

'He woke up to eat after I dropped you guys. Then he ate everything. Everything. Two wallabies and all the horse. I thought that would be impossible, even for him. And it was disgusting. Anyway, that's not the problem. He went back to sleep and he hasn't woken up.'

Luke's heart plummeted. He started to speak, but Shona hurried on. 'I don't think his temperature is higher and his heart rate and breathing are no worse, but he's not responding, whatever I do. And the skin over his shoulders and chest feels like it's going to slough right off.' The pitch of her voice rose. It was an odd mix of steel and pleading. 'But Luke, he's stable. You don't need to come straight away. What you need to do first is get some antibiotics for those cuts on your face. I'll text you Rosie's advice as soon as I get it, but you need to get into town and see a doctor.'

'Okay Shona. But I can't let Gatta ride up on her bike. Not after yesterday.'

'I've sorted it. Bec will pick her up about nine.'

They rang off.

Should he tell his mother? Luke wasn't sick yet; he might not even get sick. Telling her would mean revealing Alexander, which meant selling him. Luke coming up with Mum's money instead of Ty. He'd be buying his mum. When he closed his eyes, he saw the rotting golden horse.

Luke's GP practice had no appointments for three days, so that left the Royal Hobart Hospital Emergency Department. He'd have to wait, but at least he'd be seen today. They'd have all kinds of antibiotics on site and there was little chance anyone would know him. He woke Gatta, told her the plan and set out on foot for the bus stop.

Luke waved to Audrey in her yard. There was no sign of Ty. No car roared up and smashed him against a tree-trunk. No car even passed him. Outside Anthony's house, a man sat inside a silver Corolla holding his phone to his ear. He had a white-sprinkled ginger beard and hair and wore an azure blue suit and tie. He didn't look like any of Anthony's friends or workmates, who wore nothing but polar fleece vests, except for the ones with spade beards and checked shirts. He ignored Luke as he passed, and Luke didn't see the car or the man again, though the 448 bus was nearly full and he couldn't get near the back window.

After triage, Luke waited in Emergency. All morning, ambulances with priority patients came and went. Shona texted with Rosie's recommendation for an antibiotic. He waited some more. His thinking stopped.

When his name was called in the late afternoon, he missed it, but the receptionist pointed him out to a passing nurse. The nurse moved him through some doors, to a chair in a corridor. There the noises were different, with variations on machine alert sounds – beeps, parps and buzzes – and the voices were louder and younger.

'Luke! You in there?' A young man in scrubs with a brush of vigorous black hair crouched in front of him. His eyes were concerned but mostly impatient.

'Uh, yes, sorry,' said Luke. Crap. In all those catatonic hours in the waiting room, he hadn't rehearsed his story at all.

'You were bitten by a dog,' said the doctor, crouching again to examine his jaw.

'Ah, yes, and a friend of mine was too, and he got an antibiotic. He, ah, just sent me the name. It's Azithro…myacin.'

The doctor frowned. 'That's *unusual*.' He didn't bother to conceal his sarcasm. 'Dog bites don't need antibiotics unless they're punctures, and Azithromycin isn't what you'd use. Yours looks pretty superficial so I doubt it needs anything.'

Luke flushed. 'Someone else was bitten by the same dog and they're really sick.'

The doctor now looked suspicious. 'Are you sure that's your story? Treatment really does work better if you give me the right information.'

Luke's mind was a panicky blank. If he said anything approaching the truth, the most likely outcome was a psych ward. He shook his head. 'It was a dog. And my friend's doctor says I really need this antibiotic.'

'Sounds like you should have gone to the friend's doctor.' This doctor rolled his eyes. 'Okay, I shouldn't do this but I'm giving you an antibiotic – something got you, whatever the hell it was – but not Azithromycin. And a tetanus shot. Got any allergies? No? Good.'

Just as the doctor returned with an IV and a nurse, Luke's phone bleeped again with a text from Gatta.

Elliot dsnt know Taylah antibx. She's better. Going home tmrw.

Luke groaned. The doctor already thought he was a liar and a complete dickhead. 'Ah, Taylah Simon, who got an infection in that thing with the huskies. The antibiotic she got, can I have that one?'

'Celebrities don't get celebrity antibiotics,' said the doctor, prepping Luke's hand for the IV. 'I think you should get yourself a better taste in celebrities.'

According to the discharge letter they gave him with a strip of follow-up tablets, he'd been given ceftriaxone. When he finally left, ripping open a packet of machine-dispensed sandwiches, it was dark and the wind had risen, strong enough to stream out the street trees. He felt drained, even though he'd spent the whole day sitting down.

On the way to the bus terminus, he rang Shona and filled her in.

She replied, 'Elliot is still trying to find out what Taylah was given. Are you okay? Feeling sick?' Her voice warmed his belly. 'Maybe someone can sneak up to Taylah's ward tonight while we're at the hospital. I can't believe I just said that. Do you want someone to come get you? Bec and Adam have volunteered.'

'Adam?'

'He rang earlier. He's worrying about how Rosie is and how much energy she can afford. He wants to talk to you.'

And maybe he was worrying about how Luke felt about Rosie? And she about him. Luke didn't want to have that conversation in a car. Or at all. Anyway he was nearly at the bus terminus on Elizabeth Street. 'No, it'll take longer. I'll be there in twenty minutes.'

The space under the sandstone arches of the post office building was filled with lace-up Doc Martens and Converse, floral print shifts, torn jeans and hoodies, which was why the blue suit stood out. Luke only saw it for an instant before it slid behind a yellow pillar. Not obviously furtive, but quick. Luke's heart sped up. Was this the man he'd seen that morning? If someone wanted to follow him, surely he'd wear something less eye-catching. How could he possibly have tracked Luke out of the hospital?

When the bus arrived, Luke fiddled with his phone until the last person had got on the bus, then he boarded. Once the bus swung onto the road, it was impossible to tell what was behind.

Chapter 33

Luke stepped off the bus on the Huon Road and watched its tail lights disappear into the dark. If a car had followed, he couldn't see it. He put on his hoodie, pulled the hood up and stuck his hands deep in the pockets. The wind was piercing cold. Above him, the treetops streamed towards the south and clouds scudded across a slender moon. The noise slid down the valley like a breaker in the surf, drowning out the night. As he turned down Shona's drive, Luke felt more than heard his sneakers crunch on the gravel. The moon slipped away. The world turned almost black.

He didn't consciously detect the attack, but a sleeping part of him sawheardsmelledsensedtasted a falling shadow, an indrawn breath, a block to the wind, a sharp animal stink, which made him pause and half-turn. The knife tip that was a millimetre from his chest instead slipped sideways, scored his chest and speared his left tricep.

The pain accelerated his turn; his right elbow reflexively flung back and crunched into his attacker's face. Blindly, Luke staggered to his right, down the hill into the deeper darkness, and he already knew he was running the wrong way, away from the house. And then he tripped on something and rolled and kept rolling till he whumped against another something and stopped.

He gazed up at stars and held his breath. The wind dropped. He let his breath out slowly and strained to hear above his thundering heartbeat. Silence. Something small rustle-hopped away. Gingerly he inspected his left arm: slick and warm with blood, but it moved okay. The wind rose again. The treetops rushed, ribbons of bark rattled against their trunks. Under the forest noise, Luke heard the scrape of a foot. Gravel. The man with the knife was up the slope somewhere, keeping to the driveway, staying between where he thought Luke was and the house. Luke's only advantage was the man couldn't see him. He needed a weapon, any weapon, a branch, a stone, even a roofing nail. He cast his arms around, ran his fingers silently over grass and twigs, slender branches, felt a rock. Eased it out of the dirt.

That improved his position by one rock, but his target was invisible and behind trees. Luke needed the man to make a mistake.

And he did. He turned on his phone torch.

From where Luke lay waiting, breathing, clenching the stone in his fist, he saw three things shine out of the dark, ten metres away: ghostly tree trunks, between them a light, and a little to the right, the gleam of a blade.

A half metre above the light and the blade would be the man's head.

Luke threw the rock with all his strength. He heard a thunk and a grunt, and the light winked out.

Luke was on his feet and running for the man. The stone must have glanced off, though, because the man snorted through his broken nose. Luke dodged right and the knife point swished past his face. The man was Ty's height. Ty's speed.

Luke kept swerving, moving. Staying out of reach, but again he was slipping downhill. He was losing. The man was staying between him and the house. Ty's patience and calculation.

Luke had to do something different.

He crouched. He had to give up trying for the safety of the house and escape the back way, down through the rainforest.

He thought, then acted. Was up and floundering blindly downhill, was descending in complete dark, navigating purely by the slope of the ground, till his feet hit harder ground. The track.

He heard his pursuer's breath bubbling through the blood in his mouth and nose, less certain than Luke in the dark, but gaining. Luke's left foot slipped and he splashed into icy water. He was at the fence. Trying to be even quieter, he scrambled on hands and feet under and behind the fence. The man should run past him.

But he didn't. Luke heard the bubbling breathing slow, then stop altogether as the man held his breath and listened, assessing.

Luke's heart nearly failed then. He pressed himself down, his cheek, tears, against the wet riverbank, soil in his nostrils. The cuts Alexander had made on his cheek flared as they scraped on something. Something colder than the soil, and hard. He outlined it with his fingers. The spare star picket. The means to become a combatant. If he remained prey, he was finished.

Luke rose to his knees. He didn't have long because the man couldn't see what Luke was doing, but would know he was doing something. Luke wrenched at the picket. It came up with a soft sucking sound and the smell of rotting vegetation. He stood to his full height and gripped it, his mind now clear, even calm. When he had attacked Ty with the shovel, he'd done it in mindless desperation. This time he was logical. Whoever it was, there in the dark, was trying to kill him. To defend himself, Luke had the right – the necessity – to do the same.

Luke shifted his weight, tested his footing and ran his hand quickly up the steel. It was icy cold and slimy but the three rusty flanges provided a good grip. He shifted his hold further back; his advantage was his reach. Then he waited.

Somewhere in front of him, his enemy breathed. Another wet gurgle through the blood still running from his crushed nose down the back of his throat. Luke cast his ears and eyes across the sound, trying to centre it, urging his night vision to adapt.

Then he saw it: a faint silver line, 20cm long. It was the cloud light reflected off the blade.

All at once, the pattern formed and Luke saw the arm and the body of the man, only three metres away.

Luke hurled himself forward. The man coughed. A human sound: for that instant he was no longer only a shape or a monster. It was enough to make Luke hesitate the tiniest fraction.

The man was prepared and fast and didn't need more than a fraction. As Luke drove the stake towards the point below the man's sternum, he met resistance – the man grabbing the steel, fending him off. Luke shoved. The man thumped into a tree. The knife blade swished past Luke's face. Luke strained harder and the man grunted. The knife clattered onto the stones. Luke heaved with all his weight and there was a sudden give and the stake slid off to the left and he followed, landing on top of the man.

Then there were struggling limbs and the stink of blood and sweat and a blinding agonising light exploded in Luke's skull.

He lost his grip on the stake. He rolled to his knees, pushed upwards, still blinded, but that didn't matter, it was dark anyway. He staggered uphill. He heard a groan and knew the man's head-butt hadn't gone so well for him either.

Uphill, uphill towards the cabin, light, his friends, safety. He ran doubled over, forearms hitting trunks. Over his gasping breaths and his erratically hammering heart, he heard the man smash towards him. With the stake or the knife or both.

The crescendo of hammering stopped. It hadn't been his heart drumming but the *Flaming Dongers*, whose house must be just to his right. He'd been running ninety degrees in the wrong direction. He veered left.

A block of light fell across the ground beside him. Light from an open door.

'Hey man, you're lost!'

Luke stumbled, confused by the light, and hit a tree dead on.

Behind came a slow laugh. 'Hey guys, man's got a fencepost. He's fencing. Fencing in the dark.'

The Dongers must have seen not Luke, but the other man. Who had the fencepost. Luke gave no thought to going back. He could see a thinner part of the forest and he aimed for it.

'Like the song by that filthy rich Yank with the jeans? Bruuuuuuce! ' A cackle. 'Okay, mate, fencing man – if you don't mind, there's gunna be pissing in the dark.'

Luke accelerated. Ahead of him, the yellow glow of Shona's cottage appeared between the trees. He plunged headlong towards it. The man was bailed up by the Dongers but who knew if he thought this was his last chance at Luke.

Luke crashed in through Shona's doorway. Five shocked faces watched him slam the door and wrench home the bolt. He rapidly scanned the windows, looked across the big room. 'The glass in the conservatory, how strong is it?'

'Virtually bulletproof,' said Shona slowly. 'What's out there, Luke?'

He sank down on the stairs. If Ty hadn't chased him after being seen by the Dongers, he wasn't in a blind rage. He wasn't going to attack a house with five witnesses.

Every muscle jumped and twitched, lungs taking in great gulps, guts shrunk down to a tiny hard ball. He forced himself to slow his breathing.

'It's Ty. I think. It moved like him, thought like him. And I don't know why anyone else would try to kill me with a knife.'

'It looks like he came close,' said Shona.

Gatta hurled herself at him and buried her face in his chest. His lacerations shrieked, but that was all right, good, wonderful. It was Gatta. And it meant he was alive.

'We need to call the police,' said Shona.

'No, we don't,' said Luke. 'He's gone. There's no proof. A couple of the Dongers saw him but they're smashed; they won't remember anything, or be believed. And we need to take Alexander to the hospital, tonight.'

There was silence, except for Gatta breathing in gulps.

'Where's Rosie?' said Luke.

'Not sure if she's coming,' said Shona, frowning. 'She's not been well since yesterday and Adam's trying to talk her out of it, I think. We'll hear from her if her phone is working.'

Bolly rose from the table. 'Luke, you have wounds. First we must treat them.'

She led him off to the bathroom, with Gatta holding his arm. Under the hoodie, blood had soaked through his shirt and into the waistband of his pants. He winced as Bolly peeled the cloth from his chest. She stood back, made a practiced assessment of his injuries.

'He put the knife through your shirt in here and out here, then into your arm. But he meant to put it into your chest.' Her eyes were so large and dark under the lights, he saw himself in them, a ghost with wild hair.

'He tried to kill me. I tried to kill him.' Luke's voice rasped. 'People have the right not to be murdered, but he lost that right when he tried to kill me. So I was going to... I had a star picket. I was going to put a stake through his heart.' His throat was so tight he could hardly make the words.

'Like Dracula,' said Gatta.

'Like Dracula,' said Luke. 'Except at the very last moment, he wasn't Dracula and it got really hard to actually do it. And, anyway, he stopped me.'

Bolly's face was cool and still under her cap of tight curls. She resumed sponging the blood from his skin. The cut on his chest was shallow and the one in his triceps deep but with a small entry. An impressive bruise was forming on his forehead but the skin wasn't broken. Adeptly, she applied stick-on dressings.

'I am Nuer, from South Sudan,' she said. 'Shona is Dinka. We fight the Muslims from Sudan, even now we are killing each other and the Murle. For water. For cattle. We kill because these things are our lives. My father, he tried to help everyone, with negotiations, with gifts, and he did this work.' She held up the dressings. 'But our family could not escape being killed by being peaceful.'

'You helped him with the care?' asked Gatta in a much smaller voice than usual.

'Yes. I am the oldest and my mother,' Bolly held up her hand in a stop gesture, 'she would not.' She smoothed down the last dressing and rose to her slender height. 'My father could not kill a man. I do not know if I could. But the man in the night, who might be your uncle, he can.'

'Yes,' said Luke. 'And I don't think he's going to stop trying. I think it's only me he's after but it's dangerous for all of you. So I think I'm going to have to find somewhere else for Alexander and myself. If he survives.'

'We can talk about that in the morning,' said Shona from the doorway. 'I think by then we'll know about Alexander. I know a place if we need it, at least for a short time, with good security.'

She shook her head at their questioning faces. 'First we need to eat and discuss how we are going to do this,' she rolled her eyes, 'ridiculous plan.'

While the others foraged, Luke went to Alexander. The lizard was still; body and mind. Not unconscious, but he had lost sensation, memory, identity. All that remained was awareness. When Luke joined his mind, he entered a space that was pure being: featureless, borderless, white.

Luke wondered whether this was the tunnel of light described by people who returned from near death; a state of peace that wasn't life or death but something in between, from where they could meet it or turn back to resume their lives. Alexander could no longer make nor influence Luke's decisions about him. His own choice became clear. He pulled out his phone.

'Hi Luke.' Holly's voice was clipped, a mix of anxiety and anger. Not at him.

'Hey, Mum, let me guess. You haven't heard from Ty.'

'Not quite. I have, this morning, but he said nothing about finance, or Paladin. He only talked about the DNA analyser, of all things, to delay calibrating it, but it takes days and I've already started. He sounded angry with me, which he never is. And why? I haven't heard from him since. What's going on, Luke?'

He's wanting to run dinosaur DNA on it. And we've been trying to murder each other. 'Ah, we're not getting on.' The sensible thing would be to tell her. 'You should ask him. But about your meeting. I can tell you he won't be up for it.'

'Not up at all?' She couldn't hide the despair. Luke knuckled his forehead.

'Mum, I know he's the one who gets in first and doesn't give up. But you're his sister, made of the same stuff. Go yourself. Do it yourself.'

'Go alone? Negotiating isn't my—'

'You don't negotiate. You're Ty. The one who wins the fight is the one who is prepared to hurt more.'

'Hurt? Luke—'

'Hurt. They don't have the right to exploit you. They want 80 per cent of the company? Offer them 20 per cent. They're still going to make millions, billions.'

'They'll think I'm crazy.' Her voice was high-pitched, incredulous. 'They'll say start-ups have a 95 per cent failure rate. They do.'

'But not yours, Mum. They'll think you're confident. And if they don't take their chance, they'll lose you.'

The silence stretched out.

'Oh, Luke. I don't know what's happened to you. Anders would be proud, and I'm not sure how I feel about that. But I believe in you. I'll go to the meeting alone tomorrow and I'll ask–'

'Tell.'

'*Tell* them I'll take 80 per cent.'

They rang off.

Alexander had never been Luke's to sell.

If Holly got her money, Ty wouldn't need Alexander. And for murder attempts on each other, maybe Ty and Luke could consider themselves even.

Chapter 34

Luke brought his thoughts back to the wooden cottage; to Alexander and the slender thread that held him to the world.

'Is he here?' asked Gatta, coming up to lean on her brother. She still had a smudge of his blood on her forehead.

He rubbed at it gently, then cupped her head and pulled her in. 'Some part of him is.'

'Is the rest of him ever coming back?'

'I don't know. But we're not giving up till he tells us to. Now we have to think about how we're going to move him.'

Alexander lay still as a mountain, two and a half metres long and the weight of the two of them. He looked like a skin full of molten stilton cheese, the ugly bruised bulges over his shoulders threatening to burst. The only hard outlines were his skull, the ridge down his back and his splayed claws. Luke no longer registered the smell; his brain had simply switched it off. He didn't know about the others; nobody mentioned it anymore.

'We'll take a door off a shed to carry him' said Shona. 'But first we're eating the truckload of instant noodles Bec's brought. And figuring out who's doing what.'

While snarfing down calories and polysyllabic chemicals, they decided Luke, Shona and Bolly would take Alexander in the ute to the hospital's back entrance, where Gatta had arranged to meet Elliot. Bec, with Gatta, would park the Falcon a less audible block away, then they'd help transfer Alexander from the ute to the promised hospital stretcher. Gatta elected herself for the job of infiltrator – locating and sneaking into Taylah's room to discover the name of her antibiotic. 'Like the Black Widow, but I won't sting or shoot anyone.' She agreed to take Bec as backup.

If any of them got caught? They were smuggling a prehistoric monster bulging with deadly bacteria into a hospital. Too late, Luke realised that Elliot, whose judgement they were relying on, actually had the most to gain if they were discovered. He would lose his career but he'd be a martyr and undying hero in the animal liberation community.

If they were caught, all they could do was try not to incriminate anyone else.

Luke, full of noodles, felt like he could keel over and sleep until next Thursday. But they gathered torches, screwdrivers and shed keys and trooped outside to find their makeshift stretcher. By torchlight, the first shed's steel doors loomed huge, strong and extremely heavy. Luke regarded them doubtfully and Shona shook her braids. 'Let's have a look at the hinges, anyway. The other doors aren't any smaller.'

The hinges groaned as the doors swung open. 'There's a light switch in here somewhere,' said Shona, fumbling in the dark. There was a click and a loud hum and they all jumped out of their skins: in an instant they were drenched in light and heat.

Bec laughed gleefully. 'Skunk weed lamps. Wow, warm as shit!'

Nyabol and Gatta turned their faces wonderingly into the glow as Luke and Shona crouched to examine the hinges. Luke picked at the rust with his screwdriver. This was looking way hard.

'What about these shelf things?' said Gatta.

'The frames!' said Shona. 'Genius!'

Planter boxes, still filled with earth, sat in rows suspended off the floor on long metal racks.

'Will they be strong enough?' asked Nyabol.

'Are you kidding? They're holding up about a ton of earth,' said Bec.

The frames turned out to be ideal in size and weight but pungent in the open air.

'That's why it goes by "skunk",' said Bec. 'If we brush off all the dirt, it'll be less rank.'

It wasn't. Even after a vigorous scrub, the smell still made them want to scrape out the inside of their noses. Close up, it was eye-watering. And now they all smelled of it.

'Here,' said Bec, offering the tail of her dusty shirt to Bolly. 'Want to take a hit?'

'We all need to wash,' said Bolly.

'We can't, we're out of time,' said Shona. 'We still need to get him onto the truck. We were always going to need luck for this, we're just going to need a bit more. Except for Gatta and Bec, who'll be up on the wards: two minute shower and some of my clothes.'

In Shona's oversized white tee and faded lowrisers gathered in the belt,

Bec could have been a hip hop artist, minus the gold chains. Gatta wore a cobalt blue western shirt as a tunic, playing dress-ups, though usefully it made her look even more waiflike and vulnerable.

Sliding Alexander's bulk on his tarp onto the frame was easier than they expected. His tail was stiff with swelling. Luke winced as he bent it gingerly around in a U and tucked a sheet around him to fit his length onto the shorter rack. With the tailgate down and the tonneau cover on, they could have been carrying bags of cement. Or several dead bodies. Or a crocodile in a shroud.

The whole operation took them half an hour, so it was after midnight when they left. Gatta and Bec were a couple of minutes behind. The wind had dropped and the still air felt smothering under the low cloud. Mist thickened in Shona's headlights as they swung down the Huon Road. Luke only saw the silver shape loom up for a second before it was swallowed again. He scrambled for his phone.

'Gatta.'

She answered immediately. 'Yo.'

'There's a silver car parked on the left side just when you get onto the main road. Tell me if it's still there and what it is.'

She groaned. 'Me and cars? Bec might know. Hold on, I'll put you on speaker.'

Luke heard the crackle and roar as Bec nursed her engine over ruts, then the more even burble as she hit the local road. He heard Gatta breathing, an exclamation, a brief conversation.

'Yep, still there. Someone in it, we think. Silver hatch, Bec says something Japanese or Korean.' More mumbling. Shona frowned at him but he held up a hand. 'Wait, engine's started. There are headlights behind us now. What should we do?'

'Fuck,' said Luke.

Bec said, 'What, now? Us?' followed by manic giggling.

'Those two should never have been together,' he moaned, his fragile sense of control slipping away again.

'Sorry,' said Gatta. 'Do you want us to drive a different way?'

'Yes,' he said. 'But if he follows, don't take too long trying to lose him. Park on Liverpool in front of the Royal if you can. The police are opposite so that should be safe. Take the Argyle Street side to meet us around the back of the Private. Stay together. And if he tries to get close, run.'

'Who is he?' Gatta was serious now.

'I don't know. Maybe nobody. Maybe Ty. But don't take any risks.' Luke was sick with panic at the thought of Gatta being hurt. 'If anything, *anything* feels bad, go straight back to the police or into the main hospital.'

'Okay Luke,' said Bec. Her tone gave him more confidence. 'We'll look after each other.'

They slid through the sleeping city without further incident, though there was a bad moment when they saw the steep ramp up into the back of the Hobart Private. Luke imagined their tray tilting a few degrees too far, Alexander's dead weight sliding and a great unconscious lump of reptile deposited onto the footpath.

Luke hopped out and stood behind the ute as Shona shifted into low gear. The Courier complained its way to the top of the ramp; Alexander's sheet-shrouded mass visibly sagged backward but didn't shift. A pair of brunettes in bling and tiny leather jackets wrinkled their noses as they passed.

'We stink,' said Luke as he hopped back into the cab.

'Nothing we can do,' said Shona. 'It'll work or it won't. I should hear from Elliot in a minute or two. I wish Gatta would call in.'

She pulled up at the far end of the narrow carpark in a dark canyon of buildings, dotted with pools of blue-white light. In front, the wall was barred with silver ducts, and meticulously tagged white poly pipe and brazed copper pipes: medical gases. The exposed guts and arteries of the hospital. Signage plastered the walls and tarmac, all forbidding parking. The large red and white one directly above their bonnet read "Ambulance".

'We'd better move,' said Luke. If an ambulance came now, the ambos would be mightily pissed. And Gatta and Bec would probably turn up at exactly the wrong moment and try to argue with them. Alexander floated in the back of his mind, so nearly not there. His jaw throbbed.

'Where to?' said Shona.

The door to their left swung open. A young man carrying a yellow bundle stepped under the light. He looked like he'd climbed out of the pages of an outdoor clothing catalogue, with his Arcteryx fleece and square stubbled jaw.

'Hi,' he said to Luke, who opened his passenger side door. The rugged handsomeness peered expectantly past him into the back of the twin cab and looked startled to see Bolly, folded into the small space like a caged gazelle. 'Where's Gatta?' he said, and Luke twigged how his little sister had used more than one form of animal passion to enlist Elliot.

'Not here yet.'

'Uh, okay,' said Elliot then drew his head back. 'You all had a toke before you came?'

'No,' said Luke.

'No offence, man,' said Elliot. 'Hey, I've got gear for you all, infection control stuff. Put on everything and get some over your lizard. It keeps people away.' He thrust the yellow bundle into Luke's hands and peered towards the rear of the ute. 'He's in back?' Elliot's eyes lit up. 'I can't wait to see him; he sounds totally awesome. I'll be back with the trolley.'

They got out of the cab and put on their gear, all paper: shapeless pink caps, blue overshoes, huge billowing yellow gowns, and masks, close-fitting and stiff, standing out from their faces like beaks. They arranged a cap and the mask over Alexander's head to resemble a human body under the yellow gown, in low light, from a distance, if an observer wasn't expecting to see a crocodile.

Strong headlights hit high on the pipe-crossed wall and swept down to pick them out as an ambulance topped the ramp. It pulled up behind them and a bristle-headed paramedic wearing blue rubber gloves stepped out.

'That says "Ambulance",' he said. 'But it doesn't stop idiots, evidently. What are you doing here? Why aren't you round the front?' He stepped closer. 'And you've got a patient there, in the back of this filthy truck? What is that stink?'

Shona stepped towards him. 'I'm a landscape gardener. The smell is blood and bone,' she said truthfully. 'And we didn't have an ambulance handy.'

'You should have called one. You need someone competent to look at your patient. They're not looking lively.' He made to push around her.

'We have not asked you to examine him,' said Bolly with freezing authority. 'And we are all wearing biohazard clothing because he presents a biohazard.'

The paramedic stopped short. Bolly could sound exactly like the head of a UN mission because she had unfortunate vivid memories of several.

'Someone is getting us a trolley,' said Luke. 'We'll get out of your way.'

'You do that,' said the paramedic.

Shona moved the ute to a loading bay to let the ambulance in. The hospital door snapped shut behind the paramedics and their patient. Luke sat down on the tailgate, the sweat cold on his neck.

'We're not going to get away with that too many times,' said Shona, sitting down next to him. 'Nice work, Bol.'

Bolly shook her head, just as Gatta and Bec appeared over the top of the ramp and immediately burst into laughter.

'It's three giant ducks!' yelped Gatta.

Shona and Luke turned to each other. Big floaty yellow bodies. Duckbill masks. Yes, okay, ducks.

'What happened to the silver hatchback?' said Luke, ignoring their waddle walking.

Bec straightened up. 'Not sure. The lights went past when we parked in front of the cop shop. On foot, didn't see anyone.'

'You're looking for a medium-sized guy with red hair and a beard, all short, a bit grey. Or Ty, and you both know him.' Luke's left arm and chest burned. 'He might have a smashed nose.'

Elliot appeared again and Gatta instantly changed from a teenager into a mop-haired waif.

'Elliot! Dude! You came through for us. You're a legend.' She tilted her face up to him. Elliot was shortish and Gatta was making him feel taller. 'Savage!' she said, touching his stubble, which Luke thought was a bit much, but he was wrong. Elliot's shoulders visibly swelled.

'No sweat. He's totally worth it, right? We'd better get him inside. The old duck that just came in?' he patted the side of the ambulance, 'there's gunna be a chest X-ray, maybe a hip, so there'll be a wait. Got a trolley for him.'

They wheeled the trolley to Alexander, who was just a shape under the yellow gown and sheet, but had a definite aromatic presence.

'Wow! He's kind of out there, isn't he?' said Elliot, standing back.

'It's the infection he's got which stinks,' Gatta said. 'He's like a pig in a piggery – only smells because of his bad situation.'

'Natch,' said Elliot. He grasped his corner of the tarp. 'The sweet smell though – you gave him medical cannabis for pain?'

Shona laughed. 'We might have if we'd had some.'

Three giant ducks, a couple of homeys and a radiology professional eased Alexander's silent bulk through the back door of the hospital. Overhead fluorescents picked out the doors to a stairwell and lifts to their right and three other doors to their left. The middle door had swipe card access for Radiology; the far end dog-legged to the left, open to the lights of the Emergency Department. Alexander seemed to grow in the small hallway and Elliot's swagger dropped away.

'Let's get you out of here into my department.' He waved his badge at the Radiology door. Through it, they entered into a smaller corridor, lined with curtained alcoves and more doors. He opened the nearest into a windowless room, which was half-filled by a bed, two chairs and a sleek machine with a screen and a console.

'You'll have to wait in here. The CT is warmed up and ready, but I'll need to do the patient in DEM first. Nobody should come in here. It's our spare ultrasound room.'

Voices and footsteps grew rapidly louder from the other end of the corridor. They didn't have time to manoeuvre Alexander into the room. Elliot yanked aside the nearest curtain, shoved the trolley into the alcove, jerked his head towards the room and hissed, 'In there.'

Luke tugged the trolley fully behind the curtain as the others tumbled in through the door, a last billow of yellow gown catching as it was pulled closed.

A female voice said, 'We'll be needing a chest X-ray, AP, because she can't stand up, and a wrist.' A pause. Though his muscles were tight as bowstrings, Luke tried to lean casually on Alexander's trolley. A stifled giggle came from the ultrasound room. Luke imagined Shona strangling Bec or Gatta in the dark.

Just outside the curtain, the female voice said, 'Kinda smelly in here, Elliot. What have you been X-raying, week-old corpses?'

Luke heard Elliot rustling paper. 'Ah, farmer. Got gored by his boar.'

'Smells like the boar was still attached.' The voice receded.

Rapid footsteps came towards him and Elliot's stricken face poked through the curtains.

'I blew it. The biohazard story was supposed to also cover you if someone saw you. I panicked and forgot it. I'm sorry man, I can't do this.'

Crap.

Gatta's small hand touched the radiographer's forearm. 'It's okay, Elliot, great liars are bad people. Almost always. Someone sees us? You tell them we're the second stinker in your stinker of a shift. How could one guy be so unlucky, right?'

He smiled weakly.

'We'll wait in the little room for as long as it takes,' said Luke. 'If we're going to save Alexander, we need your pictures.'

Shona loomed up behind him. Her green eyes and dreads managed to look imposing even in duck costume. 'You're doing great, Elliot. This wasn't your fight and you're taking a big risk for us.'

Elliot looked at Gatta who gave him a sickeningly adoring simper. His brown fists clenched the curtains and he exhaled slowly. 'Okay.'

'Well, we'd better get him in there then.' Shona grasped the trolley handles. 'Bec and Gatta, you guys get going.' Her eyes skewered them. 'Stop enjoying yourselves and be careful. Bol, you'd better move the ute. Stay with it and we'll text you when we're done. Let us know if you see Luke's red-bearded guy.'

Luke sat with Shona in the ultrasound room, alone together on a bed in the almost-dark. The silence prickled. He could feel Shona's warmth, single out the scent of her skin despite the increasingly suffocating heat and smell of emanating from Alexander. His hands tingled and his breathing deepened.

'I've heard from Rosie,' Shona said. Her voice veered from strained to amused. 'She really is too old for you.'

'Ha, thanks.' Was he red enough to glow in the dark?

Shona went on, her voice serious again. 'She sent me a text. She said nothing of what she'd done had actually helped us, she was sorry for what happened, thought she would have killed Alexander without you.'

Luke was stunned. 'But she's been so... None of that was her fault! So, she's not coming?'

'It's worse than that. She said she shouldn't have been a part of this, shouldn't even be practising.' She swallowed. 'Then I got a text from Adam, on Rosie's phone. He was furious. She's on an incredible guilt trip. Her anorexia is out of control. He's needs to admit her to hospital. He blames us.'

The light under the door gleamed on the steel legs of the trolley, lost itself in Shona's gown and formed a smooth V on the muscles of her neck. Luke focused on that. It calmed him.

'Is there anything we can do?'

'I tried ringing her earlier, but no answer. I sent her your number in case she would talk to you.' She tried for a light tone. 'Being her hero and all.'

'Has she had to go to hospital before?'

'Last year, our team lost a semi-final. She was stressed and made some mistakes but we all did. It was nothing. Anyway, it's just footy! I got a text where she made all these apologies, it was ridiculous, then she just disappeared. I didn't see her for months. Apparently she nearly died.'

Wheels and footsteps squeaked by on the lino on the other side of the door.

'So Adam is being completely realistic.' Rosie had asked for scans. When would she see them? In weeks, months? Never?

'Possibly.' Shona read the worry in his voice. 'She's safe where she is, Luke. And it's not your fault.'

Who could interpret the scans for them?

The door opened and Elliot was framed in the light. His curls seemed bouncier again. 'We're sweet. I just need to process the old duck's films. You heard from Gatta? We could use some more guys to transfer Alexander.'

'I'll text,' said Luke. Elliot's head disappeared. Gatta wrote back:

Trying. Black Widow could do without She-Hulk.

Shona shook her head mutely. They slid off the bed and squeezed themselves at either end of Alexander's trolley. Shona also received a text. 'It's Bolly.' She showed Luke.

All quiet. I have locked the doors but I have not seen a man with a short red beard. Good luck to everyone.

Elliot opened the door again. 'Let's party.'

Chapter 35

The CT room was through a small passage plastered with yellow triangular radiation warning signs and PR posters of smiling radiologists. The room was warm, hummed discreetly and smelled of metal.

They positioned Alexander's trolley parallel to the scanner platform. Elliot, now businesslike, closed the door and ducked behind a glass partition to activate a console. The scanner emitted polite sets of beeps, in threes.

Alexander's mind floated faintly in Luke's. It hadn't responded to any of the activity. Luke touched his pale green tail where the sheet didn't quite cover it. The skin burned with fever and was drier than it had been yesterday, flaking off under his fingertips. Was he progressing from slug to mummy?

Something was making irregular insistent thumps. Elliot jumped up, irritated rather than alarmed. He opened the door a crack, laughed and let in Bec and Gatta.

'Sorry, we tried to text but it didn't work. We brought you this.' Gatta thrust a red plastic folder at Luke. 'We wanted to take a pic but too many nursy-people about, so we just ran.'

Luke hugged her, too thankful to be annoyed.

'I think the answer is Azithro-thingo,' she said. The antibiotic Luke hadn't had. 'Anyway, it's in there and we can help move the Stinkosaurus.'

Together they lifted Alexander smoothly across to the CT platform, the bend of his folded tail towards the machine opening.

Elliot looked at Luke. 'He's unconscious, right, but stable and breathing?' Luke nodded.

'Because we all have to go into the control room, out of the radiation.'

'Okay,' said Luke, but it wasn't.

'If you need to be with him, you can wear one of those lead gowns.'

Elliot gestured towards a rack of smocks, the front one gaily patterned with pink cartoon dalmatians.

Luke was relieved. 'I can sort of tell how he's doing if I'm nearby. But I'll put one on if he needs help.'

They crowded into the control room, lined up to look through the window. Alexander suddenly looked very alone and vulnerable, the machine's opening more like a maw. Elliot pressed buttons. The background hum grew in pitch and volume, like something was rotating very fast. The sound steadied, was overlaid with beeps like a backing truck, red lights flashed, and the platform jerked and began its slide into the scanner.

'This'll take about fifteen minutes,' said Elliot.

Luke was closest to the door, so only had a distant view of the monitors. The first picture came out as an oval – white surrounded by a complicated rim of greys.

'Anyone know how to read one of these?' said Elliot.

'Very sort of,' said Shona.

'No,' said everyone else.

'It takes the images in slices, across the body, like a salami,' Elliot said. 'I can format them whichever way you like later, but the raw information comes out as cross sections.' He gestured at the screen. 'Starting at the tail. The white stuff is bone. The black stuff is air. The grey is everything in between.'

The new images appeared every few seconds. Now Luke was seeing two sets of concentric circles, white in the middle. He realised it was two parts of Alexander's tail as it curved around on itself: bone, muscle, skin. The platform bearing him moved further into the machine. One of the circles became smaller and disappeared while the other expanded, became oval. Grey patches bloomed inside it, the white parts suddenly grew side branches. Luke had a vague understanding he must be seeing the pelvis and whatever was in there. No one spoke.

Luke wondered if they would ever see Rosie again. If they didn't, who could they ask to interpret the pictures? The prof? With each new image, the oval shape grew, became more complex, full of shadowy forms. Luke recognised clusters of white dots as claws. Who would tell them which mysterious grey puddle was a healthy liver, or a lung, which was a bag of infection, what muscles were rotting and about to burst? Did Alexander have the infection in his brain and how would they tell?

The others were staring at the screen, hypnotised. More white dots appeared either side of the main body.

Elliot sat bolt upright. The dots were larger on the next image and there were more of them, arrayed along the inside of the skin. Elliot stood up, clattering his chair back.

He glared at Luke. At Shona. At Bec. Even at Gatta. 'Are you shitting me?'

'What?' said Luke.

The others looked from Luke to Elliot, confused. Another image scrolled down the screen.

Elliot gestured angrily at it. 'This is a joke, right?'

'No, of course not. I mean, how?'

Elliot stared at them, his black eyes uncertain. He looked back at the screen, shoved his hands in his hair. Shona hunched over the monitor. Her lips moved in a silent prayer.

'Luke,' she said, 'he's got wings.'

Marie Heitz

Part III

Chapter 36

'Where?' asked Gatta.

Exactly. Outside the body there was nothing. Especially no arched struts or spreading membranes.

'Here.' Shona put her finger on the screen, on the white dots just under the skin. The screen scrolled again and the dots moved further up. 'Can you freeze this?' she asked Elliot.

His fingers flashed over the keyboard: a second screen sprang to life.

Shona took a deep breath. 'He's pupating.' She touched the screen again. 'What was his skin is now just an outer casing. Inside it, he's been growing a new body. And it's got wings.'

'I still can't see them,' said Bec slowly.

'They're there all right,' said Elliot. 'I can do a 3D reco at the end and they'll be obvious.' His voice was screwed up to a squeak. 'A lizard, with wings. That makes him—'

'A dragon,' said Gatta.

Bec gave an uncharacteristic, high-pitched giggle.

Gatta reached out towards Alexander, spread her fingers on the glass. 'You're a dragon,' she whispered.

The images rolled over, Elliot and Shona studying them intently, faces close to the screen,

After a minute Gatta said, 'Is he sick? Can you tell where his infection is?'

'I'm not sure,' said Shona. She looked distracted. 'Elliot?'

'I can't see anything obviously bad but it's not my field. He's my first flying freakin' lizard.'

'Something else is wrong,' said Shona.

'What?' said Elliot.

She rubbed her ear through the pink cap, let a few more images pass. From what Luke could tell, they were up to Alexander's shoulders. He felt like he'd just been given a spaceship, one he didn't know what to do with, but a *spaceship*! And now… Were the engines on backwards?

'His wings are too small,' said Shona.

'Too small?' Gatta sounded injured on Alexander's behalf. 'What does that mean? Besides, they must be, like, still growing.

'They're *way* too small. But it's not just his wings – his wing muscles, his structure is all wrong. Except his bones, he might have more air sacs there, for lightness. But for his weight, there's no way he could possibly fly.'

'I don't get it.' Elliot seemed as offended as Gatta. 'Fighter jets are heavy and their wings are pretty small.'

'Fighter jets have engines,' said Shona. 'I haven't spotted an engine. He's got flight muscles – around the bone sticking out of his sternum – but they're comprehensively too small, and so's the bone. They couldn't possibly develop a fraction of the power he needs to lift himself.' She spread her arms. 'His muscles would need to be literally ten, twenty times the size.'

The images on the monitor had crept up to Alexander's skull. Luke remembered to look at the texture of the brain for infection, but of course it was another anonymous grey lump. What was he expecting? Tiny bacteria waving swords?

The others shuffled restlessly.

'I feel sort of cheated,' said Bec. 'Are you sure?'

'Sure? Comparative anatomy, mechanics of flight – major parts of my Zoology units. He's got like,' Shona glanced upwards, 'pigeon wings on a rhinoceros. I'm sorry.'

The images narrowed down to a small dot – the tip of his snout – then disappeared. Elliot pressed buttons and the platform slid out of the machine.

'I'm going to format the images for 3D,' a subdued Elliot said into the silence. 'Let's get him back on the trolley while it does its thing.'

They positioned themselves around Alexander. Luke shook himself out of his bewildered daze. 'So, forgetting the wings for a minute, neither of you saw anything nasty in there?' he said to Shona and Elliot.

'I'm not trained to interpret CTs, just to take them,' said Elliot, 'so you have to get someone who knows what they're doing, but, no, I didn't see anything obvious. His heart was kinda huge, but who knows–'

'So the fever and the pain,' said Luke, 'they could be him changing?'

'I wish we could talk to Rosie,' said Shona. 'But, yes, I think it's possible that all the breaking down and making new tissue – and he did it incredibly fast – would take a huge amount of energy. I guess that's why he had to eat so much. It would have been painful; horrible. And it would have generated heat.'

Luke was still floundering but slightly relieved. They grasped the sides of Alexander's tarp and got ready to slide him across. A few flakes drifted off his tail. At least dry rot was less messy than wet. *Rot*. Luke's hands found their grip failing.

'Shona. What about the report on the sample, the bit that came off him? They saw bacteria.'

Their eyes met for a beat. 'Yes, they did.' Her face turned bleaker 'That must be how he came out wrong. He had an infection at the time of his change and it inhibited the new growth. Stunted him.'

They looked down at the massive, recumbent shape between them. He was alive. He had survived his nightmare and would come back to them. He would emerge from his casing as something new. But not as the glorious thing he should have been. What other parts of him would come out misshapen?

Silently, they dragged Alexander across to the trolley.

Shona gave a startled bark, which became a laugh, of triumph and relief; a sunny sound which filled the room. 'No, they didn't see bacteria. What they saw were mitochondria. And he will be able to fly.'

'Mighty? Mighty whats?' said Gatta.

'Mitochondria. Yes, mighty. They make energy,' Shona said. 'And his muscles are stuffed with them. Stuffed!' Joyously, she threw up her hands like she was throwing confetti.

'Sorry everyone. I didn't see it till now, but that's because it's a completely novel physiology. Which up until ten minutes ago was mythical. It needed his wings to make sense. I'll explain it properly to you later. Elliot. Is that reco finished?'

'Probably. Outline and bones anyway.'

Elliot's fingers danced over his keyboard and a perfect model of a curled-tailed Alexander popped up and waited, floating on the screen. Elliot spun it around.

'This is what we can already see from the outside,' he said. 'But here be the cool stuff.'

The model vanished. Elliot hit more keys. Someone gasped. A creature of bones sprang from the dark it lived in; a lizard skull grinned out at them, the gaze from its empty eye socket more piercing than an actual eye, knowing and pitiless, the jaws stripped of flesh, crowded with purposeful, murderous teeth. On either side, revealed without their skin, spidery razor-sharp claws.

'Whoa!' said Elliot. 'Looks like one mean dude from that direction!'

He spun the model around and everyone relaxed. Alexander's spine stretched behind, sinuous, with impossibly many segments, his ribs curving protectively – somewhere in there, invisible, was his heart – the flanges that were his hips, the graceful swirl of his tail. And from the top of his shoulders, two long thick bones arced as far back as his pelvis, where they jointed with two thinner ones that swept forward again nearly to his neck. These in turn were attached to five more, delicate, long, each nearly the length of the long bones, tucked close around his body like cradling hands: his wings.

Gatta touched her fingers to the screen, tracing them along the gracile bones of the wings. With her other hand, she reached for Luke.

'We have to tell Rosie,' she said.

'We'll keep trying,' Shona said.

'In the meantime, we have to get him out of here,' said Bec. 'But he can't go back to Shona's now, can he?'

'No,' said Luke. Ty had discovered Shona's. Mum's meeting was today. If she got her money, Ty wouldn't need Alexander and maybe Luke could negotiate a truce about the mutual murder attempts. Until then, they had to hide. 'Shona, you said you might have somewhere.'

Shona was grinning. 'It's in Clarke Avenue.'

Bec cackled. 'I love it!'

Elliot was aghast. 'You can't go there. It's in the middle of town. And it's full of millionaires.'

'Millionaires have excellent security,' said Shona. 'I'm landscaping their garden while they're in Italy for a month. The walls are high, the neighbours can't see in, and they're used to my ute.'

Luke nodded slowly. He said to Bec, 'Ty knows the Falcon but he doesn't know the ute or Shona. The guy in the hatch followed you, not us. You take Gatta home. That won't tell him anything.'

Gatta was scowling but Luke continued, 'Gattacus. Ty is after us, not you. And we have no idea when Alexander will wake up.'

Bec said, 'I know you think Ty is only going for you and Alexander, but I think Gatta needs her new bestie to come and stay.'

Gatta's brief grin was replaced by new unhappiness. 'And I can't come visit.'

Luke shook his head.

'What will he be like, do you think, when he wakes up?' asked Gatta.

'The same, only bigger, with wings,' said Luke. But they both knew he wouldn't be the same. Luke saw again that terrifyingly purposeful skull.

Chapter 37

Getting Alexander out of the hospital was easier than getting him in.

In the car park, Elliot looked like he wanted to join the desperadoes as they rode hard for the hills, but instead he fist-bumped Luke.

'Most awesome day of my life, man. Keep me in the loop. I'll put his pics on a CD and send it to Gatta. Then I'll have to bury the originals in the database – the system won't let me get rid of them completely.' He brightened further. 'It'll be a blast watching the radiologists bring up another same-same human liver to report on when there's a dragon down in there.'

They farewelled Gatta and Bec, and Shona pulled out onto the main road. Bolly sat sideways in the back seat, staring toward Alexander under the tonneau cover, hand on mouth; she'd just heard the news.

Shona darted across the four empty lanes of Macquarie Street. 'We can't take him to Clarke Ave now,' she said. 'It's 3am and it's a small street. If any of the old folks are up, they'll wonder what we're doing and call the cops. We'll wait at Marieville and take him in at six.'

She threaded through the narrow and haphazard one-way streets of Battery Point, the suburb that grew from houses for the garrison officers of Hobart's first settlement. It was close-set, winding and much photographed by tourists – and now useful to check they weren't being followed. Marieville Esplanade lay silvery and silent. It was lined with angle parking and fronted by a shallow beach, a grassy field and a toilet block – attractions for RV owners and campers low on cash. Signs forbidding overnight RVs and camping lined the footpath. Shona pulled up in the far corner.

Luke was battered and strung out but his brain was fizzing. He wanted Alexander awake. Now. To inhabit his new body, discover himself, show them what he had turned into. Luke wanted to talk to him, but his dragon sense – could he call it that now? – felt Alexander sleeping, with no indication when it might end. Minutes? Months? Where could they look after him for months? How?

'Tell me why he can fly even though he cannot,' said Bolly.

Shona's teeth gleamed in the dark. 'Birds can only fly because they're light. Light hollow bones, small organs, huge lungs, feathers. They've got big flight muscles but if their bodies were as heavy for their size as mammals or reptiles, they'd have to be gigantic. If you guys had wings, you'd need ten metres of wingspan. And two-metre thick chest muscle to power the wings.

'But if you supercharged the muscle... Mitochondria are little power stations that live in your cells. A billion years ago, they were probably bacteria, which is what they look like under a microscope. Now they live in cells, yours, mine, all animals and they make energy. His muscles are stuffed with them.'

'Are you sure?' asked Luke.

She snorted. This was what convinced Luke. 'I can't possibly be sure of anything, but it fits. The coma he was in for the last couple of days was probably more like hibernation. The stuff on the outside is falling off, but on the CT, the body inside looks clean. And mitochondria make heat.'

Heat.

'Does that mean he'll, um, breathe fire?' asked Luke.

Shona slapped her cheeks several times. 'Just checking,' she said. 'That we haven't all wandered into a fantasy novel. Yes, we are asking ourselves how to explain all this. Seriously asking.' She opened the car door. They followed her out onto the moonlit grass. The silence was profound, with only a whisper from the nearby surf.

'Assuming we're not in some skunk weed haze, which actually seems more likely at the moment,' said Shona, 'we know flying lizards do exist because there's one in the back of my ute.'

'Where are all the other ones?' asked Bolly.

A glimmer of white wings dipped out of the darkness overhead. Pacific Gulls. They circled over the ute then swept down to join a white clump at the far end of the park.

Luke said, 'If they're like Alexander, they could be very hard to see.'

'Unseen for a thousand years? With what, eight billion people on the planet?' asked Shona.

The gulls mewed and shuffled.

'Maybe most of them are gone. There are dragon myths from just about everywhere. Except Australia,' said Luke. 'And people killed them because dragons were pretty much always nasty.'

'The Aboriginal people had a Rainbow Serpent that wasn't,' said Bolly.

They looked at her, startled.

'Before we came, my father bought us books about our new country. He was very excited that there would be black people here. Even if they had no cattle. But the Rainbow Serpent had no wings and he was not violent. Alexander, he was still making colours, a little, when I met him. He made rainbows, earlier?'

'He made rainbows,' said Luke, 'but I don't think he's Australian. He had this drive, some sort of instinct towards oak trees, acorns, from Europe.'

'*Quercus cryptogermanii*,' said Shona.

'Which doesn't have anything to do with Germans. Except–'

'Why are you looking like someone just clocked you?' said Shona.

'I read about the Hungarian Oak. In German it was the Wurmbaum. We thought the translation was Wormwood, or tree. But *Wurm* also means *dragon*. It's the dragon tree. Which means–'

'One of us needs to learn medieval German and read some seriously old manuscripts,' said Shona. 'But not before morning.' She looked at her watch. 'We might get two hours of sleep before we take him to his new digs.'

They arranged themselves in the cab in the least uncomfortable positions they could find.

Luke tried to slow all the spinning wheels in his brain, both the ones he was cranking himself and the ones that were whirling away by themselves.

Alexander had caused his own change.

But he must have started it out of some sort of instinct – he certainly hadn't known what would happen and it had terrified him.

When others of his kind endured that agonising transformation, they were surely tended by kin. *Their* kin. What would they be like? Alexander would grow into – what? Luke's mind drifted its way through scales, colours, horns – horns? Yellow eyes; were there different colours? Oh Christ; size. Luke pictured Alexander overflowing the ute, crushing the suspension; straddle-legged over Luke's home swiping at the smoking chimney; planting a foot either side of an oak on Government House lawns, plucking up the Friesian cows; leaping into the air, his claws furrowing the earth with grave-size trenches, his wings darkening the sky.

Something deep shifted, nudging Luke inside his dream. He struggled to open his eyes. Sunlight sparkled off the dew on the ute's bonnet. Plovers skittered across the wet grass. Otherwise, the world was still.

The movement wasn't outside. It was more of a surge, a welling up, water within water: Alexander had begun to waken. He wasn't conscious yet, but he was on his way to the surface, a swimmer ascending towards the light. Alexander didn't know this but Luke did, being both inside and outside the process. And it was the wrong time.

Luke groped for the door handle, fell out of the cab and stumbled around to the back of the tray. Alexander's tail had partially straightened and looped out of the back of the sheet.

'What are you up to, mate?'

A man was closing his garden gate a few doors down. And Luke looked suspiciously shabby; banged up, filthy, and seemingly interfering with a load on the back of a truck.

The man was no longer young but tall and still powerful with the beard and the authority of the Pilgrim Fathers; he looked and sounded like he could call down the wrath of God in the unlikely event his own wrath should prove inadequate.

'What are you doing?' he said again, as Shona stepped out of the driver's side, stretched and adjusted her shirt. The bearded man gazed at her appreciatively, then looked back at Luke. 'Exceptionally well done, mate!' He sketched a salute and strolled off.

'Good thing he didn't see Bolly as well,' said Shona.

Shouldn't she have been shocked at what the man assumed? Embarrassed? That they had just been—

The sheet over Alexander shivered.

'We have to get going,' said Luke. 'He's waking.'

'Is he doing anything?'

'Not yet.'

'Try sending him calm vibes or whatever ET thing you do and I'll get us there.'

They made their way back through Battery Point, past double-storey white Victorians and iron-laced red brick. A speed bump moved Alexander closer to the surface, but his mind was still unfocused, searching. A right turn revealed a silver-blue horizon framed by treetops near the river. The ute lurched sideways on its 25-year-old suspension and Alexander's mind burst up into the light. His eyes opened.

'He's awake,' said Luke.

Luke needed to be physically closer, to get in the tray. He had no connection, couldn't feel Alexander fixing on him. They turned again, ground uphill into Colville. Alexander was centring now, seeing and feeling the unfamiliar world and not understanding it.

Luke spoke out loud. 'It's okay, you're okay. Rest, be still. Just a little bit longer.'

A pause in the confusion, like a question.

'It's Luke, I'm here, you're fine,' said Luke.

Shona glanced sidelong at him and swung them right into Mona Street. Bolly shifted in the back seat.

Luke's ears were ringing. Alexander was fully awake now. Luke shook his head to clear it. He knew – how? – that Alexander was testing his legs, taking weight on them, trying to untangle his tail. The street of white pickets ended, the river rose in the windscreen.

'Nearly there,' said Shona.

Alexander's head reared up, bounced against the tonneau cover and he shook his tail free.

Luke's head was still buzzing. 'Alexander! Stop!'

Alexander's movement and the buzzing stopped together.

'We're here,' said Shona through clenched teeth. She braked by a seven-foot mustard-coloured wall with a sheet metal gate the same shade. In the neighbour's house, a curtain twitched in a second-storey mullioned window. Shona fished a remote out of the ute's console as Luke's head started buzzing again. The gate slid sideways. They bumped over the kerb, up the driveway and out of sight.

Chapter 38

It was spectacularly, intimidatingly, millionaire-ish. On their left, the house was a slightly offset three storey stack of elegant wooden boxes with windows. Ahead of them at the water's edge perched another vertically planked wooden box, a boathouse the size of a three-car garage. The high mustard walls enclosed the three sides of the property that weren't water frontage.

Shona pulled up in front of the boathouse. 'Celia the neighbour spends a lot of time looking out her upper floor windows,' she said. 'The owners had those junipers put in specifically to block her. She can't see most of the garden and she can't see us here.'

The ute's tray shook with thumps and scrapes. The three of them piled out of the cab to find a half metre of pale green tail swinging out the back. They peeled back the tonneau cover. Alexander had tangled the top half of his body through the sheet and was scrabbling at the wheel arches, trying to get purchase. He saw Luke, and stopped. His eyes shone clear and brilliant as yellow sapphires.

'Oh man,' breathed Luke. 'He's back.'

Alexander shook himself. He looked like a man wearing an elderly, badly fitting rubber suit.

Luke's head was buzzing again, he badly needed to piss, and he was exhausted, but part of him was running into a knee slide, hugging Shona – well nothing new on that front – and leaping into the water.

'Wait on,' he said. 'We'll get you down.'

Shona unlocked the boathouse and returned with two planks. With Alexander staying more or less still, they slid him on the frame to the ground.

'Let's get him inside,' said Shona. 'Celia can still see about a third of the yard.'

They dragged tarp and lizard up the planks into the boathouse. It smelled of cedar and lemons and a little of diesel, because it happened to have a boat in it. The boat, ten metres of teak and stainless steel with fridge-sized twin outboards, was winched up on runners on the right. The rest of the space was twice as wide, flooded with morning light that sparkled in the bottles on the bar on the left and streamed through the glass-topped table and leather-strapped steel chairs at the far end. The lemons were in a bowl on the table and behind them was the deck and the river.

Luke went outside to piss. When he got back, Alexander was propped on his front legs on the polished boards, peering and sniffing and looking exceptionally bedraggled in his tattered, sagging skin. Luke sat down in front of him next to Bolly. His head still buzzed. Alexander stopped sniffing, fixed Luke with his ice dagger stare. The buzzing had the same repeated sound, a sound which was oddly familiar. Insistent. Meant for him.

His name.

'Luke.'

'Alexander?'

The lizard looked him full in the face. His eyes glittered, their yellow gleam refracting among a hundred facets, splintered mirrors in a maze of light that went ever deeper but seemed to have no end. Behind them lay a will that was entirely its own.

'You're *talking* to me!'

Bolly raised a graceful eyebrow. Shona looked quizzical.

'Yes.' Alexander's head bobbed. Laughter? Impatience? **'You are hearing now. Where is Gatta?'**

'She's not here. Things are dangerous now. We have to hide for a while.'

The voice in Luke's head was silent. It sounded like his own voice when he had his fingers in his ears, except it wasn't his own voice.

'You talk to me, I talk. I learn and talk.'

'Er, yes, okay. Can you talk to Shona and Bolly?'

When he shrugged his shoulders, Alexander looked uncannily like Gatta.

'We can't understand anything,' said Shona. 'I can feel a sort of vibration in my head but that's it.'

'I don't feel anything,' said Bolly.

Luke felt obscurely guilty. 'I've known him for longer. Maybe we have a wavelength.'

Alexander turned his yellow eyes on Luke. **'Sun,'** Luke heard.

Luke was rocked by sudden knowledge. And weight. He felt he was carrying a huge backpack he'd lugged through knee-deep mud for an entire drizzling day. He was filthy, aching, unpleasantly damp with rain and cooled sweat; he longed for sunlit riverbank rocks and clean water.

'He needs to go out into the sun,' he said to Shona. 'Is there a spot he can do that? Can you show us which parts of the garden can't be seen?'

'Yes,' she said. 'I can even mark them out. Do you think he'll understand?'

'Yes.'

Shona watched Luke's face. 'Did he just say yes? Jesus!'

Alexander followed Shona, treading gingerly like an amputee testing his new prosthetic legs, feeling them for fit and performance. Every few steps he wriggled impatiently, shimmying the skin that was no longer his skin but old clothes.

The second-storey deck of the main house looked over a gently sloping lawn, a small beach and the river. Up against the wall opposite the boathouse was the close rank of junipers. Fresh earth and yellow stone were piled at the foot of the trees and under the deck. Shona placed three stones to mark a diagonal line between the last juniper and a spot halfway along the beach. When Luke stepped over the line, he could see the neighbour's window.

'Okay, ah, Alexander,' Shona said. 'If you step over this line the neighbour will see you. So don't step over it.'

Alexander moved his head slowly up and down: nodding.

Shona inclined her head uncertainly back – how do you address a dragon? 'By the way, Luke, you should step over the line holding a shovel or something, and wave to her. You are my new labourer. I'll take Bolly home and find us some breakfast.'

Bolly turned to Alexander. 'I am glad you have awoken,' she said. 'I hope you will find a place here to live peacefully but it will be hard, I think. I will help if I can.'

Alexander stood up formally and bowed with one bent leg – an Elizabethan courtier holding a plumed hat in one hand. Where had he learned that? He and Gatta must have been watching pirate movies.

The gate slid closed behind the Courier. Luke could sense a suburb waking up around them, houses packed with listening ears and seeing eyes, all now open, pop pop pop, but kept out by the high walls. He felt secure, even gleeful. Was this what it felt like to be rich? Not money in piles – but space and silence and privacy. And their own beach.

Alexander had stretched out into the grass beside him, tail pointed at the sun's path on the river and the yachts, motionless on their moorings.

The spinning wheels in Luke's brain slowed, came to rest. The sunshine seeped through his body, loosening the knots of worry and injuries.

The voices preceded them, jerking Luke awake. Three white surf ski hulls slid into view from the right, not ten metres offshore, the men stroking easily and talking.

'Negative gearing, decades of it. Two percent rise in interest rates? Will bring down the banks.'

One paddler glanced casually at Luke – propped on his elbows next to two-and-a-half metres of mostly-pale green dragon – dipped his paddle blade in for the next stroke and glided on.

Luke sagged with incredulous relief. Alexander wasn't in camo. What had the paddler's brain seen? Obviously not a basking crocodile. Another pile of clay? When you take in a cloudy sky on a lazy day, you don't see actual flop-eared rabbits or one-armed clowns or maps of Africa – you see clouds, because what would a map of Africa be doing up there? You see what you expect.

Alexander had turned his head, his barely open eyes on the wake of the departed paddlers.

'You say I must hide from people?'

'Yes.'

'Like before?'

'Yes, but even more. Now they will really want to catch you, capture you – they may not kill you but they will never let you go.'

Alexander gave no response, neither in words nor feelings. Luke felt the withholding as strongly as he'd felt the flow of feeling before Alexander's change.

'This is the river.' Alexander raised his scaly head and breathed deeply, taking in a hundred smells he knew, and a thousand new ones: diesel, salt, baking shoreline mussels, floating kelp, algae, the neck feathers of cormorants. 'I will swim.'

'There are people, and boats.' Luke could see Alexander being sliced in half by one of the keels of the Peppermint Bay catamaran.

'I must swim.'

Luke felt the thick pelt of wet stinking clothes fall briefly back on his shoulders.

'You can dive, hold your breath, go deep?'

Alexander nodded.

How did he know? Gatta had dumped him in a fountain once.

'Do you know you are different, now?' Luke asked.

'I know that I have,' Luke felt him looking for the word, 'passed.'

'Did you know when you ate the acorns what would happen?'

'No.'

'But you kept going.'

'I followed you.'

Luke had an awful vertiginous moment. What if he had faltered in his totally unfounded belief that Alexander could be cured of whatever illness he had? Would Alexander have given up? *Died*?? 'And now, do you know about–?'

'I have a new body.'

'And?'

'I have wings. I will fly.'

With this, a tiny flash of uncertainty slipped out. To Luke, the new dragon suddenly felt more human again.

'Can you feel them?'

Alexander writhed and shuffled his shoulders, eventually shrugged. 'I saw them, when I was–'

For a moment, Luke hung in the white space of Alexander's *passing*. He had not been totally insensate but seeing, dreaming. 'Did you see anything else?'

'I saw others.'

Others. 'More dragons?' Luke's new world unfolded another dimension. 'How many? Do you know where they are?'

This time Luke felt Alexander's full confusion and sadness. 'I do not know where. Or when. Or if they are living.' The glittering wells of his eyes swallowed all their light.

'We'll look for them. We already have some clues. Maybe you'll remember more.'

Alexander pushed up from the grass and nosed about restlessly, as though he meant to begin the search right away.

'Now I will swim.'

'Be careful,' Luke said. 'Stay mainly underwater. Don't get lost.' He felt like his mother.

Alexander flicked his tail in response. Luke snorted. Typical teenager.

Luke's channel into Alexander opened again as his front claws sank in wet sand and a wavelet slapped him in the face. Did he need reassurance after all? Luke gasped as the cold water flowed down his back. For a moment it seemed that Alexander's weight would keep him walking on the river bottom rather than swimming, but then he inhaled, rose, broke free of the sand and floated. A burst of anxiety and a scrabble of legs, neck erect like a periscope, then his tail found purchase on the water, he melded his limbs to his body and dived.

He was gone. The channel between them was closed. Did it not work under water, or over distance? Or had Alexander deliberately closed it?

Their communication would be different now. Alexander could talk, in words! He could share with Luke what he *thought*, not just what he felt.

Luke got up, grabbed a shovel, and moved across the Celia line. He paced up and down the grass, toeing at the rock piles.

Alexander was choosing what feelings to share now. That was being an adult. What else had changed about him? Not just what body would he have – what kind of person would he become?

Chapter 39

Shona returned with coffee and fresh bacon rolls. They sat on the boathouse deck, Luke in three kinds of heaven.

Shona's eyes went to the shallow groove in the sand flanked by lines of gouges leading into the water. The unmistakeable signs of a crocodile sliding down a riverbank. 'At least it's the right side of the Celia Line,' she said, but left her breakfast to scuff out the marks.

An early north-easterly was ruffling water that stretched to the mouth of the estuary and Storm Bay, and over the horizon to albatrosses and Antarctica. Luke's mind spread gratefully out into the space. He could look past Shona's profile and downriver at the bushy skyline of Mt Nelson, and say, 'So that guy, back at Marieville Esplanade, he thought we were…'

Shona paused with her bacon roll at her lips. 'Well, why wouldn't he? We just got out of a car looking like we'd been busy all night.' She took a bite, continued, less distinctly, 'Of course, you're a bit young for me, but we've established you're older than your years. And you blush beautifully.'

Great.

'And you're very blond, but I mustn't be racist – one of my grandmothers is Danish.'

Luke tried to ignore feeling like he'd stuck his face in an oven. He opened his mouth and out came: 'Danish. Um, so have I. My dad's mother. You could be related to Princess Mary. Er, by marriage,' he said, pointing past her to Taroona, birthplace of Mary Donaldson, the Crown Princess of Denmark.

'Luke,' said Shona. 'I never thought you were a complete idiot, well, except for a little while, but it sure is fun when you act like one.' She put her long-fingered quarter-Danish hand on his arm, making his nerves fizz and pop, and he decided that he was probably ahead, though he couldn't figure out how. The four years between them seemed to vanish. When she let go to drink her coffee, it was both a disappointment and a relief.

He told her about the other dragons Alexander had seen. 'He must have some kind of ancestral memory,' he said, 'because he couldn't know what he'll look like himself yet, so he couldn't have imagined them from that.'

'Unless he and Gatta have been watching dragon movies. He was in a delirium. He could have dragged stuff into it from anywhere.'

That hadn't occurred to him. 'I'll ask her.'

Shona laughed at his crestfallen face then fist-bumped his shoulder. 'I'd like him to have relatives as much as you do, though maybe not as much as him, but what are the chances? Of undiscovered dragons – *dragons* – in a world this crowded?'

'If they *are* here somewhere, though?'

'That would be amazing, incredible.' She shook her head. 'But you know he's not magic, right? This isn't *Game of Thrones*. That amazing stuff he does, it's not magic, it's physiology. What was that saying about sufficiently advanced technology? Mobile phones would look like magic to people from the Middle Ages? He's doing the stuff, so it exists. It only seems like he's doing magic because we don't know how it's done.'

Luke loved the fierce and perfect symmetry of Shona's brows and cheekbones and her unconscious graceful strength, but mostly he loved her intensity and seriousness. She was alive with it, leaning towards him. She spread her palms across the air, miming an invisible screen.

'The pictures he makes on his skin look impossible, but LCD screens are possible. He'll have chromatophores under his skin, like squid and salamanders, but how does he run them? The computing power to create the background in real time when he's moving, in relation to observers, speed, light... He must have a complete neural network under his skin as well, like a second brain.' She leaned back and grinned. 'A tiny part of me – well, maybe not tiny – really does want to get him into a lab.'

What would she say if he told her he'd thought about putting Alexander in a lab for his profit? For Mum. He flushed again. How was Mum going in her meeting?

Shona's smile disappeared. For a moment he thought she'd read his mind. She hadn't. 'It should be Rosie here discussing magic and new physiology. She's got such a brain. All the facts and open-minded with it.

'You still haven't been able to get her? What about Adam?'

'I don't have his number. The texts I've got from him were when he was with her, using her phone. I thought about ringing Phil – the other coach – to get it, but he's such a busybody. Rosie hates anyone knowing about her mental health. That's why she disappeared like this last time.'

Luke remembered Rosie clinging to him after Alexander's seizure. Sharing their relief. 'What can we do?'

'I'll try ringing the hospitals later but they're very cagey with non-relatives.' She smoothed the empty paper bags against the table, ironing out the creases. Then she lifted her gaze to the water. 'Do you have any idea where he is?'

Luke shook his head. 'If he's just popping his head up, he'll be hard to see. He'd look like a small seal or a very big cormorant.'

'A fur seal. Or a leopard seal. That would turn out badly.'

'A shark wouldn't be great either.'

'They're mostly gummy sharks, though you're right – there are great whites in the Derwent.'

'If I start worrying about that, I'll run around screaming. Just now I'm wondering how he's not going to get lost. Can he navigate by smell? The biggest bit of water he's been in is the fountain at the RTBG.'

'But you let him go?'

'He's his own self. From the very start he just naturally seemed – was – a person. We have no rights over him.'

Except that I nearly sold him. Luke's face prickled again and he wondered what colour he was.

Shona pushed her chair back. 'He's too big to stop anyway. There's likely lots of nasty things we can't prevent. You could borrow a kayak and go look for him.'

Shona pointed over Luke's head into the boathouse. Suspended high against the rafters was a brace of golden Huon pine Greenland kayaks – 3000-year-old Inuit technology originally using seal skin and whalebone, here made from a wood that could be the same age as the design, a timber now so rare and so slow-growing it was illegal to cut a living tree.

'I can't borrow one of those!'

'I don't see why not,' said Shona. 'You're about to put a lot of work into their garden and they're not paying you.'

Luke looked out across the estuary. A distant fishing boat returning with its aerial wake of gulls, a few poised or plunging terns. A huge empty expanse of water, teeming with multitudes under the surface. Alexander could be anywhere.

'We should do some work,' said Shona. 'Celia will see you and establish who you are. Morning is her time to sit in the front room and take tea.'

They gathered tools and carried them down to the earthworks. Luke was glad he felt natural wielding a pick and shovel, courtesy of last summer's Reticulation Project. His many cuts and grazes stung, but his muscles felt okay. It was better to be moving. He felt eyes on him almost as soon as he and Shona stepped over the Celia Line. Shona lifted a hand to the neighbour's window, where behind the reflections Luke glimpsed a helmet of pale gold hair, a silver blue shift and a frail hand that waved back. It looked like a hand that might drop the phone while dialling 000 to report a monster in the Marizzi's garden, but probably also had a personal emergency alarm.

Shona left him to dig reticulation trenches and wait for Alexander. He found digging soothing. It freed him to wonder how Alexander did his other "magic". How did he cast his voice into the inside of Luke's head? It was an actual sound, low-pitched, not quite distinct, like from old bone conduction headphones. Maybe he was creating a vibration, a radio wave the right frequency for Luke's skull, or those tiny listening bones buried in his ears, but not exactly right for anyone else's. Luke stopped shovelling to catch his breath. The breeze that cooled the back of his neck darkened the incoming tide. At least the tide was now in the right direction to push Alexander home. Was he still expanding into his element, brushing his belly on the seagrass, slithering through kelp, scaring timid rays, being investigated by leatherjackets? Had he been able to associate propeller noise with the destructive power of engines he already knew about in cars? Or was he limp, drifting, one of those props having broken his neck?

Stop thinking. Ring Gatta. He sat on the beach and dialled.

'What's happening, Lukey?'

'The place is good, Gats, but he went swimming and hasn't come back.'

'He woke up!'

'Oh, yes, sorry. And he talks.'

'Like in real words?' The thumps were Gatta hammering the table.

'Yeah. About the second thing he said after hello was that he wanted you here teaching him.'

Shrieking, probably running in circles. 'And he's okay – otherwise you would have said.'

'Yes, except he's been out in the river somewhere for over two hours. I'm wondering if I should go look for him.'

'Chill bro, he'll be totally okay.' Her voice held the complete lack of doubt she'd always had in Alexander. She'd always been right.

'Okay. You guys good?'

'No sign of Ty or evil redheads. Bec took me in to get books, now she's dug into your computer, been there for hours. I didn't know sister could even read. Ow!' A scuffle. 'You need anything?'

'No. Yes. Clothes.' *A plan.*

Bec's voice. 'I made Gats put you on speaker. We'll get Shona to swing past and pick up clothes.'

'Cool. Uh, Gatta, did you and Alexander watch any dragon movies?'

'What? No, of course not. They're stupid.'

So Alexander's dragons were his own, not Disney's or Dreamworks'. They existed. Luke related his conversation.

Another scuffle of girly celebration which Luke wished he could be sharing, though it probably included a headlock. 'What do they look like?' asked Gatta.

'I don't think he's got enough language yet to describe them.'

He returned to trench digging. Gatta's confidence in Alexander was inexplicable but it was infectious.

Chapter 40

Ten minutes later, Luke stopped again. Kelp gulls wheeling and squabbling out on the river had become a dogfight around a black head – a small seal or a very big cormorant – pecking and tearing at strips of its pale flesh.

It wasn't a seal. A demented screech and convulsion of fleeing wings rent the air as Alexander grabbed the leg of a gull and pulled it under the water.

Alexander's head surfaced again ten metres away. He heaved himself onto the sand.

He was nearly unrecognisable. Protruding from the pale pulpy mass of his old skin clinging to his midsection were his neck and head, his legs and a length of his tail. Stripped of the rotten old skin, they gleamed obsidian black. He wobbled for a moment and Luke stepped forward, but it was his legs readdressing themselves to bearing weight. His brain plainly worked: he lumbered up to a patch of green where the shadows of the junipers broke up his outline.

'Alexander?'

Not quite everything was in order. Luke felt a hum that he recognised but no actual words.

'Are you okay?'

Luke got an impatient nod, and understood that Alexander's speech was a technique he was still learning and required effort.

Alexander wriggled his head like his collar was itchy. 'Yes.' The sound scratched and grated in Luke's head.

Again, Luke felt disturbingly like his mother: 'You've been out a long time and I don't think you can drink saltwater. Do you want water?'

'Yes.'

When Alexander arched his neck to drink from the bowl Luke brought him, his muscles rolled the black skin in iridescent shades of blue and purple. Not like his colour displays but like a starling's feathers, refracting the light. Its immaculate sheen looked almost comical against the undignified sodden mess of his midsection. His *much bigger* midsection.

'You must have eaten some fish,' said Luke. 'A lot of fish.'

'I travelled. I saw. I ate fish.' His words were smoother. '**In the grass, I ate soft things with eyes and long hands.**'

Alexander had discovered squid. Luke received a short burst of what he himself felt when he ate bacon, which was bad news for the squid. '**I saw fish with wings.**'

Fish with wings? 'Cormorants?' asked Luke.

'**Not cormorants. Not pelicans. Not birds. Fish.**' Alexander stretched his front legs out sideways and waggled them, looking ridiculous.

'Rays!' said Luke. He sketched a diamond shape on the grass. Alexander scratched in a whiplike tail and a blunt head. 'Yes, you saw rays.'

'**Rays. They dream. They are not brave. But they fly very fast and do not move their wings except a little.**' He sounded puzzled and annoyed. Luke hoped his amusement wasn't showing. Or his realisation that Alexander was unsure about how flying was actually achieved, insecure about how he was going to use his wings once he had them out

'It's different in the water. I think you will fly like a pelican,' he said.

Alexander shuffled his shoulders and Luke felt again the encasing sloppy mess of disintegrating skin.

'**I heard. Engines. Many engines. And…**' A series of pops and crackles.

'I think that's crayfish. And prawns and things.'

'**And…**' Squeaks, whistles and an immense long booming moan that rose and fell and trailed into echoes.

'**Whales! You heard whales!**'

'**Whales?**'

Excited, Luke traced an arching back and flukes.

'**Like dolphins?**'

'Yes like dolphins, but much bigger.' He pointed up at the boathouse. 'Maybe bigger than that.' A not entirely welcome thought struck him. 'How big are you going to get, Alexander?'

'**I am becoming.**' He spread his talons like a concert pianist. '**I will know.**'

So he wasn't sure about that either.

Chapter 41

They slept on the grass through the afternoon, equally exhausted. Luke was much hungrier. He also badly wanted a shower; his sense of filthiness was now wholly his own.

By the time Shona arrived, the grass was deep in shadow and Luke was cold and ravenous. As she stepped from the cab she looked uncharacteristically apologetic, especially given the backpack which smelled of clean clothes and the cooler bag which smelled of dinner. Gatta tumbled out, followed by Bec.

'There was nothing I could do,' said Shona, hoisting a bulging hessian sack which smelled of things raw and bloody out of the back. 'They made me pick them up from Wentworth and they say they couldn't have been followed.' Wentworth Street was two blocks behind Luke's street. They must have gone through a lot of backyards.

'We met a few dogs,' said Gatta. 'But Bec is a dog goddess and she had chicken strips.'

Alexander was up on all fours like an ebony statue rolled in cheese. Gatta bounced over to him and laid her cheek on his neck.

'Stinkosaurus! You look boss. You'll look unbelievable when we get all the batter off! Doesn't he look like a half-eaten parmi? And you don't even stink that much.'

Happiness flowed.

'Hello everyone.'

At first Luke heard only crackling rumbles. It took him a few seconds to sort it into speech. The women looked like startled cats.

Shona said, 'I heard that! In my head.'

Gatta said, 'He's talking. Do it again?'

Alexander pulled his head in and his eyes almost rolled with effort. 'Hello Gatta. Shona. Bec. Luke.' He put gaps between each name. It was the speech that Luke had heard but the words were lower, fuzzier, like they came out surrounded by multiple tiny echoes.

'*We've got brains in our heads, feet in our shoes*, Dr Suess. Dead white guy but spot on anyway,' said Gatta. 'The places we will go, now we can talk to each other.' She stroked one of Alexander's claws. 'Maybe you won't need the shoes.'

'He's talking to all of us at once,' said Luke. 'It sounds staticky compared to when he's just talking to me, like he's doing it on a lot of slightly different frequencies.'

Shona turned her palms upward. 'Processing power again!'

When a much cleaner Luke stepped out of the bathroom, the women and Alexander were on the boathouse floor, unpacking dinner, Alexander's was on his tarp to protect the floor from bloodstains. Surely he didn't need more food! But he was already less round in the middle than a few hours ago. Was he longer? Could he possibly be growing that fast?

'You look adorable towelling your ears,' said Bec.

Luke successfully refused to blush. 'What's the fastest growing animal?' he asked everyone, but mainly Shona.

'Probably a bacterium,' said Shona. 'Let's ask Google.' She reached for Luke's laptop, which they'd brought as the second necessity after clothes.

'That might give you an answer by next week,' said Bec through a custard tart. 'It's slow as.'

Alexander had cracked and gulped his way through a leg with a hoof by the time Luke typed in "fastest growing animal".

'It might as well have been "fastest eating animal". I should have guessed. Lufengosaurus! A dinosaur. Good thing he's started to find his own lunch.' He told them about Alexander's morning.

Shona was paying attention but mainly she was frowning at his computer. 'It's slothy slow. I wonder – does anyone know anything about spyware?'

They all stopped. The buttery pastry in Luke's mouth turned to cardboard. He'd barely used the laptop since Ty had broken into it, so if Ty had loaded something on it, surely he couldn't have learned much. 'No, but you're right, it could be running a background program,' he said. Had he researched anything? Emailed anyone?

'I'll ping Elliot,' said Gatta.

His answer came in minutes. 'Get off the net,' said Gatta.

Luke disconnected.

Gatta's phone rang. She put it on speaker. 'Hey man, you think it's your uncle?'

'Could be.'

'Okay, you're offline? Good. This could be easy or hard – depends what 'ware he's used. Let's start easy. Control Panel, programs and features, scroll through them. Any you don't recognise, tell me.'

Everyone, even Alexander, watched as Luke ran his eye down the list of names, mostly capital letter salads, not really sure what he was looking for. If you were naming a spy app, surely you'd call it something innocuous. 'There's something here...MSXML 4.0 SP3 Parser. What's that?'

'Parseltongue!' said Gatta. 'Must be spy stuff.'

'I heard that,' said Elliot. 'No, it's a program that, ah, reads programming languages. Normal stuff.'

'Here's something that looks like a joke,' said Luke. 'I-eye-bot?'

'Shit,' said Elliot. 'Yep, that's a keystroke reader. It's a crude one. Either your spy isn't very smart or he doesn't care about being discovered.'

'Bec was on it all day, so the spy's brain would be smothered by cat videos,' said Gatta.

'Muscle cars,' said Bec, but she wasn't smiling. She shook her head quickly. 'Nothing about dragons. We didn't know exactly where you were, but no, no Google Earth of Clarke Avenue. Some searches and emails to some people...he couldn't possibly connect them with this.'

'No harm done then, you're sure?' asked Shona.

Bec nodded but was still troubled. Luke let it ride.

'Can I get rid of it?' he asked.

'That one, a factory reset will wipe it,' Elliot said. 'I'll run you through it.'

Now that it was no longer busy recording and bundling and sending off his private information, the laptop zapped through the restart. But—

'Um, Elliot, could this thing have been tracking the location of the computer?'

'Totally, it's one of the basic functions.'

'Even if I had location turned off?'

'Um, maybe not then. Some of the newer ones can still do it, but I-eye-bot is really last week. I can check it out for you.'

The evening sun slanting through the skylights lit the suspended kayaks like Huon pine chandeliers. It felt festive and warm as they ate, but now it was less a reunion and more the night before returning to the front lines.

Gatta wasn't letting any pissy threats dampen the night. 'Alexander. We're frothing to hear about the other dragons. Are they family? What do they look like?'

Alexander licked a claw clean of the last custard molecule then turned his face to them. The high tide sighed under the boat behind him, made the light slide back and forth along the polished hull and glance off the surfaces of his eyes. His flow of emotion to Luke abruptly ceased. In Luke's head, the voice scraped like gravel. 'I do not know if they were family. They came when I could not find Luke to follow him. They showed me their faces so I would know them.'

'Do they look like you? What colour were they?' Gatta edged backwards. Alexander looked rigid and remote. Like he needed space.

'They were not a colour. They were very long, with wings around their bodies. I do not know how big they are, in the world.'

He looked without seeing at the thick-moted air, like he was struggling to be at once in two places, infinitely far apart.

'I heard their voices. They did not all have the same voice. They asked me my name.'

'What did you say?' asked Luke, suddenly dreading the answer.

'Alexander.'

Luke swallowed. Even if only a little, some of him did belong to them.

'They searched inside me.'

Luke saw a flash of being naked and powerless. Gatta must have seen it too. Her face steeled in preparation to beat up a group of giant dragons in an unreachable dimension. 'Were they mean to you?'

'I was not afraid.'

Luke had no idea whether that reflected on the nature of the dragons, or Alexander, or whether it was even the truth or only the truth Alexander told himself.

'They had to find if I should go on.'

'And if you shouldn't?' Shona's voice was neutral.

'I would not become. I would stay in white.'

He would have died.

Instead, some kind of tribunal had made a decision on unknown evidence and he had come back. To resume a transformation he was following by instinct, with no idea of where it was heading. Instinct was deep brain patterning, like computer hardware. If that was a pattern, what else was? It was a difficult question to ask.

Shona asked it: 'Alexander, do you think the dragons were real?'

'They were themselves, not me.' He understood the question at least. Even if he didn't know the part of the answer that meant most to them: whether somewhere in the world, there were more living dragons.

'They did not show me how to use my wings.'

Luke didn't need an open channel to read his insecurity, resentment, longing. He didn't know how to respond and Gatta, for once, looked uncertain.

'Hah,' said Bec. 'If pigeons can fly, you'll do it day one. They're peanut-brained. We'll take you up to the Lakes where there's no one – only stupid pommy deer – and you can go crazy doing loops over water. Then next time you see dragons, it'll be you who shows them.'

Alexander perked up and showed all his teeth.

'As long as you haven't eaten so much you don't fit in the ute,' said Shona.

It was possible for a saurian face to look shocked and piteous. Luke laughed. 'You'd better just hurry up and shake those wings out.'

Shona was packing up. 'We have to go before it gets much darker. We can't plausibly be landscaping at night. I've got a sleeping bag which you can use in the cockpit of the boat.'

Luke returned to the subject they'd put aside. 'If Ty has tracked us... Shona, how does the security work?'

Shona pointed to a wall-mounted box inside the boathouse doorway. 'That's the control box. There's an alarm and a gate opener, as well as a button that'll secure all the doors and windows here and in the main house.'

Luke walked up to the stern of the boat. There was a metre-and-a-half of dark water between it and the doors onto the river. 'There's room here for Alexander to slip into the water and escape under the doors,' he said. With Alexander gone, what could Ty do to Luke that mattered?

'Hug, Lukey,' said Gatta, and then they were gone. The gate rolled shut with a clunk, followed by the softer click of the boathouse door.

Alexander arranged his distinctly bigger self onto his tarp. With his tail curved up to his face he could continue to admire the gleaming midnight perfection of his scales.

Luke settled on the perfectly plumped cushions in the boat cockpit and inhaled the leather. The smell of money. If Mum's product was successful, she could buy ten of these. Was that what she wanted?

He took out his phone. When Holly answered, her happiness poured out. 'Luke! Luke, it worked! It worked. I so wish you were here, my beautiful son.'

Luke's smile nearly cracked his face in half, though her tone spoke less of victory than overwhelming relief. How awful her last ten years must have been. Would he ever be able to tell her that her success dissolved some of his own fears too?

'So you've got your money, and your 80 per cent?'

'Yes! Well, nearly. Sorry, I've had a little glass or two. I wish you and Gatta were here.'

'So do I.' Luke had never seen his mother drunk. He pinged the gleaming rail next to his shoulder with his fingernail. 'Here's to UC186.'

'Salut to Oozy! She's beautiful, you know. The way she folds and unfolds herself to ooze through cells is quite miraculous. I feel like I discovered her, not made her. I'd like to show her to you.'

'I'd love to see her, Mum.' His mother was unfolding too. That dedicated, passionate person. Why hadn't she shown him earlier? Luke felt angry again at everyone who bullied her. Anders. Ty, even if she couldn't see it. And the company that thought they had the right to take control of her invention. But together, she and Luke had resisted and won.

Or had they? 'Ah, what do you mean by "nearly"?'

'Oh. One more hoop to jump through.' Holly sounded less drunk. 'Roger Hicks, the Paladin partner I met with. He said he had the delegated authority to approve the money, but not the terms, which are "extraordinary".' She was completely sober now. 'I need to present my business case to a full committee of the partners. Day after tomorrow. 2pm. He's sure I'll get approval, with his recommendation.'

'They'd be idiots not to snap you up.' The mahogany decking was perfectly smooth and cool under Luke's bare toes. 'Mum, once you start making money, what will you do with it?'

Holly laughed. 'Do? Invest it back into the company. Build my own lab and do more research.'

'But that's not what Ty would do?'

'What a funny question. But no, I suppose for Ty money is about showing he won, having a higher tower of coins.' She sounded sad. 'It'll never be high enough.'

Luke sank into the leather. Victory, well nearly, after a decade of hell for his mother. But for him? Would Mum getting her money be enough to stop Ty chasing Alexander?

Chapter 42

Luke settled down to sleep, soothed by the long hiss of waves on the sand. As he drifted, among the ghostly shapes of the two hanging kayaks came other, longer shapes, with no colour but glittering eyes and bass organ pipe voices that spoke to each other but not to him. Then out in the wide sky they flew, but with their wings against their bodies, like snakes swimming through air, and because they were no colour it was the sky itself which was flying. Luke didn't know whether it was his dream or also Alexander's.

In Luke's morning half-sleep, there was a soft scrape, followed by a splash as the dragon slid into the water next to the boat, impatient to shed what remained of his clinging decayed hide, to free his imprisoned wings and step upward into the sky.

Luke woke. No one had tried to come in during the night, and he smiled all through making coffee in his boxers and walking outside to examine the poly pipes, elbows and T pieces Shona had brought for today's work. Then his phone beeped. Rosie's number.

It's Adam. Rosie is in ICU. She's critical. Where are you?

ICU. Near death.

A fissure opened in Luke's heart. He discovered he'd intended to know Rosie not for weeks, but for years, a lifetime maybe. She was a person who offered help with all her brain and spirit, to everyone, human or animal.

Luke sat on the step to feel the solid wood underneath him. And if Adam blamed him before, how would he be feeling now? He needed more information or maybe just to gain time. He found the number for the Royal Hobart Hospital, which had the only ICU he knew of, called and was put straight through to the unit.

He didn't know Rosie's surname.

The man at the other end was detached but not unkind. 'You're obviously not a relative, then.'

'Yes, no, I'm sorry, but…' the words came out sticky through his dry mouth.

'I'm also sorry, but we can't give you any information. Our policy is for families to nominate one contact person and a password they need to give to staff.' The voice was softer. 'I'm so sorry.'

Did his gentleness imply…? Luke shook his head, refusing the thought.

He stared out at the empty river. Alexander would probably be gone for hours, but when he came back… Well, Adam had already seen him, albeit much smaller. And if Adam saw him again, and Rosie survived – she had, she would – Adam could describe to her what she had helped to save. Maybe that would help her recover.

He texted Adam the address.

I'll open the gate.

I'll call when I'm close.

Luke dragged on a shirt and shorts then went back to the box of parts and sat staring at Shona's planning diagram without seeing it.

Adam called only a few minutes later, before Luke was ready. His voice sounded thick, clotted with emotion. Luke's chest clenched again. He reached through the boathouse doorway and pressed the gate release. The gate slid open.

Adam came down the shaded driveway between the main house and the high wall. He was in his paramedic's uniform with the white shirt and badges and the broad-brimmed hat the country ambos wore. His head was bent under the hat, as if its weight was too much for his neck, and his sunglasses threw long blue shadows down his cheeks like tears. But as he passed the corner of the house and the sun hit his face, the shadows weren't shadows but bruising from his broken nose.

Luke's brain moved very fast then, but not far. In less than a second all Adam's close and solicitous care of his wife slid into its proper focus.

'Rosie's dead, isn't she?'

'Yes,' said Adam at the same time as his left hand came up from his side, holding a gun with a silencer.

'You killed her.'

'As good as,' agreed Adam. The gun seemed important, but Luke's brain was resisting its presence. How could a gun be here, on a blue morning on Clarke Avenue under the viburnums?

But Rosie was real. Beautiful sad clever loving Rosie was dead and vanished from Luke's future. The crack in his heart became a vast desolate pit. 'Because you were losing control of her.'

'Every time she went near you, she lost a bit more belief in being sick.'

Not near me. Near Alexander.

Adam threw his hat and sunglasses aside still looking bizarrely trustworthy in his crisp uniform shirt with the epaulettes. He jerked the gun twice to the left. The little movements jolted Luke back to the urgent present. Adam was ordering him into the boathouse because he didn't want to shoot him in the open, even with the silencer. Luke had to stay out of the boathouse.

'I wasn't doing it on purpose.' Luke didn't have to put much effort into sounding whiny.

'Inside,' said Adam, and gestured with the gun again, making Luke's stomach flop. Now it was the green of the viburnums that looked imaginary and the gun hyperreal, scratched and sullen and sickening.

Luke put up both hands. Placating. Slowing. He stepped up onto the landing, legs shaking, not having to pretend that bit at all. He reached across his body with his right arm to the left of the doorway, looking unnatural but he couldn't help that, fumbled for half a second to find the door closing button. He pressed it and in the same movement launched himself off the landing.

It all took much too long. Adam was only two feet away.

Luke was in mid-air, hurtling towards the grass. Already he was too slow, too late. His skin felt inadequate as wet paper waiting for the punch of a bullet.

It didn't come. Instead there came a snick. His hands jolted on the ground. Behind him, a clatter. He kept moving in an awkward somersault and his face hit the earth of his trench. There was a flat thud, and another, and two bullets peeeowed past his ear, sounding exactly like in the movies. An arm's length away, two little fountains of earth spouted from the soil. Over the Celia Line.

Adam was faster on his feet than with his Glock, which Luke learned later needed a slide action to chamber the first round, the action Adam had forgotten. Adam leapt off the deck, and in three steps stood between Luke's spreadeagled body and the water. His eyes above the swollen blue nose were indifferent. The gun waited, horribly still at Adam's belt buckle, hidden from any viewers behind as he scanned the terrain. Luke was pinned down by its eye. He stared at the lovely patch of ground that was

Celia's triangle of visibility. Even if he could get his feet under him fast enough to jump, even if Celia were watching, Adam would shoot him anyway. But maybe there'd be a witness. Adam saw him look, registered the screen of junipers and the watching window, made a decision. His trigger finger knuckle whitened, just as the background noise registered as voices. Behind him, three white hulls nosed into view.

'No, you don't get it. The ASX 200 doesn't include share buybacks.' Without breaking breath or stroke, yesterday's lecturing paddler led the group, trailed by the other two. 'It's a con by the Yanks. Their dividend yield on the S&P shows 2 per cent when ours is 4.4 on average.'

Adam sank to a squat, casually, so the gun was between his knees where the paddlers couldn't see it. His eyes locked on Luke's.

'The investment markets here are starting to realise, but too late. My advice to you is...'

If Luke yelled to them for help, Adam would shoot him. And probably them. If he didn't, Adam would shoot him after they passed.

They passed.

Adam rose to his feet. The wakes of the three paddlers had merged into a single black ridge. A gull cried.

Gatta. Mum. Shona. Alexander. Rosie. Anders. Anders? His brain was letting Anders in? Giving up, dying early?

The black ridge swerved towards the shore and broadened. A black head surged from the surface, water streaming off it, followed by a long black body now sleek and gleaming down its whole length.

Adam moved his feet apart and clasped two hands over the grip. As he stilled, prepared to fire, the dragon's head rose up over him.

The quality of Adam's stillness changed. He froze, like he was seized by a paralysing vision of another world. Then a circular torrent of fire erupted around his head. It blasted toward Luke in a scalding roar of red and yellow, with Adam's white face in the middle. The face, punched with three black holes that were his eyes and mouth, dissolved into the cataract of flame that streamed around it. For long seconds his body hung in the air, then the flames vanished and it dropped.

The circle of flame was burnt on Luke's retinas, scorched into the sky. When sensation returned to him, his hands were clenching the cool grass. He lowered his forehead onto it, tried not to think, just feel, feel the soft dew.

Alexander breathed fire. Tell Gatta he can breathe fire.

Alexander had dropped to all fours. His walk now was sinuous, graceful, without the sodden mass of his old skin. While his scales glittered midnight blue, the membranes curving close around his body were pure black. His face came close to Luke's. His breath was still hot, clean, and his body smelled of the river and something flinty, metallic.

'Are you hurt?'

'Yes. No. I'm not hurt.' If Alexander thought he'd been injured, he'd go back and give Adam a second blast. Even though he was dead. He must be dead. 'He missed me. I tripped. You got him before he could shoot me again.'

'Shoot you?'

'He was holding a gun. You didn't know he had a gun?'

'I smelled him. I came to kill him.'

'But how did you know— how did you know you wanted to kill him?' Luke swung his legs around, and sat up carefully.

'I smelled him before, but I was small. I had little teeth and no fire.'

'You smelled him? What do you mean?'

Alexander shifted restlessly. In his yellow eye, deep within the maze of mirrors, there was a flick of orange.

'He smelled very strong, with Rosie.'

Luke stared at Alexander, suddenly cold. When a lizard, he had smelled – *smelled?* – the monster in Adam? And because of that he'd come to kill him today? Was Alexander now going to roam around roasting the heads of people he didn't like the smell of?

'And before I killed him, I searched him.'

Luke's frown deepened. 'Searched?'

From the lizard brain, Luke felt indecision, reluctance. The yellow eyes turned far away. Then came apology. Apology?

A moment later Luke's whole being was crushed in a monstrous grasp, his heart was flayed open and every corner exposed to pitiless light. Every impulse of selfishness, any cruelty, greed, every last thought that meant exploitation of others, was made naked. Weighed and inspected. And measured, against generosity and kindness – which, in Luke, was most of him.

It lasted less than two seconds but Luke felt eviscerated, like his organs had been ripped out through his ribcage. His hands fluttered ineffectually at his chest.

'I'm sorry. I did not need to do that to know you. But to show you. Do you see now?'

Luke gave a tiny nod. Alexander was genuinely sorry, but Luke was struggling to reassemble himself. He closed his eyes to feel his breath move and his physical person reform around it. Reopened them to see Alexander was thoroughly miserable, his tongue flickering anxiously.

So Luke said, 'It's okay,' though it wasn't, yet. 'I understand,' though he didn't. Then, with a flash of insight, he did.

'You wouldn't have that ability... You wouldn't have to show it to me unless you had it for a reason. That's your purpose, isn't it? That's what you're for.'

'Yes.'

'But you haven't always known that.'

'No. Before, I was small. That time was for growing, seeing, smelling.'

'So, now what are you supposed to– How?' Luke swallowed. 'Who?'

'I do not know. I think other dragons get instruction. They do not grow up alone.'

Luke had a pang, which he thought he repressed successfully.

'I'm sorry,' Alexander said. 'I am not alone. I mean grow up without instruction.'

Luke's mind was flailing. Alexander thought he had an inborn obligation – to kill people. A *right* to kill people. To take on what humans had a justice system for and apply a punishment most countries had rejected. The first example lay behind him on the sand.

The smell...

Alexander turned his black head to Adam's body. 'That has another place now. I will take it. It can become fish.'

Maybe a lot of the body was also about to become dragon, but Alexander was being considerate. He grasped it somewhere near the shoulder and dragged it into the water. It floated there, dipping and rising gently, so Luke alternately saw the knees then the buttons on the chest, and beyond, something black and indistinct. Alexander adjusted his grip and in a flowing surge drew it with him under the surface.

Luke waited till he was certain all would remain hidden, then he got up and mechanically erased all the signs of the struggle in the sand, though who could have read them?

Then he sat back on the edge of the deck and folded his hands carefully on his thighs. He needed to talk to somebody.

Shona. He texted her.

Something has happened. Can you come?

He wiped his mouth with the back of his wrist, then added:

I'm okay.

After several minutes there was no reply. Luke was piloting his body by remote control, from a galaxy far away. He fetched the box of reticulation parts and laid them one by one on the grass in a calming pleasing order.

Chapter 43

Ninety minutes later, Shona and Bec rattled down the drive and got out.

'I was taking my tutorial group. I—' Shona stopped.

Luke stood facing his array of parts, white plastic on green grass, with a column of elbows and T junctions down the middle, all their side arms pointed precisely to the left. The arrangement was strictly ordered, pleasingly symmetrical. And purposeless.

Hand on the ute doorhandle, Shona frowned. 'And all this is for?'

But Bec went to Luke's shoulder, surveyed his work with him. 'What happened, Luke?'

'Adam killed...' he toed a pipe. 'Adam killed—'

'Adam killed Rosie, didn't he?' said Bec.

'Adam?' said Shona.

Luke nodded. He didn't care how Bec guessed. His brain and heart had no room left. Rosie. He cried silently, tears and snot flooding his face and soaking into his t-shirt. Then Shona's arms were around him, which should have felt wonderful but feeling had maxed out. She held him out at arm's length then, to examine him, with a grip that was frighteningly strong. 'Rosie's dead? You're sure?'

He nodded again, blinded by tears.

Bec stood back, dry-eyed, lips thin and white.

'Tell us,' said Shona.

Luke looked at the columns of white angled plumbing parts, broke Shona's grip and walked mechanically away and sat down by the water. They sat with him, trying not to let impatience show. He still felt remote, like the world was a distant assembly of fragments.

He wanted to keep flying further away, blindly, far enough till everything behind wasn't real anymore, went back to being okay. But he couldn't and it wouldn't.

'Rosie is – was – in ICU,' he mumbled finally. 'I rang them. I don't know how Adam killed her, but *he* said he did.

'Did he mean to?' asked Shona. 'Was Adam here? *What happened?*'

'He tried to shoot me. Alexander killed him.'

'Hooray,' Bec clenched a fist. 'He deserved it. But how did Alexander do that? Where are they?'

Luke saw again the scorched circle on the sky. 'Alexander can breathe fire. He immolated him. He pointed his toe at a black smear on the sand which wasn't a wash of diesel oil. The women pulled their legs up. 'Then he took the body away,

Shona's lips had trouble framing the words: 'Alexander saved you from being shot by Adam?'

'Yes, but Alexander didn't know Adam had a gun or that he was going to kill me.' Luke hesitated. Everything farfetched about Alexander so far had been physically obvious. The new part wasn't. It had to be taken on trust. 'He, he said he did it because he can smell evil.'

Luke was right. Shona's face went from shocked to frankly incredulous.

Luke went on, to get the worst of it out. 'And he's going to do it again, keep doing it. That's his purpose, he says.'

'Alexander thinks he's some kind of psychic vigilante?' said Shona. 'Presumably he didn't know that Adam had killed Rosie either. And none of us knows how or why.'

Dismay crept up on Luke with the steeliness in her voice.

'We don't know that Adam was evil,' she said. 'He could have gone nuts, not coping with the prospect of losing a wife all over again. Euthanised Rosie, came to shoot you because he thought you caused her last breakdown.' She didn't quite glare at Luke. 'And you believe Alexander can smell–'

Bec broke across her, snarling. 'Adam has been killing Rosie for months!' Her words came out in a torrent: 'And I could have stopped him. Fucking gaslighting her. Outsiders usually can't pick it, but of anyone I should have.

'Then I found that morphine ampoule. The one Adam brought that nearly killed Alexander, that he was so eager to find, remember? Something felt very hinky there. I picked it up. I found later its label was soaked off something else. It wasn't morphine, or it was a different strength. Adam tried to have Rosie kill Alexander to wreck her confidence.

'That was the first concrete sign, but all that "support" stuff he did? That was to suck out her self-respect, make her weaker. Did you notice he was always telling her she couldn't manage? And Shona, remember that her footy only started going backwards *after* Adam joined the coaches?'

Shona's lips thinned. She nodded.

'And food,' Bec went on, 'he always gave her too much. No anorexic could get her brain around that.'

Bec leapt to her feet and kicked viciously at the water. 'I put off telling Rosie about the ampoule till I had more evidence. *She loved him!*' Her jaw trembled with fury.

'I should have done something. Straight away! Removed her. Got her to move in with us. I thought I was being so fucking smart. I emailed Rosie's sister in Darwin. I found stuff about Adam that–'

Rage overtook her. No word was enough to express her contempt. She spat. 'I got her to look up his first wife, the one who supposedly died of cancer. There's no record of her on the RDH cancer ward.'

Shona's bright, challenging eyes were now hooded, her shoulders hunched.

'Alexander was bringing Rosie back to her real self,' Luke said to her. 'Adam thought it was me doing it. When that man tried to kill me that night on the mountain, I broke his nose. Adam turned up today with a broken nose, so I knew that man was him. Then he really had to kill me.'

Shona stretched uneasily. 'So Alexander picked a target who probably was evil. But we can't know for certain; it's not like we can interview Adam now. And you said he was going to keep doing it. Why? To whom? How can he know he's right?'

Luke's insides began to dissociate. 'He does an – examination. He did it to me, to show me.' A patch of water in front of them darkened. 'You can ask him yourself.'

Alexander's progress out of the water this time was graceful but leisurely, even somnolent. His eyes were half-lidded and he seemed to take several seconds to register the three of them, before his head rose smoothly to the height of Bec's waist.

'Luke, Shona, Bec.'

None of them moved for a moment. Luke was still finding it an effort to think or respond; Bec was still plainly in the throes of self-disgust for not saving Rosie. And Shona? She was remote, had retreated as far from Luke as she'd ever been. Numbly, the three of them stared at the new Alexander, a creature so much more than physically changed from the one they'd known.

Bec was the first to react. All her doubts were about herself; about him, she had none. Her focus shifted gladly to him and his transformation.

'Alexander! Is that really you? You've ditched the horrible cheesy coat!'

His neck stretched longer as he preened, peered back over his shoulders at his wings, like they were precious passengers.

'Come on,' said Bec. 'Show!'

He swivelled his head quickly, scanning for watchers, then his shoulder muscles bunched, the tendons coming alive under the skin. He hesitated, shimmied the metre-long bones. Then he unfolded.

The wings sprang out and snapped taut into a span as wide as he was long, deepest black and quivering, already restless. He looked at them with bursting anxious pride and gave an experimental flap, which lifted Luke's hair.

'Awesome,' said Bec.

They were. The sun and half the sky disappeared behind them, enveloping the humans in their shadow.

Luke shivered. An obscure fear stirred within him. He must still be in shock. But Shona must have felt something too; her face grew bleaker. Even more than Alexander's flame – which had killed – his wings presaged the creature he was becoming. Flight increased his reach, his power, manyfold.

'Alexander, you saved Luke, you eliminated Adam, saw his arseholeness when we didn't,' said Bec. She showed no evidence of a fear, and she rejected the doubts: she was defiantly on the side of the dragon. 'How do you do that?'

'How?' Alexander's tail quivered. He folded his new wings.

'I don't know if "how" is the right question,' Luke said, facing Bec, but speaking to Shona. Maybe he could reengage her into trying to work out the mechanism of Alexander's search. And if they determined that, it might somehow resolve the morality issues. 'It's a sense he has, like vision or hearing. It's like his emotional sense, I think, magnified a thousand times and focused for details. It can see everything, *everything*, even the stuff you hide from yourself. The only way he can explain is to demonstrate and he doesn't want to do that to you.'

Shona looked sad, like she was regretting something lost. Luke wondered whether it was respect for him.

But Bec persisted. 'Why not? How can you tell I'm not really an arsehole without doing it,' she asked Alexander.

'You smell good.'

Bec laughed. 'So smelling good is solid, end of story, but smelling bad needs further investigation?'

'Exactly.'

'I know there are a thousand ways to be an arsehole, but why would you want to tell them apart?'

'Because some arseholes do not need to be killed.'

They all blinked.

And Shona finally spoke. 'But the others do?' This was new information.

'The only thing required for evil to succeed is for good men to do nothing,' quoted Bec, then looked embarrassed. 'Or some shit like that. Except it should have included women and I should have done something.'

'Maybe we all should have,' said Shona. 'It's not like I wasn't worried.' She looked Alexander in his yellow eyes. 'But I still don't see why you make the distinction. Or how.'

She also meant "Or if you really can" but left it unsaid. Luke tried to warm himself with the thought. Despite her clear moral stance, she was allowing them a little leeway. She didn't shy from conflict but didn't enjoy it for its own sake.

'The people who smell bad are those who only act for their own selves. They do not see other living beings except to use for themselves. But some of them only grew like this because of fear or hurt and they can grow differently. Better.

'The ones I need to find cannot grow differently. They were maybe wrong in the seed and the root. But they will not grow differently.'

Bec's eyes were wide and bright. 'So you sort out the poor bastards who can't help themselves from the swamp predators?'

'Yes.'

'And you clean up the swamp predators?'

'Yes.'

Satisfied, Bec inclined her head, sat comfortably down and swept the flat of her hand over the grass, a gesture that could have meant benediction or decapitation. Shona's face remained unreadable, except for the implications ticking over behind her eyes. For her, the legal and moral questions had multiplied.

Luke couldn't face any more of it himself, now. In the course of the morning, his every thought and emotion had been bashed to an unrecognisable pulp. He had no strength left to engage with Shona on questions he wasn't even sure about himself. And he could tell Gatta about it all later. Now he needed to lie unthinking in the sun. He closed his eyes and enjoyed the silence in his brain, while over unknown walls and hedges, a car door slammed, a dog barked.

Alexander was growing sleepier too, sinking to the ground, his tail curled placidly and his eyes darkening to ochre. His wings fluttered restlessly and then settled.

Pop. Luke's eyelids flew open. The noise sounded both far away and very close and had a stomach-dropping familiarity.

Pop, pop, pop. Pop pop. Poppop.

Alexander looked startled, then mildly offended, then extended his neck and gave a reptilian smile and a burp. There was a waft of toffee. Luke would have expected sulphur, brimstone, but he didn't know much about firearms. He hadn't given any thought to Adam's gun, but now he knew where it had ended up.

'That was – the gun?' said Shona.

Luke nodded.

She peered speculatively at Alexander's distended abdomen as it worked on its contents.

'What does he have in there that can dissolve metal cartridges?' Her voice had regained some of its warmth. Luke realised it was a relief to her too, to put the tangle of moral questions aside, if temporarily, and engage with the fascinations of chemistry. '

'It would be great to be able to have a look, take a sample with an endoscope or something, but he'd probably dissolve anything you put down there to do it with. And what's his stomach made of that it can even contain an acid like that? We'd need a biopsy.'

Alexander's open eye was now glaring at her.

Bec giggled. 'It's okay, Alexander. Shona will have to wait till you die of natural causes.'

Shona waved an impatient hand at her. 'How do you make the fire?'

Alexander blinked slowly and closed his eyes. The work of digestion demanded sleep and it was creeping through him. The tip of his tail twirled once, acknowledging the question but dismissing it till later.

'Probably methane,' said Shona, to herself but including the other non-dragons. 'Maybe ammonia; that would be nasty!' She frowned. 'But how does he ignite it?'

The buzzer when it sounded could have signalled a submarine dive.

'It's the gate,' said Shona.

'It's the cops,' said Bec. 'Ambo missing. They're closely tracked. I think the police are door-knocking the street.'

Chapter 44

'Alexander!' Shona hissed.

Next to them, nearly two hundred kilos of saurian, of which possibly seventy kilos was rapidly dissolving evidence, lay comatose in the sunshine. He could have been polished black stone. Luke had a brief wild image of leaving a life-sized dragon shaped garden ornament on the grass. Followed by one of Alexander searing his second emergency services worker of the morning.

He put his mouth to the patch behind Alexander's eye. 'You have to wake up!'

An outer eyelid dragged upward but there was no comprehension in the gaze. The buzzer sounded again.

'Celia will have told them we're here,' Shona said. 'We have to open up.'

Luke bared his teeth. 'I can hardly hit him with a shovel.'

'You might have to.'

'Try this,' said Bec. She reached to the base of Alexander's left wing and squeezed. Both black spars sprang out, knocking her off her feet. The flailing tail whistled savagely over the back of her head. 'Ow!'

He was up on all fours swaying, his eyes unfocused.

'He can't go in the water like that,' said Luke.

'But he can go in the boathouse,' said Bec. 'Come on, tiger.' She grasped him cautiously at the wing base and pulled. He shivered hugely but didn't hit her with anything and after a pause he followed onto the deck. His tail slid to rest with a foot of it still protruding from the doorway.

Bec reappeared, toed it inside and gave Luke a grin of feral glee, which vanished at the clenched white of his face. 'Luke! Except for your name and address, you don't have to tell them anything.' She disappeared back inside.

Shona was already striding up to the gate. Luke darted down to the edge of the lawn and shuffled through Alexander's drag marks on the sand, thought too late of whether it looked like something had been deliberately obscured. The tableau of pipes was odd, very, but wouldn't lead anywhere useful. The bullets must have gone deep somewhere. Adam's shoe prints had been wiped by the advancing tide, all but one, which he trod on. Adam's hat and his glasses he kicked into the nearby trench and followed them with soil.

What else? Was Adam's gun the sort that popped out things when fired – casings? They'd be somewhere near the deck. A quick scan: no winking metal. And he was out of time. A blue-capped head was peering around Shona in the open gateway. Luke picked up a shovel to give himself something to hold.

There were two of them, both men, in blue overalls and fluoro safety vests festooned with nylon pouches and shoulder radios. They sauntered down the path, the one behind meaty, heavy-treading, looking like he'd had the same cropped haircut since high school; the younger, taller one in front with an open face, casual, dangly hands, and ears that might once have made him the class clown.

'You must be Luke,' the younger one said. His eyes were alert – no, not casual at all. He'd instinctively straightened on facing Shona and now Luke equally unconsciously slumped, so they were nearly the same height. 'I'm Constable Damien Hart.' He touched his name badge, 'And that's Sergeant Cresswell, Tas Police. An ambulance officer has gone missing near here this morning. We don't like our ambos missing, so we're trying to find him as quickly as possible.'

Luke nodded, attempting a neutral face.

Constable Hart laughed. 'It's okay, mate, that really is what we're doing. We're not about to search the place for your baggie.'

The other cop's eyes were sweeping the garden, his brows and eyes and mouth in horizontal lines. The brows tented briefly when he came to the poly pipes.

'This won't take long,' said Hart, 'because we don't have a lot of time. Shona tells us you guys are doing the garden, you've been here all morning, but you don't live here. Can I have your name and address?' He took out a plastic-covered notebook and pen.

The most innocuous question, but if the police had his address and they followed him up at home for some reason, could that help Ty to find him? 'Do I have to give it?'

'Yes,' said Hart steadily enough, though two sets of eyes were on him now. Three, because Shona behind them was grimacing and shaking her head minutely. Unhelpfully.

He stumbled through his name and address, spelling his surname. He couldn't have underlined any better that he was guilty of *something*. He could only hope they still thought it was a stash. He needed to help them leave. 'I can't help you find your ambulance officer.'

Even a baby policeman would have effortlessly recognised the lie-by-evasion. Their instincts sharpened further. They only needed to ask him the right direct question. Hart had produced a mobile phone. He turned its screen towards Luke. 'He might have been out of uniform. Here's a picture.'

On screen, Adam's face was the textbook ambo's picture of compassion and competence. But Luke saw down the well of fire, Adam's eyes in his last second of awareness, his silent screaming mouth. Luke's own face turned ice-cold, a peculiar patchwork of red and white with the flush creeping up his neck and blooming on his cheekbones. It was hopeless to pretend anything.

'I can't help you find him,' he repeated in a strangled voice.

The policemen exchanged looks and an understanding. The sergeant nodded once and ambled off, his eyes roaming the house, the yard. Hart made a show of putting his notebook away.

'Something has spooked you here and I don't think it's just us. I do think it has something to do with Adam. But you can't tell us for some reason.'

Luke hunched miserably.

Hart waited, his eyes clear and patient, concerned but not pitying. He opened a space between them.

'Were you planning the irrigation plumbing this morning? You look very organised.' He glanced at Shona. 'Maybe a bit too organised.'

She peered back stonily. Luke watched Hart making a mental note.

'I think sometime this morning you saw Adam.'

Luke twiddled the handle of the shovel and shifted on his feet, head down. There was no point hiding his anxiety now. On Hart's question, his knuckles whitened on the shovel, a reflex, signalling an affirmative. Except it wasn't an affirmative, it was a reaction to, just a metre away in the longer grass near the deck, one step from Shona's boot, a glint of brass. He grunted, his feet propelled him away from the tell-tale casing, and he started poking the ground with the shovel. Movement, movement drew the eye.

Hart followed up on his apparent success. 'Okay, you did see him. Something happened. Something you can't tell us about. Maybe involving somebody you're scared of?'

Luke was making thrusts with the shovel, precise perpendicular cuts, marking out a square. Acting out his anxiety, encouraging Hart, making him watch the shovel. Not the bright shiny casing. The sergeant, the one whose eyes were everywhere, he had been watching the shovel too, but now his gaze was drifting down to the shore, examining the scuff marks, then turning to the house and the patch of too-sparse lawn. Any moment now, he'd spot the brass.

'You don't have to tell us exactly what you saw,' said Hart. 'Just give us a hint that points us in the right direction, then we find it out ourselves and the information won't be linked to you.'

Luke made segmenting slices across his neat turf square. He couldn't do this forever. What was their next move?

Cresswell was walking towards Shona. She took one step forward. The sergeant's chin cocked. Had he seen the casing, seen her step on it? Luke's brain stalled. Static. The sergeant's blunt hand came up; he grasped his shoulder radio and swivelled, listened, talked.

He dropped the radio again. 'Take him to the station,' he said to Hart. 'No more off the record.'

'Hold on.' Shona turned without moving her feet. 'You have no right to do that. You haven't said you're arresting him. And Luke is a minor.'

The air crackled with ice. Science decreed no temperature lower than absolute zero, but science was full of errors like that.

'Is that right, son?' said the Sergeant. 'How old are you?'

'Seventeen.'

The station. Not good. But away from the brass casing and an unpredictable dragon. What if they found Alexander? And he thought they smelled *bad*?

'We can't question you without the presence of a parent or guardian.'

'Luke's got a single mum and she's in Sydney.'

'It's okay,' Luke said to Shona. 'You can be my guardian. We'll go.' Belatedly, 'Why do we have to go?'

'Information that changes the situation. Over my pay grade to question you now,' said Cresswell. He sounded reluctant. Wondering why Luke was eager to talk at the station?

'Take pictures,' he said to Hart. To Shona: 'The owners are away. Does anyone else have a remote for the gate?'

They were leaving, but the police wanted the scene not disturbed. The problem wasn't solved, just pushed down the road, unless Bec remembered about the casings, which she wouldn't. They couldn't call her – the ringer would be heard through the boathouse wall.

Shona fished in her pocket and held up her remote. 'This is it. Nobody else can get in.' She lied by evasion like Luke; she was just better at it.

'Can I call my sister?' asked Luke.

'Luke's got a little sister he's caring for. I take it we might be a while,' said Shona.

'Do it,' said Cresswell. Hart was snapping photos industriously. 'Make sure you've got the whole beach. Then we'd better go.'

Luke could keep his face down, dialling. Gatta answered.

'Hi Aggie. Something has happened and I need to go talk to the police about it.' The forbidden name shocked her into silence. 'It's all okay, but I might be late. Call Bec and ask her to take the beast for a walk, will you? And help with those chemistry cases.'

A pause. 'I'll do that. Totally,' said Gatta. No freakout. What a star. 'Are you okay, Luke?'

'Yes. Thanks, Aggie.'

In the police car, Cresswell sat next to Luke on the back seat with its clear shiny cover while Shona sat in front and Hart drove. Did that mean Luke had transitioned from witness into suspect? What was the further information the police had? Without a corpse, there was no evidence of a crime and surely now that was beyond reach. Alexander had obviously swallowed a huge something and his guts melted the bullets.

Then Luke's stomach flopped like a flathead in a bucket. What if the Alexander had left portions for the fish after all? Identifiable body parts? A waft of old vomit from the footwell rose up, slid into his mouth, mingling with the taste of coffee. Luke scrabbled at the window but of course he couldn't open it.

'Nearly there,' said Hart, eyeing Luke in the rear-view mirror. Maybe it was his job to mop out the patrol car. When they pulled up on Liverpool Street, he darted around to open Luke's door and murmured, 'Sorry about the back. Cresswell's car is the only one with plastic on the seats and the only person who's ever puked in there is his three-year-old.'

Luke's stomach subsided, though remained mutinous as Hart led them through a maze of hard-used corridors deep into the building

They were left alone in an interview room. It was bland, windowless and cramped, with a table and four brown plastic chairs. And two cameras in opposite corners of the ceiling. There was no way of telling whether they were turned on. Luke and Shona exchanged glances, made an unspoken agreement not to talk.

They sat in silence, their chairs at right angles, which let Luke stare uninterruptedly at Shona's profile. Figures, in and out of uniform, went by the open door. A few glanced inside. Restless, Shona got up to lean on the wall by the door. In faded khaki drill, she radiated energy, physical work and sunshine, and made the room smaller.

She didn't sit when the two detectives came in.

'I'm Detective Auld and this is Detective Simpson,' the male detective said.

Detective Simpson carried a laptop and had a trick of disappearing from notice as soon as she sat at the end of the table. Auld carried a file and looked like a distance runner. The sports watch on his lean muscled forearm bristled with knobs and had a face large and shiny enough to shave in.

He sat opposite Luke, nodded at both of them then pointed at the cameras. Simpson hit a button on her laptop and a red eye sprang to life in each corner. So they hadn't been turned on.

'This interview is being recorded, both audio and video. If you do not wish it to be recorded, you should say so now.' He paused. The unwinking red eyes recorded Luke not protesting. 'Could you state your name for the record, please?'

Luke gave his name and address, Shona gave hers. He agreed on the date and time, nodded when he was told he was being interviewed as a witness, not a suspect. After that he couldn't answer anything. He'd already figured the police tactic would be to get him into a rhythm of answering before springing the important things, but all the questions were unanswerable anyway: 'What time did you get to the property this morning?'

It was yesterday. I stayed overnight with my fire-breathing cannibal friend. Is it cannibalism if a human-like dragon eats a human?

'Were you by yourself till Shona came?'

No, Adam was there, and he still is, as molecules. What is it that you guys know?

How fast could his heart go?

Auld persisted for several minutes, neither friendly nor hostile. Eventually he fell silent, gazed at Luke for a few seconds, as though the outcome was what he'd expected but he'd needed to give him a chance. He folded his hands on the file on the table.

'You're not talking to us as you have the right not to. But this isn't some schmuck we're looking for. Adam Cain is an emergency services officer, one of us, and we're going to find him; for us, as well as for the community's sake, and for his friends and family.' He was speaking reasonably but his eyes – wintry grey – drilled into Luke's. He waited.

'Or at least we need to find out what happened to him.'

They knew Adam was dead. How did they know? What was it they'd found? Luke had a vision of a floating hand, white, swollen and trailing torn tendons at the wrist. He swallowed.

Auld waited, letting the silence thicken till it pressed into Luke's ear canals, then all the other openings in his head. Shona's head was tilted back against the wall. Deliberately she laced her fingers in front of her thighs. Saying to Luke: *Wait it out. It's okay to say nothing.*

Finally, Auld said, 'This morning we got the call from Tas Ambulance that they'd lost contact with Adam Cain. His first intervention vehicle has a transmitting GPS and we found it parked at the bottom of Finlay Street a hundred metres from where you were working.' His eyes remained level. 'This information doesn't appear to be a surprise to you.'

What had they found? Had someone linked Shona to Adam through football? Did paramedics have their fingerprints on file?

'Our patrol officers have been doorknocking Finlay, Clarke and Secheron Streets and searching the CSIRO carpark and foreshore.'

And they found an arm. Adam *had* been disarmed. Luke clamped his lips over a hysterical laugh.

'And they obtained a description, from a credible witness two houses down from you–'

Of a floating torso with Tas Ambo epaulettes.

'–of shots fired. Silenced shots, two of them.'

The sludge-thick air suddenly loosed, flowed freely into Luke's lungs. The police had shots. Not a body. Or part of one.

Auld noted the drop in tension and paused, evaluating. 'We think that can't be a coincidence. We think that Adam Cain has met with harm. Two shots close together indicate that harm was not self-harm.'

No body. No proof of murder. Though what was that woman's name, the one on the boat, her partner's body never found – the one who'd only just been paroled after 13 years? Whose supporters seemed to be in the media every second week. Sue Neill-Fraser.

'You were outside, next to the water, which carries sound. Did you hear shots, Luke?'

Luke gazed back, expressionless.

'Did you see someone shoot Adam?

Luke's head was shaking before he could stop it. Auld scratched his upper lip and regarded him wryly. 'You really are bad at evasions.' He leaned back, stretching. 'But you seem like a bright kid. What are you doing out of school, anyway?'

Luke found himself saying, 'I'm doing a self-directed learning unit.'

Shona's laced hands stiffened. *He's making you talk. Be careful.*

'Well, that must be because you're smart and trustworthy, not because you're stupid.'

Luke said nothing, shrugged.

Auld sighed and leaned forward again, straightened his rolled cuffs. 'Let me summarise. Our patrol officers believe, and I believe, not that you committed an offence but that you witnessed one and that something has you afraid of answering questions about it.'

Luke just managed not to nod.

'That's not uncommon with witnesses to serious offences, so there are ways around it. This is where I have to explain some options to you.'

Luke did nod, then wondered whether he should have.

'If what you are afraid of is implicating yourself, you should ask to talk to a lawyer. And in the meantime, I need to tell you that you are not obliged to answer any questions, but anything you say or do can later be used as evidence in a court.'

Luke blinked.

'If you're afraid of implicating someone else, you need to know that you can be charged with withholding information about an indictable offence if you don't have a reasonable excuse, and you can go to jail for two years. Being a minor is taken into account.'

He swung around suddenly to Shona. 'But it isn't in your case, Miss Garang. These warnings fully apply to you, if you know what Luke knows, which I think you do.'

She didn't bother about not looking hostile; she glared at him.

Auld rose fluidly to his feet. 'We'll suspend the interview at this point.'

Detective Simpson seemed to rematerialise at the end of the table. She hit a button on her laptop. The red eyes faded.

'There is no other recording in this room, so you can have a chat about your options. And sandwiches and coffee if you want them.'

The door closed behind the detectives. Shona raised an eyebrow at Luke. Unspeaking, they agreed on continued silence. Luke put a palm to his chest. *I can breathe now. And thanks.*

Shona replied with two straight fingers on hers. *We're doing this together.* Her hand became a fist. *Hang in there.*

Galaxies were born and died while Auld and Simpson didn't return. The sandwiches came and went. Luke lay his head on the table. He could eat for an hour and sleep for a week. His head was so full of things to think about he refused to think about any of them.

He must have finally fallen asleep because when he raised his head, Auld was talking to him.

'Miss Garang says neither of you have anything further to say.' He pointed at the cameras, which were on.

'Can we go home?'

'Yes.' Afternoon stubble had hollowed Auld's cheeks. 'But this is not going away, Luke. We're getting a lot more information and, somewhere, you are going to feature in it. You need to tell us your side. Soon.' He gave them each a card.

Detective Simpson, whose first name was Briony, drove them back through the 5pm traffic in an unmarked car. They'd made it past St David's Park, nosed around a plumber's ute, before Luke's brain woke up. Shona's ute. If Bec had understood his message, she'd had plenty of time to carry out his instructions. But what if she hadn't? And what had she done with the Courier? If it wasn't on the property when they got there, surely Simpson would twig?

The Courier was parked next to the boathouse, as it had been that morning.

Simpson expressed her admiration of the view and the convenient situation, the precision of their earthworks and the layout of pipes and the laburnums, which surely were flowering very late. Shona and Luke waited till the gap in the gate had slid completely shut behind her before Shona said quietly, 'That woman is scary. She should be with ASIO.'

The beachfront showed no signs of the morning's violence. The sand had been wiped clean by the tide, smooth and golden in the afternoon sun, marked only by the prints of a single departed oystercatcher.

'Rosie's really gone,' said Luke. 'The man in ICU was trying to tell me without telling me.' *I'm so sorry.* 'Makes all the shit we're in feel trivial.'

'Yes.' Shona wrapped her arms around herself, her face infinitely bleak. 'It feels even more shit that grief will have to wait while we're still in it.'

Chapter 45

Luke's phone pinged. Bec.

Cops gone?

Yes.

The boathouse door slid open and Bec and Alexander emerged. Alexander bulged less in the middle and was possibly longer at the ends. His tail shimmered but he was dusty forward of his wings and Bec had thrown on a pair of grubby jeans and some elderly trainers. Between them they looked very un-Clarke Ave.

'Got the chemistry cases – *casings*,' said Bec, grinning. Luke and Shona grinned back. They couldn't help it. 'Alexander sniffed out a very suss hat and sunnies in a trench. Got those too. How'd you guys do? Looks like the police didn't bang you up, anyways.'

'The police searched you?'

They all flinched. Alexander's first words in a conversation were still unsettling, like a large beetle scratching around in your head.

'Not quite like you do it, Alexander,' said Luke. 'Lots of questions but not remotely as effective. And they take a lot longer.'

'They discovered no facts?'

'Not much. But somebody nearby heard the shots and I couldn't hide that I saw something. They know, and they'll definitely be back. They'll ring Mum and probably get on to Ty and he'll know where we are.'

What do I tell Mum?

'The cops need a warrant to do a search,' said Bec.

'But if they can locate the Marizzis in darkest Sicily, they'll get permission instead, so, Ty or not, we need to find somewhere else for *you*,' Shona, engaging with sorting out the shit, nodded at Alexander, 'pronto.'

Alexander was regarding his dusty chest with displeasure. **'I am dirty. I will have a bath before I go somewhere else.'**

He vanished into the river. At least there he had an almost infallible escape route. When the wind blew, his head was indistinguishable among the dark wavelets. Even electronic eyes couldn't see him. Half a kilometre out at sea, the slab-sided hull of the icebreaker *Aurora Australis* blazed orange as it turned across the sun. Its sonar arrays would detect him but conclude he was a leopard seal.

'We've been for a drive. I've found new digs for him,' said Bec, tracing her finger along the fender of the ute, which had acquired a fine yellow-grey coat of gravel dust.

'A friend's place? The friend not in residence?' said Shona, sitting on the deck.

'Jules Charny. A man I used to know.' Bec sat next to Shona. 'He was one of Mum's boyfriends, classier than her usual. He used to buy me ice-creams. He called himself The Emperor of Ice-Cream.' She smiled benevolently down at an imaginary child.

'He behaved like a dad, he'd sit down and listen to me talk; no one ever had. I chattered at him about everything. I knew he was making nice with Mum's girl so he could get into Mum's pants. I didn't care But I had it wrong.' Her voice was light. 'It was the other way round.'

Shona looked like Luke felt: that she had spiders crawling on her. And why was Bec telling them this now?

'It didn't take him long. He had money, he smelled nice, he talked about London and Amsterdam and shit, and I'd never even been to Launceston and I was so proud that it was me he wanted.'

Luke's stomach shrivelled to a hard clenched fist.

Bec's voice was even lighter. 'I felt so beautiful and important and interesting. You know *The Emperor of Ice-Cream* is a poem? It's about big cigars and wenches and horny feet and I thought he meant it for me, about what to do. I would have done anything for him. And I did. So when his friends thought I was beautiful and he said he didn't want me letting him down with his friends and I thought he wouldn't love me... There's a part in the poem about covering the face with a sheet, and he had me do that part. It wasn't ice-creams by then, it was morphine and that helped.'

She jerked up and did a grotesque twirl and a skip on the grass. 'He'd go to school sports days with me as my dad. It was our secret and he was so good-looking and I was so proud to run for him, nobody could beat me. But it wasn't me he was watching: it was the Year 8s. And one day he told me I'd been sleeping with all these guys because I was a whore and a slut and he'd tried for a long time to still love me but he couldn't do it anymore.'

Luke and Shona, sick with horror and pity, hadn't noticed Alexander had returned until Bec looked past them, down at the river. 'I was taller than him by then, but mainly I'd got too old.'

The light picked out rainbow colours across Alexander's wet body and ignited his eyes, two tiny fires against the charcoal water.

'You heard Alexander say this morning he could tell which bad ones were made that way by life happening to them? We went to see him – Julie was my name for him – today.' Now her voice was saturated with self-disgust. 'I thought I wanted revenge, but pissweak little girl, I still thought – can you believe? – there was a chance he'd pushed me away because he was *damaged*, he'd been hurt once, he was *afraid of love*.'

Luke couldn't bear to hear any more.

But Alexander showed no signs of having eaten a whole paedophile. Luke peeked again for reassurance. No, not even one shorter than Bec. Maybe meeting Alexander had made him apologise, or something.

'His main place is down near Birch's Bay, lots of trees, a fire pit, places to play hunting games; no little girls were hurt in the making of this movie. I texted him. He hadn't heard a single fucking word from me since the day I left – I wasn't quite… broken enough to let him ghost me – so he was curious about what I wanted. He never thought about people so he couldn't have expected I'd be dangerous or even different. And who would expect Alexander?'

Shona's face was the colour of clay.

'Alexander was in the trees, not even I could see him, and Julie was outside by the fire pit. How convenient. He was just the same. I was hoping he'd have man-boobs or dyed hair but of course he didn't. He was just picking up my not-happy vibe when Alexander turned on his searching thing and Jules went…

'It was a total mind-fuck just watching. It was like Jules saw everything Alexander was seeing, and he knew himself for the smear of dogshit he was.'

Luke rechecked Alexander's middle.

'No, Alexander didn't eat him,' Bec said.

Luke's stomach unclenched slightly.

'He couldn't manage two psychos in one day. He incinerated him.'

'It was wasteful.' Alexander sounded apologetic.

'He's gone, ashes, blown away. It was windy.' Bec ran a finger down the Courier's door panel and laughed. 'Don't worry, Shona, this is driveway dust. Mainly.' She looked absently at her shoes. 'I don't mind walking all over him for a while. I don't mind that at all.'

Shona was gripping the deck, arms rigid, neck bent so low her face was lost in shadow, her voice so soft they hardly heard her: 'Bec, I'm so sorry. There are no words...' Then she looked up. 'But Alexander, you're two for two. If they smell bad and there are no redeeming features, they get executed?'

'Ah, not exactly,' said Bec. 'Marko and Fourby rocked up and saw Alexander doing cremate-while-you-wait. They're a couple of low-lifes who used to fetch and carry for Julie – he called them *serfs* – coming today for who the fuck knows, but they didn't have enough brains to run, or probably thought they were having a bad trip flashback, whatever. Alexander searched them.'

'They were mostly rotted, made wrong by others when children, but some good was still in them. They can grow right again.'

Shona said, 'So they're still alive?'

'Yes.'

'Are they different now? I mean do you change anything?'

'I cannot make change. But what I see, they see. I uncover everything that is buried. Maybe they know they can grow better and now they will do it. Maybe they will not. That is not my affair. My purpose is to remove those that cannot grow better.'

'But they're alive, awake, functioning?'

'Yes.'

'Which means they could tell someone about what happened and who killed the bastard?' Shona's voice was stony.

Bec shook her head. 'When we left they looked like their brains were firebombed. Who are they going to tell? Who would believe them? I don't think they're even going to be able to tell themselves.'

Shona turned into the twilight and raked her braids off her face. A lopsided moonrise spilled wan light down Droughty Point. Shona's conflict wrung Luke's guts. She didn't believe Alexander could see inside a true self, so his executions were murder. And Bec had just instigated an execution. But Bec's story; what had been done to her. She hadn't pointed a living blowtorch at an old boyfriend because he'd merely dumped her.

The moon sucked itself free of the horizon. Shona turned back to them. She couldn't challenge Bec, her friend, with her private wounds laid open, but she could disagree about the threat level.

'When the police catch up with them – Marko and Fourby – they will notice two separate healthy men going missing in one day, leaving three fugue-state non-witnesses, the other one being you, Luke. They'll be back here. They're coming back anyway. You said you had somewhere for Alexander to go.'

Bec dug in a pocket of her jeans and produced a pair of keys. 'Asshole had a bolthole. It's on acreage on Garden Island Creek, behind the Clennett Hills. None of his serfs ever went there and it's not in his name.'

She turned to Alexander, who had become a coiled darkness in the shadows on the deck, the last light capping the ridge of his back. 'It's got a field in the middle of a forest, buckets of air, good for checking out those wings.'

His eyes lit like tiny headlamps. 'Will we go soon?' He flared his wings, two great hands with immensely long skeletal fingers, black sails billowing between the tips. He beat them a couple of times for emphasis.

Luke's phone pinged. Gatta. It seemed he'd travelled a thousand miles since he'd last seen her. Yesterday.

> Luke, what's happening?? Weird Ty stuff here but he's gone now. Come home tonight?

'I need to go home.'

'Looks like everyone needs to move,' Shona said. 'We can all go in my ute to the uni, I pick up Bec's car to take you home Luke, and Bec can take Alexander to the bolthole.' Her voice had a stilted quality that nobody missed. Alexander's eyes went dark, but he was still rehearsing flying movements. The swooshes of air smelled faintly coppery.

Chapter 46

'We're going to need a bigger truck if he keeps eating people,' Shona said as she climbed into the driver's seat of Bec's XH. Her Courier's tail lights receded. 'Or you are.'

A sickening chill in his guts. No better because he knew it was coming. Luke nodded. He thought he'd vomit if he tried to talk.

'He's turned into a monster, Luke. What he says about judging people? I've got no doubt he believes in what he's doing, but he's not even a human, he's a lizard. How can he possibly understand humans? Society? Morality? Let alone set himself up as a judge?'

'He sees…' But Luke couldn't find any words to describe the naked exposure of Alexander's *search* – the feeling of being completely, dispassionately understood.

Shona waited but he couldn't get any further. 'He sees? But what is he doing really? It certainly sounds like he does something to the heads of the people he *sees*. From the external manifestations it sounds more like a kind of ECT, putting a current though their brains, something like how he talks to us but a different frequency.' She put a forefinger on either temple, miming electrodes and stared at him, challenging him. Then she slid her hands up to clasp her head.

He'd held one of those hands. Only once.

'I know you believe it, Luke, and he believes it, but there's just no way it could work. And he uses this to justify killing people.' When they'd parted with Bec, she'd hugged them with a new, unburdened warmth, which Luke had awkwardly returned. Shona's response had been even stiffer. Now she was as cold and remote as the moon.

'He said the truly evil may be bad from the start, the root and seed he said, and he can tell. Does that mean he's going to kill *children*? *Babies*?'

Luke hadn't imagined this nightmare could possibly get worse. A horror more unspeakable. His brain batted away images.

'I don't know,' he whispered.

She went on. 'And if he does, are you going to accept it?'

It was the worst silence of his life. Shona relented a little, by breaking it. 'Adam, I could accept, sort of. Only because the other option was you'd be shot dead. But this man that Bec– Yes, he's the worst kind of serial paedophile, but the legal penalty for that isn't death.'

Outside, one of the streetlights popped and flickered.

'I'm not going to rat you out. I can't do that. But I can't be a part of it anymore, except to help you get him somewhere where he won't do any more damage.'

The streetlight flared, unnaturally bright.

Luke found words, because he had to. 'But he does see, and he understands. He showed me, I know what it feels like, like you can hide absolutely nothing. It's like the brightest light ever on everything you've ever done, not only what you've done but what you thought about doing it. He understands down to the last neuron. So he *can* make a judgement.'

'Luke! You can get exactly that experience from an LSD trip! He's put some kind of current through your brain and that's how it reacts, those are the coloured lights you see. Think for a moment. How could he possibly, conceivably, get all that detail in one instant, from your brain into his? That's mind-reading, which is impossible. This is not a fantasy, Luke. Alexander is as real as you and me. And he's really going to kill more people, maybe innocent ones.'

Luke said nothing, but stared back, frozen with misery. Then the heat boiled up in his chest. He punched the glovebox. 'Unexplained is not inexplicable. How could you know? How could you possibly know?' Suddenly she didn't feel four years older. His tongue was thick with anger. 'Just take me home.'

She started to say several things, stopped. She started the engine.

Haloed lights blurred past in the night. He wound down the window and stared out, trying to control his breathing, all the way to South Hobart. His rage propelled him out of the car, drowned out whatever Shona said, almost inaudible anyway. He stopped short of slamming the door. But as the XH drove away, he watched the tail lights till they disappeared. He kicked the kerbstone. His anger sputtered out.

Gatta burst out of the house wearing a long-sleeved green velvet dress with white frills at the wrists. And Docs.

'Luke! Ty was here and he's not the guy you hit! I mean, yes, with the shovel but not the one with the knife whose nose you splatted. It's a different guy. Get inside, now! McSplatterface could be out here.' She grabbed his arm. 'Urgh. You're freezing and you stink.' She dragged him into the hallway. 'And Ty's gone super weird, new-weird. I don't know what he's up to. He– Lukey, what's happened?'

Luke felt like only shivering was keeping him upright. 'Is there anything to eat?'

'Ty brought curry. Amazement! It's green but I'm guessing it's safe to eat. I don't think his plan is plutonium poisoning.'

Twenty minutes later, two-thirds of the Thai curry down, Luke was starting to revive. The Luke-zombie reflected in the kitchen window was more lifelike and moving pretty freely despite the gravel rash and the knife wounds. The scar on his jawline was healing. But the eyes were still hollow. It was his insides that felt most battered by the day.

Rosie. *Would Alexander kill babies?* Luke would have to ask him. Would he get the chance to tell Shona the answer?

Gatta had been impatiently quiet. 'So, Luke, you good to spill now?'

He nodded. This was his warm kitchen with the lemon tree nudging at the window and the table littered with half-full bowls, and this was Gatta and he didn't have to pretend anything. He got to the part about Rosie.

'Adam admitted killing her – "as good as" – but she got into ICU. He must have made it look like not murder. I hope it wasn't; that she didn't suffer.'

Gatta went to the window and rubbed noses with the lemons on the other side. She leaned her forehead on the glass. Luke went on to Adam's attempt to shoot him, which wasn't the worst thing that had happened today. Alexander's judgements. The detectives. Bec's history. What she and Alexander had done. He told the trip home in four words: 'Shona's off the team.'

'She'll be back, she'll work it out and, besides, she likes–'

Luke made a cutting motion with one hand.

While he was talking, Gatta had picked up a spoon and bent it nearly double, then back, so the inverted bowl became a head with a sinuous neck and a silvery body. She bared her teeth at it.

'He breathes fire,' said Gatta. 'Of course he breathes fire. He's going to fly. He's a real dragon.'

'Apparently.'

'Flying, fire. Checking you out for evil. How did it feel?'

'Totally munted. Like I'd opened up my brain, and everything.' He opened both palms like a book. 'But I believed it. If he did it to Shona, she still wouldn't believe it. She'd still think it was some kind of trip.' His hands clenched. 'I know this is all big, but can we talk about something else now?'

Gatta placed her spoon dragon on the windowsill so it was facing itself in the glass.

'Yes. Ty. He was just *wrong*. Like someone had taken control of his body. Maybe he was a beetle colony, Ty-shaped, walking around wearing his skin.' She sighed.

'No, it was really him. You know how he makes no noise, he sneaks in and he's just suddenly there and you don't know how long he's been there for, looking at you? Well, he did that and I finally saw him, then get this, he said, "I never knock." Then he said, "Hello, Gatta". When has he ever, like ever, called me that? Then he said something like, "I'm not staying but tell Luke I want to talk to you together. We've got matters to address and I don't want to do it twice". Then he said you could "nominate a venue" but he didn't want anyone else there. Then he put the curry on the sink he looked at me and he said, "I'm sorry about Thatso". I just said "Whatevs" because I had to say something and he said, "Will you ask Luke?" like him being sorry would make me do it and I didn't say anything and he left.'

Gatta traced question marks on the nap of her green velvet sleeve. 'What does he want, Luke?'

'I don't think he wants to kill us now, if he ever did. He wants Alexander. He's got his DNA. The results will just look like a mistake but that'll only make him keener. He can't get him with money or threats. He wants to cosy up, make some kind of deal, but with what?'

'He doesn't want any witnesses. Which means it might be shysty. Can he blackmail us?'

'With what?'

'What should we do?'

'I think we have to meet him. Better to find out what he's up to. Tell him we'll meet tomorrow at 6. It might as well be here, but we only tell him that at 5.30.' He stretched. 'I'm wrecked.'

He had his hand on the hall light-switch when Gatta paused at her bedroom door.

'Luke, what are we going to do?'

He knew she didn't mean about Ty.

'We have to keep looking after him, protecting him from people. But now we also have to protect people from him.'

Chapter 47

The morning brought more complications. Luke slumped at the kitchen table, scratchy-eyed with his hair in yellow haystacks. Gatta wandered in with her feet doing the navigating, eyes riveted to her phone. She thrust it at him. 'This is trending its arse off.'

In the footage, a young ABC reporter was standing in front of a cosy house, with a flagpole flying a flag with a winged sword-wielding golden lion on a red field. The house looked familiar but not the flag. The reporter held back her streaming hair as she spoke.

'The mystery surrounding the disappearance yesterday of ambulance officer Adam Cain took a macabre turn this evening with the discovery of body parts on a Battery Point beach. They were identified by prominent retired emergency physician Dr Bryan Walpole.'

With a jolt, Luke recognised the man who had challenged him and Shona that morning at Marieville. He was looking somewhat embarrassed.

'No, I didn't find them myself. The neighbour who found them ran to find me, goodness knows why. What did she think I was going to do, resuscitate? A couple of feet chopped off just above the ankles would be beyond even the clever young docs at the Royal. But I recognised the type of shoe: it's a black shoe with steel caps. They've brought me a lot of patients. The ambos wear them.'

'Oh crap,' said Luke.

The camera was back on the reporter. 'Anyone with information relating to the body parts, or Adam Cain, is asked to contact Crime Stoppers on…'

'They have to be his,' Luke said gloomily. 'Now he's not just a guy who is missing, possibly shot, he's also half-eaten.'

'Nine-tenths,' said Gatta. 'And cheer up, they won't think of animal teeth, it'll be a saw or something they'll think the ambocide was done with. I'd better have brekky. Bec's coming to get us soon. We have to see Alexander fly!'

Bec was the next startlingly-changed person. Having skipped out to greet her, Gatta clattered back into the kitchen.

'Sheesh!' she said. 'It's Mary the West Coast Eagle, wearing a Bec suit!'

Luke followed Gatta back out. Bec was in the XH. Her sun-bleached hair was loose on her shoulders and one forearm dangled over the wheel. She was tranquil as the Blessed Virgin. Unnervingly unlike herself. It was a relief when she blipped the engine and yelled, 'Hurry up you two, or he'll have flown to Poatina by the time we get there!'

Bec hummed as she wound through sunny, pretty, busy Woodbridge and past squadrons of fruit pickers in Birch's Bay. Could there possibly be a place secluded enough for covert aerial practise by a winged creature that now couldn't be mistaken for a large bird? The Channel was repopulating. The fish farms had revived Electrona. Rows of slim fruit trees had joined the gnarled few that survived the long depression of the orchards. Multi-coloured play jungles had sprouted in Margate Park and skateboards rattled down the footpath before the *Snug Aged Care Facility*. Which all added up to a lot more people. The queue for the Bruny ferry at Kettering extended to the main road, and was clotted with minibuses bearing sharp-eyed tourists with telephoto lenses.

'You know,' Bec said, '*The Emperor of Ice-Cream* wasn't about sex at all. It's about a wake. For an old woman. But it doesn't matter anymore.' She swung the wheel to the right and they climbed away from the sparkling water through a meadow of uncut grass and into a forest. 'Clennett Hills,' said Bec. Rapidly, the trees grew closer and were filled in with undergrowth. By the time they rounded three more ascending curves and came to the gate, the wall of vegetation was so densely matted a wallaby couldn't have slipped though.

The gate was huge – a single, four-metre-high slab of steel with an inset lock, and painted dark brown. A sleepy driver would have slammed straight into it. Bec unlocked it and relocked it behind them. The forest surrounded them for a dozen metres before they burst back out into the sunshine and another meadow. They climbed to the brow of the hill and found themselves at the lip of a small grassy valley, with a small stream running through its base, enclosed all around by big old trees. The drive dropped through the valley and ascended the opposite slope but any house at the end was invisible.

'See?' said Bec. 'Perfect. Even if some bastard found us, he'd need an oxy torch to get through the gate – or a chainsaw to get through the trees.

The only way in is the drive and you'd see him coming. ISIS, or ASIO, could train a swarm of terrorists in here.'

On the far high ground, the tops of the waist-high wildflowers shivered in the still air. Alexander must have heard them. His head popped up, meerkat-like. Gatta leaped out of the car and careered down the hill with her arms out, like a baby aeroplane. Bec and Luke took the XH down the drive.

'He was up at dawn, watching the honeyeaters,' Bec said. 'I'm not sure how much good it did him.'

They crested the hill. They had nearly reached the treeline before the forest revealed the house, dull green with salmon and mustard uprights exactly the colour of the trunks of the surrounding yellow gums. Not juvenile-dragon-level camouflage but pretty good for humans. Had Alexander's adult skin retained any of that ability at all? There hadn't been any sign of it. Against a blue sky, he was going to look like a giant black bat.

Bec and Luke found chairs on the veranda. Gatta and Alexander were conferring in the tall grass. Luke didn't join them. He needed to talk to Alexander: *Will you kill babies?* But he wanted to do that privately. The conversation with Shona did another fruitless loop inside his skull. Did he have to choose between Alexander and Shona? It would be like cutting himself in half. Could he even do it? Trust his own senses over Shona's undeniable logic? Had that excoriating searchlight really been Alexander looking at his brain or just his stupefied brain looking at itself?

Gatta scrambled up to them. 'He's sorry he didn't eat the feet. They got away while he was dealing with the rest. And he didn't know whether his fire would work until it did, so that was probably on his mind.'

Luke stood up. 'I need to talk to him.

'I don't think he wants any flying advice,' said Gatta.

'I won't give him any.' Luke pushed through the flax lilies to where Alexander sat on his hind legs and tail, studying high-flying ravens.

Luke wasn't sure how to phrase his question. 'Alexander, could you search – and maybe kill – anyone?'

The dragon's gaze stayed fixed upward. **'Nobody can withstand me.'**

Was that hauteur or statement of fact? Maybe both. Anyway, it didn't answer his real question. Best to just ask. 'I mean children; babies. If you say evil may be from the beginning, could you detect it in a child?

Luke caught the hint of unease before the dragon closed himself off.

'When I search a child, I will find if it is evil.' Which meant Alexander didn't know.

Luke knew he wouldn't get any further. 'If you ever do, or think you're going to, could you let me know before you start?'

'Yes, Luke.' Alexander met Luke's eyes to underline his promise. Then he set off downhill.

Luke turned and stared unseeing back toward Gatta and Bec. It would have to do. How powerless Luke, or any of them now were to compel Alexander to do anything. Luke was relying on – what? A trust, no, a hope, that dragons had an intrinsic moral sense, and that it was somehow close to the human sort. Or that Alexander had gained one from himself and Gatta. Luke walked slowly back up to the house and prepared to watch his dragon fly.

Alexander had positioned himself on a low rise halfway down the slope. His tail swayed. He tasted the air. Then he reared and flung out his wings with an audible snap. A flock of native hens scattered. Doves rose in a hoo-hooing cloud. He leaned back on his haunches, gathered, then sprang. His wings gripped the air, thrust triumphantly, and his body was free of the earth, in the air, flying. Luke's heart soared with him. Bec was grinning fiercely. Like herself again.

Alexander's wings swept forward for their second beat. He slowed. The wings struggled for purchase, the black body squirming vainly, and suddenly he was just a horse-sized lizard who happened to be in mid-air. He thumped to earth.

Everyone winced.

The dragon scrabbled up immediately and shook himself. He examined his spread wings in turn, might have muttered some words of encouragement. Then he sprang up again. He made it higher than the first time. A couple of currawongs flew overhead, observing him, and swooped on gracefully to a high branch. The air on which they had flown supported them, had substance. Under Alexander's wings, the same air dissolved and dropped him again.

He went no higher the third time, or the fourth. He tried smaller faster flaps, an ungainly flurry which barely lifted his claws above the grass, then reversed the strategy to try great lunging gulps which only tilted him forward and speared him head-first into the ground. The currawongs, fascinated, moved to a lower branch.

Luke, Bec and Gatta watched with growing anxiety. 'He just doesn't have the power or speed to lift his mass,' said Luke. 'Maybe Shona was right the first time – he's too heavy for his wings.'

Gatta shook her head. 'He's only a baby, his muscles aren't strong enough yet. He'll get there.'

The currawongs departed. Alexander watched them glide overhead, their white fringed tails forming precise arcs, wings motionless, letting the air bear them up and wave them forward. A mysterious, effortless collusion. His upturned gaze wasn't longing, like Luke's – it was calculating. He needed to be high enough to glide.

Alexander turned a preparatory circle, positioned himself with his tail curled under his back legs and his wings tight against his body, crouched on his haunches. Then he uncoiled, exploding upwards like a rocket, tail giving the extra shove, the afterburner. He made it to about thirty feet, then flung his tail back to try for horizontal. Managed only a desperate aerial comma and fell tail-first back to earth. There was a complicated whump and silence.

Daisies nodded brightly. A kookaburra glissaded over, landed in a downslope gum without a single wingflap and lifted his tail in a gesture of derision.

Alexander bellowed. The dragon hurled himself headlong downhill, legs flailing like four paddlewheels, reached a slight ski jump lip and sprang for the jeering kookaburra. Just as his wings locked outward, the wind gusted under them and bore him up and just like that he was flying, the obliging air sweeping him straight at the kookaburra. But it was only a brief gust. It dropped, he sagged in the air, managed a single flap and crashed into the gumtree. He fell down through the branches with a series of tearing thuds and a terrible screech.

Luke and Gatta and Bec were already running down the hill. When they reached Alexander, he was on his back, stunned, showered in leaves and dust. His front claws were opening and closing vaguely.

'Alexander!' Gatta leaned up close to his chest, carefully not to tread on his wings. He howled and his tail lashed, smashing straight through a couple of boxthorns, and thumped into the trunk of the gum. She leaped away, dodging the second swipe and the convulsion of clawed legs as he squirmed onto his feet. They stood back warily.

'I can't fly any better than those brainless cowards.' He hissed at the native hens, spectating from an insultingly close distance. 'And such stupid little things like that can do it!' He jerked his head at the inoffensive doves.

'You can't fly like doves do,' said Luke. 'You're built differently. You're an eagle, an albatross, not a pigeon. You need wind.'

'And you're not strong enough yet,' said Bec, possibly unhelpfully. He glared at her. 'Meaning when you get stronger, you will.'

Treetops swayed. 'The south-westerly is coming in,' Luke said. 'Have a rest for a bit and try again after lunch.'

They trailed back up the hill, Alexander swiping bad-temperedly at the taller broom shrubs and eyeing off the dragonflies. Luke was glad the kookaburra hadn't laughed; Alexander might have burnt down the forest.

The storeroom had been stocked for a nuclear winter or the climate apocalypse, and they helped themselves to provisions. They sat on the veranda while Alexander brooded in a sunny spot away from the native hens. He accepted a frozen chicken from Gatta, possibly on the basis that he was eating one of the hens' fatter cousins.

'Flight-wise, he's at about overachieving chook level,' whispered Bec.

Gatta didn't laugh. 'Do you think he can do it, Luke? Or did he really come out wrong?'

'I think he will, eventually. He needs to work out what technique works. I'm more worried about what it will mean if he succeeds,' said Luke.

'He'll crash, or the army will shoot him down?' said Gatta.

'No, he'll go out into the world, killing people.'

'Bad people,' said Bec. 'And that's a problem how?'

'The death penalty,' said Luke. 'Do you believe in it?'

Bec and Gatta hesitated, then shook their heads.

'Why not?' said Luke.

'I can see where you're going,' said Bec. 'There are utter arseholes out there who have no right to be part of humanity. They got no respect for us, they deserve no respect back. We can get rid of them, no question. But innocent people on death row, that's the bummer.'

'But isn't that exactly what Alexander can do? Sort out which are the innocent ones, or at least the fixable ones?' said Gatta.

'Exactly,' said Bec.

'What if he can't really tell the difference?' said Luke.

'What do you mean?' asked Bec, losing her tranquillity. 'I saw him do it and you freakin' felt him do it! And I know who he did it to.' She tied up her ponytail with quick, jerky movements. 'Shona's got to you. I thought you were over being a puppy dog, Luke.'

Luke felt angry words rise up, push to get past his lips. He walked away. Bec had no choice but to believe in Alexander's scrying – she was culpable in his second killing. She'd suffered horribly then relived it in the telling. He understood attack was her defence. But *puppy dog? Unable to think for himself?* He stalked into the yellow gums. Smooth, sympathetic, unjudgmental, calming. Gradually he slowed.

This thing was far bigger than his ego or Bec's. People were going to die, maybe lots of them. Luke had to fix what was breaking before their group fractured further. He turned back towards the house.

Bec stood rigid in a corner of the veranda. She couldn't have projected the fend-off better with her elbows out. Gatta watched her anxiously, looking small and sixteen.

Luke said to Bec, 'What happened to you was so awful I can't imagine how you even survived it. Look, I don't know how or if – sorry – Alexander's judgement works, but you believe it does and you acted in good faith.'

The tropical blue of her eyes swarmed with sharks.

'Can you help me figure out what it is he's doing?' Luke said.

She dropped her eyes. 'I'm not Shona.'

That wasn't disagreement at least.

The wind had filled in now and was blowing the grass in a steady wave against Alexander's hind legs and flowing over his wings. He tilted the leading edges up and down like horizontal sails tacking through the wind. At the far end of the field, a stronger gust bowed the grasses like the stroke of a giant invisible hand, approached up the slope till it swirled up and filled the bellies of his wings, lifted him free of the ground. Lifted and lowered him in a slow-motion ballet, complete with involuntary eggbeater from his back legs.

'To da moon!' called Gatta.

Alexander gave a triumphant look over his shoulder then concentrated on the next gust approaching over the sea of grass. This time he launched himself to embrace it. He was borne upward and swept gracefully down the valley, even managing a staggery but effective left turn just before the wind dropped out at the bottom. He executed a four-point landing and swarmed quickly uphill, tail high in victory.

The next gust advanced in a sudden silvery rush from the far side of the hill. It bent the treetops, slapped down the grass. Luke expected Alexander to let it past, but he didn't. It tossed him vertically nearly twenty metres, helpless, a giant black paper bag. The gust swept on without him and he hung for a moment with as much grip on the air as a rock, then fell, only this time he managed to scoop the air under him, flip over his length and dive – not stalling – diving! But steep, too steep. His wing tendons snapped tight as he strained to pull out. Strained further and he rocketed over at grass height, his tail brushing it. Shot forward, flying again. Gatta gasped with relief. He was still gliding, had gained height. But not enough. The forest edge was a barred wall directly in his path and he banked, too slow and too shallow. A wingtip tore through branches and he gave a last desperate twist, which became an uncontrolled, vicious pirouette. He cracked himself like a whip. With a heart-stopping shriek and in a tangle of claws and tail and membranes, he fell.

They pelted down the hill. Hillocks of dragon were piled in an untidy jumble. His left wing drooped on his flank; his right was crumpled under him. The coils of his tail were strewn in the grass.

'Alexander!' shouted Luke. 'Are you hurt? Open your eyes.'

Leaves dangled over the motionless black body. The wind gust had disappeared over the hill, job done.

Something toed the jelly of Luke's brain. A yellow dragon eye opened. The black mailed ribs rose and fell, quick shallow breaths. A pause. The light in the yellow eye wavered.

Luke was light-headed with panic. Alexander was badly injured, they were only three, and they knew nothing. And they didn't have Rosie. A hollow ache in his chest. Wishing wouldn't bring her back. *What did they have?* Her example.

'Okay,' he whispered. Louder. 'Okay. Can you breathe? Take a big breath.'

Alexander stopped panting. He took a slow, deep breath, which caught, but only at the end.

'Good.' What next? Start at the head. 'Can you move your neck okay?'

No! Neck injuries you had to immobilise till safe. 'No, wait!'

Too late. Alexander had cautiously lifted his head from the ground and was swaying it right and left.

'My neck is not injured.'

What next? 'Try your legs.'

Alexander picked up and waggled each limb in turn then arced his spine in a slow wave that began from his neck, hitched at his shoulders then continued down to his tail.

'My body is undamaged but my wing is broken,' he announced.

Luke swallowed. 'Ah, your right wing?'

Bec and Gatta looked at Luke.

'Yes.'

'Okay, let me look.' His voice came out artificially deep. He crouched by Alexander's flank. The long delicate wing bones, the ones Luke thought of as fingers, were wedged under Alexander's stomach, bent downward at a sharp angle, but they looked clean and undamaged. The two shoulder bones had no unsightly bulges. Luke shuffled back on his haunches.

Gatta leaned over his shoulder. 'That joint doesn't look right.' She pointed at the one that looked like a shoulder. Luke frowned. How could he know what a dragon's second wing joint was supposed to look like? Alexander was no help.

'It doesn't look like the one on the other side. It's dislocated,' said Bec.

'**Can you fix it?**' Alexander remembered to speak to everyone now.

No, thought Luke.

'Yes,' said Bec. 'It's like a popped finger. We put them back all the time at footy.' She scowled at Luke's expression. 'Adam used to say–' They both grimaced. She shrugged. 'Being evil doesn't make you crap at your job. Adam used to say that if you pull in a straight line you can't damage anything. He was good at dislocations.'

Alexander's eye flared. '**I am sorry I could not save Rosie from him. I was not grown.**'

'I was grown and I could have saved her and I didn't,' said Bec.

Gatta touched both of them. 'He did the evil, not you guys. And she's still here anyway, in our heads, helping.'

Bec smiled wanly. 'She'd get on with it. So let's.'

Bec placed herself at Alexander's left shoulder and Luke and Gatta at his right wing. He extended his neck on the grass, eyes closed. They heaved, grimaced at each other, found better footing, heaved again. Alexander's mind was so blatantly shut to Luke he might as well have been screaming.

'Stop wincing, Luke,' said Gatta.

'**Yes. There is no room for softness, not in Sparta.**'

'What?' said Luke.

'We watched 300. I thought he needed some history.' Gatta shrugged.

But when they heaved again, she was muttering, 'This so sucks; *sucks sucks sucks sucks.*'

Sweat beaded on their faces and ran down Luke's back. Alexander's neck and tail quivered in his efforts to relax but the harder the humans pulled, the harder his muscles clenched around the ugly joint. The heat poured off him, through his skin, into their hands. Gatta's fingers were bright red and her face was white.

'No,' said Luke. He dropped the wing, grabbed her shoulder, dragged her across the grass to the stream and thrust both her hands under the water.

'It wasn't working,' he said. 'You, we, would have burned our hands for nothing.'

She slumped against him. 'What are we going to do?'

'Not this,' he said. 'Sit down and think. Alexander, can you make it here? We could all chill a bit. Literally.'

Alexander's body was wider than the stream but he managed to submerge his head. Bec copied him. Wet and cooler they sat together, recovering. Taking stock.

'Rosie would do – what?' said Luke.

'She'd use drugs,' said Bec.

'We don't have any drugs.'

'No.' Then Bec smiled a slow smile. 'We do have alcohol.'

Their faces were blank, including Alexander's, then Gatta mimed an all over wobble, ragdoll-like. 'You mean make him floppy like a drunk?'

'Exactly that.' Bec grinned evilly. 'Julie has a case of overproof Overeem. No better use for it.'

Luke felt a rise of mixed unreality and hopefulness. 'You want to fill him up with whisky?'

'Yep. Till he either relaxes enough or goes unconscious. A Slav bouncer I knew, big as a Mack truck but really stupid, too stupid to be a bouncer, used to pop his shoulder. His brother, the bright one who owned the nightclub, would make him lie on the bar and drink vodka till he passed out, turn him facedown and pull down on the arm to get the shoulder back in. Then he could vomit, sleep, whatever, not choke. Wake up and go back to being an arsehole.'

'**I will sleep and vomit and I will be an arsehole?**'

'You might. But your wing will be back in. Probably.'

Alexander stretched out his neck and head and tongue in a long line, rehearsing. Luke imagined a stream of dragon vomit. '**I will drink this Overeem. It will help me. And maybe I will not do the other things.**'

Luke tried not to think of all the other things Alexander might do. Alcohol. The fuel of chaos. They were about to pour it into a creature which functioned in ways that were mostly a mystery even to itself. Bec's thoughts were obviously similar; her grin was now a little glassy. But what were their options?

'Where's the whisky?' he asked.

Chapter 48

The whisky glowed copper in squat, soft-shouldered bottles on shelving that ran the length of the cellar. At the other end of the cellar were spare car batteries and leads and black nylon sacks, one containing Kevlar body armour and the other, complicated webbing strap-harnesses.

'Best not to ask,' said Bec. They dumped the gear and used the sacks to carry the whisky – twenty bottles. They had no idea how much they'd need.

Alexander craned his neck, regarding the first bottle with a mix of suspicion and curiosity. When Luke popped off the seal, he retracted his head swiftly. After a moment he reopened his nostrils to slits.

'**People drink this? Fire burns people. How can they drink this?**'

'I don't know,' said Bec. 'I suppose they put their minds to it. But if soft white slugs like humans can drink it, dragons probably piss it.'

Luke and Gatta and Alexander frowned at each other, but Bec was already dumping the bottles out of her sack. She folded the sack along its length. Deftly she wound the bottle in the black nylon, took a big swallow herself, and placed it in Alexander's claw. 'Let's smash this.'

Alexander's tongue poked delicately into the shimmer that rose from the bottle's open mouth, and shrivelled.

'Julie never shared this stuff with anyone,' Bec said. 'You reckon you could bring him back so we can kill him again?'

A growl came from Bec or Alexander or both. Alexander's claw rose to his uptilted mouth and he emptied the bottle in one long red-gold stream. The facets in his eyes shattered into a thousand sparks. Each scale on his body trembled, came alive, like a cloak of ants.

'**Am I burning?**' Alexander looked back along his body in amazement. '**Fire cannot burn me but everything inside is burning.**' He poked a claw cautiously at his stomach. Curled his tail forward and regarded the tip with suspicion.

'**I am not on fire. Maybe I am feeling frozen.**' He hit his stomach harder, waiting for it to tinkle. His eyes still had their shattered texture; compound eyes – a dragonfly rather than a dragon. They rolled uncertainly. He waited some more. Guardedly he wiggled his injured wing.

'This does not feel loose.'

Bec took the empty bottle and gave him a second one. 'It doesn't work that fast. And we're going to need a lot more.'

The second bottle went down much like the first. It was Gatta who handed him the third, after wafting the open neck under her nostrils, drawing the visibly coiling vapour up through her nose. Luke watched it expand behind her face like a slow firework. This time Alexander let the whisky pool in his mouth before swallowing. The flicker in his eyes slowed and his lids drooped.

Flaring them open, he said, 'The sun is going through me! But how does it have oranges in it?'

'The mob who make this are clever fuckers,' said Bec. 'Secretive. Maybe they're magicians.'

Gatta opened the next bottle. She proceeded to hand them to him one by one, inhaling each one first like the king's taster. Gradually Alexander's head bent skyward and to the right, and he peered meditatively at the middle branches. Suddenly he flicked the latest bottle aside.

'I am flying on the ground!' His voice had filled out into an entire string section, though not everyone was playing strictly in time. He lurched to his feet. 'I can fly through the trees. Not between. I am air, I am less than air.'

Next to him, Gatta stretched into a winged Victory pose. Dramatically, Alexander swept up his wings. The right hung from its deformed joint but he ignored it.

'Alexander, sit down,' said Luke urgently. 'You can't fly. And, Gatta, neither can you.'

'I can't fly.' His head swept from side to side, stopped at his ruined wing. 'No, I can't.' He lifted his throat and howled, a real sound, like a wind through catacombs, shrieks and rumbles, building in intensity.

The voice in Luke's head was howling now. Unbearably loud. 'Why did you not come? Why did you refuse to teach me, then judge me for not knowing? Why did you not show me how to use my wings?'

Luke felt a slap of wind. The ground was a rush of wheeling shadows. He looked up. The sky was empty. But whirling all around him was a tumult of different voices, melodious and harsh, words he couldn't understand, the clamour of many wings close to his head, his nostrils assaulted by great wafts of sweaty leather, sulphur, flint. He covered his head.

'Why do you only come when I am broken, not show me how not to break?'

Gatta's knees buckled. She crouched, looking up wildly at nothing, arms over her face in horror.

'Why am I alone?'

Then the inner voice slipped back into that terrible inhuman roar, directed at the sky, endlessly, till he took a breath, his head descended and a gout of red and yellow flame gushed from his jaws, setting fire to the air for fully ten metres.

'Alexander. Stop it!' yelled Luke. 'There's nothing there!'

The dragon heard the new voice, swung his head blindly and the sheet of flame scythed over the grass. Luke threw himself to the ground, yanking down Gatta as the flame swung past them, razed on through branches, bringing one crashing to earth.

'Alexander! Stop. You'll kill us!'

Alexander raised his head, shook it back and forth in blind rage, turning the air above him into a massive arch of pulsating red. Bec darted forward and seized the fallen branch, still on fire at its thick end, reversed it like a club.

'Yes!' shouted Luke. 'Hit him!'

She flat batted the branch with all her strength at Alexander's head. It smashed into his skull with a sickening thump, and shattered into fiery fragments that rained down around him. Alexander's head stalled. Trembled. The flame and the dragon voices died away. Luke's shoulders dropped with relief. Gatta hauled herself up, turned back to Alexander, her arms outstretched, just as his head lifted. The crowd of voices swelled up again into a many-throated shriek. Alexander ducked, then reared up again, thrashed blindly with his front claws and flailed out another torrent of fire.

'Christ.' Luke grabbed the neck of the second black sack, swung its weight behind him and heaved it with all his strength at the core of the fire. There was a great crash of breaking glass. Somewhere maybe a clever fucker distiller howled in grief, but the dragon shivered and went boneless as his brain winked out. The fire vanished, along with the ululating voices and the wings.

Over the incinerated waste, the air was draped in smoke which writhed and shimmered where it mingled with the departing spirits. The unburnt grass around them waited.

'Quick!' said Bec. 'He's out now, as limp as he'll ever be without being dead. Let's get that bloody wing back!'

Luke jolted out of his daze. He reached for the wing splayed on the ground, jerked his hand back.

'It's about 500 degrees!'

'Ah shit!' Bec stared at him in dismay. 'I don't know how long we've got.'

'Or what he'll be like when he wakes up.' Luke jerked around. The stream. Could they pour water on him? What with? God, to submerge himself in that water. If only. He plucked at his filthy T-shirt where it clung to his body. The shirt. He wrenched it off – Bec's eyes widened – and thrust it into the running stream.

'Wet the sack,' he said. 'We'll have to do this quickly.'

Seconds later, they stood on opposite sides of the dragon, hands wrapped in dripping fabric.

'Together, smooth, but hard as we can,' said Bec.

The fabric under Luke's fingers steamed against the dragon's skin – he heard Gatta's indrawn breath – but he dug them in and heaved. He and Bec pulled in a straight line of human arms and dragon wing and shoulder. The joint extended, the ugly knot dissolved and was gone. Luke and Bec were on their knees by the river plunging their hands into the water. Bec's teeth in her blackened face were white and wide.

'Cool Hand Luke.'

He grinned in return and flexed his fingers under the water.

'Down!' Gatta cannoned into him and he saw, or remembered seeing, a last tiny tongue of flame from Alexander's snout lick the pale pool of overproof alcohol he lay in.

With a *whump*, the air exploded.

Chapter 49

The three of them lay tangled together half in and out of the stream. Someone's leg was across Luke's back and his teeth were against a white arm. Gatta's.

'Sweet baby Jesus,' groaned Bec. 'I'm cured forever of barbies. Crackling. Ribs.'

'Not marshmallows though,' said Gatta. 'Not the pink ones.' She pulled out her arm and rolled on her back, sat up.

'Is he okay?' asked Luke.

'Looks like he's just getting comfortable.'

Alexander's coils were sunk into the earth like the roots of an ancient forest giant, a fire-blackened myrtle in a scorched field. But he was breathing.

'For real,' agreed Bec. 'But we're a mess. Especially you, Luke.'

They left Gatta, who was the cleanest, to sit by the smashed dragon, while they walked back up to the house in search of clothes and food. Luke was almost getting used to being assaulted. Every day or so he seemed to be slashed, stabbed, skinned or battered, though burned was new. The right side of his back felt like it was still on fire and he was being followed by a sickening smell. He passed his hand over his head. On the left, his hair felt congealed with ancient motor oil – sweat, soot, dragon lighter fluid – the right side had been burnt down to a wire brush. Rubbing it made his eyes water with the smell of rotting fish. His burnt hair stank!

'Don't worry. We'll give it a number two cut,' said Bec.

She had a swinging, hippy stride, bouncing with energy. Grinning, she gestured at his bare torso with her chin. 'And you're still pretty.'

He looked down at his shoulders and chest. Muscles. Not huge, lean, but there. And the scars could be manly.

Bec's grin grew wider. 'Shona had better make a move or she'll find herself standing in line.'

He refused to blush, surprised to find that Bec made him feel good.

She disguised her courage as recklessness, but it was deep and real, and she didn't try to hide her faults. She always gave all of herself, unstintingly. Whereas Shona remained mostly contained, dealing with the world from behind her high observation ports. Luke smiled back at Bec.

She took his wrecked T-shirt from his hand. 'Shower thataway and Julie's shirts are in the closet.'

The stink of his burned hair did not wash off, but his burned back, which had fortuitously plunged straight into a cold stream, wasn't blistered, just a scalded red.

Back in the kitchen, he microwaved pastries. Bec came up behind him. 'We could be twins,' she said. Or siblings. They both had blond hair and chosen identical blue chambray shirts. Like Ty and Holly, who underlined their sibling status with styling. Ty's styling. What was up with that, anyway? They gathered up the pastries and coffee to take to Gatta.

At the brow of the slope, the scene stopped them. Alexander was the centre of an aerial conga line of crows, swooping down to hover in the intoxicating exhalation from his snout, reeling away at random angles, yodelling, some colliding happily with trees, while the more determined looped back for another turn. The ground was a burlesque of native hens, flaring their feathery bottoms as they dipped their beaks in his breath, occasionally aiming an approximate peck at a crispy-toasted upturned beetle.

Luke and Bec joined Gatta in the front row and they ate. After a time, he said, 'Do you think we should stop them?'

'Stop them?' said Bec. 'What bird ever gets to do this?'

'But one of his eyes is open and he really likes roast chicken.'

'Maybe he'll only roast the evil ones,' said Gatta. 'Do you think there are good and evil chickens, Luke?'

'Probably. But I'm not sure we can leave His Leglessness by himself till we know what he's like awake.'

'About that,' said Bec. 'We could have flaming crows spewing out all over the forest.'

'He's looking pretty chilled, I think,' said Gatta.

Alexander's eyes were both open now, surveying the scene with unfocused but benign interest. Unconscious birds were strewn across the ground, while those still upright swayed together, ruffle-feathered ravers. He switched his gaze to the humans and said very slowly and carefully:

'I will not vomit or be an arsehole. My wing is better. I will say thank you to the Overeem.'

'It definitely helped, but that was mainly us,' said Luke.

Alexander lifted his head in puzzlement. '**I do not remember.**' He closed his eyes and opened them. Peered around. Bobbed his head mimicking the crows' variable flight paths. '**Did the Overeem bring these? They do not fly well.**' His eyes narrowed at the hens. '**Some of them mocked me.**' He lurched to his feet and took a breath. More flame looked imminent.

'You can forgive them, Alexander,' Luke said hurriedly. 'You are much bigger than they are. Be magnanimous.'

The dragon hesitated. Then he breathed out an eye-watering but fortunately unlit gust, and flung a wing out in a grand gesture. '**I am magma…magnum…**' Both wings swept wide. '**You are all my friends. You are beauuuutiful,**' he bellowed. '**I love you!**'

The humans winced. 'I don't think they speak English,' said Luke.

'**Then I will speak to them in hen!**'

The sound in Luke's head became a grating squawk, wobbled higher in pitch to a squeal which had the humans grabbing their ears, climbed higher still and disappeared. The remaining airborne crows veered off course and crashed and all the upright hens abruptly fell over.

'**I cannot talk to them. Their heads are too small.**'

'And maybe their skulls are too thin. Better stop trying, Alexander.'

The dragon had already lost interest. He was gazing at the charred earth and broken glass. '**Everything is burnt. Bottles are broken. Luke, you are burnt! The dragons were here! They did this!**' He crouched low and inhaled again.

Luke soothed the air with both hands. 'You dreamed the dragons.'

'**But you must have seen them.**'

'You dreamed them so hard we saw them too,' said Gatta.

'**If I dream them harder, maybe they will stay. More Overeem…**'

'No!' The three humans spoke in unison. Luke stepped closer, though inhaling made his head spin. 'Lie down, Alexander. You need to relax now. Enjoy your friends.' Most of the birds were back on their feet, though the crows, with typical corvid good judgement, hadn't taken off. Slowly Alexander sank back to earth, lay his chin on the ground. His breathing slowed. Occasionally he bared his teeth at the nearer birds.

'Hopefully that was a smile,' whispered Bec. The dragon's eyelids were drooping.

'Not sure,' said Luke.

The breathing became whistles and rumbles.

'Those dragons he brought down,' said Gatta. 'Do you think they could have been real but like, transmitting themselves into his head from far away?'

'You mean like shortwave? And he was just rebroadcasting them to us?'

'Yeah, that.'

'I don't know. I wish I could ask Shona. Though even if she'd been here, she'd probably have interpreted it as a trip. What's more LSD than a cloud of dragons?'

Alexander let out a deep sigh. The air above him shimmered with exhaled spirits.

Luke groaned. 'We have to go home sometime but I don't think it's safe to leave him.'

'Not safe,' said Gatta, usually Alexander's greatest defender. 'When he wakes up, he'll have a Godzilla hangover.'

'I can't do breakfast burritos,' said Bec. 'But the house has, like a thousand cold pizzas.'

'I will eat pizza, not hens.'

'I think we're being manipulated here,' grumbled Luke to Gatta, walking back down to Alexander with a stack of frozen pizza cartons.

'He's had a very hard day.'

'Harder than us?'

They dumped the pizzas a snout's length from Alexander.

'I think we're good to go,' said Luke.

They were by the XH when his phone beeped. Shona.

Luke. The police have asked us to stay in the Hobart area. They will want another interview soon. Take care.

His fingers, on their way to touching her name or her last two words, stopped. She wasn't sending affection; she was warning him. He showed the text to the others.

'I think we're going to have to be careful with phones,' said Gatta. 'The cops can track where your phone was if you make a call.'

'Not the content, though?' asked Bec. 'Not like Adam was tracking Rosie. He had one of those fucking apps on her phone. She showed me, thought it was sweet! And can the police track where the person you're calling is at?'

'I'm not sure,' said Gatta. 'I'll ping Elliot.' She arrested her fingers halfway through their autonomous activity. 'But not here and now, numpty.' She looked up. 'We need to go home. Remember we have to meet Ty.'

At home, Luke gave his putridly scorched hair a number two cut, which rendered the bathroom uninhabitable by giving it a smell like charred long-dead chickens and burnt rubber.

He opened all the windows to share the stench with the neighbours. Then he showered again and put on a shirt that fit. He didn't feel ready to confront Ty, but Ty was coming anyway.

Chapter 50

Ty had them off balance from the moment he arrived. Always, he'd appear in the kitchen, exuding ownership and faint disgust that Luke and Gatta were displacing useful air with their bodies. Today he knocked, opened the front door and waited on the threshold.

He was what? Surely not seeking permission. An acknowledgement, maybe?

Luke felt Gatta consider a fanfare. 'Hello, Ty,' he said.

His uncle bent his head decorously and followed them into the kitchen. Luke's uneasiness grew. Ty had always emitted a personal ionosphere of invisible crawly things. It was unpleasant but routine, and now it was gone. Why did he have to choose today to be a new kind of weird?

Ty moved to the kitchen table and sat. Luke and Gatta couldn't sit. They stood at the window in front of the lemons. Ty nodded, put his hands flat, symmetrically, on the table.

'Two matters,' he said. 'First, I am not your uncle.' His face was empty, uninhabited, as though the previous occupant had left and no one knew how to live there now. 'In the sense that I'm not your mother's biological brother.'

Gatta could have fired off a dozen sarcastic comments but had nobody recognisable to aim them at. She managed only, 'Juicy. Does she know?'

'Yes. She was calibrating our new DNA analyser in Sydney and I knew she was using our tissue. So I told her before she found out.'

Suddenly, someone was looking out from his face, but they didn't know who. His ice-blue eyes looked clear all the way through. 'And she doesn't care.'

'If it doesn't matter to her, why are you telling us?' The floor felt slanted beneath Luke. He leaned on the window, trying for negligence.

'Because I discovered that you and I are alike. Or perhaps you have latterly become like me.' The words were cut with the familiar precision and his voice remained flat as his hands. 'I was surplus to my birth parents, then became surplus to my adoptive parents when they finally got what they wanted – their own daughter, Holly. But I was never surplus to her, not from the day she was born. My life starts and ends with her. I wasn't going to lose her to anyone, not to bureaucracies or human garbage when we were children, not to Anders or Brendan, not to you. Who I am – everything I do – is to protect that.'

Now the presence behind his eyes challenged Luke. 'You are doing the same thing. Protecting something. Not because of your hormones. Possibly for money, possibly for itself.' A faint smile. Ty touched the green bruises on the left of his neck. 'I couldn't let you kill me. It would have been bad for your mother.'

'Hmph!' Gatta.

'So let's agree not to murder each other. Instead, I tender a proposition. Congratulations on convincing Holly and the Paladin representative on retaining 80 per cent. As I might have tried when young. However, as it stands, the Paladin board has not approved Holly's money and they won't in the absence of evident investment from her principal financial partner.' He smiled gaily. 'Me.'

Gatta's mouth stalled.

'My proposition: you show me your creature and I engage in looking after it; I gift Holly a 49 per cent interest in Flexig and email the Paladin chairman accordingly.'

Along with anger, Luke felt unexpected rising bubbles of want. He could transfer, share the burden of Alexander. He was already hopelessly out of his depth, and without Shona; and who knew what was coming?

No. He swatted all the wanting down and pushed off the window. 'We haven't the right. He's not our creature, he's himself.'

'Really? Aren't you already commodifying the creature? Tasmania Police have spoken to Holly and me about the incident yesterday. The ambulance officer and Miss Garang from the university. Who are they? Intermediaries between you and unsavoury buyers?'

Luke tried to control his face. Why would Ty think that? Because selling Alexander is what Ty would do?

'Are you not in over your heads? Perhaps an alternate path may benefit you both. All of us.'

Luke hoped he was glaring stubbornly. He couldn't speak in case he found himself agreeing. Because he wanted to. For himself and for Alexander, who needed more care than they could give. What stopped him was their – his and Ty's – history. And Ty's proposition was blackmail.

After a long moment in which he seemed entirely at ease, Ty tapped his fingertips lightly together once and stood. 'The field stays open. The next move is yours.' He gave them a wide smile, which they couldn't process. A mirage? 'I transferred half the company to Holly this morning. Still your move.' And he left.

Brother and sister gazed blankly at each other.

'Slap me twice and sideways,' said Gatta. 'I have no clue who that even was. It's like someone whacked him right out of his head with a shovel. And someone else moved in.' She scratched her head. 'The stuff about not being Mum's brother must be true though, cos why say it otherwise?'

'I nearly said yes,' said Luke.

Gatta stopped mid-scratch. 'For legit?'

'He was wrong about the details, but right. Alexander is chaos and destruction. We've never known what to do with him and we don't know now. People are getting hurt and dying and I don't know how to stop it happening to more of them, including him.'

'Okaaaaay. You nearly said yes. But you didn't.'

'That bargain about Mum?' Luke rubbed his hands through his strange hair. 'Emotional blackmail. And he profits by it anyway.'

'You don't think he might have meant it positive for her and us, for reals?' She held up both hands, fending off his incredulous look. 'Okay, so the Overeem might have over-revved me.'

'I'd better call Mum before she—'

His phone rang. 'Luke? The police called me! Are you okay?'

'Ah, yes.' When your mother asked you questions, you didn't have a legal right not to answer. He couldn't revert to silence; he'd never had a silent phase. Neither had Gatta, though Ty had suggested it to her. But he'd had a crash course in evasion in recent weeks. So from her questions, she learned he hadn't been shot, shot anyone, or seen anyone shot, and he wasn't being threatened. He managed to divert her to Ty and Paladin, and found that Ty hadn't lied about anything. Flexig had underwritten Holly and she was invited to meet the partners for a final decision tomorrow.

And she truly didn't care about Ty's genetics. 'It's actions, nothing else, that define a relationship. Ty has never failed me in the smallest thing.'

'You can fly solo now, Mum.'

He didn't say, *I've never failed you, either. And I'm your son.*

Chapter 51

Luke gasped awake in the night. A thirty-metre concrete woman with slots for eyes strode through his dreams, sweeping the earth with searchlight beams of icy green light which shone clear through him. For an instant, the giant followed him into the waking world where he lay on his bed under the window, spreadeagled by moonlight.

Shona was indeed sending beams, but on a different part of the spectrum: his phone was ringing.

'Luke. The police want to talk to us first thing in the morning. I'll pick you up at 7.30.'

She hung up. She didn't ask how he was or what had happened. He reached vainly into the empty space she'd left, couldn't get back to sleep.

He got up to have another shower, scrubbed his hair again, trying to drown the smell of dead chickens in citrus shampoo. Alexander felt very far away. Was he being battered by dragon demons that poured out of his subconscious or wherever it was they existed? Snoring gloriously? Or prowling through the forest, ambushing bandicoot snacks?

He considered leaving a note for Gatta, but woke her at seven instead, an hour which she considered sub-adjacent to The Middle of the Night. Her eyes creaked open above the sheets, blinked to agree Bec would come and fetch her. 'Elliot says don't call us,' she mumbled, already falling back to sleep. 'Cops can nail callee location, more calls, sharper nailing...'

The Courier was on his drive at 7.25, Shona standing next to it. She had shrunk by over twenty-eight metres. Her eyes looked as tired as his. They widened when they saw his hair. 'I'm not sure I want to ask.' Her glance lowered to meet his. She passed both hands back over her braided crown.

'You were right and I was wrong. Unexplained doesn't mean inexplicable.'

Without dropping her eyes, she gently ran her fingers over his cropped head. The tingle that went through him made every single hair on his body sit up and beg. Before he could get up the courage to hold her hand against his cheek, she removed it.

'Like a shaved cat,' she said. Strange harmonics ran through her voice. Her work boot scuffed the gravel. 'The way you just accepted Alexander's brain reading, I thought you weren't thinking, that were you being uncritical like a child.' Her hand brushed over his shoulder, delicately, like flicking off dust. 'You're not a child.'

I'm not a child.

'I looked at the idea properly.' She grasped her elbows. 'Let's assume he can detect evil minds. How does he do it?'

He found his voice. 'You came up with a theory?'

'Yes. I'd like to test it. I'll keep helping. If you want me.'

If you want me.

Luke couldn't speak. He just nodded.

'Good. We'd better get going.'

As they turned down the Huon Road, she said, 'You look like a Jesuit. You could convert an entire South American country with that haircut. All the women, anyway.'

'It'll be good for going to jail,' he said, lightly

'If the police manage to tie us to Adam, there's a good chance we might.'

Luke's hands stung and his back felt like he'd been branded. He caught the animal tang of Shona's sweat. Unlike him, she was not a minor in the eyes of the law. Her future could be far grimmer than his.

'I'm sorry,' he said.

Her profile was impassive. The moment in front of his house, her hand stroking his head, might never have been.

They parked. Walking down Liverpool Street, Shona said, 'They might separate us. Do you have another guardian you could ring?'

Another guardian? Mum was in Sydney and Brendan still down a hole. Ty? Luke stifled a hysterical laugh. 'No.'

'Thought not. I've rung Prof, just in case. I tried Bolly, whose major is criminal law. She's in Melbourne helping her sister with a modelling contract. You okay with Prof?'

The Prof. Fearsomely competent. Could cow a bully with a glance. 'Awesome! But how has she got time?'

Shona gave a tiny smile. 'This morning is supposed to be our monthly PhD meeting.'

At the station, a civilian receptionist directed them to the familiar interview room.

Simpson was already seated at the table, hands hovering over her laptop, grey pouches under her eyes. She looked up, unsmiling, and gestured at Luke's hands. 'More fires?'

Fires? What did the Ds know? Did Celia in her eyrie have a gap through the poplars, through which she saw Adam's head aflame?

'Jobs he should have been wearing gloves for,' said Shona.

Simpson's eyes were bright and hard. 'Yeah, shovels. Rough.'

Luke's brain gibbered. Was that an accidental hit? What had Ty told them?

Auld came in at that moment. His shirt was crisp and his cheeks freshly shaved, but they were hollow with fatigue. He nodded curtly. Luke sat in his previous place. Shona stayed standing against the wall.

Auld said, 'We saw you two days ago, when you told us essentially nothing. Since then, this investigation has wasted a massive amount of manpower uncovering facts which you already knew but didn't tell us. And we've heard accounts that show both of you in quite a different light.'

He sat down. The muscles in his arms were stringier and the creases in his rolled sleeves sharp. Maybe he ironed them himself. 'Withholding facts which may prove to be of material assistance in securing the apprehension of an offender is a crime. So is murder.'

Simpson pecked at her keyboard and the red eyes of the cameras sprang to life. Luke barely heard Auld as he took them through the identification process. Murder?

'The first thing you didn't tell us: you both knew Adam Cain,' said Auld. Simpson swivelled her laptop to show a photo of a beaming Phil, Shona and Emily holding a trophy, in front of the team. Adam was off to the side, head turned but unmistakeable. 'You withheld that fact, which means his disappearance in your vicinity was not a coincidence.' He paused to acknowledge their expressions. Blank. Not disagreeing.

'And the things I'm about to tell you won't come as a surprise. Feel free to stop me at any time. Anything you might tell us at this point will count in your favour, even if we already know it.'

The air in the room felt like it had been trapped for years. Murder? Us?

Simpson rotated her screen again. A new picture: A pair of short, muddy and maniacally grinning girl footballers and between them, taller, smiling, showing a healthy swell of muscle before the anorexia ate it all, was Rosie.

'You know this is Rosemary Cain,' said Auld.

Luke felt his lips open, heard a small sound. He bowed his head.

'And if you know that, you probably also know that she died two days ago in the RHH ICU.'

Luke almost gave up on controlling his reactions. He could only hide his face, look straight down and watch the scarred plastic blur with his tears. He wished he still had hair.

'I don't suppose you want to tell me about the connection between her death in hospital and his murder, later that morning?' Auld leaned forward. 'Remember this helps you.'

Their faces remained silently averted, Luke's at the table, Shona's at the ceiling.

Auld sighed. 'Adam Cain murdered his wife. Facilitated her anorexia then straight out killed her. With insulin. We don't have all the proof yet, but from his house we have the aperient bottles and insulin ampoules, and the testimony of the paramedics who responded to his emergency call and couldn't make her blood tests fit.' He leaned forward in his chair.

'We know we'll get the proof. Because we now know he's done this before. In Darwin. The coroner returned an open verdict on his first wife's death. Adam's colleagues here all thought she'd died of cancer. Why would he let them believe that when the records from her hospital admissions say anorexia? And the blood test discrepancies from her cardiac arrest at home are the same as Rosie's.'

Auld paused now, because Shona had stepped forward, put her hand on Luke's shoulder then sat down next to him. To the detectives, she was steadying his emotions, helping him hold out. But in the squeeze, Luke felt her acknowledgement: Yes, Alexander had known. Luke counted back through Alexander's spasms of rage. He had detected Adam's nature from the first meeting.

Auld went on. 'The next thing we have is a statement from a relative of the man who sold Adam an illegal firearm, on the day of his wife's death. Adam Cain was a psychopath. He committed at least two murders for no gain that we can see except control and it looks probable he intended to commit another. But somebody stopped him. Which brings us to you.'

Auld regarded Luke, fingers steepled at his lips. 'You were in the vicinity of his last known sighting, at the time of the gunshots. At the first interview, you looked like a sensitive young man shocked by something he'd witnessed. Which he was withholding. But what if you had a different role?

'When we asked at your school, they said you were "mild, industrious, studious, public spirited" – words rarely associated with the operator end of a firearm. Then we heard something different: "An overdeveloped sense of his own moral righteousness".'

Luke went scarlet. Someone thought he was a prissy prick. Who? Hansen? Ty?

Auld hunched forward, three fingers laced, forefingers aimed at Luke. 'We heard you'd predicted the mountain fire, had high stakes on it. And it started within the week. At the Cascades. Not three k's from your house.'

Hansen, then.

Shona pushed herself back from the table. Her bored look had vanished. 'I didn't start it,' said Luke.

Auld continued as if he hadn't heard him. 'So, an intense young man with rigid views on moral issues, possibly willing to back up views with action. Especially possible if influenced by a charismatic person.' He swung the forefingers at Shona. 'Could he have come by his own gun?'

Simpson's next photo. Four people in biker leathers who made the picnic table they were sitting at look like kindergarten furniture. Shona, two men who could only be her brothers, and a white man – beard, tatts of skeletal fingers meeting on the tip of his nose.

'The Garang siblings and friend. Friend never apprehended in possession of firearms, always in possession of extreme luck or prior information. Garangs reside at premises formerly owned by a dope dealer.'

The veins had swelled in Shona's neck. 'Garangs collectively in possession of no firearms, no drugs and four university degrees. Three with honours.'

'Ah, Miss Shona Garang of UTAS.' Auld spread his hands. 'Undeniable brains and charisma but divides opinion. Doesn't suffer fools. Doesn't participate in student activities—'

'Drinking,' said Shona derisively.

'Except AFL – W.' Luke had never heard a single letter sound so patronising. 'But encourages people of questionable background to participate in the Uni team. Her PhD supervisor is similarly described as a maverick. Has a number of people evidently afraid of her. Does she collect dirt on them?'

'She is a geologist.'

Simpson coughed.

Auld, unruffled, changed tack. 'Has intense and influential relationship with schoolboy, nature obscure. Why haven't you mentioned Shona to your mum, Luke?'

Luke glanced at Shona who looked as curious as Auld did. 'She's been busy with something else.'

271

'Yes, I heard about that too, the advice you gave her. Quite the high-stakes financier. You're a long way from mild and studious, Luke. You're a doer and a risk-taker. And you were at the scene when Adam Cain was murdered. At the very least you witnessed it. You probably were an accessory. Or you may have done it yourself.'

Shona snorted.

'Are either of you ready to say something?'

'No,' said Shona.

'No? Not yet?' Auld raised an eyebrow. He nodded at Simpson, who began typing again. Who knew that a keyboard could sound bullying? 'You'd better hurry up and help yourselves because we know the killing didn't stop at one.'

Jules! What had Bec and Alexander done that linked him to Adam?

At this point, Auld did something neither of them anticipated – he laughed.

'You have no idea quite how awful you are at hiding your reactions. You already knew there'd been more killing. You could at least try to look surprised.' His voice darkened again. 'But the second murder isn't public knowledge. Except to you, apparently. If you didn't do it, you know who did, or something close to that.' He thrust his hard, open hands towards Luke – a proxy for wanting to beat Luke's head against the table? 'So, for once, why don't you stop making this so fucking slow?'

Luke looked mutely back. He couldn't see Auld's angry, intent face, only Bec's, when she was telling them about Jules.

'Why don't you humour us,' said Shona humourlessly. 'Tell us about the other killing we apparently know about.'

'At least you only mentioned one,' said Auld. 'So we can stop looking for more pairs of feet.'

Luke's heart gave a double tap. Had Bec mentioned leaving Jules' feet? Or had Alexander, in the long hours he'd been missing presumed swimming, been interviewing other potential execution subjects instead?

Auld looked at Simpson, who shrugged. She flicked up the next photo. Luke saw a stranger. A headshot of a man with a likeable grin and large untroubled eyes.

'Uh, what's his name?' Luke said.

'You don't know this man?' Auld's attention sharpened. 'He owns several businesses around Hobart, some hotels and a laundromat. He's got teenage kids, supports sporting groups.'

'I don't know him,' said Luke.

'We found his feet and his shoes near his property in Birch's Bay—'

A knock on the door. Sergeant Cresswell slipped into the room.

'You were in this room at the time he was killed, but you evidently knew about it. His name,' Auld gestured at the screen, 'is Julien Charny. And there doesn't seem to have been any reason for anyone to separate him from his feet.' He stood up. 'I've had about enough. You need to know that Sergeant Cresswell has just interviewed eyewitnesses to his murder.'

Cresswell's dour eyes took in Luke and Shona. Luke exhaled. He couldn't think of anyone less likely to believe a dragon sighting.

Auld went on, 'And we are about to examine the security footage from Charny's computer.'

And Luke discovered he hadn't been afraid before now.

'If you tell us what you know is on that footage before we tell you, maybe we can get you off these charges. Because let me tell you, as of now, you are both going to jail.'

Chapter 52

Shona's lips looked riveted together. *Jail. Risdon.* Was Risdon where women went? Luke stayed silent.

'So be it,' said Auld. 'Time to separate you.'

'In that case,' said Shona, 'shall I ring Prof Cantrell to be your guardian, Luke? Yes,' she added blandly to Auld, 'the maverick geologist.'

Simpson smiled behind her screen.

The detectives left with Cresswell. They were replaced by a young female uniform who waited while Shona made her four-word call – 'We need you, Joy' – then asked for their phones.

Shona rose. 'You can't do that. We haven't been arrested.'

The young woman looked like Luke's adored second grade teacher. Her clear brown eyes gazed up – a long way up – into Shona's green ones. 'We can if we have reasonable suspicion you may use them to allow an offender to escape custody.'

Luke clamped his fingers around his phone. What would Gatta do? 'We can give you our phones but we don't consent to a search of them. You can't do that without a warrant.'

She smiled at Luke like she was approving his red crayon drawing of his dog. 'No, we can't. We won't.'

Reflexively, Luke smiled back. He gestured up at the waiting cameras. 'And you can't record us without a warrant or consent either.'

'No, we can't.'

The door closed behind the policewoman and their phones. And Shona.

Without *her* the air subsided to dull and flat. Time grew old.

When Joy Cantrell arrived, Luke picked out her footsteps among the others in the corridor. They were quicker, sharper, more precise. A male uniform opened the door for her. She wore a tailored dove-coloured skirt and cropped jacket. Her iron-grey hair was in an immaculate French twist, the reverse engineering for which looked impossible to Luke.

She thanked the policeman, who left, and sat down next to him. 'Are you okay, Luke?'

'Yes.' She didn't sit opposite, but at his shoulder. She was on his side, with all her dispassionate intelligence and toughness. She could help him to stay out of jail. And also tackle the moral problems. If he wanted.

'Well...no, I'm not,' he admitted. 'Thanks for coming to help.'

She settled herself. 'You seem to have appropriated my administrative assistant lately. Now you're appropriating me. I'm assuming it's a good cause.'

'Ah, yes. Should I start at the beginning?'

'An excellent place.' She folded her hands: short, polished nails, ropy veins draped over tendons, arthritic fingers. The age in her hands looked like authority, not weakness.

So he told her all of it. He left in Ty and Holly and Taylah and the acorns. And Jason and the racehorses because they seemed relevant. At first she nodded encouragingly. When Luke reached disappearance-level camouflage she stopped nodding. She showed no external scepticism, only asking the occasional clarifying question, but at the description of Alexander's deliberate mood-casting, one hand began tapping an invisible pencil. At "wings" she held up the hand to stop him.

'Um,' he said. 'At this point I might as well tell you he talks. And, ah, breathes fire.'

She stood up. All her warmth had vanished. 'Enough. I can only assume you have chosen to recite this farrago to rehearse an insanity defence. You could have asked someone with less to do.'

'No, Professor, I'm sorry but–'

'And you're continuing with it?' Her heels rapped sharply on their way to the door. 'I shall request the police provide an independent person to replace me. I advise you at your interview to say nothing.'

Luke jumped up, his chair clattering backwards. 'Professor, stop, wait, let me–' What could he possibly think of that was remotely like evidence? 'Alexander's egg! It's unlike anything else. Isn't it?'

She turned, voice clipped: 'Yes. Admittedly. But on one small unexplained object, you balance this edifice of nonsense?'

'His DNA sample was stolen. And Shona! Why would she tell you nothing, spend so much time...'

She hesitated, hand on the doorhandle.

Luke stayed behind the table, afraid to go nearer. 'Here, he burned me, yesterday.' He dragged up his shirt to expose the swathe of red, now blistering, across his back. 'Professor, Alexander has murdered – killed – two people. I don't have another story to tell the police, and this one, I *can't* tell them.'

Her knuckles on the doorhandle went white. 'You can't tell them the story, because it's true? You could actually show me…Alexander. And he can demonstrate these things?'

'Yes.'

'Great God!' She took a couple of steps back into the room. 'Give me a few moments.' She looked into the middle distance while a thousand wheels whirred and clicked behind her eyes, then turned her face to the heavens above the little room.

Her voice was soft and deep. 'That I should have lived so long and seen such wonders.' She turned glistening eyes on him. 'What are we doing in this little room, Luke? Excuse me if I walk. Continue, continue.'

So he went on while she paced. When he paused to allow questions, she waved him on impatiently.

Luke was able to relate Adam's attempt to shoot him and his fiery execution fairly steadily, but stumbled when he came to Alexander's explanation of searching and the search of himself.

'Shona had trouble believing he really can see a person's thoughts,' he said.

'Yes, I can see why. But tell me the rest. The police give interviewees thinking time to discomfit them. This habit has served us well so far, but we may have little left.'

When he reached the end, which was when the detectives left the room, Joy paced and he waited. When she sat down it was opposite him. She took off her glasses. 'Sixty-six impossible things before breakfast.' She rubbed her eyes. 'But immediate questions first. How would you summarise your legal situation, Luke?' She waited patiently.

'I haven't murdered anyone, and I don't think they can prove I have.'

She nodded.

'I haven't even been an accessory. He did it all himself.'

'We might come back to that. Go on.'

'But I suppose I have – no, I have – withheld information.'

'About Alexander. By the way, Luke, you realise that as a scientist and a human being, I am capering about, casting my cap over the windmills at your discovery?'

'Ah, yes.' Why did real life have to be so difficult? Why wasn't he sitting in a sunny field with the Prof, she and Alexander discovering each other, the occasional cap being flung? 'Alexander. He's killed people.' Luke thought hard. 'Whether you call it murder depends on whether you classify him as a person. How sentient he is.'

'Precisely. If only my honours students could think so clearly.'

'But if Alexander isn't sentient, then that makes me more culpable because I'm responsible for him.'

'Yes. Excellent. I'd agree with that assessment.' She rubbed her glasses. 'Now we're getting close to the bigger moral problems. Why have you taken so much trouble to hide Alexander, Luke?'

'Um, at first because of Ty, I suppose. Because he would take him and get rid of him. Or try to sell him.'

'And you didn't want to do either of those things.'

Luke hadn't mentioned his temptation to use Alexander to erase Holly's debt. His guilt made him speak. 'Ah, I did want to. For a bit.'

'But you didn't do it. Why not?'

'I never thought Alexander belonged to me.'

'*Laudato si.*'

Latin? Luke's sense of receiving a tutorial in a wood-panelled, book-filled room tripled. 'Loud...what?'

'Latin for "Praise be to you". It's the second encyclical issued by Pope Francis. He wasn't directing the praise at you personally but he was agreeing with you. Genesis 1:26. God gave man dominion over the fish of the sea and the birds of the air and the livestock and the earth. Francis says that dominion doesn't mean the power to do what you want, but the responsibility to look after these things, which responsibility humanity is executing particularly badly.'

Joy sighed. 'Unfortunately, for you it's not a defence that will go down well in a courtroom. Never know more Latin than the judge.

'But your story is about power, who assumes it and what they do with it. You took on Alexander, saw that as responsibility for him. Using your power to allow him to live as he wants.

'Ty uses power for control. Adam and Jules used their power for satisfactions of their own. Corporations, Paladin, use power for money and for itself. People use power over animals mostly for their own benefit.

'You, and now I, have a responsibility towards Alexander.' She grasped the lapels of her jacket. 'To act in *his interests*. We also have a responsibility towards society.'

Towards society. Luke grew still.

'Alexander has power. Which he believes he has not only a right but a duty to use.'

Luke nodded glumly. They were far from the sunlit field, back in a cramped, dank room.

The lines in the Professor's face grew deeper. 'He is administering a death penalty. To be morally defensible, his selection process must be 100 per cent accurate. Every single time. He must kill only people who have no hope of remorse or reform. Unfortunately, his *process* is doubtful at best. So we must protect society from him. And him from himself, given society will exact retribution on him.'

'His process... He, it felt...' How could Luke describe having his mind uprooted and turned upside down for examination?

'Did you ask Alexander for details of what he'd seen inside you?'

'No. But it was... I wasn't thinking the thoughts on purpose. He was making me think them. That made them visible to him.'

'The qualia of *your* experience is not proof. Mind-reading not only has never been proven, there is no believable theory of how it's neurophysiologically possible.' Joy didn't look at all triumphant.

'Shona decided it could be done.' His pulse pounded in his throat. *Am I wrong and he really can't do it?*

'Shona has emotional reasons for giving credence to mind-reading.'

'She has a theory.' *Emotional reasons?*

'She wants very much for you to be right, Luke.'

He shook his head to untangle the implications. 'But...she trusts logic, not emotions.'

The professor looked amused.

He was on the edge of tears. 'She worked out some logical way, how it would work. That's when she came around.'

'Oh hell,' said Joy, 'and forgive me, Shona. Of course she's a scientist, Luke, a very, very good one. She also makes men feel puny. Height, strength, brains. Beauty. Honesty. The men she hasn't intimidated had huge egos. But you, Luke, to her you're not puny or intimidated, maybe because your heart is bigger than your ego. If your genders were reversed, the age gap wouldn't be an issue. And youth is temporary.'

Luke's heart sped up. He felt light-headed. 'Are you saying—'

'The important point now is that, even though she advised me to believe you, for once I don't trust Shona's judgement on this. Alexander's *searching*—'

Footsteps. Simpson, Auld and Cresswell burst through the door.

Experienced senior officers, they looked both profoundly shaken – almost fragile – but scoured of all softness. Without speaking, Simpson and Auld pulled out chairs and sat together at the head of the table. Cresswell remained standing. Simpson opened her laptop, stabbed at the keyboard. The cameras winked on.

'You knew about this,' said Simpson. It was inconceivable that she'd ever seemed insignificant.

The professor glanced at Luke. He knew their evasion was over. The detectives were no longer guessing – they knew. Auld's reaction was the opposite to Simpson's. They'd almost switched characters. His persona no longer matched the crisp white of his shirt. His hair was greased with sweat. He finger-combed it back, and Luke knew no explanation he could give was going to erase what Auld had seen on the security footage: vision of a living man burned away to nothing as he stood.

'You knew,' repeated Simpson, emotionless and terrifying, 'and now you're going to tell us.'

The cameras waited.

'We couldn't–' began Luke. But where, how to even start? And what was Joy going to say? She'd judged Alexander as a murderer, thought they had a responsibility to give him up. His brain scuttled about for ameliorations. How to get in first, convince them of the real Alexander before they mobilised an army unit to capture him. 'We didn't know... what he was; who – that he was even a *who*–'

'We knew what?' said Joy, with the authority of her professorial office.

Luke recognised another truth about power – you only held it if the other party ceded it to you. He subsided but Simpson ceded nothing.

'You are not helping Luke,' she said to Joy. 'Stop it.'

Luke sat up, straightened his sticky shirt, tried to look trustworthy. Why was the professor stalling? He needed to distance himself from her. Stop helicopters, snipers descending on Alexander. Bec and Gatta. 'He knows people's–'

'What's on the security tape?' asked Joy.

Auld lifted his eyes from his hands. 'There's nothing on the security tape. The cameras were turned off.'

The four of them stared at each other.

'I don't understand,' said Luke

'We're not going to–' began Simpson.

'On Charny's computer,' said Auld, 'we couldn't find the relevant time on the security video, but we could open his encrypted files. Some other videos. Alannah Hayatsu and Lily Dee. We never stopped looking for them but we can stop now. And another little girl we haven't identified yet.'

His voice was harsh and remote, distancing himself from his words. 'Charny was selling the videos on a Tochka marketplace.'

'What happened to them?' said Luke, but he knew. Alannah and Lily had disappeared three years apart. The media attention had never completely stopped.

'At least they're dead now,' said Auld.

Joy's hands trembled on the table. She closed her eyes and let her head drop.

An image struck Luke behind the eyes: the bag of webbing straps and the batteries in the cellar, neatly stowed away. Without thinking, he asked, 'Were the girls on the video restrained?'

'All of them were,' said Auld. 'Some kind of black harness. Made to size.'

Luke's fingers turned cold. They had lifted the straps out of their bag, touched the fabric.

Then Joy's cool dry hand was on his arm, silently saying *humanity, humanity was greater than evil*. And that she understood. *Alexander had killed with reason and he had found the reason inside Charny.*

Simpson reverted from remorseless fury back to middle-aged detective. 'We seem to have discovered one thing each: you have established that we haven't seen the security footage, and we find that you haven't seen Charny's videos. And were unaware of what was on them. Correct?'

Luke nodded.

'But you know what would have been on his security footage?'

'Why was the footage missing? Who has it?' asked Joy.

'Nobody,' said Auld. 'Someone turned it off thirty minutes before. Charny was expecting someone he didn't want to appear on a recording. Who almost certainly was the killer.'

Bec.

'So, Luke,' said Simpson. 'We have no security video but what we do have is a trademark identical to that left at Cain's murder. And an identical motive, one that fits *your* character.'

'But you've already admitted that you don't believe Luke knew what was on the encrypted videos.' Joy was back in charge of herself and by her tone expected charge of the interview to follow. 'I think you've had enough questioning time.'

Simpson said, 'He and Miss Garang knew Adam and Rosemary Cain–'

'This is Hobart, detective. How many gatherings of eight people haven't contained your dentist or your son's ukelele teacher?'

'—and concealed their association.'

'Charging Luke with murder is a blatant ambit claim. You're not serious. Surely.' Her voice, not loud, would have been clear in the back row of a lecture theatre.

'Yes, we–' said Simpson.

'No,' said Auld.

'You're accusing him of being an accessory but all your evidence is coincidence and supposition. Are you going to charge him with that?'

Simpson stayed silent.

'No,' said Auld.

'Are you going to charge him with withholding evidence?'

Simpson nodded. 'Yes,' said Auld.

They had almost forgotten Cresswell. He coughed. 'Ah, maybe not, sir.' The landscape of his face was a granite plateau.

Auld's eyebrows rose. 'How so?'

'It may not be the best way of obtaining his evidence and may present negatively to Joe Public. I conducted his initial interview as well as those of Charny's associates who witnessed his murder.'

Charny's brainfried serfs. It appeared the police had managed to hotwire enough of their remaining neurons after all.

'Marko Ilic refused or was unable to provide meaningful information. Fourby – no other name – it seems to be related to timber – talked but much of his statement was emotional and frankly useless. He appears to have been threatened.' He consulted his notebook. 'And I quote: "The mofo that did Charny. He eye-fucked me. I've done shit. I've done shit. For the love of Christ, put me inside".' Cresswell looked up.

'The second lot of shit was in his jeans. He insisted on confessing to decades of offences. And his request to be incarcerated may not be remorse but for his own protection.

'When pressed for a description, the witness became extremely emotional.' Cresswell glanced at his left sleeve, which was streaked with something pale green and crusted. He sighed. '"Seven feet tall. Bald. Eyes, red. Had a fuckin' flamethrower",' he added tonelessly, '"Wearing a black cape".'

'Your point is, sergeant?' said Auld.

'The witnesses to this second killing – habitual criminals with extensive experience of violence – were intimidated to the point of delusion.

281

Breakdown. Luke Schache, a juvenile without such experience, was in a similar state of shock when I saw him. I just don't believe charging him would be productive. Sir.'

Auld was playing with the buttons on his sports watch, focus already directed elsewhere. Maybe on Charny's film crew or customer base. Or the conversations he, as the senior officer, would be having with Alannah and Lily's parents.

His wiry fingers stopped on the only red button. 'Okay. I agree. You're free to go.'

'But,' said Simpson, plainly more reluctant to disengage, 'you are required to notify us if you intend to leave the state for any reason.'

Five minutes later, Luke and Joy were waiting for Shona in the empty reception area. They both started to speak just as Sergeant Cresswell advanced across the floor. His face was shuttered.

'You know the killer,' he said. 'You weren't like those other two. You had the willies, but not from him.'

'So why did you—'

'Alannah Hayatsu played T-ball with my kids. In my back garden. I'm not interested in putting away the man who removed her murderer. Get out of here. And tell your friend to stop with the signature.' He wasn't smiling. 'Get rid of the feet, for fuck's sake.'

Chapter 53

Outside the glass doors on the greasy footpath, in her glossy heels, Prof looked as unlikely as an impala. People with lank hair and torn black jeans skirted her. She ignored them. 'I apologise, Luke. I nearly failed you in there. Alexander very likely discriminates evildoers. We heard an excellent description of him doing just that.'

Luke rubbed his neck. 'You were right to doubt, though. Shona did.'

Did she really stop doubting for my sake? He blushed, unfortunately at the moment Shona emerged through the doors. Then her arms were around both of them and he felt nothing but Prof's raw silk jacket and the burn of Shona's arm across his back. Every Luke particle was dancing with happiness.

She released them. 'Shona doubted what?'

'The *searching*,' said Joy. 'As you know, I was still debating whether we should tell the detectives about Alexander. I nearly did.'

'But you didn't,' Luke said, 'and you helped get me out. I'm very grateful.'

Joy stretched up to kiss his cheek. So like but unlike his mother. He smelled her perfume: a flower he didn't recognise, but something sharp and sweet and growing only in inaccessible places. When in life had such toughness come to her? How deep did it go?

'Do you think Alexander is a pterosaur?' Joy said to Shona. 'An azhdarchoid? Did he have pneumatised bones on that CT?'

'Probably. Didn't do a detailed survey. But he'd have to anyway, to fly.' Shona grinned hugely. 'If he's a Quetzacoatlus variant, his wings could grow wider than this street. But breathing fire is entirely new. Wait!' She looked stunned. 'How do we know the allosaurs didn't? There's no way you could tell one way or another from the bones.' Joy and Shona shared a look of incredulous glee. 'A cow could breathe fire: it's got the methane, it only needs to figure out how to ignite it.'

'And not set fire to its tongue,' said Joy. 'Most regrettably, I have a class now. Luke, if we study Alexander, everything we do is up to him. He has dominion over himself.' She kissed him on both cheeks and jaywalked briskly across Liverpool Street.

'Don't get ideas,' said Shona. 'Her first husband was French. That's how they say goodbye. Besides, I'd get jealous. She doesn't do that to me.'

Luke's face cycled through colours like a nightclub strobe.

Shona laughed and handed him his phone. 'Detective Simpson gave me the short version and cautioned me not to leave town. Fill me in?'

They walked, passing *Artizan Café*, habitat of court and hospital workers. As he spoke, Luke saw the patrons skirt Shona the way they'd skirted Joy. Then in the café window, he caught his own reflection – his shorn blond head and scars. Add Gatta's Docs, and he'd make a neo-Nazi enforcer. Maybe he was the one making people cautious. Shona's face, when his story reached Charny's videos, created an even wider no-go space, but she didn't look surprised.

'He had to have done something like that,' she said, 'for him to fail searching. My theory of the neurophysiological process by the way, is that when Alexander is searching, he isn't examining every detail – he can't be, even if he thinks he is. What he could be doing is stimulating an intense self-examination in the subject, then assessing the results. To confirm that, we'd have to ask him to describe the details of what he saw, in you, for example.'

She laughed, forestalling Luke. 'You could do that in private. But my theory is, he won't be able to. It's like when you have a "warm glow" level of understanding of a subject; you think you understand it when really, you only have a superficial grasp.'

Shona strode faster, manipulating an imaginary brain with long expressive fingers.

'Someone like Jules would recognise massive wrongdoing but express zero guilt. I think. We need a neuroscientist.' She shook her head and laughed, half-rueful, half-gleeful. 'Another field of science where Alexander makes the wheels go wobbly. Let's go talk to him.'

'See whether dragons advance the science of hangovers?'

They were at the Courier. Luke woke up his phone. It showed no signs of forced entry, but how would he tell? Splinters and crowbar marks? The phone pinged. 'Missed call from Mum. Voice message.'

He played it. Holly's voice was curt. 'Luke? You and Ty are worrying me. What's going on? Call me.'

Texting wouldn't be enough; she'd want to hear his voice. What was he going to say? *I was in the police station, safe from Ty and btw I've got a killer bodyguard?* Or *Ty died but he's happy running the underworld.* If only. He dialled and it went to voicemail. 'Ah, Mum? The police wanted a follow-up interview. Routine. I'm all good. Hope you aced your meeting. Loveyoubye.'

'Mum issue just pushed down the road?'

Luke sighed. 'I'm wondering whether I could just tell her. The old mum would have freaked. The new one, I'm not sure. And Ty, he's the original Terminator. He won't stop, ever. The solution to it all is finding somewhere safe for Alexander. Clennett Hills isn't it. The police are going to find it soon, when they look at Charny's books. They'll have whatchamacallits.'

'Forensic accountants.'

'Yes, those. We'd better warn our mob.'

'Think Gatta will be on the air?' asked Shona.

'I'll text. It depends how far she's taken the conversation about phone tracking.'

Gatta didn't reply in the five minutes it took them to reach the ute.

'She must have turned her phone off,' said Luke. 'For her that's like walking around with her head inside a sleeping bag. I once lost a bet with her that she couldn't text with her eyes shut.'

'Doesn't matter,' said Shona, sliding into the cab. 'We'll be in Clennett Hills inside the hour.'

Her smooth hands rested wide on the wheel as the ute filtered down Campbell Street. 'I accept that I don't have to understand how Alexander does it to believe it.' Her smile flashed white. 'Yet.'

'I think,' said Luke slowly, 'that he has two different things – abilities.' His mind went back to a floodlit uni oval and an inquisitive lizard on his shoulder. 'I think he gets a smell, or something, like from Taylah and the rappers, and he got it the first time he was near Adam at training, and he tried to hide his reaction. His signal turned off completely. Then at your place, twice he woke and smelled Adam after Adam had left. That's why he went nuts.'

Shona swung up Davey Street and the sea breeze over the moored fishing boats passed through the open windows. 'Some kind of pheromone thing?'

'Yes. But the mind searching is completely different. It's the adult dragon making a serious decision. It's directed and it has major consequences. He did nothing to Adam till he'd searched him. Even though Adam was pointing a gun at me. I don't think Alexander even saw the gun.'

'And with Charny,' said Shona, 'it was the first time he'd seen him. Bec might have told him their history but they didn't know about the kids. Oh, the kids.'

They were pulling up the Southern Outlet before anyone spoke, passing Fitzroy Gardens and its graceful sandstone Federations among old spreading green branches and old money.

'He sees evil,' Shona said. 'How did he put it? People who see only their own selves? Ha! If we let him loose on executives from, say, Big Tobacco? Big Pharma? Oil companies?'

People who chose to use their power for themselves. Luke pictured a polished boardroom table, a semicircle of burning Italian wool suits. A few spared faces.

'It wouldn't be all of them,' he said.

'I don't know how we'd introduce him,' said Shona. 'In the sense of finding them.' She pulled out to overtake a log truck. 'Or how we'd get him in a lift to a fiftieth floor.'

Young green forest slid past. She sounded whimsical, but Luke realised she was completely serious. Having absorbed the concept of Alexander's purpose, she'd advanced with it further and faster than he had. He wasn't there yet. Wasn't sure they *should* ever be there. But it might be out of his hands already. Alexander was beyond his power to compel.

At Kettering, the queue into Ferry Road stopped them and a minibus heaving with teenagers reminded him of Gatta.

He delved for his phone. 'Still off the air.'

'Contact from you now could look like the cops trying to find her,' said Shona, unperturbed. She accelerated around the last of the queue.

'If we can't get hold of her or Bec, I'm not sure how we're going to get through the gate.'

'We'll solve that when we get there.'

How would they solve it, though? The property must have a serious fence. Electric? Razor wire? They'd probably have to get over the gate, which was just short of the height of both of them combined. They could leg up. They could climb each other's bodies...

He had to wind the window down and look up at the cool sky.

His head hit the window frame as Shona swerved to avoid an oncoming van.

'Sorry,' she said. 'Looking for a flying dragon? So was I.'

'No.' But a part of him *was* looking. Seeing the sky filled him with an almost physical longing. 'Yes.' They had reached the meadow at the bottom of their road. 'Turn up here.'

'I can't wait to see him do it. Fly,' said Shona, 'and I haven't even seen him try yet.'

They plunged into the forest, rounded the shaded curves. The gate stood open.

'They were expecting us?' said Luke. 'How could they know?'

'There's a camera at the gate,' said Shona, driving through. 'Maybe there's one further up the road too.'

'Maybe,' said Luke, but apprehension was creeping up him. They emerged into the field spread bright, silent and open in the sunshine. From the brow of the hill they could see the empty valley, the scorched circle near the forest's edge and, ahead, a glint of something in the direction of the house.

'This place feels really remote,' said Shona.

They crested the opposite hill. The glint was from the windshield of the XH, standing in front of the house, unnaturally still without the burble that usually charged the air around it. Nobody ran out onto the deck.

'Have they gone to try more flying?' Shona got out to scan the slope.

'There's no wind. He can't even get off the ground without it.'

'Hunting breakfast?'

'Maybe.' Alexander so far had only killed people, squid, and some gulls who deserved it. He would need to diversify sometime.

'He's not here, or anywhere nearby,' said Luke. 'The place feels empty of him. And I don't think Bec and Gatta are here either.'

'Let's check inside,' said Shona.

A few minutes later, Shona had explored the ground floor and Luke the cellar.

'You okay?' said Shona, seeing his rigid jaw. He hadn't told her about the webbing straps.

'Yes. Nothing, nobody.'

'Bec's clothes are still here, so they haven't cleared out, but something's odd. The kitchen looks like they were about to cook for twelve.'

The kitchen benchtops were immaculate. Gatta had premiered Ironic Tidiness at the age of eleven. The irony had gone unappreciated, sadly for her, but the tidiness continued, conceding not being her style. So the surfaces that met Luke and Shona were normal. The stacks of cookware were not.

Shona frowned at them, hands on hips. 'The *Marie Celeste*. Interrupted while cooking breakfast?'

'No,' said Luke. A pair of saucepans were nested inside each other, next to them a pair of frypans. 'Once is an accident, twice is a pattern, three times is a habit. Gatta told me once how she always beat me at poker.'

'It's a pattern?'

'Yes. Pans.'

'Double boiler? Overcooked?'

'No. Two pans. Pan-pan. She wants us to talk to Elliot.' Luke scrambled for his phone.

'Luke? Hi, man. You're not in the cells then? Er, like, are you?'

'No. But we need to find Gatta and our friend.'

'Yeah. She said he can baby fly! Those wings I saw, they're out now, hey? But I'm not sure how much I can help. She messaged this morning that they needed to find somewhere else to crash. Oh, wrong word. Alexander crashed. Some high place with a lot of wind. Then only, like, half an hour ago, she texted me: "Ty's coming. Laters." End of transmission.'

'Nothing else?'

'Zip.'

'Can you call as soon as you hear anything else from her? Better, get her to call me. It's safe.' Luke pushed down the voice which said that it wasn't. He hung up, and repeated the conversation for Shona.

'So they're gone, but we don't know where or how or whether Ty's got them. Could they have gone bush, up into the Tiers?'

'I don't know. Any of it.' Luke spun around to the valley window. 'I just know he's not around. I've got so used to feeling his presence that I don't know I'm doing it. But I can tell when he's not here. I haven't felt him since...' He slapped his cropped head. 'Since we passed that van. At the bottom of the road. That big whoosh of flying vibe we got? And the van, didn't it turn out from here?'

They locked eyes. They'd both seen the van turn and not registered it.

'Who was driving?' Luke's brain revved up. 'If either Bec or Gatta had been in the front, they'd have seen us and stopped.'

'Unless they were restrained or threatened somehow. Ty doesn't know me or my car and he might not have seen you.'

'If he did, he'd have kept driving. And he knows we didn't recognise him.' Or we'd be right up his arse now, trying to force him off without killing anyone. 'He's taken them! All of them.' Luke banged out of the house.

Shona found him by the XH, hands laced on his head, staring sightlessly over its roof.

'What can we do?' she asked.

'Nothing here,' he said, slapping his hands on the roof in defeat. 'Take me home. He'll be in touch with whatever his deal is.'

They didn't speak as they got in the ute and drove back through the bush. Luke's brain was numb. The greens and browns and blues passed in front of his eyes like a silent movie. Shortly past Woodbridge they crossed Schemer's Creek and the sign woke him up.

How had Ty managed to control Alexander? Through Gatta? Maybe the red-haired man was with him and they had weapons. They had Bec and Gatta to contend with as well as the dragon. Someone to drive...

'Hey! It's the van!' Shona braked violently.

'What? Where?'

'Getting on the Bruny ferry.' Shona stamped the throttle, hurled them past the next three cars, saw the queue and swore. 'Hang on!' She crashed the Courier over the median strip, grievously injuring what remained of its suspension, took the space made by two oncoming trucks which had dodged prudently into the weeds and roared onto Ferry Road. The queue to the imminently departing ferry, the *Mirambeena*, stretched another half-kilometre.

'You sure you saw it?' said Luke.

'What do you think? I've nearly killed my truck, let alone us. Ferry won't let us on, though. There's no chance all these cars will make this crossing. We can go as foot passengers.'

But they couldn't.

They were stopped at the foot ramp by a diesel-stained hi-viz vest and an upraised palm. Luke wondered how many languages Shona could curse in. The *Mirambeena's* engine note rose, preparing to take Alexander, Gatta and Bec out of reach.

'Half an hour to the next boat,' the ferryman said.

'We're not waiting for it.' Shona slapped Luke's arm and sprinted back up the road. He trailed her past open-mouthed faces towards the marina and cannoned into her when she stopped at the base of the first quay. A double row of boats stretched in front of them.

'We're looking for a white converted fishing boat with a high blue flybridge tacked on top. Ugly. Called *Madeleine*, in loopy letters. On the third pier, I think. There's, god willing, a scooter on the foredeck. And if, on the way, you see a crescent wrench or a hammer or something big and solid, grab it.' She loped up the quay.

Shona wanted weapons? But you were either serious or you weren't. Ahead of Luke was an old big-bottomed cruising yacht. Old boat meant old owner, old-style tools. He leaped aboard, rummaged in the sailcloth pockets, fished out a huge steel winch handle. He hesitated. Stealing.

'Found it,' yelled Shona from across the marina.

He grabbed the handle, vaulted the rails and ran.

Shona was crouched in the cockpit of a timber mongrel-boat slathered in white house paint aeons ago, running her hands under the wooden gunnels. She came up empty-handed.

'I didn't think we'd find the key. That's why you brought the lock picker.' She seized the winch handle. A single blow took out the padlock.

Luke followed her into the cramped cabin. The small varnished wooden steering station held encouragingly few controls and a spiked wooden wheel. Shona was frowning at the blank dials.

'See anything which turns on the lickity?'

Luke reached past her, lifted the hinged lid, groped for a tear-shaped knob and twisted it. The dials sprang to life.

'Can you drive one of these too?' she asked, hopefully.

'Nope.'

'Better go and cast off then. And find something to fend off with. I last did this when I was six.'

They wove a drunken path through ten million dollars of floating marine hardware. By the time they reached open water and Luke on the afterdeck heard Shona shove the throttle fully open, the stern of the *Mirambeena* was fingernail-sized. On it was everything that mattered.

Was Ty restraining Alexander through threatening Gatta? How much did Ty truly hate her? Luke shivered. Or maybe the dragon had been sedated somehow? Alcohol certainly worked, as did morphine. What was it Rosie had done? Pressure over his eyes?

If he woke up now, a growing adult dragon, confused and furious and blindly sensing an enemy… Luke's mind saw white-hot flame punch through the wall of the van, scythe a couple of tourist-filled Kia Rios and erupt through the hull of the ferry.

Shona caught his glance and his thought. 'This thing won't go any faster.'

'Okay,' he yelled back. 'Where's the scooter?'

'On the foredeck somewhere.'

It was under a disintegrating tarp, lashed to the front of the wheelhouse.

The right-hand mirror drooped and patches of the crazed black paint had been splashed with a solvent. It looked like a border collie with one floppy ear. 'Go Lassie,' muttered Luke. He unscrewed the fuel cap and shook the scooter.

He joined Shona. 'Key in the ignition, tyres not flat, not much fuel.'

She grimaced. 'I hope you can ride one.'

'Nope, but how hard can it be? Justin Bieber does it.'

Across the glittering water a sudden dark patch rose, spread and swept towards them – the rising southerly, bringing clouds. The ferry had docked. The first car emerged and began to wind its way up the green slope of Roberts Hill.

'Great,' said Luke as the wind hit and slowed them. With screwed-up eyes he could make out the colour and size of the vehicles but not the shape. Was that a van or an RV? Bloody RVs.

He hadn't definitely seen the van by the time they pulled alongside the ferry dock and the small wooden wharf next to it. And the sign: Mooring Strictly Prohibited. A heavyweight pro wrestler in a beanie and hi-viz tight over his middle was rocking his way down to intercept them.

'I was hoping one of Ilo and Tomasi's fishing mates would be on duty,' muttered Shona. 'No such luck.'

'Youse can't tie up here. And what are you doing with Fowkesy's boat?'

'Tying up,' said Luke and leaped onto the wharf to throw a bight around a bollard near the *Madeleine's* bow.

'Not here you're not. Fuck off before I make you.'

'It's an emergency.' Shona stepped out onto the deck.

Luke sprang back onto the boat. There had to be a means of getting the scooter onto land. His heart sank when he realised the three metre plank tied up behind the scooter was it.

The man snorted. 'Well, it's your emergency, not mine. Where did you come from anyway, freak?'

'Kettering,' said Shona. 'Are Denny or Frank here?'

Luke threw the plank across the gap between the boat's gunnel and the wharf. It was only half a metre in distance and fairly level. He just needed to aim at where he needed to go and keep momentum. And figure out how to start the scooter.

'I don't care who you know, you're getting off my fucking wharf.'

Two other men in blue overalls at the ferry ramp turned towards them just as a white van clanged over the steel plates onto the shore. Luke seized the scooter, turned the key and stabbed the button. It started with a belch of smoke. He grabbed the brake to stop it lurching forward. He didn't hear what Hi-viz-Man said next. He muscled the scooter round to the bottom of the plank, fixed his eyes on the shore end and accelerated – just as the gap under the plank abruptly widened. Hi-viz-Man had thrown off Luke's mooring line and the southerly was pushing the *Madeleine* off the wharf. Luke's grip on the throttle jerked, the back wheel lost traction.

'Luke!'

And the scooter dropped down into the d'Entrecasteaux Channel.

He followed.

The water was very cold. Suspended down in the green, Luke's brain saw the white van crest the top of Roberts Hill and disappear to where they would never find it. And he saw clearly what he was prepared to do to prevent that. He surfaced with a gasp, swarmed up the wharf timbers and heaved himself out onto the wharf, water streaming off him and strode up to the wrestler.

'Your keys. Give them to me. We're taking your car.'

The bully's fists balled, went slack. He fumbled in his pocket.

Chapter 54

Luke plucked half a festering sausage roll off the passenger seat and threw it out the window of the Nissan Navara. They took off in a cloud of burnt oil and bourbon fumes.

Shona glanced across, eyes still wide. 'Yes, you are Luke again, I think. Who was that you just turned into?'

'I don't know. My father? Ty? Alexander? Not Alexander.'

'How did he happen?' Concerned, but still Shona, wanting to know how things worked.

'I just knew, absolutely, that I was about to harm him, no matter how much he hurt me, till I got what I needed.'

'And you made that lump know it. I nearly wet my pants; I think he went right ahead.'

Luke shivered. He was cold and shaken. The person – bully, monster – he had briefly been was gone, but he had slipped into Luke's mind so easily down in the water. And the purity, the freedom, the power of being him. A secret part of Luke had liked that very much. He didn't want to think about it and they had no time to think about it. The van was out of sight. The water of Barnes Bay was dropping steeply away to their left. Crossroads decision soon.

'The scooter – god, that was funny. But we'd never have made it. I'm glad you got us this.' Shona floored the throttle as they crested the hill. 'It's actually pretty grunty.' She crashed the brakes as they nearly slammed into the back of a bus. The back of another queue.

'What's going on?'

'I don't know, but it might help us,' said Luke. 'Hold on.' He jumped out and ran to the driver's window of the bus. 'Hey, mate, what are all you people here for?'

A wind-reddened face beamed down at him. 'You haven't heard? It's the Shy Albatrosses! A pair nesting on Cape de Sorty. They mate for life, you know, funny bastards, but never this far north. David Attenborough is here!'

Luke got back into the Navara. 'Where's Cape de Sorty?'

'Cape de la Sortie. It's opposite Dennes Point.'

'I reckon everyone here is going that way. And there's no chance Ty will have gone where everyone else is. I think you can overtake all of these.'

'We're making this a habit,' said Shona, gunning the engine up the wrong side of the road, past the line of stalled traffic. 'I could get to like it.'

'Are we forming bad habits?'

'Absolutely.'

Did bad habits make bad people? Worry later.

Car windows flashed past them, most drivers bemused, a few of them glaring. No white vans. Shona slowed as the queue snaked off to their left up the turning to Barnes Bay and became shrouded in gravel dust.

'I can't see them in that lot,' said Luke, 'and I don't think they would have gone that way.'

Shona nodded agreement. 'So the other direction. As fast as we can.'

Luke grabbed for the Jesus handle as the back tyres did a squealing shimmy. 'I don't think there's any point in turning off anywhere until we get across the Neck. If they leave the main road before we spot them, we're stuffed anyway. This way, we might catch them.' Luke's anger surged. 'We have to catch them.'

'And when that happens?' Shona paused, tongue between her teeth, as she nursed the Navara out of a rocketing weave. 'This thing isn't as fast as it thinks it is. I think the back end was trying to overtake the front.'

'I'm just counting on there being more of us; you, me, Gatta, Bec, Alexander. Make it harder for Ty and whoever's with him. And Gatta won't have let on that Alexander can communicate. Ty still thinks we have a *Tasmaniosaurus triassicus* with wings, yep, surprising, but not something that talks and breathes fire and eats people.'

'Two of those skills would be pretty surprising,' agreed Shona. Woolly backsides pogoed away in every direction as the road plunged between sheep pastures. 'But we have to find them. I agree they won't be north of the Neck, too many farms. When we get over it, though, if we haven't caught them?'

'We–'

A gust of wind caught the Navara and Shona slowed, gentling the startled back end. 'At least this will slow them down more than us.'

'If we still haven't caught them, I'm just going to have to try seeing whether I can feel him or not, on whatever road we take. I have no idea what distance it works over.' He grimaced unhappily. 'I can't even tell that it's happening, whether I'm making it up, or what.'

'So without the woo-woo, we'll just call it guessing?' Shona took the next three corners in a barely deviating straight line, throwing out alternating rooster tails of gravel shoulder.

From there through the rest of North Bruny, she slowed only for three blind corners and a tractor with a harrow. For a flock of silver gulls she used the horn as a snowplough, scattering them in a frantic wave of white to either side. They hit the potholed gravel of the Neck with a whump which pitched Luke into the ceiling.

'Sorry,' said Shona. 'You won't be much use with a broken neck.'

The engine note dropped fractionally, then further as a wave of spray blew over the cab. The long ribbon of isthmus stretched in front of them, ragged streams of spume and sand blowing horizontally off the tops of the dunes to their left and gouging furrows in the waters of the channel.

'Is that them?' Luke pointed. In the far distance, intermittently through the veils of streaming salt water, was a blocky white shape. Ty's van or an RV?

'Could be.'

Shona gritted her teeth and launched them into the maelstrom. It was less the gusts – they were signalled by the stormbirds on the wing being thrown wildly upwards a fraction before the wind hit the Navara broadsides – than the sudden lulls, which had Shona careering across the road in the opposite direction. But they stayed mostly on the gravel until the moment they crested a rise – to confront a white wall. Shona wrenched them left to a stop.

A swaying white RV with Queensland plates was stopped diagonally across their lane, the wind trying to push it off the eroded road shoulder. Two women were photographing a carpet of orange butterflies sheltering under the heath.

'Bloody butterfly nuts.' said Shona. 'Not a practical neuron in their heads. Nice Xenicas though.' She accelerated around the RV.

Luke rubbed his bashed knees and growled. The RV had lost them time. But, mainly, they were driving onto South Bruny and soon he'd have to make a decision that mattered. The road left, to Adventure Bay, or right, into the depths of the national park? And all he had to go on was some nebulous absence in his gut. Or between his ears, or floating above his head. Just the thing a tinfoil hat would block, he thought sourly. He craved facts, something he could work out. He punched at his phone again, brought up Google maps, contours, earth. Where would Ty be heading? One of the lighter cleared areas, but surely protected by forest? On a peak for security? Or by water? Did Ty know Alexander could swim?

'Could he have gone up Mt Mangana?' he asked.

'They'd never get the van up the road,' said Shona, plunging headlong over corrugations. She let the wheel buck under her fingers. 'Why did he come here anyway?'

He slapped the glovebox. 'I don't know! It doesn't make sense. Most of this is National Park.' A trickle of driveway marked by a milk-can letterbox swept past. 'And who knows who owns the rest...ah shit, I'm an idiot!'

He stabbed at his phone again. 'Mum mentioned once that Ty owns property all over the state. Some of it will be here!'

No reception, but he could at least text Holly and pray to the mostly absent gods of Optus that one of them would deign to glance down at some point. He punched out his text and waited, glaring at his phone, willing it to respond. The reception bars remained sullenly blank.

He went back to interrogating the map, swiping and zooming at sandy bays and swathes of dark green, the black roads that snaked through them, suggestive lighter lines that might betray unmarked roads, roads Ty might have taken. Until he realised he had stopped assessing and was instead scouring the screen for a tiny moving white rectangle, as though he would see the physical van!! Dickhead! He threw the phone down in disgust.

'Left or right?' asked Shona. Ahead, bright perky white under the avenue of stringybarks and black peppermints, was the sign to Adventure Bay. Shona slowed. 'Luke?'

'Right,' he said desperately, and they were past. He didn't feel any different. Should he? Should they turn and try the other road, to see whether it made him feel something? If that didn't work, what then? He scrubbed his stubbled head and moaned. They could only go onwards, at breakneck speed, their guide an ungraspable feeling of emptiness inside him that could just as likely be hunger for a ham sandwich.

His phone pinged. 'It's Mum!' No wonder men called for their mothers in foxholes.

The message was uncharacteristically terse. Her Paladin meeting! She must be still in it.

Ty owns land on Bruny. He's never told me where.

'Secretive bastard!' Luke snorted. 'I wonder why he's never told her.'

But he had reception, however briefly, and one more try at hard information. He dialled Elliot.

'No, man, I haven't heard from her.' Elliot spoke before he could. 'Where are you?'

'On Bruny.'

'Have they gone to check out the albatross? Cool!'

'Ty has kidnapped them. We know they're on the island but we've lost them. Is there anything else she might have said, any way you can track her, knowing her number, anything you can think of?'

The silence was so long, Luke thought the Optus gods might have drifted off to sprinkle their meagre reception bounty elsewhere, but Elliot's voice came back. 'No, I'm sorry, Luke. Her phone is off. And I can't think of diddly.' His voice softened. 'Before the last text, she sounded really upbeat. She's ballsy, Gats, such a babe. I hope you don't mind if I say it.'

'I don't mind. But she's sixteen. Bye.' He smacked the phone on his leg and said to Shona, 'She's sixteen. And she's tried to piss off Ty since forever and… You know the thing I did with the ferry guy? Now I know what it feels like to be Ty. We can't *not* find them.'

He stared at the stained grey tarmac disappearing into ever taller, denser forest, feeling for what? The tunnel the van had punched through the air? A winking trail of tiny motes it had left? The last molecules of their breaths? The residual heat of Alexander's body? Vibrations of his dragonness? Whatever the fuck it was. Feel. Track. Find. Find.

But the road remained just a road, rattling under the Navara, and the earth-smelling air rushed by, invisible, revealing nothing. Luke wasn't going to gain powers he didn't have.

'Slow down,' he barked. 'Take the road to the left.'

Shona punched the brake and swerved them off camber up an unmarked gravel drive. 'They're here?'

'No, I think they're not. But we have to test whether this woo-woo works and, if it does, what that feels like. So far I've had nothing but I've got no idea what that means.'

'Fast?'

'Fast as you like. I'll know sooner.'

Shona nodded and kicked the reluctant engine to greater effort up the increasingly muddy ruts. Luke tried to suppress the surge of anxiety that they were wasting time. The Navara fishtailed, caught, ground on.

'Anything?' said Shona, rapidly working the gears.

'No.' Luke shook his head in frustration. 'Not a fucking thing. And I hate the idea they're getting further away while we're doing this.'

'Maybe they are.'

Luke felt a flush of anger. All she had to do was drive. 'You could be more—'

He stopped. Alexander wasn't here. And he'd been ignoring what he'd known for several minutes. That they were going the wrong way. His Alexander-tracking was doing its thing. 'Oh shit, you're right. Turn around!'

The ute did a perfect stone-spitting 180-degree swivel and they were slithering back down the slope.

'It works,' said Luke. 'It might be woo-woo, but it works.'

Shona bottomed out the Navara's shocks at the base of the hill and pointed them back south. From the moment they rejoined what he now knew was the trail of Alexander, Luke's being divided into two. Only half of him was braced in the cab across from Shona. His inner self floated high above, in the space of things not of earth: gods, Google Earth, eagles, saw the silver tray of the ute speed under the restless canopy of trees, winking in and out under dark glossy ripples, now bursting out into green grazing land, closing on Alonnah and the coast. Perfectly, vividly real. His mind straining so hard after Alexander, Luke was becoming him, or the being Alexander yearned to be.

'Keep left.' Ahead, hidden to him but definitely there, was the van.

Now Luke was over the shoreline, up with the high riding gannets and the swamp harriers, heads and eyes miraculously still in the howling air. From higher still, with the sea eagles, he saw all of South Bruny, a long, ragged shield embossed with mountains, and bolted to its upper rim the great scythe of the Labillardiere Peninsula, and glinting from the curve of the scythe, a lighthouse. The eye of his mind saw all of it. The island was no longer his enemy's refuge but a place where Luke could track and find him.

Already they were at Lunawanna. Cloudy Bay Road. To the left up into the mountains, or to the right to the lagoon and the sea cliffs?

Luke was down in the cab with Shona again. 'Go right,' he said.

The Navara popped and juddered in the turn and Shona had to wrestle it back on course, the light rippling on her forearm muscles and sparking her eyes as she glanced across at him. 'Shocks are gone. Struts might be following. It isn't all our fault. Ferryman wasn't nice to his car either.' A moment later, 'You good with the direction? We're on track?'

'Yes,' said Luke. 'You're all over this rally driving.'

'Practice. Getting field geologists into town before the pub closes.'

'We might even make it.'

Their wrong options diminished with every fork they took, the blind search now a pursuit. Again Luke floated above them, kestrel hunting the field, falcon patrolling the rolling carpet of ironbark, bluegum, feathered blue-green silver wattle. This was the chase. When they reached the end, which he now knew they would, would he need that brutal merciless Luke he'd discovered, underwater at the ferry landing?

Next to him, Shona forced the groaning, increasingly wandering Nissan onward, driving it with muscle through the corners, letting it drift in the straightaways, but always fast.

They crested a rise. To the left, far below, the blue churning cauldron of Cloudy Bay opened into the Southern Ocean. Ahead, against the sky over the dark hills of the peninsula, the Cape Bruny Lighthouse. And crawling up towards it, on a road too small to see, a speck of white.

'It's them,' said Shona.

Chapter 55

'Yes,' said Luke. 'It is.'

'What are they doing up there?' The Navara rolled in a gust and Shona took the steep downhill a little more cautiously. 'Do we have time to make some kind of plan?'

'Some kind.' The lighthouse had disappeared from view. 'What I've been feeling from Alexander… There's no fear, no anger, confusion, nothing. Only presence. He's got to be unconscious; asleep, drunk, drugged maybe. Gatta is going to be scared and furious. Bec? Furious at minimum.'

Luke stretched calming hands toward his distant sister. 'When he wakes up, Alexander's going to absorb all that emotion – Ty hating and Gatta scared – and there's going to be,' his hands flew apart, 'a fireball.'

'We have to stop that.'

'We have to stop that. And Ty and his helper are sure to have something else – knives, a gun – to make certain of control.'

They had topped the final hill before the ascent to the lighthouse. Across the valley gleamed two shapes caught in brilliant light: the whitewashed stone tower and, a hundred metres of brush below, the side of the van.

'I can't see anyone, yet,' said Shona, scanning briefly. She launched the ute down the last, steepest incline. 'When we get there—'

'We'll have to draw them out of the van somehow, but stay separate, divide their attention,' said Luke.

Their bonnet pitched steeply down. Steeper. Too steeply. Luke fended himself off the glovebox. Trees, wind rushed past the windows. Their tyres broke free of the gravel and they were skating, skiing, floating. Falling.

'Shona! Slow down!'

He had time to register Shona's puzzled glance before she touched the brakes. The Navara slid, slammed into a pothole, and, with a splintering crunch, the front suspension surrendered and sent the ute juddering sideways over the shoulder.

Into the arms of the brush.

The final smack against a boulder.

Ancient cigarette butts, girlie mags and an open packet of something that could have been weed or beard clippings rained down on Luke from the parcel shelf. Shona had already unbuckled and was struggling with her door. Luke opened his door and fell out. He couldn't remember hitting his head, but the world seemed hazy and distant. Blue was above. A writhing tangle of brown flew across it. A peregrine pair? No, white gum bark on the wind. Then all was white.

'Luke!' A voice. Gatta's voice. 'Luke, you'd better wake up now, or Shona is one dead rally driver.'

Luke opened his eyes. Black pillars. Above his face dangled curved bronze knives, scimitars. He blinked. They turned into a burnt white gum, leaves turned copper. A fire had been through here too. In the foreground, out of focus, shaggy black hair and a white, Gatta-shaped face.

'See?' Bec said. 'Did the trick.'

Then he couldn't breathe because Gatta was crushing him. He groaned.

'Oh, sorry. Are you actually okay?'

Luke checked himself for injuries, a process that was becoming distressingly familiar. He wished that sometime soon he would stop having to do it. 'Yes.'

'Shona says the police let you go!' said Gatta.

'You took to the life pretty quick!' said Bec, admiring the detritus that had followed him out of the cab.

'Luke, what just happened to you, on the way down?' Shona was leaning in the Navara's window, testing the steering.

Luke looked up at the road behind her. Steep, yes. Super-scary, no. 'I don't know. I just suddenly felt we were out of control.'

Gatta and Bec shared a glance.

'Just before you tried to park…' said Bec, jabbing a thumb at the ute.

'Alexander took his first look at the downwards view,' said Gatta.

And shared with me how that went for him. Luke's heartbeat still felt like it was approaching from a distant place but he sat up.

'Think you can walk?' asked Shona. 'This thing won't steer.'

'Typical Navara. Sulking. Passive-aggressive prick,' said Bec.

'I can walk,' said Luke. His brain was ahead of his heartbeat. 'What are you doing up here, Gatta? And why didn't you see us and stop?'

'Ty drove us.'

'Ty?' Luke stood up. Quivery and sick in the middle.

Gatta held his arms. 'This morning, I thought you could be gone, you and Shona, like forever and we had to look after Alexander. We were knackered, the police looking and us with nowhere to run. And Ty was out there, crazy dangerous, right? But what if he wasn't dangerous? Who would know? *Alexander would.* That's what he's for! Alexander could suck his brains out to look at them and if he found only *mostly* troll, the non-troll part would help us. Or he's all troll and Alexander would eat him, *oo naturel* or fried, and we'd be rid of him for good. Either way, problem sorted. So I called him and he came.'

'And since he drove you here, Alexander didn't eat him.'

Gatta rubbed her streaming nose on his shirt. 'Freakin' cold up here! Yeah, it was batshit weird. Alexander was flat in the grass when Ty got there, and then he stood up. Went ginormous – Ty thought he was going to be, like, poodle-sized – and he's got teeth, right, and claws? And Ty was like, is that all you got? But mainly Ty thought Alexander was the coolest thing in forever, which he is.'

Even for Gatta, she sounded frenetic. She seized Luke's hand and tugged him up the hill. 'Come see him!' Then she stopped. 'The next bit, though…

'*Bwaaaahhhh.*' She shuddered. 'Alexander tasered him through the eyes and Ty, it was like he had a death-thrash track skewering the middle of his head while his brains were getting ripped out through his ears. I'm glad I saw it!' She bit her lip. 'No I'm not. It was private.'

She squeezed Luke's hand and he realised what a relief it was for her to share the decisions again. 'And then everything stopped and Alexander showed all his teeth and I thought Ty was gunna be chicken nuggets and then he – Ty – laughed.'

'He's got a great laugh.' Bec was behind them with Shona, who was limping.

'Never heard it before.' Gatta was pulling Luke uphill again. 'He was happy! But, whatever, we had to be out of there quick. Once the Ds had you, we didn't know how soon they'd get to us. Alexander had to be elsewhere.'

'Why here?' Luke's legs were reluctant to walk. The wind was making his ears ache.

'Ty's got a place here. Not here here – back there – but Ty saw the wings and we told him that Alexander's flying wasn't going so well, and Ty said he knew somewhere that would make it easy, and Alexander wanted to come here right away.'

Luke's stomach reminded him it was queasy. Ty? Ty had been talking to Alexander. So soon? Befriending him?

'In the back of the van, he was singing! Swooshing his wings like he was up there already. He nearly took Kim's eye out. Oh, Kim's the man with the red hair.'

Swooshing his wings?

Luke heard his own words: *What I'm getting from Alexander? No anger, no fear, confusion, nothing.* Such an idiot! Not nothing: *flying.* Not yet airborne, but wanting it, his yearning so strong it had put Luke up among the kestrels.

'Shame you couldn't text, worrying about police phone tracking. We've had a hairy trip,' said Shona.

Luke was partly listening. Flying. Scary trip. He stopped. 'This place is high, sure, and windy and there's no big trees to bump into, but the landing area is *small*.' He gestured at the flanking cliff edges, the peak ahead.

Gatta's teeth chattered. 'I think Juvie-jaws secretly thinks that too. But he needs to be told it's okay not to try this.'

Next to them, Bec was waving at three figures on the ridgeline: Ty in shirtsleeves, a taller redhead and, above them, swaying restlessly, an oval of gleaming black.

Every time he saw Alexander in new surroundings, Luke's sense of unreality was renewed. That he existed. That he had not been photoshopped into Luke's world. A deeper sense followed. That Alexander belonged, had been present for millennia beyond human memory. That it was the humans who were out of place.

Ty looked casual, as in control as he always was. How did Kim, who'd just met Alexander, feel? He was coming down to meet them.

'This guy's got an even better laugh.' Bec's hips did a cha-cha.

Kim was large and loosely assembled, his red hair brightly sprinkled with white. He looked like he drove the bus for a second-grade cricket team. 'I need to have grandchildren, just so I can tell them,' he said. 'Sorry, not tell them.'

'Kim's a private investigator,' said Gatta. 'I think he should employ me for shadowing and shit because, unlike him, I don't look like a strawberry lamington.'

'I told her she should look up *agent provocateur*—'

'It means rat-fucker,' said Gatta.

'Because it's more her role. Right now, you need logistics, planning and concealment, not UXBs. And you probably don't need flying.'

Luke didn't get a chance to answer. A windy blast of gravel peppered his calves. They had reached the carpark. Alexander's whole length was winding back and forth, feeling the flow of the wind, his burnished scales turning blue and indigo and white in the sunlight. The energy that came off him was intense but erratic.

His eyes went incandescent. **'Luke and Shona! You escaped! You are on the lam? But you did not grass first.'**

Ty and Kim reeled, clutching their heads exactly as if there was suddenly a large creature shouting from within their ears. The rest of them just winced, but Luke wondered whether you could go deaf from the inside.

And Gatta had clearly shown Alexander too many English heist movies. 'No, Alexander, the police let us go. And no, they don't know about you.'

'Miss Garang.' Ty, cream linen shirt, the cold outlining the fine bones of his face. Not intimidated. Not puny. He could have been one of the aristocratic French discoverers of the land he stood on. The smile he gave Shona was astonishingly charming. 'The real woman far exceeds the police description. But you are hurt.' He gestured at her injured leg, then included Luke in his smile. 'Not Luke, was it? He has acquired a habit of afflicting his friends and relatives.'

'Luke is hurt too. It was the police! Making suspects soft.'

'Tas Police don't do softening up, Alexander,' said Shona. 'We did the injuries ourselves.' She appraised Ty. Any lighter and her tone would be flirting. 'We stole a boat, drowned a scooter and crashed a car, trying to save Alexander from *you*, Ty.'

Shit. We did. Luke's poverty worries resurfaced from under all the exciting new ones. *How are we going to pay for them?*

Ty's eyebrows rose. 'Somebody will need to pay for all that.'

Shona matched Ty's earlier smile. 'Perhaps "Robert Coombs" from Aalto who visited our lab and walked out with Alexander's DNA sample could find the cash. To maintain his reputation in the Hobart lab community.'

Ty laughed gaily. 'He might well do. It could be a gesture of goodwill, a seal on the partnership it'll take to look after Alexander. But he has deeds to accomplish first.' He slapped a casual hand on Alexander's mailed flank.

Like he was a cow!

Alexander was too excited to notice. **'Now all my family is here to see me fly. Gatta, my namer. Bec, my defender. Luke, my father-brother. And Shona, you have dragon blood. But are wiser and kinder.'**

'Thanks,' said Shona. 'I don't think I eat quite as much as one.'

'And Ty, who I am glad I did not have to eat. Because then I would be too heavy to fly until tomorrow. And he has a van and a house.'

'Does he make jokes?' asked Ty.

'No,' said Gatta.

'And this place, it is the right place.' The pitch of his voice rose. 'So high, so much air, so much wind.'

'Yes, Alexander,' said Luke, 'but clear landing space is tiny, and there's a lot of wind, maybe too much.' The wind had swung due north, heading straight down the peninsula towards them and the lighthouse. It pushed an icy shank between Luke's shoulder blades.

Alexander arced his neck to a high curve. 'I will look into its voice. I will understand it. I will make it not my enemy but my friend, like they do.' He jerked his head to the side.

Either side of them, the land fell to the Tasman Sea. To the east, across the mouth of Cloudy Bay, the wind dipped to the water, driving it into rushing points of light. Inside the wind were the birds. Resting within it, motionless at speed. Flicking free and slicing through. Turning into its face and shooting upwards. A vast wheeling dance of wings.

'They didn't just make friends, Alexander,' said Luke. 'They were introduced to it, had instruction from their parents. And they took it in small steps.'

Alexander's crest quivered. 'I had no instruction from those dragons. They searched me. I could not question them.'

Luke needed to head him off the subject of the other dragons. 'We can't ask them now. But you could do like young birds do and practise first, with a lot more room to land, without–'

'With the Overeem, the dragons came.'

Gatta and Bec flinched, remembering.

'We could make it bring them again.' Alexander scanned the sky.

'Alcohol is a really bad way to fly, Alexander.' An acrid draught from the burnt hillside below reminded Luke of yesterday and how narrowly they had escaped disaster.

'If we walk up to the lighthouse,' said Ty, 'we can at least scope out the landing area. And maybe the wind will be manageable.'

Luke's teeth clenched. Was Ty testing the dragon's allegiance? Between himself and Ty?

'It is higher. We will see more.'

If so, Luke had lost. Alexander had already turned. He was giving off bravado and defiance in little bursts of static. As though the dragons he craved and feared and resented were watching, judging him. He made for the access road, with Bec and Gatta and Kim, who hadn't supported Luke. Ty followed.

Shona fell into step with Luke. 'We're going to have to find those dragons, if they exist.'

What? Why wasn't she worrying about Alexander flying in these conditions? And didn't she see that Ty was challenging Luke? Or was he just jealously paranoid?

'Uh, yeah. Or he'll go crazy,' he said. 'But how the hell do we do that?'

'Our best clues are in his egg. Prof is still on it. There's a chance the egg might have been brought in by an early explorer.'

'Oh, uh, great,' said Luke. 'But just now we have to talk him down from here before he breaks his neck. That gust that nearly did yesterday it was smaller than these.'

'Yes. He's got no protection from that wind. If he takes off into it, he'll go backwards over the cliff and then just fall. No chance to get control.'

The wind razored Luke's cheek but he felt a little better. 'I don't know why Ty agreed to bring him up here. I need to talk to him.'

To this new Ty, the one he didn't know, the one who'd laughed after Alexander turned him inside out in searching him. And then again at Shona's Robert Coombs blackmail. Maybe he was still the old Ty. 'Wish me luck.' Luke increased his pace and caught up with his uncle.

Ty saw Luke beside him, but didn't turn. 'He was never a *Tasmaniosaurus*, was he?'

'What? Ah, I don't think so. Evolved from one maybe; I don't know.'

'But his physiology is completely unique. You got any idea how any of it works?'

'Shona has some theories.'

At least they were talking neutrally. Were they?

'I don't know how we're going to test them while keeping him a secret.' Ty held a palm up to stop Luke's protest. 'We will, we will. Keep him secret. His freedom comes first – always.'

His eyes shifted back to Alexander, above them on the path. 'That thing he did to me–'

'He did it to me too.'

Ty looked surprised. 'He needed to?'

'It was a demonstration.'

Ty nodded, then said, 'Each man must give an account of himself to

God. It wasn't God, but I've got mine out of the way and I'm not even dead.' That laugh again. An open, confident sound.

They came up onto the high promontory, the brilliant green dominated by the white tower of the lighthouse. And all about, boundless air and water. To their left, halfway to the horizon, the dark vertical folds of Tasman Head where the wind was tearing the veil over the Friars into rainbow shreds and, nearer, the surf exploding at the feet of East Cloudy Head.

'Why are we here?' asked Luke.

'Alexander wanted to come. And it's the best place for him.'

The best place? For what?

The dragon stood in front of them, head swinging. His body rippled, giving off sulphur and metal. **'Those dragons, I cannot smell them here. They cannot speak to me. I do not need them. I will fly here and become myself.'**

Alexander opened his wings a little. The wind bellied the folds of them, sought to force them wide open, toss them and him up into the sky to be its plaything. The dragon staggered back, tried to make it look a dance of anticipation.

'Yes, here, Alexander, it's a good place. But not today,' said Luke desperately. 'It won't be you that's in charge. It'll be the wind. And if the dragons are watching, somehow, don't you want to show them brains over bravery?'

Ty watched, hands in his pockets.

Alexander went still, as did the sputter from his mind. His eyes were mustard. **'You want me to behave like a dragon or like a human? How do you know what dragons value? How to be a dragon?'**

I might have some idea, thought Luke, but this wasn't the time to relate humanity's dragon mythology – a parade of cruelty, violence, deception, self-aggrandisement and greed, reflecting badly on both species.

'I don't know,' he said, miserably. 'I just don't want you to crash.'

Alexander dropped to all fours and turned away, his wing-roots hunched around his neck and the membranes wrapped closely around him. He stalked off towards the lighthouse.

Ty said, 'A man makes his own choice on what to value,' and followed him.

Gatta put her arm around him. 'Don't worry, Lukey, it's just yoof. A stinky teenager without a dad. He has to stomp and swear. You never do that 'cos you're too prissy-lips. I have to do it for both of us.'

Ty and Alexander had crossed to the other side of the lighthouse and were forcing their way through the low brush to the cliff edge. The wind plastered Ty's shirt against his back. Their two heads were close together. Luke grappled with the sight of it. Ty was everything that was wrong, opposite, alien, to Luke. How was Alexander not seeing that? Was he talking to Ty? Luke heard nothing in his head, not even a buzz. Alexander had closed his emotions off completely. To Luke at least. Could he direct them at others, specific people – Ty – and exclude Luke? What had happened between Ty and Alexander in the van?

'Has Alexander talked to Ty?'

'No,' said Gatta. Her face against his chest was icy.

Bec was on Luke's other side: 'Blue is not Gats' colour.'

'Nor yours.' Kim was close behind Bec, acting as windbreak.

Bec grinned over her shoulder at him. 'Hey Luke, it's spectacularing its tits off up here, but the cold is doing the same to mine. Do we suppose Alexander could finish his scope-out quick?'

Luke hugged Gatta. So she and Bec had been supportive of giving Alexander space, not approving of him flying. 'I wish I could make him. What's Ty up to?'

Ty and Alexander were outlined against the sky and the Southern Ocean, the water below them an impenetrable midnight blue untouched by the sun and wind. Further out, all the way to the horizon, the sea was turquoise streaked in white, crazed by wind into patches of steely brilliance. As Luke watched, Alexander's head rose suddenly, turning silver in the sunlight, then disappeared.

At first Luke thought he'd lost him against the backdrop.

Then a bolt of terror smashed into him. A tremendous rushing. And a cry. His name. In his ears, through his head. Then all of it rapidly tailed away into nothing. Luke's mind reached vainly after the dragon. The terror, sound, presence – all of Alexander had vanished.

Ty bent forward, peered over the cliff edge for a few seconds, then up to the horizon, then he turned idly around.

Luke ran, tripping through the brush toward him. 'What's happened? What have you done?'

Ty smiled, satisfied, peaceful. 'I made him jump. It was for the best.'

Luke's foot slid to the crumbling edge. Far below at the foot of the cliffs, the water, nearly black, had closed over its secrets.

How? How had Alexander, the mind invader, not seen Ty clearly? Not known that Ty could never have accepted being searched; if some creature penetrated into his private self, he'd have to kill it. Or had Ty managed a deception; with his supreme ego, turned the window to his soul into a mirror?

Whichever, Alexander was gone. The only dragon in the world.

Ty waited, gazing at the wide water, serene and unmistakeably satisfied. Luke moved away from the edge and turned to face him. Luke's being - past, future, cause, consequence - was swept away into the endless space, here high above the world. By loss.

'No,' he said.

Unacceptable loss.

Luke stretched out an arm towards Ty. Clean angry power surged up inside him. He pushed.

Shona's hand was abruptly on his, her right hand on his left. Stopping him.

'Ty's right, Luke. This is the best place for him. But doing the take-off downward instead of upwind. Height, protection from the gusts, this cliff is a launch ramp.'

'No, Shona, he's gone. I heard him call me. He was terrified. Now I can't hear or feel him. He's gone.'

'That's because he's flying so fast.' She pointed with her other hand.

Far out against the torn opalescent sea, a silver shape arrowed away, a low-flying jet. As they watched, it rose skyward and extended its wings, turned to black.

And the dragon Alexander swept up into his kingdom.

Then another hand grabbed him, not gently, and yanked him away from the edge. The same hand dragged in Ty.

Holly! In a jade silk blouse, slim navy skirt and jacket.

'What the *hell* do you two think you're doing?'

Ty stepped over a cushion plant and said agreeably, 'Oh, hello, Holly. I persuaded Luke's friend to jump and Luke got mad.'

Holly stared at him coldly. 'Jump? He was, what, base-jumping? Into the water? Hang gliding?'

'He's fine,' said Ty, shading his eyes. 'He's flying okay up there, just needed some encouragement. What are you doing here?'

'Finding out what's going on. You – both of you – have been giving me identical evasions for the last week. The blander, the scarier.'

'But…shouldn't you be in your meeting with Paladin?' said Luke.

'Don't you fob me off, too. After your *pathetic* message: *routine follow-up*, my arse.'

They all took a wary step back, including Shona. 'I knew whatever was up with you two couldn't wait. I upped and left their meeting. Told them if they didn't make a decision now, I'd find someone with more balls and less greed and just as much money. Got on a plane. Then I tracked you, Ty, on that app you put on both our phones.'

She broke off. 'You must be Shona. The police told me about you. I'm Holly. Nice to meet you. I think.'

Why haven't you mentioned Shona to your mum, Luke? He hadn't discussed his mum with Shona either. Was he worried they'd compete? Or collude?

Shona grinned. 'I wonder why Luke has been keeping us in the dark about each other.'

Collude.

Holly mirrored Shona's amusement. Then, she turned her glare again at her son and her brother. 'So...'

In the plant of her feet and the jut of her jaw, Luke found he had a different mother. Her attention had always been scattered amongst regrets and anxieties and obligations. To schedules, employees, children, Ty. Now, with her powers gathered into her own self, she was formidable. And very irritated.

'So. This friend. I presume it is he who has caused you both to behave like lunatics.'

'Yes,' said Luke and Ty meekly.

'And you've received all these injuries fighting each other?'

'To me, yes. To Luke, no,' said Ty.

'Yes and no,' said Luke.

'Now you're going to stop fighting.' It was fully a command, but demanded acknowledgement.

Luke and Ty looked at each other.

'Yes,' said Ty.

'Yes,' said Luke, with a prickling neck. He had no idea of the small print.

'The friend will be staying with me from now on,' said Ty.

'What?' *Permanently?* Luke looked at Gatta, who was even bluer with cold, despite being in a huddle with Bec, sharing the shelter of Kim. Had there been a discussion on residences in the van? The girls shook their heads tightly. No, no discussion.

'I think I'll have better control than Luke,' said Ty.

Control?

'That appears the best solution, all round,' said Ty.

Control? What did that even mean? How was he going to exert it?

Luke's shoulder muscles bunched. Then he felt Alexander tug at his mind, open their channel, send his exaltation down from an immense height. Luke looked up. Soaring above the gulls, so much higher he looked the same size, a shape of silver blue against blue, inside the wind, looking down, seeing Luke, sharing his joy.

'**Luke. I am flying.**'

He felt like saying, *Go. Fly. Escape.* He looked at the faces around him, the people Alexander would return to, if he *did* return. Gatta's was smeared with bliss, feeling his high, as bound to Alexander's heart as Luke was to his mind.

Ty, all smoothly amiable surface now – would it be possible, ever, to get a realistic grip on him? As for control of Alexander – ha! *Ty had no idea*!

What of Kim? Gatta liked him, which was recommendation enough.

Bec, guileless and passionate. Alexander had set her free; she'd be loyal unto the death. Would have been anyway.

Shona, ferociously intelligent, whose beauty caught his heart off guard, no matter how often he saw it. She'd let him in, a little, down in the rainforest. He hugged that precious moment fiercely to himself. However her easy response to his mother, her teasing dance of a conversation with Ty – Luke's twist of jealousy was deep and ugly. But the professor had seen a future for them.

Hope and confusion made him dizzy so he looked away, at Holly: biotech potentate-in-waiting, visionary, sister, mother, grown back into her whole self at last.

They, all of them here – for better or worse – were responsible for Alexander now. He could fly away but there was nowhere he could escape humanity; or they him. His human friends had to find him a role in the world involving the fewest fatalities.

'Shared responsibility,' Luke said.

'Agreed,' said Ty immediately.

Yep. The bastard was still three moves ahead. It would have to do.

'This wind is getting over-fresh,' said Holly, taking Kim's place as Gatta's shelter, wrapping her jacket around her daughter, who snuggled into her. 'Your flying lunatic, will he rejoin us?'

'Yes,' said Luke. 'He'll come down for his friends.'

About the Author

Marie Heitz

Marie has spent 35 years writing what she fervently hopes is nonfiction, given it is doctor's notes. Dr Heitz' medical fields have ranged from Immunology (The Department of Obscure Diseases) to Remote Area Medicine, in Kakadu National Park, and a lot of time in city Emergency Departments. She claims that her handwriting has survived.

Marie is fascinated by how animals work: the how and why of what makes different species function. She is troubled about human responsibility towards animals and the planet; and she loves where she lives. Unsurprisingly, these things are what her first novel, *The Diemen Alexander*, is about.

She thinks *The Diemen Alexander* is funnier and more charming than she is.

Acknowledgements

Nelli Noakes and Suzy Cooper were subjected to the first draft as it came out. Strong unflinching women both, their support never flagged. No matter how I jammed Alexander headfirst into unreversible plot thickets, or strangled and choked and drowned him in overworked prose (sic) they retained their belief in him and in me. Their style and creativity remain my inspiration.

Lindy Cameron of Clan Destine Press left the door ajar one Sunday night and Alexander took his chance and slipped inside. She didn't evict him, rather gave him a home, for which both of us are profoundly grateful.

Narrelle Harris, my editor at CDP, is the consummate contract killer. She was insightful and comforting while ruthlessly slaying some of the words I treasured the most. But keeping the best ones.

Sgt Reece Duffield of Victoria Police gave invaluable insights into police procedures, including entire sentences which I lifted verbatim. He definitely does not condone any dubious behaviour by my officers. (I haven't told him.)

Dr Sandy Gale, anaesthetist and martial artist, who knocks people out for a living, (very gently,) helped choreograph my fight scenes and provided insight into the psychology of hand to hand combat.

Bryan Walpole unknowingly contributed his inimitable self. I wouldn't have been able to make him up. Once he found out, he graciously allowed me to keep him.

Romey Ward, as well as providing scrupulous and detailed feedback, gifted me the most encouraging words a new writer can hear: 'It's 2am. I can't stop reading your book and I'm laughing.'

Bronwyn and the Hobart Bookshop, with their extraordinary enthusiasm, kindness and generosity to authors, show that selling books is far more than a business to them.